# Harold Arlen and His Songs

# Harold Arlen and His Songs

WALTER FRISCH

# OXFORD
UNIVERSITY PRESS

Oxford University Press is a department of the University of Oxford. It furthers the University's objective of excellence in research, scholarship, and education by publishing worldwide. Oxford is a registered trade mark of Oxford University Press in the UK and certain other countries.

Published in the United States of America by Oxford University Press
198 Madison Avenue, New York, NY 10016, United States of America.

© Oxford University Press 2024

All rights reserved. No part of this publication may be reproduced, stored in a retrieval system, or transmitted, in any form or by any means, without the prior permission in writing of Oxford University Press, or as expressly permitted by law, by license, or under terms agreed with the appropriate reproduction rights organization. Inquiries concerning reproduction outside the scope of the above should be sent to the Rights Department, Oxford University Press, at the address above.

You must not circulate this work in any other form
and you must impose this same condition on any acquirer.

Library of Congress Cataloging-in-Publication Data
Names: Frisch, Walter, 1951– author.
Title: Harold Arlen and His Songs / Walter Frisch.
Description: New York, NY : Oxford University Press, 2024. | Includes bibliographical references and index.
Identifiers: LCCN 2024000929 (print) | LCCN 2024000930 (ebook) | ISBN 9780197503270 (hardback) | ISBN 9780197503294 (epub)
Subjects: LCSH: Arlen, Harold, 1905–1986—Criticism and interpretation. | Songs—United States—20th century—History and criticism.
Classification: LCC ML410.A76 F76 2024 (print) | LCC ML410.A76 (ebook) | DDC 782.42164092—dc23/eng/20240109
LC record available at https://lccn.loc.gov/2024000929
LC ebook record available at https://lccn.loc.gov/2024000930

DOI: 10.1093/oso/9780197503270.001.0001

Printed by Sheridan Books, Inc., United States of America

# Contents

*Preface and Acknowledgments* — vii
*About Arlen Sheet Music and the Companion Website* — xiii

1. Introducing Harold Arlen — 1
2. Inside the Rainbow — 18
3. Arlen and Ted Koehler — 29
4. Arlen and Yip Harburg — 62
5. Arlen and Johnny Mercer — 98
6. Arlen, Leo Robin, and Dorothy Fields — 134
7. Arlen, Ira Gershwin, and *A Star Is Born* — 147
8. Arlen, Truman Capote, and *House of Flowers* — 167
9. Arlen Sings and Plays: Recordings and Performances of the 1950s and 1960s — 190
10. A Late Style? Arlen, Dory Langdon, and Martin Charnin—and Harold Arlen — 206
11. Singing the Arlen Songbook — 228

*Notes* — 249
*Selected Bibliography* — 277
*Credits* — 283
*Index—General* — 287
*Index of Arlen Songs* — 303

# Preface and Acknowledgments

In the fall of 2018 I was invited to attend a small reception in New York hosted by a friend who, knowing of my work on Harold Arlen, told me that a great admirer of the composer would be present—Stephen Sondheim. I brought along a copy of a book I had recently written on "Over the Rainbow," with the hope of giving it to Sondheim at an opportune moment. When such a moment came, I introduced myself (we had met many years earlier, but I don't think he remembered). His eyes lit up and he became animated as we chatted about Arlen. He told me proudly that Arlen had attended the original production of *Pacific Overtures* several times. (I already knew about this from the Sondheim literature.) When I presented my book on "Over the Rainbow" to him, Sondheim astonished me by raising it to his lips and kissing it. Then he looked directly at me and said, with a glint in his eye, "That's for Harold Arlen, not for you!"

I cannot be sure Sondheim ever read my book or whether it would have earned even a fraction of the affection he held for Arlen's music. But his spontaneous gesture was enough to reassure me I was on a worthwhile journey. That journey had begun some ten years earlier, when I took off my shelf a book I had long owned but had not read closely, Alec Wilder's idiosyncratic but keenly insightful *American Popular Song: The Great Innovators, 1920–1950*, originally published in 1972. I was drawn into the long chapter on Harold Arlen. I had been familiar with only a few of Arlen's best known songs, like "Stormy Weather" and "Over the Rainbow," but now found myself reading about many other numbers. Wilder reveres Arlen. He inscribed a copy of his book to the composer: "For Harold Arlen / I can only say what I've said over and over again in these pages: I love you and every last note you've ever written or shall write. / Alec Wilder." In the book, Wilder almost apologetically elevates Arlen above Gershwin: "I've carefully examined the music of both composers . . . without prejudice," he writes. "I respect Gershwin, but I envy Arlen." Comments like these—and there are many more in Wilder's chapter—piqued my interest. I began to sense that there was much more to discover, that Arlen's greatness might be hiding in plain sight. Although Arlen's name is not as familiar to the general public as some of his peers, his songs have long been championed by distinguished composers like Sondheim and André Previn, as well as by great vocalists, including Ethel Waters, Judy Garland, Frank Sinatra, Tony Bennett, Barbra Streisand, and Audra McDonald.

I purchased the two available Harold Arlen songbooks in print and began to acquire other sheet music, published and unpublished, from libraries and from generous collectors and musicians with whom I became acquainted. I tracked down many of the probably thousands of recordings made of Arlen's songs. I wrote an analytical article about Arlen's longer "tapeworm" songs and the short book about "Over the Rainbow," each as a kind of down payment on a larger study of Arlen's work that I knew had to be pursued.

Arlen has been well served by three biographies, two of them written by his friend and amanuensis Edward Jablonski (1961 and 1996), and one by Walter Rimler (2015). Although all devote some attention to Arlen's music, beyond Wilder's chapter there has been no sustained critical or analytical discussion of his songs. That is the goal of *Harold Arlen and His Songs*. The book traces a roughly chronological trajectory through Arlen's career. It includes biographical information which I draw partly from Jablonski and Rimler and have supplemented with (or verified from) other sources where appropriate. But my focus is on the songs, which form the best network through which Arlen's life and career can be understood.

A basic premise of this book (despite its title) is that Arlen's songs are not "his," but, as the composer himself frequently acknowledged, "theirs," created with some of the finest lyricists of the twentieth century, including Ted Koehler, E.Y. ("Yip") Harburg, Johnny Mercer, Ira Gershwin, and Dorothy Fields. One shortcoming of Wilder's book—something that justifiably annoyed Harburg and Ira Gershwin—is that he rarely discusses the lyrics. I hope to redress this imbalance, as well as another: when recreated by vocalists, Arlen's songs are also "theirs" in an important sense.

While the main focus is on the songs, I also consider where appropriate their placement in films and shows, especially in the book musicals *Bloomer Girl, St. Louis Woman,* and *House of Flowers,* and films like *The Wizard of Oz* and *A Star Is Born,* where the music is an integral part of the story. In the case of some shows, including *St. Louis Woman* and *Softly* (a musical never completed), I provide deeper context by incorporating sources that have not been previously discussed.

Having spent a good portion of my career writing about the music of Brahms, I have sometimes been asked how I traveled to Arlen. The two composers share certain qualities that resonate with me. Both Brahms and Arlen, although confident artists, were relatively modest craftsmen concerned with writing works at the highest level—what Brahms called *dauerhafte Musik*, music that would endure. The high level of technique displayed in their music never stands in the way of its expressive power. Indeed, the emotional impact seems inseparable from the technical mastery. The music of both Brahms and Arlen is often tinged with a melancholy or longing that speaks to many listeners (including myself). "There is enormous sadness in his work," Alex Ross writes of Brahms. "His heart is always breaking," Sondheim says of Arlen.

Brahms and Arlen also seemed to work most comfortably on a smaller scale. Brahms famously never wrote an opera; Arlen never had a hit Broadway show. Yet for Brahms, each individual song or piano piece, or a movement (if it forms part of a larger work), creates a kind of emotional-narrative arc that often feels complete in itself. Similarly, most Arlen songs have a powerfully expressive trajectory. Sometimes, as in "The Man That Got Away," "I Had Myself a True Love," or "I Never Has Seen Snow," Arlen (with his lyricist) takes us on an extended journey, with several moments of climax or catharsis. We may end up close to where we began musically, as often happens in popular song, but we are emotionally in a different place. Arlen's sense of expressive architecture shapes even songs of more conventional length, like "Over the Rainbow," "Last Night When We Were Young," and "My Shining Hour."

One difference between Brahms and Arlen: Brahms's music has always occupied a large place in the standard classical repertory, while much of Arlen's music has remained more obscure in the realm of popular song. The present book explores an extraordinary body of work that needs more than Sondheim's kiss to emerge from the shadows.

*** 

Over the years that I have worked on Arlen's music, many institutions and individuals have been extraordinarily generous and helpful. Columbia University, my own academic home for more than forty years, has been supportive with leave time and research assistance. Columbia's devoted Music & Arts librarians Elizabeth Davis and Nick Patterson have often tracked down materials or brought resources to my attention. The Library of Congress Music Division has for much of my career been a kind of home away from home. For my work on Arlen, I am especially grateful for the assistance and deep knowledge of the library's Senior Research Specialists Mark Eden Horowitz and Ray White, and also for the help of Reference Specialist Paul Sommerfeld. I have greatly benefited from visits to or sources supplied digitally by many other institutions (especially during the pandemic), including the New York Public Library (Main and Performing Arts Libraries), Yale University (Beinecke Library and Irving Gilmore Music Library), Boston University (Howard Gotlieb Research Center), Tulane University (Amistad Research Center), Georgia State University (Johnny Mercer Papers in Special Collections), Emory University (Stuart A. Rose Manuscript, Archives, and Rare Book Library), the University of California, Berkeley (Bancroft Library), the University of Texas (Harry Ransom Center), and the University of Southern California (Cinematic Arts Library). Nick Markovich, executive director of the Yip Harburg Foundation, has provided me with much information and many sources, as has Jane Klain at the Paley Center for Media.

The late Rita Arlen, who became a friend, generously allowed access to materials in her possession, many of which are now on deposit in the Rita Arlen Collection in the Music Division at the Library of Congress. I regret she did not live to see this book. Sam Arlen has responded promptly to my queries. Michael Feinstein is unique in the world of American popular song as a keeper of the flame. His immense knowledge and talent are matched only by his generosity in sharing some of the many materials he has collected over decades. Michael Lavine, Eric Comstock, and Alex Hassan have shared sheet music from their vast personal collections.

I am also grateful to the following individuals, who responded to queries and shared materials, and with many of whom I have had many fruitful and informative exchanges: Sarah England Baab, Joby Baker, Richard Barrios, Ken Bloom, Laura Lynn Broadhurst, Dominic Broomfield-McHugh, Carla Cantrelle, David Chase, Eric Davis, Todd Decker, Thomas DeFrantz, William Ecker, Kevin Fellezs, Martin Fridson, Will Friedwald, Aaron Gandy, Lynn Garafola, Howard Green, Julia Greenberg, David Hajdu, Leo Holder, Matt Howe, Robert Hurwitz, Velia Ivanova, Marc Kligman, Jeffrey Koehler, Nancy Koehler, Miles Kreuger, John Lahr, Daniel Lazour, Peter Lefferts, James Leve, Jeffrey Magee, John Mauceri, Peter Mintun, Michael Owen, Nathan Platte, William Rosar, Bill Rudman, Phil Schaap, Loren Schoenberg, Lawrence Schulman, Lesley Shatz, W. Anthony Sheppard, Nate Sloan, Evan Smolin, Ted Sperling, Larry Stempel, Judith Tick, Glory Van Scott, Elaine Sisman, Scott Warfield, Chris Washburne, and William Zinsser.

Michael Gildin read the entire manuscript of this book in an earlier draft and offered perceptive remarks based on his deep knowledge and love of the popular song repertory. Sean Smither also read a draft and helped me considerably with the finer points of harmonic analysis. Rebecca Zola worked through all my musical examples and assisted with chord labeling and syntax.

I have known and worked for years in various capacities with the wonderful editors at Oxford University Press, including former Editor-in-Chief for Humanities Suzanne Ryan and current Humanities Editor Norm Hirschy. As the book has moved through the editorial process, Norm has continued to offer encouragement and enthusiasm. The staff of OUP, including Project Manager Meredith Taylor, has helped make the production of this volume as smooth as imaginable.

Finally, I am deeply grateful to my family for their love and support over many years. My partner Marilyn has come to love Arlen's songs as much as I do, and as a singer she has offered me many insights. My sons Nicholas and Simon, both excellent musicians, have followed me appreciatively from Brahms, through Schoenberg, to Arlen. Simon read through many parts of the book and shared keen musical insights with me, some of which I have incorporated here (often tacitly but with paternal pride). He also prepared the handsome musical examples.

# About Arlen Sheet Music and the Companion Website

www.oup.com/us/haroldarlenandhissongs

Some readers will not have ready access to the scores of Arlen's songs referred to in this book. As with his contemporaries, many Arlen songs were originally published as individual pieces of sheet music and have not been reprinted. These can be hard to find, except in libraries and private collections. Fortunately, a selection of Arlen's songs has been assembled in two anthologies that are more easily available, *The Harold Arlen Songbook* (Hal Leonard and MPL Communications, 1985) and *Harold Arlen Rediscovered* (Hal Leonard and MPL Communications, 1996). (There is some overlap between the two volumes.)

In the text of this book I have included short musical examples to illustrate some analytical observations. In most cases, unless otherwise noted, I discuss a song in the key in which it was originally published. Most singers transpose songs to the keys that best fit their vocal types and ranges. (For example, "Over the Rainbow" is printed in the key of E♭, but Judy Garland always sang it in A♭, a fifth below.)

The Companion Website offers readers a fuller context for the songs that are discussed in the text. References to these brief audio and video excerpts are indicated with the ▶ symbol. In most cases I have sought to use recordings or film excerpts from about the time the song was written. But where those are not readily accessible, I have opted for more recent versions by leading vocalists. Recordings of many of Arlen's most popular songs, as well as cast albums of most shows and films for which he wrote music, can be found on streaming services like YouTube, Spotify, Apple Music, and Amazon Music.

# 1
# Introducing Harold Arlen

"Like counting the gold bars at Fort Knox." That is how in 1963 the composer, conductor, and pianist André Previn described hearing a medley of Harold Arlen's songs. Previn and his wife Dory reported starting "to laugh at the incredulity of the fact that, you know, he [Arlen] wrote this one and he wrote that one, and we didn't know he'd written this, and it went on and on and on."[1]

A year earlier, in 1962, *Variety* published "The Golden 100," a list of "all-time pop standards" based on "performances, sheet music, and disk sales." Arlen has seven numbers on the list, exceeded only by Richard Rodgers (nine) and Irving Berlin (eight).[2] This result is striking in that Arlen's output comprises about 450 songs, less than half of Rodgers's and only a third of Berlin's.

In the year 2000, "Over the Rainbow" was voted the greatest song of the twentieth century in a survey conducted by the National Endowment for the Arts and the Recording Industry Association of America. It also tops a list of movie songs prepared by the American Film Institute.[3] Many reports about these surveys name Judy Garland and *The Wizard of Oz*, but fail to mention the song's composer, Harold Arlen, or lyricist, E.Y. ("Yip") Harburg.

Previn's comments and the statistics and surveys make clear that Arlen suffers from what I call anonymous immortality: his songs are far more familiar than his name, especially when compared with other giants of American popular song like Berlin, Rodgers, Jerome Kern, George Gershwin, and Cole Porter. This situation was acknowledged by Walter Cronkite in his introductory remarks to "The Songs of Harold Arlen," an hour-long television program broadcast in 1964, from which the Previn comments cited above also come. Cronkite intones: "Harold Arlen is a shy, retiring man, which perhaps explains the paradox of his fame. People know and love his music but they do not know his name. They do not connect Harold Arlen with 'Over the Rainbow' as quickly as they connect Irving Berlin with 'White Christmas' and Richard Rodgers with *Oklahoma!*"[4]

There are several explanations for Arlen's low name recognition relative to the high number of standards he wrote. One, as Arlen mentions to Cronkite, is "the privacy I cherish"; he notes that getting name recognition "necessitates doing a lot of things that don't come naturally [to me]," like interviews and publicity. Arlen lacked the kind of profile Berlin and Gershwin pursued—and achieved—as iconic "American" composers. Without envy or resentment, Arlen tells Cronkite that Berlin "made himself an institution" and Gershwin was "catapulted" to fame with *Rhapsody in Blue*.

Some of Arlen's shows had decent runs, and one film with his songs, *The Wizard of Oz*, is a beloved classic. Yet he never had a hit stage musical on the order of *Oklahoma!* or *My Fair Lady*. Arlen often characterized himself as a craftsman writing the best music he could; he was not inclined to protest the indignities songwriters often suffered at the hands of producers and directors, especially in Hollywood, but also on Broadway. When MGM executives cut "Over the Rainbow" during a preview *The Wizard of Oz*—it was, of course, later restored—Arlen came home and told his wife, "From now on I'm just going to write the best I can, turn 'em in and forget 'em."[5] In many respects that was Arlen's stoic attitude throughout his career. After his musical *Saratoga* flopped in 1960, he wrote, "That's the way of the theater and we will have to take it in our stride."[6]

Another reason for Arlen's relatively low name recognition is that there is no easily definable Arlen "style." His melodies can be as readily singable as "Over the Rainbow" or as tricky to navigate as "I've Got the World on a String." His catalogue ranges from the infectious "list" song "Lydia the Tattooed Lady" (memorably premiered by Groucho Marx), to "Blues in the Night," an expansive number built from a succession of twelve-bar blues. Much of the variety, as will be discussed below, is the result of Arlen's close collaborations with different lyricists.

## Harold Arlen—Composer, Craftsman

The range and unconventional aspects of Arlen's oeuvre led Previn to call him a "composer" rather than a "songwriter"—and mean it as a compliment. In the interview cited above Previn observes:

> Harold is more of a composer in the accepted sense of that word than he is a songwriter. Harold does not simply go on and on with a song. It never becomes filler. In other words, even if, let us say for the sake of the argument,

that he has a song that's twenty bars longer than the norm. It then becomes fascinating to me that you cannot take out one bar of that supposedly extra twenty bars and still make it come out, because every single note that he has put down seems suddenly the only logical next move. And that's really a great accomplishment.[7]

Previn refers here to how the composer often tweaks or stretches the standard thirty-two-measure forms of Tin Pan Alley into what Arlen would call a "tapeworm."

Alec Wilder, another Arlen admirer and, like Previn, an accomplished songwriter, emphasizes less Arlen's distinctive approach to form than the "thoroughness" of his songs, as reflected in the carefully crafted details of melody, harmony, and accompaniment:

> The most specific reason for my affection for Arlen's music is that his songs suggested a greater thoroughness than those of other writers. By "thoroughness" I mean the sense of a finished product. Within the piano part was evidence of the song in its performance. One sensed the seeds of orchestration, one knew somehow that he had thought the song through to its final phase, the performance of it, whether by a singer, a piano, a band, a jazz group, or a band with a singer.[8]

Arlen was indeed one of the most "thorough" among his contemporaries in almost all the capacities mentioned by Wilder. In the 1920s, before he took up songwriting seriously, Arlen worked as pianist, singer, and arranger for a number of bands, including his homegrown Buffalodians and the New York-based orchestra of Arnold Johnson. These activities distinguish Arlen from songwriters like Berlin, Kern, and Gershwin, who had far more limited (though valuable) experience as "song pluggers" performing and promoting new numbers for music publishers. Ray Bolger, a close friend of Arlen's who would play the Scarecrow in *The Wizard of Oz*, made explicit the connection between Arlen's early professional pursuits and his songs: "Maybe because he had been an arranger, Harold could write the song complete, with all the wonderful musical ideas written in—so that no arranger was really required." Bolger pointed especially to Arlen's tendency to "make the afterbeat part of the melody," by which he appears to mean the presence of strong syncopations that push a tune off a square metrical-rhythmic grid.[9]

Although he certainly had the ability to do so, Arlen, like most of his contemporaries, rarely notated his songs in full. Piano accompaniments in the published sheet music, replete with the kinds of details admired by Wilder, often represent transcriptions taken down from Arlen's playing. But this process, typical for many songwriters, does not make him any less a "composer." In his recorded performances, Arlen often reproduces quite closely the details we see on the printed page, which thus conveys his intentions quite faithfully.

If Previn praises the variety and formal innovations of Arlen's songs, and Wilder their completeness, another fan, Stephen Sondheim, stresses their originality and emotional power. Arlen was Sondheim's favorite songwriter (along with Jerome Kern). "Arlen kills me," he told James Lapine. "He's as inventive a composer as there ever was." When asked to characterize an Arlen song, Sondheim replied, "It's about seduction and warmth and yearning.... What I love about Arlen's work is that his heart is always breaking." Sondheim explained on several occasions how he sought to emulate those qualities by creating an Arlen-inspired song "in every score I write."[10]

Encomia like those from Previn, Wilder, and Sondheim lift Arlen's songs to the highest realm of popular music. During a visit with Arlen in the early 1970s, the music critic Gene Lees touched on that issue with a question which, "to judge from his [Arlen's] air of surprise, had never been put to him before." "I said, 'Mr. Arlen, when you and George Gershwin and Rodgers and Hart were writing for the theater in the thirties, were you consciously aware that what you were writing was art music?' He looked at me for what seems in memory a long moment and then said, softly, 'Yes.'"[11]

Arlen's delayed and laconic answer reveals that he and his peers understood the value of their creations, even while working amid the commercial hurly-burly of Broadway and Hollywood. Here another observation by Sondheim seems relevant. His interlocuter Mark Horowitz asks, "Is there anything you want to say to posterity about your music—listening to your music?" Sondheim at first demurs: "No, no, of course not. It's just, like all art—it's to be discovered by sampling, by listening." But then he stresses that "there's a great deal to be learned" from studying the craft of the great songwriters: "To analyze a Kern tune [etc.] or to analyze an Arlen tune is not more than a rung below analyzing the Mozart 39th [Symphony]; it's the same process.... And without craft, I think art is nonsense."[12] Analyzing

Arlen does not quite involve the "same process" as analyzing Mozart. But, as Sondheim suggests, Arlen's music rewards approaches that focus on his craft.

Arlen's work is distinctive for its many tapeworms, like those alluded to by Previn above, whose choruses (the main section of the song) extend beyond the standard thirty-two-bar span, as in "That Old Black Magic" (72 bars), "The Man That Got Away" (61), "Blues in the Night" (58), and "One for My Baby" (58). Tapeworm is probably a misnomer for such songs; it evokes not only a gooey pathology, but also a structure that evolves freely. Yet in most cases Arlen's tapeworm songs have a standard formal frame (like AABA), which is expanded through an increase in the length of the component sections, or the interpolation of additional ones. When Jablonski asked him whether he was trying to be "different" from other songwriters with such frequent departures from convention, Arlen replied, "I don't think I'm trying to be different. Sometimes I get into trouble; in order to get out of trouble I break the form: I start twisting and turning, get into another key or go sixteen extra bars in order to resolve the song. And often as not I'm happier with the extension than I would have been trying to keep the song in regular form."[13] Arlen was certainly not alone in writing tapeworms; Cole Porter created the monumental "Begin the Beguine" (108 bars), and Irving Berlin the expansive "Cheek to Cheek" (72). But Arlen wrote more tapeworms than his contemporaries, pushed by a compositional impulse to do justice to the musical material as it unfolded.[14]

## Arlen's Jots

Most of Arlen's songs began life as a tune or a fragment thereof, set down on music paper as what he called "jots" or, more explicitly, "melodic springboards to be developed into songs."[15] Many jots were never used; few of the surviving ones can be readily associated with completed songs. Some jots are only a few measures long, others more extended. They might have a title, a generic indicator like "ballad," a designation as "verse" or "chorus," or no annotation at all.

Early on, Arlen seems to have made his jots on full pages of manuscript paper.[16] Figure 1.1 shows one such sheet, undated (as almost all are) but most likely from the 1930s.[17] The top five staves appear to sketch out a tune,

6  HAROLD ARLEN AND HIS SONGS

**Figure 1.1** A page of jots for unidentified songs, most likely made in the late 1920s or early 1930s (Rita Arlen Collection, Music Division, Library of Congress, Washington, D.C.)

probably for the chorus of a song, with no lyrics; here, as in most Arlen songs, the music (or the beginning of it) came first. There is a clear indication of key (F major) and meter (cut time or alle breve, ¢). The jot consists mainly of a tune, but under some measures Arlen sketches in chords or a counter-melody, which suggests he had the harmony and full texture in mind, as we might expect from someone with his experience as an arranger. The opening motive and the dotted rhythms in the fourth measure of this jot bear some resemblance to "I Gotta Right to Sing the Blues," which Arlen wrote with Ted Koehler in 1932. On the sixth and seventh staves Arlen sketches a "verse" or introduction, presumably intended for the same song. He writes "1–4" to indicate measures that are to be repeated literally; this kind of shorthand becomes characteristic for Arlen.

Near the bottom of the page, Arlen fills three staves with heavier pencil. He probably made these jots at a later time, but they appear intended for the same song as the melody higher up on the page, with which they share a key and meter. These later jots are heavily syncopated, with accents on the off-beats; Arlen seems to explore different notational possibilities for the rhythms. The jots also feature one of Arlen's signature gestures, an octave leap (like the one that opens "Over the Rainbow" or "It's Only a Paper Moon"). And the melodic fragments end on a distinct "blue" note, the flatted third of F, A♭, another Arlen fingerprint.

Arlen also made jots on small pieces of music paper cut from larger sheets. Some have holes punched in the left margin, which suggests they were fashioned into booklets that Arlen might carry with him when away from home. In his 1964 television interview, the composer pulls out of his pocket what appears to be a folded music sheet similar to the small jot pages, and he tells Cronkite how he often gets an ideas for a song while out walking: "They may not be useable, may not work. . . . The momentum, the rhythm of it sets up something in me . . . and if I can find a wall where nobody's looking, I take out the manuscript and put it down."[18] Arlen's story lines up with those of other composers, including classical ones like Beethoven and Brahms, who often got their best ideas while strolling out in nature. Song composers likely did too. George Gershwin, for one, kept notebooks of various sizes into which he sketched melodic ideas.[19]

Figure 1.2 reproduces a piece of pocket-sized manuscript paper with jots most likely intended by Arlen for two separate numbers. The first, on the top two staves, is striking for its key, G♭ major, rarely if ever encountered in sheet music for the American Songbook, and for its verbal annotations. "Clock strikes twelve (witch)" evidently refers to the song's dramatic function; "Finish down Chromatic" is a more technical remark. It is tempting to imagine this jot was intended for *The Wizard of Oz*, which features the only witches in the Arlen canon. But in neither the film nor L. Frank Baum's book

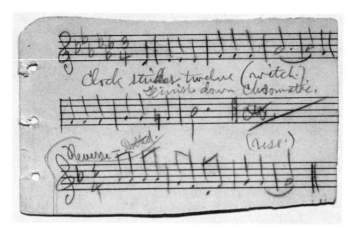

**Figure 1.2** A portable jot, for an unidentified song (or songs) (Rita Arlen Collection, Music Division, Library of Congress, Washington, D.C.)

does a clock strike twelve. (In the film, when the Wicked Witch turns over the hourglass to mark the moments until Dorothy's demise, there is no song or melody, only dissonant underscoring, with which Arlen was not involved.) Beneath the "witch" jot is another, in F major and duple meter, with the annotation "Reverse—Dotted." It is not clear from the context what would be "reversed," but "dotted" might be an indication that the tune would have dotted rhythms. Over the last measure Arlen writes "(Use)," which suggests he was pleased enough to want to retain this jot.

The most famous Arlen story about a small jot involves a song that *was* intended for *The Wizard of Oz*. The moment of inspiration occurred not on a walk, but, as we might expect in Hollywood, on a drive. In June 1938, the composer was having a hard time coming up with a ballad for Dorothy to sing near the opening of *The Wizard of Oz*. As he told the story to Cronkite:

> I said to Mrs. Arlen, I said, "Let's go to Grauman's Chinese [Theatre]." I said, "You drive the car. I don't feel too well right now." I wasn't thinking of work. I wasn't conscious of thinking of work. I just wanted to relax. And as we drove by Schwab's Drug Store on Sunset [Boulevard], I said, "Pull over, please." And she knew what I meant, and we stopped and I really don't know why, bless the muses, and I took out my little piece of manuscript and put down what you know now as "Over the Rainbow." Of course, it needed Mr. Harburg's lyric.[20]

## Harold Arlen—Collaborator

What appears to be almost an afterthought in Arlen's remarks to Cronkite about "Over the Rainbow"—"it needed Mr. Harburg's lyric"— in fact reflects his core belief as a songwriter. Arlen insisted that no song was his creation alone, but rather the product of close collaboration. "A good lyric writer is the composer's best friend," he once noted.[21] As he told Cronkite, quite humbly:

> It's not a tune, it isn't *my* composition that you remember, if I can put it that personally. . . . If you sing [he hums the opening melody of "Over the Rainbow"], you won't do what I just did. You will subconsciously think of "Somewhere over the rainbow," or sing it or some phrase in it. Well, somebody wrote that, and those little phrases are what make—not just those little phrases—those are the memorable things that stand out and cling to a song and make it a happy wedding.[22]

Arlen always emphasized the give-and-take between composer and lyricist. When asked by Cronkite the proverbial question, "Which comes first—the music or the words?" Arlen responded:

> I would say that through the years I've written every which way: written to titles, written to lyric—a complete lyric—written tune first, the lyric writer suggesting a phrase, or several phrases, written backwards. . . . A lyric writer might have a resolution that sounds awfully good and work from the top down. There's no set pattern. But I will say this: for the pro writer, lyric writer, I should think—and I've only worked with six lyric writers, I believe—that when they hear a stunning tune, if you're fortunate to have one, or an exciting one or something, and it gives them something, they're ready. Something snaps and the little wheel starts turning.[23]

Like all composers of his generation, Arlen had many "trunk" tunes, songs without lyrics, which he wrote without a specific purpose or commission, or which may have been intended for inclusion in a specific show or film but then set aside. Arlen would hold on to what he deemed the best of these songs for use on some later occasion. "Last Night When We Were Young" and "A Sleepin' Bee," two of his greatest numbers (to be discussed in Chapters 4 and 8), were originally trunk tunes, created well before lyrics were added. But even in such cases, songwriting would remain a fundamentally collaborative process for Arlen. In 1961 he told his biographer Edward Jablonski: "Each lyricist is an individual and I have to work with each in his own way." He goes on to give an example of his work with Harburg on the musical *Jamaica*: "About 90 percent of the songs began with an idea or a title. We'd jump around a lot, begin a song, leave it, begin another. . . . Once we'd set the mood and point of the song, we knew what we still had to do when the time came."[24]

Although he wrote most of his songs with four different lyricists—Ted Koehler, Yip Harburg, Johnny Mercer, and Ira Gershwin—Arlen had a total of almost two dozen collaborators over his career, considerably more than the six he references in his remarks to Cronkite.[25] In a 1965 interview Arlen attributed his range as a composer specifically—and generously—to working with different lyricists:

> If I hadn't had the very group of collaborators, I wouldn't have had the variety of songs that I have. I think it was healthy all the way, because they all write differently, they all think differently, they all listen differently. And I think most times I was in tune with them and it made me reach, where had I been with one collaborator all the time, I think it would have probably stunted my growth.[26]

Arlen also felt he owed his "reach" to the different venues for which he and his lyricists wrote, including Harlem, Broadway, and Hollywood. "I have never liked to stick to one groove," he told the radio commentator Dave Garroway in 1955. "I like to what I call 'complete the circle.'"[27] Arlen went on to explain how he moved from the "blues and hot rhythm" of Harlem and the Cotton Club in the early 1930s, with songs like "Stormy Weather"; to Hollywood in 1933, with a "simple" lyrical number like "Let's Fall in Love"; to a jauntier Broadway style with the 1934 show *Life Begins at 8:40* and songs like "Fun to Be Fooled"; to the "pure line" of "Over the Rainbow" for *The Wizard of Oz* (1939); and then back to jazz- and blues-inspired music for all-black cast shows *St. Louis Woman* (1946) and *House of Flowers* (1954).

Too much commentary on popular song, especially when composer and lyricist are not the same person, concentrates on either music or lyrics, not their intersection. The "poets of Tin Pan Alley," as Philip Furia has called lyricists, rarely get adequate recognition for their work.[28] The present book, the first to discuss Arlen's songs in detail, will be organized around the partnerships with his principal lyricists. Such a structure, conveniently but not coincidentally, yields a largely chronological trajectory, stretching from the Cotton Club and Ted Koehler in the 1930s, through Arlen's work with Yip Harburg on Broadway and in Hollywood later in that decade, his collaboration with Johnny Mercer beginning in the 1940s, to the briefer but no less significant partnerships from the last two decades of his active career, beginning with Leo Robin (1947) and Dorothy Fields (1951–1953), then Ira Gershwin (1953–1954), Truman Capote (1954), and, finally, Dory Langdon (1962–1964) and Martin Charnin (1964–1967).

These partnerships do not always follow a neat timeline: Arlen worked with both Koehler and Harburg at various points over several decades; and he teamed up again with Mercer in the 1950s after collaborations with Robin, Fields, Capote, and Gershwin. Some Arlen songs will thus be studied out of the order of their creation. But I believe that focusing on the special bond of the composer and his steadiest collaborators offers the most fruitful approach to this repertory, because, as noted above by Arlen himself, he developed a distinctive sound and style with each. In that sense Arlen differs from composers like Jerome Kern, Harry Warren, Vincent Youmans, Vernon Duke, or Jule Styne, for whom it is difficult to identify stylistic distinctions arising from their work with different lyricists.

Arlen held each of his collaborators to the same high standard as he held himself, and he might express displeasure if the "happy wedding" of music and lyric was anything less than perfect. Arlen could even become frustrated with an experienced, long-time collaborator, as is clear from an entry in a diary he kept for a short while in 1966.[29] Though there is little context given, the passage reports on a meeting with Yip Harburg about a song for Harry Belafonte to be included in a film version (never made) of the 1944 Arlen-Harburg show *Bloomer Girl*, which had been optioned by 20th Century Fox. (We will discuss *Bloomer Girl* in Chapter 4.) Belafonte would be likely have been cast as the escaped slave Pompey, a role played by Dooley Wilson in the Broadway show. In the diary Arlen notes discussing with Harburg the first song Belafonte would sing, presumably newly composed for the film. He then remarks that he finds Harburg "one of the greatest lyricists of my generation," but that "when it comes to songs that have or need a rhythmic base— I'm always troubled by his presence—He do lack rhythm—"

Harburg's poetic imagination, responsible for "Over the Rainbow," "Last Night When We Were Young," "Happiness Is Just a Thing Called Joe," and "Cocoanut Sweet," was indeed unsurpassed among his peers. But he did arguably lack the kind of "rhythmic base" needed, for example, for songs like "Blues in the Night," "Come Rain or Come Shine," or "One for My Baby," created by Arlen with Johnny Mercer. Perhaps the number Arlen was envisioning (or had already drafted) for Belafonte in 1966 was closer to those songs in style, where Harburg's talents would not work as well. Above all, Arlen's diary comment about Harburg reveals not only how essential it was for him to have the right lyric and lyricist for the task at hand, but also how he would work differently with each partner.

Several lyricists note both the inspiration and challenge of collaborating with Arlen, especially of fitting lyrics to his "tapeworms." Mercer observes that Arlen "won't let a simple phrase take him where it would ordinarily lead somebody else. He'll take a phrase and he'll say, 'Now where can this phrase be—how can it be different? How can I take it that it'll interest the public in a new way?'"[30] Ira Gershwin writes, "Arlen is no thirty-two-bar man. As one of the most individual of American show-composers he is distinctive in melodic line and unusual construction." Gershwin goes on to explain that anyone collaborating with Arlen "finds himself wondering if a resultant song isn't too long or too difficult or too mannered for popular consumption. But there's no cause for worry. Many Arlen songs do take time to catch on, but when they do they join his impressive and lasting catalogue."[31] Charnin calls the composer "one of the great spaghetti writers of all time," whose "melodies would go places you wouldn't expect." He adds, "You'd find yourself trying to accommodate them rather than telling him to turn it into a thirty-two-bar song."[32]

## A "Realist" versus "Replicative" Approach to Popular Song

In recent decades, scholars of popular music have reminded us that songs exist in a complex network of composers, arrangers, improvisers, performers, and listeners. The printed musical score is just one part of that network. In a thoughtful consideration of the ontology of "standards," songs that are the most performed and recorded, Brian Kane notes:

> American popular songs are composed of small, often interchangeable parts. Even before their premieres on radio, film, Broadway, or recordings, songs from the era of Tin Pan Alley were never integral. They would go through many alterations: a verse might be added or cut; new lyrics might be written, or re-written; the melody line may be altered to accentuate the strengths of one singer and hide the weaknesses of another. Once in

the public, the song might circulate in performances by a wide variety of musicians, each "testing" the tune, making alterations or additions to it.[33]

Kane distinguishes between a "realist" approach, which views a song as thing, an object that has essential properties, and an approach that acknowledges the mutability of the song in the process of "replication" by performers. "A standard requires that others participate in its perpetuation and stabilization," Kane writes. "By reproducing the standard, it is transformed at the same time that it is transmitted."[34]

Although the basic thrust of the present book is a "realist" one, comprising close analyses based on the notated music, two complete chapters (9 and 11) and portions of others treat Arlen's songs in performance, by himself and others. Most songs by Arlen and his contemporaries were published as sheet music that enables analysis of structural features; and yet each performance will differ, and with it the song's identity will change. In this sense there is no essential "Over the Rainbow"; it is a product of continuous "replication."

## Harold Arlen—Jewish and Black-Adjacent Composer

Two photographs capture important dimensions of Arlen's musical identity, as acknowledged by him and many who knew, worked with, or have written about him. The first, from about 1910, was taken at the Buffalo synagogue where Arlen's father was the cantor and young Harold worshipped and sang regularly (Figure 1.3). The second, taken in 1929, shows Arlen with bandleader Fletcher Henderson, composer Will Marion Cook, and several other leading Black musicians (Figure 1.4).

Like several of his songwriting contemporaries, including Berlin, Kern, and Gershwin, Arlen was the offspring of first-generation Jewish immigrants. (Berlin was born in Russia.) His father Samuel (Shmuel) Arluck and his mother Celia Orlin both arrived in the United States as children from Vilnius, in the Polish part of the Russian Empire. Arlen was born in 1905 in Buffalo, New York, as Chaim (or Hyman) Arluck. He changed his name in the 1920s, initially just his given name (the first compositions were credited to "Harold Arluck"), and then his surname ("Arlen" blends the surnames of his parents).[35]

Samuel served as cantor of Buffalo's prominent Brith Sholem synagogue (also called the Pine Street Shul after one of its locations), where Arlen often

**Figure 1.3** The Brith Sholem synagogue in Buffalo, New York (ca. 1910). Cantor Samuel Arluck is at center; smallest boy at right is his son Hyman Arluck, later known as Harold Arlen. (Courtesy of the University Archives, University at Buffalo, State University of New York)

sang in services as a child. In 1924, Samuel took a similar position in Syracuse, New York. Arlen pointed to his father's vocal and improvisational practices as formative. "My father was the best of cantors," he told William Zinsser in 1960. "He improvised wonderful melodies to fit the texts that had no music, and that's undoubtedly where my sense of melody comes from."[36] Arlen heard his father's cantorial improvisations as resembling Black styles of singing, even though Samuel had no familiarity with those traditions. When asked by Max Wilk about "the unique meld of two cultures [Jewish and African American]" in his music, Arlen replied: "Oh *boy*, I don't know how the hell to explain it—except I hear jazz and gospel in my father's singing. He was one of the greatest *improvisers* I ever heard. . . . I never dreamed of aping my father, but I know damned well now that his glorious improvisations must have had some effect on me and my own style." Later on, Arlen recalls, Samuel would sing his son's songs in the synagogue: "It got so that his congregation would expect to hear him sing one of my so-called 'hits'. . . . Whatever of mine

**Figure 1.4** Harold Arlen (second from left) with Fletcher Henderson (at the wheel) and Will Marion Cook (standing in front of the car) in Atlantic City, New Jersey (1929). Next to Arlen is the actor Roscoe ("Fatty") Arbuckle, and the other musicians are Lois Deppe (waving hat), Bobby Stark, and Rex Stewart. The car is a Packard. (Courtesy of Bill Ecker, Harmonie Autographs and Music, Inc., New York)

was going at the time, he'd use it in the musical text of the service. He'd sing 'Stormy Weather' or 'My Shining Hour' as one of his solo passages!"[37]

Arlen's closest collaborators, although likely unfamiliar with Samuel's singing, claimed to hear Jewish inflections in the composer's music. Ira Gershwin observes, "To me the Hebraic influence is the big one in his [Arlen's] music, and it's something that my brother George didn't have. Our parents, like Harold's, came from Eastern Russia, but there was no Jewish religious music in our family." Mercer comments, "Harold's melodies are way out because Jewish melodies are way out—they take unexpected twists and turns."[38] Harburg spoke of Arlen bringing to music "his Semitic background."[39]

Even as he acknowledged the influence of his father's improvised melodies, Arlen avoided identifying Jewish features in his own songs. The composer and critic Jack Gottlieb took on that task, seeking to link Arlen tunes directly to Jewish liturgical chants. As an example, he adduces "Come Rain or Come Shine." Arlen's tune is (unusually for him) almost anti-melodic, featuring the chant-like repetition of a single note ("I'm gonna love you / like nobody loved you"). Gottlieb hears in this an "echo" of a passage, also featuring repeated notes, from *The Song of Songs* sung during Passover services. Both, he also writes, "are about love." Gottlieb finds similarities between another melodic motive in "Come Rain or Come Shine" and a Jewish folk song.[40] Such analyses are problematic. Repeated notes are common in many different repertoires, and countless songs in both sacred and secular traditions are "about love." It seems likely that for Arlen any connection with Jewish cantorial style, at least his father's, runs through the practice of improvisation rather than the melodic shapes Gottlieb identifies. Improvisation also provides the link with Black musicians and musical practices.

Even as he was studying classical piano as a child in Buffalo, Arlen was drawn to ragtime and jazz. He played in and provided arrangements for various local bands. By his early teens he began forming his own groups, first the Snappy Trio, then the Yankee Six and the Buffalodians. The other players in these ensembles were, like Arlen, white, but in 1925 he sang with the Blue Ribbon Syncopators, a Black band in Buffalo, an interracial pairing unusual at the time.[41] Arlen would continue to work closely with Black musicians for the rest of his career. By the mid 1920s he was preparing arrangements for Fletcher Henderson, who in 1929 brought him into contact with composer Will Marion Cook. The following year Arlen began to write for the Cotton Club in Harlem, where Ethel Waters would admiringly call him "the Negro-est white man I know."[42] Among his white songwriting peers, Arlen was the one who engaged most deeply with Black musical styles and genres. (We will return in later chapters to Arlen's Cotton Club activities, his several Black-cast musicals, and his long association with prominent Black singers.)

The historian Jeffrey Melnick has suggested that Arlen, Berlin, Kern, and Gershwin were "the composers most responsible for repositioning African American music as a province of Jewish art." Melnick characterizes Jewish composers, jazz musicians, and music publishers of the early twentieth century as figures who often "traded in a Blackness which did not benefit African Americans and often actively worked to exclude them from positions of cultural power."[43] Such claims are legitimate in many cases. But we might also, with the critic John McWhorter, view Arlen and other white composers as "Black-adjacent artists, often writing, respectfully, in Black-derived idioms" for Black singers or dramatic characters. While acknowledging a history of conflict and appropriation, McWhorter argues that some of Arlen's greatest songs—he singles out "I Wonder What Became of Me" from the Black-cast musical *St. Louis Woman* (to be discussed in Chapter 5)—represent an admirable "cultural melding."[44]

I lean more toward McWhorter's view than Melnick's. A creative figure like Arlen draws consciously and unconsciously from many different strands of music and culture. From when he began writing songs in the mid-1920s until he stopped almost fifty years later, Arlen had his ears wide open—to Jewish music, blues, and jazz, as well as the popular song of his day, including those by Berlin and Kern from the previous generation, and contemporaries like Gershwin, Youmans, Rodgers, and Porter. Arlen also absorbed much from vocalists, not only his cantor father, but singers with whom he worked closely or who sang his songs across decades, including Waters, Lena Horne, Pearl Bailey, Judy Garland, Ella Fitzgerald, Frank Sinatra, Peggy Lee, and Tony Bennett. All these musical traditions and figures are part of the world of Arlen's songs we will explore in the chapters to follow.

# 2
# Inside the Rainbow

A *National Geographic* article about rainbows begins:

> A rainbow is a multicolored arc made by light striking water droplets. The most familiar type rainbow is produced when sunlight strikes raindrops in front of a viewer at a precise angle (42 degrees). Rainbows can also be viewed around fog, sea spray, or waterfalls. A rainbow is an optical illusion—it does not actually exist in a specific spot in the sky. The appearance of a rainbow depends on where you're standing and where the sun (or other source of light) is shining. The sun or other source of light is usually behind the person seeing the rainbow.[1]

As we might expect from such a reference source, this definition is largely technical. It does not celebrate the stunning beauty of rainbows, which have inspired countless paintings, poems, and songs. Nor does this paragraph explore the many associations that rainbows have inspired—hope, healing, good fortune, cultural diversity, gay pride, and ethnic self-determination.

Yet scientific descriptions of natural phenomena like rainbows do not necessarily detract from our enjoyment or imagination; knowing how things are made can enhance our appreciation. The same is true of works of art—novels, plays, paintings, sculptures, and music. Detailed analysis of Shakespeare's *Romeo and Juliet*, Monet's *Water Lilies*, or the Beatles' "Yesterday" helps us understand why we admire these works, why we return to them again and again.

My example of the rainbow is not, of course, arbitrary. That image shapes one of the most beloved songs of all time, "Over the Rainbow," with music by Harold Arlen and lyrics by Yip Harburg. It first appeared in the film musical *The Wizard of Oz* in 1939. Since then, generations of performers, listeners, and commentators have read (or sung) into "Over the Rainbow" many different meanings. The song has become a palimpsest, a term that traditionally connotes a manuscript which has been written over many times but on which traces of the original remain. In 1992 "Over the Rainbow" was celebrated by the writer Salman Rushdie as "the anthem of all the world's migrants . . . a hymn to Elsewhere."[2] In 2013, weeks after the massacre at Sandy Hook Elementary School, it was recorded by a group of school children from Newtown, Connecticut, as a gesture of consolation and solidarity. Yo-Yo Ma and Kathryn Stott played "Over the Rainbow" on their album *Songs of Comfort and Hope*, released by Sony Classical at the height of the Covid pandemic in 2020.

Where does the appeal of "Over the Rainbow," and that of many other Arlen songs, lie? Why do prominent composers like André Previn and Stephen Sondheim admire Arlen's music so deeply? Why have great singers like Judy Garland or Frank Sinatra performed them again and again? Answering those questions invites us—compels us, I believe—to explore Arlen's songs in some depth; that is one of the principal goals of this book. In the present chapter, in order to introduce some of the relevant terminology and analytical tools, we will get inside "Over the Rainbow."[3] Try to hear the song in your mind's ear as you read on and follow the discussion.

## Formal Structure

In "Over the Rainbow" Arlen and Harburg were working within certain conventions of popular song of their day. "Over the Rainbow" has an introduction or **verse** ("When all the world is a hopeless jumble"). Verses can vary in length—the verse of "Over the Rainbow" is twenty measures long—and tend to set up the musical and poetic features of a song. (Regrettably, verses are often omitted by singers in performance. Garland rarely sang it in "Over the Rainbow.") A verse is followed by the main portion of the song, called the **chorus**, which has a more standard length, usually thirty-two measures, divided into eight-measure segments. We represent the musical structure of a chorus with uppercase letters for each eight-measure segment, **AABA**. The contrasting **B** section is also called the **bridge**, because it serves to connect the A sections. (**Release** is another common term for the bridge.)

The AABA structure, one of the most common among song composers, conforms nicely to patterns of human comprehension. A musical unit is presented and then repeated (AA), to allow it to become familiar. The ear is then ready for change, which comes with a contrasting eight-measure segment (B). This is followed by a return of the opening segment that rounds off the structure in a satisfying way (A, or slightly modified as indicated by a prime sign, A′). The chorus of "Over the Rainbow" has a typical AABA musical structure, followed by an eight-measure **coda,** a segment added in many songs to create an effective conclusion.

The uppercase letters refer to the *musical* structure, not the words, which can, as in "Over the Rainbow," change even when the music repeats, thus shaping the narrative and emotional trajectory of a song. Harburg begins the lyrics of each A with the same phrase, "Somewhere over the rainbow," but then develops or modifies the imagery. "Way up high" in the first A becomes "skies are blue" in the second, and then "bluebirds fly" in the third. These changes lead in turn to further ones in each A, such that only the first four words are the same. In this way, Arlen and Harburg capture the emotions of Dorothy, who, as a twelve-year-old child might do, remains singularly focused on the idea of getting over the rainbow but also imagines different possibilities of what might lie there. For the contrasting B section or bridge, Harburg's lyric shifts from space to time, from the "somewhere" Dorothy would like to be, to the "someday" when she hopes to wake up. For the ending of the last A, Dorothy for the first time frames her longing as a question, "Why, then, oh why can't I?"

## The "Pure Line"

We saw in Chapter 1 that Arlen was proud of his ability to create a "pure line," a melody with clear shape and direction. There is perhaps no better example than the opening A segment of "Over the Rainbow" (Example 2.1). Arlen begins with what became a signature gesture, an upward leap of an octave ("Some-where"). Then across the next eight measures the melodic line descends gradually, ending on the note where it began ("lulla-*by*"). This melody is gratifying to the ear—and to a singer who performs it—because it opens with a surprise, the upward leap, which is then resolved or, more literally, fulfilled by the slow descent to the point of origin. Arlen ends the coda of "Over the Rainbow" by reversing the direction of the pure line heard at the beginning (Example 2.2). The tune rises by step to the high E♭, the same note

Example 2.1 "Over the Rainbow," melodic arc of A section

**Example 2.2** "Over the Rainbow," coda

from which the descent began at the opening of the song. This is a kind of musical question, which Harburg matches with a verbal one: "Why, oh why can't I?"

With its broad arc, Arlen's opening melody is the perfect analogy to the image of the rainbow, which Harburg had settled on before the team began working on the song. Filling out the lyrics proved challenging, as Harburg would later recall, especially because of the opening melodic leap:

> He [Arlen] gave me a tune with those first two notes. I tried *I'll go over the rainbow, Someday over the rainbow*. I had difficulty coming to the idea of *Somewhere*. For a while I just thought I would leave those first two notes out. It was a long time before I came to *Somewhere over the rainbow*.[4]

We could scarcely imagine the pure line of "Over the Rainbow" without "those first two notes"; we can be grateful Harburg did not omit them.

## Harmony

The first two phrases of "Over the Rainbow" are shaped not only by the melody, but by what lies beneath it, the **harmony** or succession of chords. The songs of Arlen and his contemporaries share the basic harmonic vocabulary and techniques of Western music since about 1700, which were then enhanced in popular music and jazz during the twentieth century. "Over the Rainbow" begins and ends in a "home" **key,** or **tonic.** The tonic is the principal note of a seven-note **diatonic scale.** Think of the white keys on the piano, comprising the scale of C major, which can be recreated, or **transposed** to start, on any note. An expanded scale with all twelve available notes (black and white keys) is **chromatic.** Like most songs, "Over the Rainbow" draws on both diatonic and chromatic notes.

Chords are often labeled with reference to their main note or **root,** and any chord can be either **major** or **minor,** depending on whether the third note above the root is raised or lowered: thus C major or C minor (abbreviated as Cmaj or Cmin). The way chords succeed each other in time is known as a **harmonic progression**, which gives depth and direction to a melody. Progressions are often indicated by chord names or Roman numerals: the tonic is I, and other harmonies are labeled according to the position in the seven-note scale, reckoned upward from the tonic, thus II, III, IV, V, VI, and VII. A Roman numeral appearing in uppercase indicates a major chord; lower case, as in ii or vi, a minor chord.

The most basic form of a harmony is a three-note chord or **triad**. In "Over the Rainbow," as in much popular music and jazz, most triads are enriched by notes lying above the root at various distances (or **intervals**), usually a sixth, seventh, ninth, eleventh, or thirteenth, thus creating chords of four, or sometimes five or six notes, rather than three. In musical analysis, as reflected in the musical discussions and notated examples in this book, Arabic numerals after the chord name or Roman numeral indicate the distance of the added note or notes from the bass, thus C7 or V7, or $C7^{(9)}$ or $V7^{(9)}$. In the latter, the chord has both a seventh and a ninth.

Harmonic progressions in tonal music move between more and less stable chords. The most stable ones, like the tonic, are considered **consonances** (in the adjectival form, **consonant**); they tend to feature notes of the diatonic scale. The less stable chords are **dissonances** (**dissonant**), which usually contain added or chromatic notes. It is a general principle of tonal music that dissonances must eventually resolve to consonances. One of the most basic dissonance-to-consonance progressions is from V7 to I, from the **dominant seventh** to the tonic, forming a **cadence**, which usually comes at the end of a phrase or series of phrases.

Example 2.3 shows the first musical **phrase** of "Over the Rainbow" with its underlying harmonic structure. "Phrase" is used in music in similar ways to language, to characterize a coherent but not fully closed portion of a longer melody. In "Over the Rainbow" the A segment is comprised of two four-measure phrases. Arlen adds a sixth (C) to the opening tonic ("Some-"); a seventh (B♭) to the vi chord ("-where"); a seventh (D♭) to the I ("-bow"); and a seventh (G) to the IV ("up"). These added notes make for smooth harmonic transitions in that each becomes a component of the next harmony—that is, the C becomes the root of the vi chord, the B♭ becomes the third of iii, and so on.

Arlen structures the A section of "Over the Rainbow" so that cadential closure does not arrive too soon. The first phrase ends ("high") on an attenuated

**Example 2.3** "Over the Rainbow," harmonic analysis of opening bars

**Example 2.4** "Over the Rainbow," circle of fifths harmonic progression

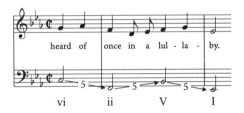

tonic or I chord, presented in an **inversion**: the third of the chord (G), rather than root (E♭), is in the bass. Only at the end of A ("once in a lullaby") do we get a full **cadential progression** leading firmly toward closure on the tonic in root position (Example 2.4). The bass notes move by fifth—the strongest progression in tonal music—from C to F to B♭ to E♭. (In Arlen's notated music, F moves up by fourth to B♭, but this is an inversion of, and thus functionally equivalent to, the fifth.) The harmonies are very typical of a cadential progression: vi–ii–V–I.

Compared with the A section, the first part of B or the bridge of "Over the Rainbow" ("Someday I'll wish upon a star") is melodically and harmonically static. The vocal part is no "pure line," but rather an oscillation between two notes. With this gesture Arlen sought to evoke the sound of a child's piano exercise. (Harburg had a different recollection, claiming that the two-note alternation was inspired by the whistling sound Arlen used to call his dog.)[5] Underneath the tune, the harmony remains constant, a tonic chord anchored for four measures by a **pedal point**, or sustained note in the bass.

**Example 2.5** "Over the Rainbow," end of the bridge

But after floating musically for four measures, the bridge builds quickly to a climax with its second phrase ("Where troubles melt like lemon drops"). The moment of greatest tension in "Over the Rainbow" comes at "that's where you'll find me," with a dissonance under each word (Example 2.5). It is here that the oscillating melodic figure gives way to more sustained notes. The most dissonant harmonies arrive at "find me," to lead back to the tonic E♭ major. The dominant seventh is enriched with an augmented fifth (F♯) and a ninth (C), and Arlen adds to the tension by displacing the bass B♭ rhythmically. The melodic note on "find" (F) is the highest in the song: Arlen thus coordinates the vocal climax with the harmonic one.

In his superb lyrics for the bridge Harburg followed Arlen's lead. To reflect the change in musical style and the contrast that a bridge normally represents in a song, Harburg shifts, as mentioned above, from spatial ("Somewhere") to temporal ("Someday") imagery and then blends the two as Dorothy imagines waking with the clouds "far behind me" in both space and time. At the musical climax Harburg uses the second person ("you'll") for the only time in the song, as if Dorothy is speaking directly to us, breaking the fourth wall. Music and lyric here come together for maximum effect.[6]

## Jazz Harmonizations

As suggested in Chapter 1, a notated score of a song will never capture the "replication," the alterations that occur in each performance. Countless jazz musicians have reimagined "Over the Rainbow" since its appearance in 1939. That practice is something Arlen himself, as a capable jazz pianist, understood, endorsed, and engaged in, as is clear from his own recordings of the song.

We can look briefly at how the opening measures of "Over the Rainbow" are reinterpreted by pianist André Previn in a solo version recorded in 1960 (partially transcribed in Example 2.6).[7] We recall from Chapter 1 that Previn admires Arlen as a "composer" whose carefully crafted formal structures resist modification by a performer. But in jazz styles of Previn's era this stricture does not apply to the harmony. While retaining Arlen's melodic shapes, Previn recasts the harmonic progressions and enriches chords with ninths, elevenths, and thirteenths, some of which are then also raised or lowered (with sharps and flats). (In Example 2.6 chord functions or progressions are shown beneath the music; chord names and descriptions appear above.) All these alterations result in an intensely rich harmonic "rainbow."

Previn reshapes the song's initial phrases to delay the tonic. Rather than establishing the key of E♭ with the opening chord, he harmonizes the first melodic note with an A diminished triad with added minor seventh, a chord generally referred to as "half-diminished" (represented in Example 2.6 by a circle with a slash). Previn approaches Arlen's original G minor, on the downbeat of the second measure ("*o*-ver"), via a succession of bass motions

**Example 2.6** "Over the Rainbow," transcribed from André Previn's jazz interpretation (1960) and transposed from D major to facilitate comparison with other examples

by fifth, A–D–G.[8] Previn's opening progression anticipates his approach to Arlen's A♭ harmony on the downbeat of the third measure ("way"). In the sheet music Arlen (as seen in Example 2.3) reaches the A♭ from its own dominant seventh, E♭7. Previn precedes that chord (which he presents in inversion) with its own dominant seventh, thus creating another chain of fifths, B♭–E♭–A♭, similar to the opening. Previn further embellishes the first phrase by filling the space between the chords with a motive based on the oscillating minor thirds of song's B theme ("Someday I'll wish upon a star"). Here these figures sound extraterrestrial, lying well beyond the rainbow: the B♮–D eighth notes are not part of Previn's opening half-diminished chord.

Previn continues to obscure the tonic E♭ across the first phrase. In the approach to the fourth measure ("high"), he avoids Arlen's IV–I cadence (often called a **plagal cadence**), underlaying the right-hand A♭ chord ("up") with a G♭ triad in the left, which then descends on the downbeat in parallel motion to E (or F♭) major. The key-defining E♭–B♭ fifth is present in the right hand, but is attenuated by the added G♭ and A♭.

Previn's inventive version of "Over the Rainbow" is just one example of how a jazz instrumentalist can reconceive Arlen's song.[9] As will become clear in the chapters that follow, the harmonies represented in the published sheet music of Arlen's songs already reflect some advanced jazz practices, as we might expect from a composer with his background. Arlen's own notated harmonic structures arguably influenced or inspired later jazz musicians.

## Texture and Voice-Leading

For "Over the Rainbow," as for many of Arlen's songs, Roman numerals and chord labels—the latter usually added by music publishers—are imperfect representations of harmonic and melodic structure. They capture only individual moments in a fluid musical **texture**. Just as cloth fabric has a texture woven from threads oriented horizontally and vertically, so too in music, texture is the result of the intersection of the horizontal (melodic) and vertical (harmonic) dimensions. Arlen's textures are often very rich.

Individual notes that make up the harmonies tend to move at different speeds, forming **counter-melodies** to the main tune. This kind of **voice-leading** is partly what gives Arlen's songs their complexity. Thus, as we see in Example 2.3 above, under "up high" the inner parts or "voices" (though they are not literally sung) move at a faster rate than the sustained notes

**Example 2.7** "Over the Rainbow," inner voice chromatic descent

of the melody and harmony, creating a different sonority at each moment. What happens under "up high" is in fact only the start of a long countermelody descending by step in the piano that our ear can trace across six measures. This inner line spans an octave from G down to G and serves to provide continuity across the two large phrases of A (Example 2.7). Here one can see exactly what Alec Wilder and Ray Bolger mean, as quoted in Chapter 1, about a "thorough" Arlen who writes many compositional details into his music.

We hear the same kind of descending inner line at the climax of the bridge of "Over the Rainbow," as discussed above (Example 2.5). It begins on F under "chimney" (the example starts a beat later at the E♭ of "that's") and continues down by step, across the song's melodic and harmonic climax, at last resolving on the G that is part of the tonic chord at the return of the A section ("Somewhere"). As in the earlier passage, this line represents a countermelody to the "pure line" of the vocal part.

\*\*\*

Reading and absorbing the above analysis of "Over the Rainbow" will certainly take longer than playing through the song or listening to Garland's original performance in *The Wizard of Oz*, which lasts under three minutes. Yet, as I have tried to show here—and will suggest throughout this book—detailed exploration of an Arlen song, with reference to the notated music as conceived by the composer, can only enhance our appreciation. We do not need to compare an Arlen song to a Mozart symphony, as Sondheim does in his observation reported in Chapter 1, to feel that it deserves similarly close analysis.

My conviction in this regard is reaffirmed by some exchanges I have had with jazz musicians. Many base their renditions of popular song on other performances and recordings, on lead sheets, or on so-called fake books or the Real Book. The latter include only the tune and chord symbols, usually added over generations by musicians, rarely the composer him- or herself.

When I have showed the published sheet music of an Arlen song to accomplished jazz or pop musicians, they often express astonishment and admiration, finding the composer's harmonies, textures, and voice-leading more inventive than what they or other performers do. I believe it does not in any way diminish the replicative value of their activities to encourage these musicians, as well as general readers, to follow my exploration of Arlen's music.

# 3
# Arlen and Ted Koehler

The decade of the 1910s saw significant developments in American popular song. Irving Berlin's "Alexander's Ragtime Band" (1911) infused the march idioms of John Philip Sousa and George M. Cohan with new rhythmic and melodic vitality deriving in part from African American traditions. Jerome Kern's ballads like "They Didn't Believe Me" (1914) achieved a new harmonic sophistication and a melodic style that could sound at once lyrical and conversational. W.C. Handy's "St. Louis Blues" (1914) enriched the standard song forms with the inflected notes and twelve-bar structure of the blues.[1]

The generation of songwriters coming to prominence in the 1920s—including George and Ira Gershwin, Richard Rodgers and Lorenz Hart, Vincent Youmans, and Eubie Blake and Noble Sissle—contributed to a burgeoning Broadway music-theatrical scene. Sheet music publishers, many still concentrated in the district of New York known as Tin Pan Alley (a term that has also long been used to describe the popular music repertory of the era), issued tunes that were often hawked to prospective customers by pianist-singers known as "song pluggers." Berlin, Kern, and George Gershwin all worked in that humble capacity early in their careers. Vaudeville, though in decline, was still a presence across the United States. The New York stage saw many new revues and musicals. As the commercial record industry burgeoned, the music of bands and singers, both white and Black, could be heard in the increasing number of homes with phonographs. Radio also developed as a medium of transmission. In 1926, the Radio Corporation of America (RCA) formed the National Broadcasting Company as the first nationwide radio network. By the end of the decade over six hundred radio stations were operating in the United States.[2]

As a pianist, singer, and arranger during the 1920s, his formative years in Buffalo, Arlen became familiar with the songs of all the figures mentioned above. Yet he had no plans to become a composer, as he later told Max Wilk: "I wanted to be a singer. Never dreamed of songwriting."[3] Indeed, Arlen enjoyed some success as a crooner on disk, first performing short vocal solos with the Buffalodians, then fronting with the bandleader Arnold Johnson in

1928, and continuing for several years to sing with other well-known bands or accompanists.[4] He recorded popular hits of the day, including "Baby Face" by Harry Akst and Benny Davis and "How Many Times" by Berlin.

But Arlen's compositional impulse was clearly growing. As early as 1920 he became fascinated by George Gershwin's "Swanee" (1919), with its rhythmic and motivic intensity (the rapid-fire "How I love you / How I love you") and bold harmonies (augmented and diminished chords). When *Rhapsody in Blue* appeared in 1924, Arlen and a fellow pianist in Buffalo played an arrangement for two pianos and orchestra. "A lot of George Gershwin rubbed off on Harold," recalled one of Arlen's collaborators, Yip Harburg. "George was Harold's deity, he really was."[5] Arlen took inspiration from Gershwin's affinity and (in several articles published in the 1920s) advocacy for blues and jazz. In the 1930s the two men would develop a close relationship; Gershwin became something of a mentor. Hoagy Carmichael's jazz-infused music was another strong influence, though he rarely gets a mention by Arlen or his biographers.

## "Get Happy"

Arlen's compositional career took a decisive turn in the summer of 1929 when he was cast in a small role ("The Piano Player") in *Great Day*, a show with music by Youmans. Like *Show Boat* from two years earlier, *Great Day* had a mixed-race cast, was set in the South, and featured songs that drew on both Black and white traditions. Unlike *Show Boat*, *Great Day* flopped, closing after thirty-six performances. Yet, almost by chance, *Great Day* marked the real start of Arlen as a songwriter. Although his role was cut at some point during tryouts, Arlen remained involved as a rehearsal pianist, a task he assumed when the regular accompanist, the band leader Fletcher Henderson, fell ill.[6] As Arlen told the story in later years (often demonstrating at the piano), he would play a standard two-bar vamp to lead the dancers into a routine. Getting bored with that formula after a while, Arlen improvised a short fanfare with dotted and syncopated rhythms, rising an octave through the tonic triad, something like what is represented in Example 3.1.

This musical phrase caught the attention of two composers: Will Marion Cook, who was serving as choral director for *Great Day*, and Harry Warren, who was working in New York as a song plugger and appears to have attended rehearsals. Both encouraged Arlen to expand the phrase into a song. Warren

**Example 3.1** Arlen's improvised fanfare, which becomes the opening of "Get Happy"

told him of the ideal man to provide the words, Ted Koehler, an experienced lyricist (and also a pianist and composer) eleven years Arlen's senior. Warren brought them together at the office of his own employer, the music publisher Jerome Remick, and there the fanfare/vamp became "Get Happy," the composer's first big hit.[7]

"I didn't seek it out, or ask for it," Arlen recalled to Wilk, marveling at the apparent serendipity that led to "Get Happy" and his subsequent career as a song composer. "It just *happened*."[8] On July 31, 1929, Arlen was signed to a one-year contract as a staff composer for the music publishers George and Arthur Piantadosi (a firm that in early 1930 merged with Remick Music, a Warner Bros. subsidiary), earning fifty dollars a week plus royalties. Koehler would become Arlen's first long-term creative partner (Fig. 3.1). Together they would write just over a hundred songs between 1929 and 1947, with the bulk of their collaboration concentrated before 1934 in various musical revues, especially at the Cotton Club in Harlem. (See Table 3.1 for a selection of important Arlen-Koehler numbers.)

That Cook and Warren both heard promise in "Get Happy" seems no coincidence. They came from two different realms of American popular music that Arlen would arguably bring together better than any composer of his generation. Cook, a Black musician who had studied with Dvořák in New York, drew in his works on a range of African American idioms from the pre-jazz era, including cakewalk, ragtime, and spirituals.[9] By contrast, Warren, a Brooklyn-born, self-taught son of Italian immigrants, was the quintessential Tin Pan Alley composer, who would create such toe-tapping standards as "Lullaby of Broadway," "42nd Street," and "You Must Have Been a Beautiful Baby."

The compositional process for "Get Happy" became typical for Arlen. The opening musical phrase has the quality of a "jot," the kind of brief musical idea Arlen would put down on music paper (as described in Chapter 1) and then develop into a full song to which Koehler would add lyrics. In subsequent years of their collaboration, this pattern of music-then-lyric would

**Figure 3.1** Harold Arlen and Ted Koehler, early 1930s (Rita Arlen Collection, Music Division, Library of Congress, Washington, D.C.)

prevail. Koehler would reportedly lie down with his eyes closed on Arlen's sofa as the composer played a song over and over. Arlen, wondering at times whether Koehler was dozing off, would call out his name; Koehler would sit up abruptly and assure Arlen that the lyric was evolving in his head.[10]

"Get Happy" fits squarely into the category of what have been called "Broadway spirituals," in which composers and lyricists evoke the traditional African American genres like spiritual and gospel. Prominent contemporary examples include the Gershwins' "Clap Yo' Hands" (1926) and Jerome Kern and Oscar Hammerstein II's "Ol' Man River" (1927).[11] The sturdy diatonic harmonies and exhortative lyrics of "Get Happy" seek to capture the tone of a gospel number

Table 3.1  Harold Arlen & Ted Koehler: Twenty Songs

| TITLE | VENUE / FIRST PERFORMANCE |
| --- | --- |
| "Get Happy" | *Nine-Fifteen Revue* (George M. Cohan Theatre), opened February 11, 1930 |
| "Contagious Rhythm" | *Earl Carroll's Vanities of 1930*, opened July 1, 1930 |
| "Out of a Clear Blue Sky" | |
| "Linda" | *Brown Sugar* (Cotton Club), opened Fall 1930 |
| "Song of the Gigolo" | |
| "Between the Devil and the Deep Blue Sea" | *Rhythmania* (Cotton Club), opened March 1931 |
| "I Love a Parade" | |
| "Tell Me with a Love Song" | Unknown, published 1931 |
| "I Gotta Right to Sing the Blues" | *Earl Carroll's Vanities of 1932*, opened September 27, 1932 |
| "Satan's Li'l Lamb" | *Americana* (Shubert Theatre), opened October 5, 1932 |
| "I've Got the World on a String" | *Cotton Club Parade* (21st Edition), opened October 23, 1932 |
| "Minnie the Moocher's Wedding Day" | |
| "Happy as the Day Is Long" | *Cotton Club Parade* (22nd Edition), opened April 6, 1933 |
| "Stormy Weather" | |
| "Let's Fall in Love" | *Let's Fall in Love* (film), released January 1934 |
| "As Long as I Live" | *Cotton Club Parade* (24th Edition), opened March 23, 1934 |
| "Ill Wind" | |
| "Sing My Heart" | *Love Affair* (film), released March 1939 |
| *Americanegro Suite* (6 numbers) | Published 1941 |
| "Now I Know" | *Up in Arms* (film), released March 1944 |

like "Hallelujah to the Lamb," recorded by the Rust College Quartet in 1927, just a couple of years before Arlen and Koehler's song (▶ 3.1).[12] In this gospel song, the word "Hallelujah" and the full phrase "Hallelujah to the Lamb" are repeated over and over again, alternating with verses, the first of which begins with the imperative "Now come my brother and sister too / Let us join in the heavenly tune." Koehler's verse for "Get Happy," which is rarely performed, makes the connection with gospel clearer than the song's chorus alone. It begins with a twofold invocation, followed by a command, as if a preacher is calling his congregation together: "Hallelujah! Hallelujah! Come you sinners gather 'round."

In African American religious services and music dating back to the nineteenth century, the phrase "getting happy" indicates not merely the experience of joy, but the receiving of the Holy Spirit. In an oral history made in the late 1920s, a Black preacher recalled of his congregation after the Civil War, "All of my people were great Christians. Shouting, singing, praying, and good old heartfelt religion make up the things that filled their lives. . . . Aunt Charlotte used to cry most all the time when she got happy."[13] A popular spiritual entitled "Good Morning" has the verse, "My soul got happy this morning, O children!" In another spiritual, called "Tell Jesus," the words read "I went up on de mountain, I didn't go dere for t' stay, But when my soul got happy, Den I stayed all day."[14]

While "Get Happy" draws on both Black and Tin Pan Alley traditions, the most immediate influence probably came from Youmans, Arlen's employer at the time of the song's creation. According to Arlen's biographer Jablonski, Youmans "didn't like to bother with collaboration," so during the creation of *Great Day* he would send Arlen to play the show's lead sheets to the lyricists Billy Rose and Edward Eliscu.[15] Youmans is today best known as the composer of "Tea for Two" and the hit musical from which it came, *No, No, Nanette* (1925). Other Youmans numbers have also come to be recognized as classics of popular song, including "More Than You Know," "Without a Song" (both from *Great Day*), "Sometimes I'm Happy," and "Time on My Hands."[16] Some of Youmans's more intricate and chromatic tunes would clearly resonate with the younger composer.

"Get Happy" seems almost a paraphrase of Youmans's own Broadway spiritual "Hallelujah!" from the 1926 show *Hit the Deck*, with lyrics by Leo Robin and Clifford Grey (▶ 3.2). Youmans's opening melody rises fanfare-like up through an octave (Example 3.2). This tune must have been in Arlen's ear, even unconsciously, when he came up with the first phrase of "Get Happy," which has an identical contour (see Example 3.1). For his part, Koehler adapts some of Robin and Grey's language: their "you'll shoo the blues away" becomes his "you better chase all your cares away." The resemblances between the two songs extend to the bridge sections. Youmans's ("Satan lies

**Example 3.2** Vincent Youmans, Leo Robin, Clifford Grey, "Hallelujah!"

**Example 3.3** Comparison of bridges in Youmans, "Hallelujah!," and Arlen, "Get Happy"

**Example 3.4** Melodic climaxes in "Get Happy"

awaitin'") is built from a syncopated theme that descends sequentially from a high E♭; Arlen takes over this pattern directly, including the basic harmonic design (Example 3.3).

Given their similarities, we might ask why "Get Happy" became a far bigger hit than "Hallelujah!" The answer lies in the combined talents that made Arlen-Koehler one of the great partnerships in American popular song. The choruses of both "Hallelujah!" and "Get Happy" follow a standard AABA pattern. Youmans's A section is a long arc generated by syncopations that group measures together into larger units. Arlen's A section by contrast is comprised of short recurring two-bar units, as if he is trying to translate directly into music the repetition and breathless pacing characteristic of a gospel preacher. "Forget your troubles," "You better chase," and "Sing Hallelujah" all feature the same rising triadic figure, which changes only on the last two-bar unit of A, "Get ready for the judgement day." Here Arlen begins on a high E♭, the highest note so far—the imagined preacher reaches the climax of his exhortation—before descending to the tonic an octave below. In the last A of the song, Arlen recreates the climax by rising back to the high E♭ on "day" (Example 3.4).

Arlen deviates from the standard harmonic structure of songs (including "Hallelujah!") by beginning the second A of the AABA up a fourth ("The sun is shining"), in the subdominant instead of the tonic, a strategy Gershwin had used in "Fascinatin' Rhythm" of 1924. Some commentators have suggested that Arlen was drawing from the blues form, where the second four bars shift to the subdominant.[17] But there are also more purely compositional reasons. Arlen understood that after four short two-bar phrases beginning on the tonic, three of them identical, a change was needed, one which would also help articulate the form—hence the shift to A♭. The second A is not a literal transposition of the first. In the final phrase ("We're going to the promised land") Arlen does not move the high E♭ up to A♭, which would be extremely demanding for a singer, but remains on E♭, reinterpreting it as a dominant.

In the bridge of "Get Happy" Arlen intensifies the use of short melodic units. It is built entirely from the reiteration, in a descending musical sequence, of the interval of a fourth (see above, Example 3.3). The downward motion of the bridge melody balances or neutralizes the upward thrust of the song's opening phrase that dominated the A section.

Jablonski has justly characterized Koehler's gift as "an easy ear for the vernacular . . . with words both poetic and simple."[18] Moreover, as Philip Furia has observed, Koehler understood from his very first collaboration with Arlen that "one way to match Arlen's wide-ranging melodies and driving rhythms was to build a lyric around short verb phrases."[19] "Get Happy" is just such a phrase (and a more memorably distinctive one than Youmans's "Hallelujah!"). It appears twice in the A section of the song, and Koehler further weaves the syllable "get" into the very fabric of his lyrics: "For*get* your troubles," "*Get* ready for the judgement day." And he creates a subtle internal rhyme with "You *bet*ter chase. . ." For the bridge, Koehler expands the lyrics to full sentences, responding less to Arlen's one-measure units than to the outline of a pure melodic descent, E♭ ("head-," "all")–D♭ ("Riv-," "peace-")–C ("sins," "on")–B♭ ("tide," "side").

## Building a Style: *Earl Carroll's Vanities* of 1930

Beside "Get Happy," Arlen and Koehler are best known for the jazz- and blues-inflected songs written for the Cotton Club in Harlem between 1930 and 1934, above all "Stormy Weather." But before turning to those, we consider the five less familiar songs they contributed to the 1930 edition of the Broadway revue *Earl Carroll's Vanities*, which premiered in July 1930: "Contagious Rhythm," "One Love," "The March of Time," "Hittin' the Bottle," and "Out of a Clear Blue Sky." Written after "Get Happy" but before the first Cotton Club engagements, these numbers provide a cross-section of contemporary song styles that Arlen and Koehler sought to master.

*Earl Carroll's Vanities* was one of a number of musical revues that appeared with regularity on Broadway during the 1920s and early 30s, including the *Ziegfeld Follies*, the *Garrick Gaieties, Lew Leslie's Blackbirds,* and *George White's Scandals.* These revues had their precedents (and rivals) in the Shubert brothers' *Passing Shows.*[20] Many composers, lyricists, and performers who would go onto distinguished careers on Broadway and in Hollywood contributed to these shows, which were essentially derived from vaudeville entertainments. The *Vanities* of 1930, which played at the New Amsterdam Theatre, was the eighth such show produced by Carroll. It consisted of sixty-six different scenes in two acts, a miscellany of dramatic vignettes, comedy, dance, and music.[21] The Arlen-Koehler songs were dispersed throughout the show, which also contained numbers by Jay Gorney and Yip Harburg.

The compact, syncopated motive of "Contagious Rhythm" appears to be modeled on the Gershwins' "Fascinatin' Rhythm" (1924); as in that song and "Get Happy" Arlen transposes the second eight bars up a fourth. "One Love" has a broadly arching melody, with sustained whole notes, showing the influence of operetta-style waltz songs like Jerome Kern and Oscar Hammerstein's "You Are Love" from *Show Boat* (1927). "One Love" also has an early example of what would become an Arlen fingerprint, the octave leap (at "you alone") (Example 3.5). "The March of Time" is a stirring number in $\frac{6}{8}$ time about accepting and even celebrating the passage of time. Although not as common as waltzes, march songs are part of a long tradition in Tin Pan Alley into which Arlen and Koehler were tapping, including numbers like Berlin's "Oh! How I Hate to Get Up in the Morning" from the show *Yip Yip Yaphank* (1918), with which "The March of Time" shares a meter. The following year (1931), Arlen and Koehler would create perhaps their best known march song, "I Love a Parade."

One other aspect of "The March of Time" deserves mention: an extra thirty-two-bar "patter" that follows the chorus, part of which is then reprised. Such patter segments, also called "trio," "trio-patter," or (less often) "recitation" or

**Example 3.5** "One Love"

"interlude," were relatively common in popular song of the 1920s and 30s. We find them in (to name just a few examples) Rodgers and Hart's "Mountain Greenery" (1926) and "Little Girl Blue" (1935); in Berlin's "Everybody Step" (1921) and "I'd Rather Lead a Band" (1936); and in the Gershwins' "Stairway to Paradise" (1922). Patter sections, sometimes featuring dialogue or a more declamatory vocal style, tend to elaborate on the main narrative of a song. In the case of "The March of Time," whose chorus encourages us to enjoy life because time moves inexorably forward, the patter, partly spoken (calling out marching steps "Left, Right, Left, Right") and partly sung, warns us "A fool is he who lives to worry . . . Life itself is only a flurry." In "Stormy Weather" and other later songs, Arlen and his collaborators would sometimes develop the patter or interlude into a significant structural and expressive element.

The biggest Arlen and Koehler hits from the 1930 *Vanities* were two strongly contrasting numbers, "Hittin' the Bottle" and "Out of a Clear Blue Sky," both recorded in July 1930 by the Colonial Club Orchestra and released on two sides of a disk.[22] "Hittin' the Bottle" is not about drinking, but rather about what the song's verse calls a "dance craze" of that name. Arlen and Koehler here evoke the dance instruction song, which in the earlier part of the twentieth century helped teach and popularize dance steps, especially African American ones.[23] "Ballin' the Jack" (1913) is one paradigmatic example: "First you put your two knees close up tight, / Then you sway 'em to the left, then you sway 'em to the right." Koehler's lyrics for "Hittin' the Bottle" contain similar choreographic directions. The listener is told to place an empty bottle on the floor: "Then you step around a bit, / Be careful not to Hit the Bottle." It is not clear whether Koehler was describing an actual dance or making one up.

In "Out of a Clear Blue Sky" Arlen writes a song, again with a precedent in Gershwin's "Fascinatin' Rhythm," that initially conflicts with the notated meter and overrides the bar lines (Example 3.6).[24] Cross-rhythms generate two larger units of six beats: first in units of three quarter notes ("Oh gosh! Oh gee! / Pinch me and see"), then of four plus two ("If I'm asleep or awake") to round out the phrase into a tidy four measures. Koehler follows Arlen with characteristic skill, creating a scheme that rhymes "gee" and "see" for the three-beat units, then "awake" and "break" (the latter not shown in the example) for the four-beat ones. The phrase "Out of a clear blue sky," the title of the song, stands outside the rhyme and concludes the first A at eight measures. Koehler would adopt a similar strategy with the placement of the title phrase "Stormy Weather" at the end of the first A of that song.

**Example 3.6** "Out of a Clear Blue Sky"

**Example 3.7** "Out of a Clear Blue Sky," modulation by thirds in bridge

The bridge of "Out of a Clear Blue Sky" uses a harmonic device, sequential modulation by thirds, familiar from some classic Tin Pan Alley songs, but less typical of Arlen's jazz- and blues-inspired idioms (Example 3.7). Arlen begins with a sudden move from the tonic E♭ at the end of the A section ("sky"), to G major ("Look at that rainbow"), a major third higher. A four-measure phrase in G then is repeated in sequence up a minor third, in B♭ ("Where did that rain go?"). That chord becomes the dominant seventh of E♭, leading back to the tonic for the last A of the chorus ("I never knew").

This kind of harmonic motion is characteristic of Kern, one of Arlen's great predecessors. In the verse to "Till the Clouds Roll By" (1917), for example, Kern moves rapidly from the tonic E♭ in a descending cycle of major thirds, to B major, then G major, before landing on the dominant B♭ for a return to the tonic. Such modulations are striking for being based on chromatic third relations, incorporating harmonies outside the prevailing key (in Arlen's song, G major). In many songs by Kern ("Smoke Gets in Your Eyes," "The Song Is You") and others (Rodgers and Hart's "Lover" and "Have You Met Miss Jones?"), as in "Out of a Clear Blue Sky," the modulations appear in the bridge, the section where we might expect the most adventurous departures from the tonic key. These techniques most likely entered the American popular song repertory via the European operetta tradition, in which Kern and to some extent Rodgers were steeped. In later jazz repertories, these cycle-of-thirds progressions become known as "Coltrane changes" because of their prominent appearance in some compositions by John Coltrane.[25]

Each of the features we have addressed in the *Vanities* numbers shows Arlen exploring contemporary popular idioms in ways that are engaging, if not strikingly original. But soon, working with Koehler on the Cotton Club revues, he would create some of the most compelling and enduring songs in the American Songbook.

## The Cotton Club

Opening in 1923 on the corner of 142nd Street and Lenox Avenue, the Cotton Club became one of the premier nightclubs of Harlem. It featured top Black entertainers—singers, dancers, and a chorus—performing for mostly white audiences in musical revues, two new ones per season. The most prominent composer-lyricist team to work at the Cotton Club in the later 1920s was Jimmy McHugh and Dorothy Fields.[26] Their departure for Hollywood in 1930 opened the way for Arlen and Koehler, who would eclipse them with hit songs written between 1930 and 1934 for five Cotton Club shows: *Brown Sugar* (1930), *Rhythmania* (1931), and three Cotton Club Parades (21st edition, 1932; 22nd, 1933; and 24th, 1934).

At the Cotton Club, Arlen and Koehler had the chance to work closely with the leading Black musicians of the day, including bandleaders Duke Ellington and Cab Calloway and the vocalists Ethel Waters and Adelaide Hall. Arlen enjoyed an especially good relationship with Waters, who, according to her biographer Donald Bogle, admired his "style, his attitude, his music, his relaxed down-to-earth way of relating to her as an African American woman."[27] Roger Edens, who would go on to become a major Hollywood arranger and composer, was also struck by Arlen's comfortable relationship with the musicians: "Singing with them, dancing with them, laughing and kidding with them. He was really one of them. . . . I was always amazed that they completely accepted Harold and his super-minstrel-show antics. They loved it—and adored him."[28]

Edens's observation about Arlen's being "one of them" with his "super-minstrel-show antics" raises the complex issues of racial and ethnic identities touched on briefly in Chapter 1. Like other Tin Pan Alley songwriters (including Berlin and the Gershwins), Arlen and Koehler were white Jewish men adapting Black musical styles and forms of expression at a time when few African American song composers had similar professional opportunities.[29] Their Jewish publisher Jack Mills and his brothers built a large, profitable company in part by exploiting Black musicians, for example, in taking fifty percent of Duke Ellington's earnings. Some scholars have suggested that both Blacks and Jews felt themselves to be outsiders, with a desire to assimilate and prosper in the United States. Jews, who could more easily appear "white," proved more successful at navigating this terrain.[30]

However much Arlen and Koehler may fit this pattern, their activities at the Cotton Club mark a special and perhaps partially redemptive moment in any such narrative. Nathaniel Sloan, who discusses the Cotton Club and its repertory with insightful sympathy, argues that "Arlen and Koehler, in using popular song to depict the everyday lives of Harlemites, contributed powerful visions of the lived experience of that urban community. In this way, their music can be seen to undermine the racial projections of the Cotton Club and other whites-only cabarets, even as their music celebrated the sensationalized Harlem vogue."[31] To be sure, Arlen and Koehler traded in stereotypes, as in "Primitive Prima Donna" ("It's the jungle that's in my soul") or "Harlem Holiday" ("Ev'ry day will be Harlem Holiday, / No more work, only play"). But as Sloan observes, they also treated topics that would have been familiar to locals. In "Breakfast Ball," Arlen and Koehler evoke the early-morning breakfast dance held often in Harlem clubs in the 1930s. In "Raisin' the Rent," the team touches on so-called rent parties, at which contributions were made to help with a resident's lodging. In these ways Arlen and Koehler differ from contemporaries who tended to idealize Harlem life in their songs, like Rodgers and Hart in "Harlemania" (1930), Berlin in "Harlem on My Mind" (1933), and McHugh and Fields in "You've Seen Harlem At Its Best" (1934).

The 22nd edition of the Cotton Club Parade, which premiered on April 6, 1933, had a typical structure, comprising fifteen different "scenes" that mixed skits, song, and dance. The settings were mostly Harlem-centered, including "Harlem Hospital," "On Lenox Avenue," "On Any Street in Harlem," and "57 Strivers Row" (an address in a well-known Harlem district, today landmarked), and "Cabin in the Cotton Club." Arlen and Koehler wrote the bulk of the songs for this Cotton Club Parade, including "Stormy Weather," "Happy as the Day Is Long," "Get Yourself a New Broom," and "Raisin' the Rent." Additional music and lyrics were furnished by Victor Young and Ned Washington.[32]

## "Stormy Weather"

"Stormy Weather" was originally intended for bandleader/singer Cab Calloway to perform in the 22nd edition show. But Calloway did not take part—Duke Ellington was hired as the bandleader—and the song became a vehicle for Ethel Waters, who premiered it at the Cotton Club on April 6, accompanied by Ellington's musicians, and recorded it on May 3.[33]

The songwriters were interviewed separately about the creation of "Stormy Weather" for Walter Cronkite's 1964 television broadcast about Arlen, discussed in Chapter 1. Even after more than thirty years, their recollections tend to align on important points, especially the speed at which the song was created:

HAROLD ARLEN: I didn't call the shot on "Stormy Weather." I didn't care to call the shot. I was doing my job and that came quickly. We wrote it in—I don't know what the time—no more than thirty minutes, with the lyric and less than half [of that] the music. And we went out for a sandwich, and that was it, and left it on the piano.

TED KOEHLER: Harold was at the piano rehearsing the chorus, I believe, and I went in the office and grabbed a piece of Cotton Club stationery and started to do the lyric on this thing and in a very short time I came out with enough—I call it a dummy—and I went over to the piano and set it up on the piano and Harold, off of this very sheet of paper [Koehler gestures toward the framed lyric sheet behind him; see Figure 3.3], read it, sang it while he was at the piano, and I think we changed three lines in the whole thing. And that was it.[34]

These comments reflect the genuinely collaborative approach of Arlen and his partners, as well as the energizing effect of working at the Cotton Club: "Stormy Weather" did not follow the pattern of Koehler reclining on a couch while Arlen played a tune repeatedly.

The primary sources for "Stormy Weather," which (unusually for an Arlen song) include original manuscripts from both composer and lyricist, supplement Arlen and Koehler's recollections. One Arlen "jot" contains the complete melody of the chorus in A♭, the key in which the song was first published.[35] (The chorus has a standard AA′BA″ design, modified in ways to be discussed below.) From this jot Arlen prepared a two-page piano score, sketching some harmonies underneath the melody, but little in the way of

**Figure 3.2** Harold Arlen, sketch for "Stormy Weather" (Library of Congress, Washington, D.C.)

detailed voice-leading (Figure 3.2). The indication we see on the third system, "1–7," is Arlen's characteristic shorthand for the literal repetition of measures, in this case the first A section. At the bottom of the second page of the manuscript Arlen has written, "Interlude to follow, then D.S. [*dal segno*] to last eight bars," indicating that the final A is to be repeated after the interlude. No manuscript source appears to survive for either music or lyrics of the interlude of "Stormy Weather" ("I walk around, heavy-hearted and sad"), which can be found only in the modern edition of the song in *The Harold Arlen Songbook*.[36]

The piece of Cotton Club stationery with the lyrics for "Stormy Weather," to which Koehler refers during his interview with Cronkite, is a revealing document (Figure 3.3).[37] The design exposes clearly the racial and social dynamics of the Cotton Club, the self-styled "aristocrat of Harlem." In the banner across the top, the grinning face at the far left and the doorman in the center feature the exaggerated white lips of blackface minstrelsy. Other stereotypes are the female Black dancers in a tight body suits who seem to slap their backsides.[38] In the image on the left, a white couple looks on, the woman peering through a lorgnette as if to keep a safe distance from some exotic tribal ritual. The white patrons in the central panel have fur or feather

44  HAROLD ARLEN AND HIS SONGS

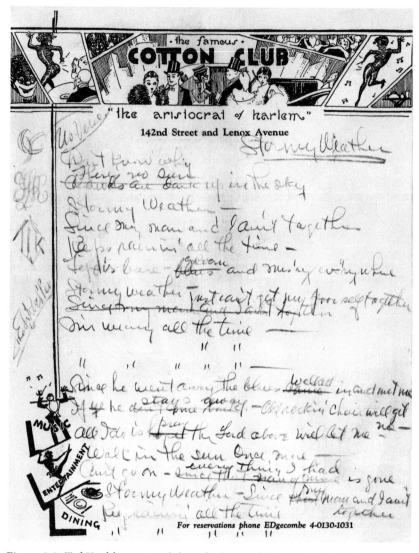

**Figure 3.3** Ted Koehler, original sheet for lyrics of "Stormy Weather," written on Cotton Club stationery (Courtesy of Nancy Koehler)

boas, tuxedos, and top hats. They engage in smooth ballroom dancing, as shown in the upper right, in contrast to the wild solo Black dancers. The images on this piece of stationery, which literally frame the lyrics of "Stormy Weather," provide an important context for the songs Arlen and Koehler created at the Cotton Club.

At the top left of the lyric sheet, Koehler has written "No Verse." Indeed, "Stormy Weather" lacks a verse, which would have dulled the impact of the unforgettable opening wail, "Don't know why." This phrase reflects Arlen's attempt to recreate what he called the "front shout" associated with Calloway, who was originally to debut "Stormy Weather" and often began his songs with a short unaccompanied scat, usually "hi-de-ho."[39] (Arlen and Koehler would begin the chorus of "Breakfast Ball," which Calloway performed at the next year's Cotton Club Parade, with an actual "hi-de-ho" phrase.)

In his interview, Koehler refers to the Cotton Club sheet as comprising "dummy" lyrics put under a melody as placeholders. But we can also see how Koehler refined and polished "Stormy Weather":

- "Clouds are dark up in the sky" was changed to "There's no sun up in the sky." The switch makes for a more concise, punchier phrase and puts the main noun, now "sun," on a strong beat, where the adjective "dark" was before.
- "Blues and mis'ry" was changed to "gloom and mis'ry." Koehler would likely have changed to "gloom" to avoid anticipating the use of "blues" in the song's bridge.
- Koehler at first used "Since my man and I ain't together" as the fourth line in both initial A segments. On the lyric sheet he crosses out the first one and substitutes "Just can't get my poor self together." In the final, published version of the song, these placements are reversed: "Since my man" appears in the first A, "Just can't" in A′. For A″ or the reprise, Koehler changed his original "Since that man" to "Since my man," bringing it into line with the earlier A.
- The first line of the bridge originally read, "Since he went away the blues came in." On the lyric sheet Koehler changes "came" to "walked." In the final version the bridge begins "When he went away."
- In the line "All I do is pray," the word "pray" replaced "hope" and provides an internal rhyme with "Since he went away" and "If he stays away" in the previous two lines. (The second of these lines was changed by Koehler from "If he don't come round.") It captures better the evocation of a spiritual in Arlen's music, and its open vowel sound sings better than the closed consonant.
- In the final A "ev'rything I had is gone" was originally "since that man of mine is gone."

Koehler uses ditto marks (") to indicate the repetition of last line of the second A, "I'm weary all the time," and its parallel line in the final A″, "Keeps rainin' all the time." These ditto marks reflect the phrase extensions that in the music stretch the standard eight-bar segments by two measures, such that the design of the chorus of "Stormy Weather" is A(8) A′(10) B(8) A″(10). The measures on the fourth system of the first page of the sketch reproduced above as Figure 3.2, marked by Arlen as "Bar (6)" and "Bar (7)," make clear that these extensions were part of the original conception of the song. With them, Arlen evokes the instrumental "break" or "stop" common in early jazz, one or two measures which are inserted in between phrases and during which a soloist might improvise briefly. Such breaks occur frequently in Jelly Roll Morton and Louis Armstrong tracks from the 1920s. Arlen himself engaged in the practice: we hear breaks in recordings made in 1926 by his group the Buffalodians.[40]

It is no surprise that this jazz technique would inform his songs and that his lyricists would seek to accommodate it. At the end of A′ in "Stormy Weather" Arlen and Koehler fill out the last measure with a varied iteration of "the time," which falls *within* the regular phrase structure, as was common in some jazz breaks. But then, as happens in other such breaks, Arlen and Koehler *add* two bars, repeating "So weary all the time" to extend A′ to ten. "I didn't break away consciously," Arlen later told Alec Wilder in reference to the extra measures in "Stormy Weather" (and it seems significant he uses the word "break" here). "It fell that way. I didn't count the measures until it was all over."[41]

During the period when he wrote "Stormy Weather," Arlen often visited Edens at the latter's home outside of New York City. Edens's recollections further enrich the story of the song's genesis:

> Harold spent many weekends with us there. . . . We like to think that, on one of those weekends, Harold wrote "Stormy Weather." Of course, this is not true. Not really. He had already found the melody, and, I believe, Ted had a first rough lyric. And, on this weekend, he sang it for us many times—each time with an added note, or a different phrase, or possible change in the lyric. I do think that he possibly found the "repeat phrases" as he was playing it.[42]

Edens seems to suggest that the composer improvised the "repeat phrases" we have discussed above and which were then written into the song. As such, they provide an example of the "thoroughness" identified by Wilder, as discussed in Chapter 1, whereby Arlen's notated score is already "evidence of the song in its performance."

"Stormy Weather" is not a standard blues, but blue notes, especially the flatted third, play a large role throughout. The front-shout melodic figure ("Don't know why") pays direct homage to the initial motive of "West End Blues," the King Oliver number made famous by Louis Armstrong's recording of 1928 (Example 3.8 shows the tunes aligned). Both tunes start on an upbeat with the blue note, the flatted third (or raised second) of the scale, which rises by half step to the major third; in both, the dominant note arrives on the downbeat and is sustained, as a kind of wail, longer than we would expect.[43] Both Arlen and Oliver/Armstrong end their first phrases with a "Scotch snap" rhythm (short-long, on the downbeat; "wea-ther" in Arlen).

George Gershwin expressed admiration for the melodic structure of the A section of "Stormy Weather." He told Arlen, "You know you didn't repeat a phrase in the first eight bars?" Arlen admitted that, as with the extra "break" measures, the process was unconscious: "I never gave it a thought."[44] But we can admire his craft all the more, because while each two-measure phrase is indeed distinctive, three of them are linked by the appearance of the blues motive (B♮–C–E♭), something Koehler accommodated by working "blues" into the lyrics. Throughout "Stormy Weather," as in "Get Happy," Koehler crafts short, pithy phrases to match Arlen's compact musical units. The title phrase "Stormy Weather" becomes a syntactic fragment, hanging off the end of the first sentence almost as a meditative afterthought.

Furia admires Koehler's ability in "Stormy Weather" to "weave an extended blues-like lament out of truncated, slang phrases." He also observes that "the omission of pronouns and connectives gives the lyric a nervous monotony."[45]

**Example 3.8** Comparison of Oliver/Armstrong, "West End Blues," and Arlen, "Stormy Weather"

What Furia misses is how these features reflect not "slang" (a term he uses four times in three pages) but rather Koehler's evocation of Black English, a rich, complex dialect.[46] Koehler was one of many lyricists—Black and white—who used elements of Black English in their songs, and he was arguably one of the most gifted, especially when working with Arlen's melodies.

The B section or bridge of "Stormy Weather" renounces the blues idiom for that of the Broadway spiritual, as discussed above, with steady rhythm, simpler diatonic harmonic motion (mainly between IV and I), and a texture that at time resembles that of a choir. The lyrics change from images of "gloom and misery" and weariness to more hopeful ones characteristic of gospel or spirituals, like "All I do is pray the Lord above will let me / walk in the sun once more." With the phrase "old rockin' chair will get me" there is also a direct homage to a 1929 song "Rockin' Chair" ("Old rockin' chair's got me...") by Hoagy Carmichael.[47]

"And that was it," Koehler notes, after describing the creation of "Stormy Weather." But that was far from it, because the song still had to be realized in performance. And here the role of Ethel Waters was critical. When Waters showed up at the Cotton Club to rehearse "Stormy Weather," she later recalled, the producers "were using a lot of mechanical devices to get storm effects."[48] A dissatisfied Waters told them "the piece should have more to do with human emotions" than "noise-making machines." She asked to take the song's lead sheet home and work on it to create a "dramatic ending." The staging of "Stormy Weather" was reshaped around Waters's own lived experience. "Singing 'Stormy Weather' proved a turning point in my life," she wrote. "My love life, my marriage, was being stormy as hell just then. I felt I was working my heart out and getting no happiness. 'Stormy Weather' was the perfect expression of my mood." For the opening of the song, she stood alone before a log cabin backdrop, under a lamppost, illuminated by a blue spotlight. In what was presumably the "dramatic ending" she envisioned, Waters was joined for a reprise of the song by fellow Cotton Club star George Dewey Washington and a female choir (the Talbert Choir) and dancers.[49]

Waters's performance of "Stormy Weather" would be made all the more powerful by the inclusion of the interlude, a twelve-bar segment sung after the chorus and followed by a reprise of the final A″. Although fulfilling a similar structural role, this interlude differs from "patter" or "trio" sections in projecting a strongly contrasting emotion. As we have seen, the interlude is not included in either Arlen's or Koehler's manuscripts for "Stormy Weather," although the former indicates it is "to come." Nor does the interlude appear in the original sheet music of "Stormy Weather" as published in early 1933. None of the earliest recordings features it, including Arlen's own version with Leo Reisman. The first recording with the interlude is Waters's own, made the month after she premiered the song.[50] These circumstances strongly suggest that the interlude was planned by Arlen and Koehler specially for Waters to sing at the Cotton Club, in response to her demand that the song reflect "human emotions."

By expanding the melodic range and level of dissonance, the interlude lifts "Stormy Weather" beyond the blues and the spiritual. (Here I refer to the interlude in its published key of G major.) The chromaticism in the A segments of the chorus is primarily linear, folded into the sinuous melody or the inner voices of the piano. Although there are blue minor thirds in the melody of the interlude, the chromaticism is more vertical, built structurally into the harmonies. With the exception of a D-minor triad on "pitterin' patterin," every chord is a dissonance of some kind, featuring clusters of seconds and sevenths. At the climax ("Love, love"), which also functions as the climax of "Stormy Weather" as a whole, Arlen reaches the highest note of the song, a G, and then dramatically drops an octave, a gesture repeated a third lower, starting on E (Example 3.9). The extraordinary chords are comprised of dense note clusters: underneath the melodic Gs, all the notes of the G-major scale except for C; under the Es, the full D-major scale. As the music lands on the dominant D to prepare the return to A″ ("this misery"), the singer's defiance quickly evaporates, and she sinks back into the more resigned mood of the chorus. In this way, like so many of Arlen's song, "Stormy Weather" traces a compelling emotional arc.

**Example 3.9** "Stormy Weather," interlude

## "Ill Wind"

In "Ill Wind," written for the Cotton Club Parade of 1934, Arlen and Koehler preserve structural features of the prior year's hit, even as they downgrade the meteorological alert from a storm to something more subtly ominous. Like "Stormy Weather," "Ill Wind" lacks a verse, features an AABA chorus with extended phrases, and includes a substantial interlude (again, not printed in the sheet music). Arlen and Koehler stretch the first two A sections of "Ill Wind" from the conventional eight to ten measures, and the third A to twelve, with techniques resembling the "break" adopted in the earlier song. In the first A, the extension is achieved by a repetition of the words "no good"; in the second, by the addition of "and that's no good"; and in the final A, by one additional repetition of "no good." Both songs begin with a three-measure phrase, after which, in "Ill Wind," Arlen continues the asymmetry by alternating three- and two-measure units: "Blow" (3)—"Let me" (2)—"You're blowin' me (3)—"no good" (2).

"Ill Wind" absorbs elements of the blues more discreetly than "Stormy Weather." In the first two phrases, the melody touches successively on conventional blue notes in the key of B♭: the flatted seventh (A♭) and the flatted third (D♭) respectively (Example 3.10). Yet these sound less like blue notes than inflections within a rich chromatic language whose harmonic progressions, displaying logic as well as constant surprise, are among the most complex in Arlen's works. In the first three measures the harmony moves from the tonic on "Blow" to G7, on "a-*way*." The progression (I–V7/ii) is common enough, but not the syntax. We do not know whether the initial "Blow" is major or minor, because the mode-defining D♮ appears only on the last beat of the first measure in the left hand. The next harmony ("ill wind") is similarly ambiguous in lacking a third and a fifth: a bare three-note D7 chord (D–C–G), where the G may be reckoned a suspension to the third, F (thus creating what is commonly called a "sus4" chord). The note F arrives not as a resolution of the G, however, but as the bass of an Fm7 ("blow a-"). When this chord leads to the G7, we begin to perceive a progression to ii or C minor. Yet what arrives is an ambiguous harmony that could be reckoned as either a C half-diminished seventh or an E♭ minor sixth. The ambiguity is heightened by the voice-leading at "Let me rest," where the left hand is not a clear bass line but a doubling of the melody (D♭–C–B♭). When a pure B♭ triad finally arrives in the fifth measure ("to-*day*"), it hardly sounds like a stable tonic. Only with

**Example 3.10** "Ill Wind"

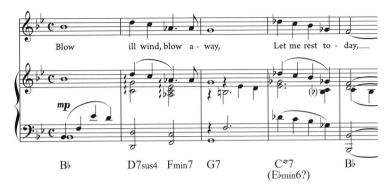

the more traditional cadence on "no good" at the end of the first A segment do we have a sense of closure.

To capture the unsettling mood of Arlen's tune, Koehler avoids the standard tropes of blues lyrics and reaches back to what appears to be an old English proverb. The phrase "ill wind" originally related to sailing. First recorded in the sixteenth century, it turns up subsequently in many contexts (including Shakespeare), often in a form like "It is an ill wind that blows nobody any good."[51] Koehler likely puzzled for a while over how to set the whole note that begins Arlen's melody and pushes the first phrase to three measures. "Blow," deriving from the original proverb but now made by the lyricist into an imperative, was an inspired choice: the "-ow," not a bright or open sound, immediately darkens the tonic note B♭. The same qualities apply to Koehler's use of "Go" and "So" at the analogous moments in the A and A′ segments.

The bridge of "Ill Wind" presents a strong contrast with the A section, as did the spiritual-inspired bridge of "Stormy Weather." After the more languid melody of A, Arlen shifts abruptly to strong syncopation, and to rapid downward octave leaps in the voice and upward tenths in the left hand of the piano. To nudge the performers out of the semi-torpor of A, Arlen writes "rhythmic" in the piano part of the bridge.

One feature of "Ill Wind" is distinctive, perhaps unique, in the repertory of American popular song. The sheet music as published by Mills in 1934 includes an alternative version of the chorus fitted out with an "optional piano accompaniment, suggested by the authors." The original accompaniment of the A section, which often doubles or shadows the vocal line, is

**Example 3.11** "Ill Wind," with optional piano accompaniment

replaced here by an independent, agitated triplet pattern alternating with steadier quarter notes (Example 3.11) (▶ 3.3). This optional accompaniment is featured in the earliest recordings of "Ill Wind," which Arlen himself made as a vocalist in February 1934: first with the pianist Arthur Schutt (February 6) and then with Eddie Duchin's big band (February 28).[52]

The accompaniment imparts a still darker, more ominous feel to the chorus of "Ill Wind." Although the harmonic outline remains basically the same as in the original, Arlen alters the chord voicings. The initial "Blow" is now underpinned by a B♭ triad with an added sixth, G♮; the inclusion of D♮ clarifies the major key at the outset. Similarly, the subsequent chord (on "ill") is also now revealed as a Dm7 (D–F–A–C), but with an A in the bass. We recall that in the original version, the harmony at "Let me rest" is ambiguous, suggesting either C half-diminished or E♭ minor. The optional accompaniment retains the ambiguity, but the strong bass octaves point us more toward the latter. The B♭6 chord arrives in the next measure ("-day") in a kind of plagal cadence, although the tonic still sounds unstable. However we parse the harmonic syntax of "Ill Wind," in either version, it is clear that the song represents a moment of extraordinary harmonic adventurousness in Arlen's early period.

Arlen and Koehler also outfitted "Ill Wind" with an interlude that has never appeared in print. Indeed, Arlen's recorded version of "Ill Wind" with Schutt contains the only primary evidence of the interlude, which extends the overall form of the song to AABA–interlude–A (▶ 3.4).[53] The lyrics for the interlude (as heard on the recording) are:

> How can I feel at ease,
> When you wind through the trees,
> Where blackbirds are singing the blues?
> You rattle my door,
> Can't stand it no more,
> Weary of hearing bad news.
> My bluebird would cheer me,
> If you'd let him near me.
> But when you are around
> Away he goes.
> The Lord only knows
> My trouble and woes.

As in "Stormy Weather," the interlude, especially when sung by Arlen to virtuosic accompaniment by Schutt, provides a strong contrast with the chorus. The "ill wind," now provoking more agitation than foreboding, has become a jittery honky-tonk piano. But sorrow lies underneath: Koehler's lyrics refer specifically to the "blues" avoided in the chorus. Very much as in "Stormy Weather," the last phrase of the interlude, "The Lord only knows / My trouble and woes," slows the tempo to prepare the transition back to the return of the last A of the chorus.

## Songs for *Let's Fall in Love*

In the spring of 1933, still basking in the success of "Stormy Weather," Arlen was in the offices of the William Morris Agency in Manhattan when he saw a teletype (an early form of computer printer) announcing that Columbia Pictures wanted to sign him and Koehler to write songs for a film to be called *Let's Fall in Love*. Arlen retreated to the men's room and, knowing only the film's title, wrote down a jot of ten measures.[54] In the fall, he and Koehler headed out to Hollywood for five weeks.

Although this would be Arlen's first experience in the studio system, his music already had a presence in film. In 1929, after Warner Bros. took over the catalogue of Arlen's first publisher Remick Music, an Arlen song appeared in the company's *Vitaphone Varieties* series of shorts.[55] In 1931 Warner Bros. began using "Get Happy" as the title tune for the "Merrie Melodie" cartoons.[56] In the same year they placed Arlen and Koehler's "I Love a Parade" in the opening and closing credits for the film *Manhattan Parade*.

Of the five songs Arlen and Koehler wrote for *Let's Fall in Love*, only three were used in the film (a typical ratio for Hollywood): the title song, "Love Is Love Anywhere" (both sung), and "This Is Only the Beginning," which appears briefly in the background score. According to Jablonski, Arlen and Koehler found life on the West Coast "less invigorating" than in New York and decamped once their time was up.[57] The composer would return to Los Angeles for longer sojourns, and he would express appreciation of the salaries and the Southern California lifestyle. Yet like many songwriters he remained ambivalent about the Hollywood system that treated songwriters as contract workers rather than collaborators, and their songs as disposable properties over which the original creators had little control.[58]

As noted in Chapter 1, Arlen was proud of the turn to what he called the "simple" and "pure" style of "Let's Fall in Love," which captures an expressive world very different from the Cotton Club. The tune of "Let's Fall in Love" is built mainly on basic diatonic harmonies (C, F, G7) (Example 3.12). With the exception of the dominant seventh, the A section contains only one mild dissonance, a seventh between the melodic E and the bass F on "afraid of it" (Koehler clearly picked up on the possibility of some word-painting here). Many Arlen melodies reveal a strong linear sense, but the pure line that Arlen valued is especially clear in "Let's Fall in Love": the melody, after initially hovering around the high C, descends steadily across eight measures to A, G, F, and then E (Example 3.13).

Example 3.12 "Let's Fall in Love"

**Example 3.13** "Let's Fall in Love," melodic arc

The bridge of the song elevates the pure style to almost operatic grandeur, with a *forte* sustained high E on "We." Again, Arlen thinks in terms of a longer line: the E moves down to D ("be") and eventually back to the high C at the return to the A section (as shown in Example 3.13). Koehler proved himself adept at adapting to Arlen's pure style, again deploying his skill with short verb phrases like "Let's fall in love," "Let's take a chance," and "Let's close our eyes." In the bridge, at Arlen's high-brow melody, Koehler winks at us by working in perhaps the most famous verb phrase in literature, "To be or not to be."

"This Is Only the Beginning" represents a still more striking departure from the Cotton Club style. It almost seems to come from the world of 1920s American operetta, recalling composers like Rudolf Friml or Sigmund Romberg. The melody has sweep, wide chromatic intervals, and several prominent fermatas on suspended dissonances. Harmonically, the song relies on half-diminished seventh chords and modal shifts that are unusual for Arlen: the chorus begins in G minor, but the A section ends on G major.[59]

Arlen and Koehler may not have enjoyed some aspects of their first West Coast experience, but they surely would have been gratified by the enormous exposure given the title song of *Let's Fall in Love*, which became a hit in the fall of 1933, before the release of the film. Arlen recorded the song with Ray Sinatra and his orchestra on November 1 and performed it live on the radio on Paul Whiteman's Kraft Music Hall broadcast on December 7. Unusually for a number in an early Hollywood musical, "Let's Fall in Love" is performed or "spotted" three different times in *Let's Fall in Love*: first at the opening when "the composer" sings it for, and then with, the cast of the "Swedish" film in which it will feature (this is a backstage film, with a plot about the making of a film); second, when the star Ann Sothern performs it, complete with the verse (also unusual), for the family that has taken her in to help her pass as Swedish; and third, when Sothern sings it at a party thrown by the producer. In each case "Let's

Fall in Love" stands out as diegetic, that is, performed before an audience within the world of the film.

## Arlen Sings Arlen and Koehler

I have referred above to several recordings made by Arlen as a vocalist during this early period of his career. These sources, as in the case of "Ill Wind," can provide important historical and musical information not available elsewhere. Arlen's performances of his music as singer and as pianist—on disk, on radio, and later on television—constitute a significant but understudied aspect of his career.[60] He was active professionally as a performer of his own songs in two main phases, in the early 1930s and then in the 1950s and 60s. (We will return to the latter period in Chapter 9.)

Arlen cut his first six sides in the spring and summer of 1926 as pianist, arranger, and singer for the Buffalodians. None of these included his own music—Arlen himself had barely started songwriting—but rather contemporary hits, including some by prominent composers like King Oliver and Irving Berlin.[61] In the Buffalodian recordings, Arlen sings in a firm and light tenor voice, with a relatively rapid vibrato, creating a sound that is distinctive but also characteristic of crooners becoming popular at the time. Will Friedwald notes that Arlen is also seeking to capture the style of Black jazz vocalists, with elements of improvisation and a tendency to rise in pitch at the end of a note or phrase. As such, "Arlen the singer begins to lay down a foundation for Arlen the songwriter."[62]

The links between singer and composer become especially vivid in the eleven recordings Arlen made between 1930 and 1934 of the songs written with Koehler (see Table 3.2). To these we should add the valuable three-and-a-half-minute film made at the same time as part of Paramount's series *Song Makers of the Nation*, where Arlen sings, plays, and conducts five of their songs (▶ 3.5). Such so-called pictorials were like newsreels, shown in theaters between features, offering viewers a chance to see their favorite radio or recording artists.[63]

Arlen made his first Arlen-Koehler recording with Loring "Red" Nichols and his orchestra; the song was "Linda," written for the team's earliest Cotton Club Show, *Brown Sugar* (Brunswick 4982). On disks of this era, the vocalist normally enters only after a full instrumental chorus. But "Linda" begins directly with a seemingly improvised front shout from Arlen: "Linda,

Table 3.2 Arlen's Recordings of Arlen-Koehler Songs, 1930–1934

| SONG TITLE | RECORDING DATE & LABEL | ARTISTS (w. Arlen, vocal) |
|---|---|---|
| "Linda" | 11/6/30, Brunswick 4982 | Loring "Red" Nichols & Orchestra |
| "Stepping Into Love" | 1/19/32, Victor 22913 | Leo Reisman & Orchestra |
| "Stormy Weather" | 2/28/33, Victor 24262 | Leo Reisman & Orchestra |
| "Happy As the Day Is Long" | 5/2/33, Victor 24315 | Leo Reisman & Orchestra |
| "Let's Fall in Love" | 11/1/33, Victor 24467 | Ray Sinatra & Orchestra |
| "This Is Only the Beginning" | 11/1/33, Victor 24467 | Ray Sinatra & Orchestra |
| "Let's Fall in Love" | 12/7/33, radio broadcast | Paul Whiteman & Orchestra |
| "Another Night Alone," "Between the Devil and the Deep Blue Sea," "I Gotta Right to Sing the Blues," "Stormy Weather," "I Love a Parade" | Paramount Pictorial, *Song Makers of the Nation*, ca. 1933 | Arlen, with orchestra |
| "Ill Wind" | 2/6/34, Victor 24569 | Arthur Schutt, piano |
| "As Long As I Live" | 2/6/34, Victor 24569 | Arthur Schutt, piano |
| "Ill Wind" | 2/28/34, Victor 24579 | Eddy Duchin & Orchestra |
| "As Long As I Live" | 2/28/34, Victor 24579 | Eddy Duchin & Orchestra |

Linda, oh, my sweet baby Linda, won't you make up your mind." The initial utterances of "Linda" are punctuated by sharp brass outbursts (▶ 3.6). Arlen then launches into the chorus, and at the very end of the recording he comes back in briefly for a tag—a kind of "back shout"—"Oh, Linda, won't you make up your mind."

Arlen made his own recording of "Stormy Weather" with Leo Reisman four months before Waters and just two weeks after the very first, by Frances Langford and Tommy Dorsey. Arlen-Reisman and Langford-Dorsey could not be more divergent in style. Langford and Dorsey emphasize the blues-derived elements, even introducing the song with a full twelve-bar blues based on the main motive of Arlen's tune and directly quoting the likely source of that motive, "West End Blues" (▶ 3.7). Arlen and Reisman, whose band was oriented more toward ballroom dance than "hot" jazz, take a "sweet," more lyrical approach.

The instrumental chorus of the Arlen-Reisman version (performed in G major) begins with a steady foxtrot-style accompaniment, after which a solo violin, probably Reisman himself, emerges to play the first two A sections. The bridge is taken by the brass in a rhythmic, chordal style appropriate to this gospel-inspired segment of the song. The violin returns for the final A, and Arlen enters in a manner that aims to match its timbre and style closely, with a light, focused tone. Arlen's improvisatory instinct comes out brilliantly in the last A of his chorus, where he alters the phrase "Ev'rything I have is gone," rising to a high G on "I" and then, avoiding the chromatic C♯–C slide, arpeggiates down through the tonic triad to a low D. He thus provides a kind of anticipation of the D-to-D octave drop that comes on "Weather" in the next measure.

Arlen's fine recording of "Happy As the Day Is Long" reveals a different kind of improvisatory skill. He delivers the opening of the song's verse, "I'm sick of love songs, Lovey dove songs...," in a speech-song that hews closely to the notated rhythm. Then at the next line ("I'm tired of tuning in on crooners crooning") Arlen begins to sing the actual melody of the verse. Beyond Arlen's elegant ability to transition from talk into tune, what is striking is his crisp and focused delivery in the chorus. As if warming to the occasion, Arlen freely reinterprets the notes of the bridge, as in "Got a heavy affair, and I'm having my fun." Perhaps among all the early recordings, "Happy As the Day Is Long" best captures Arlen's gifts. As a composer he crafted distinctive melodies and harmonies that work supremely well as notated; then as a vocal interpreter he would improvise on them at a level that at times reaches that of the best jazz singers.

At the same time, we must acknowledge how offensive the opening banter between Reisman and Arlen on "Happy As the Day Is Long" will seem today. Reisman begins by asking, in an evocation of Black dialect, "Come on, Harold boy, what you gonna sing today, a blues song?" To his credit, perhaps, Arlen avoids what Edens called the "minstrel-show antics" and answers in his own voice, "No, Leo, I'm afraid I'm not in that mood today."

In the two sides recorded with Ray Sinatra and his orchestra in November 1933, "Let's Fall in Love" and "This Is Only the Beginning," Arlen switches gears from a jazz idiom to the pure line of the songs written for his first Hollywood film, *Let's Fall in Love*.[64] Arlen's distinctive vocal timbre is still recognizable, but there is little of the improvisation or rhythmic or melodic bending we hear in "Stormy Weather" or "Happy As the Day Is Long." Arlen plies the upper range of his tenor voice with secure pitch and focus, especially in "This Is Only the Beginning."

## The Last Arlen-Koehler Songs, Including a Tapeworm

In 1938–1939, well into his partnership with Yip Harburg and contemporaneously with work on *The Wizard of Oz*, Arlen reunited with Koehler for what turned out to be a few further projects. One was a set of six numbers grouped into the *Americanegro Suite: Four Spirituals, a Dream, and a Lullaby*. The score was recorded in 1940 and published by Chappell in 1941 in an elegant edition with illustrations by Henry Botkin. According to an introduction written by the publicist and columnist Robert Wachsman, with the *Americanegro Suite* Arlen and Koehler were seeking to fulfill a "promise" they had made to themselves back in the Cotton Club days, to "produce music and songs for Negroes that would truly express the race."[65] The *Suite* seems to have attracted little attention from the press or from singers, and it has proved far less enduring than Arlen and Koehler's Cotton Club numbers, which, as we saw above, reflect some of the conditions of Black life in Harlem. In hoping to "truly express the race" with the *Americanegro Suite*, Arlen and Koehler over-reached, misjudging their audience and their moment. As Sloan has observed, Arlen's employment of the Broadway spiritual idiom and Koehler's lyrics in Black dialect here appear "backwards-looking rather than enlightened."[66]

The final collaboration between Arlen and Koehler occurred in 1943, when they contributed three numbers to the wartime film *Up in Arms*, with Dinah Shore and Danny Kaye in the cast. Shore's ballad "Now I Know," though not well known among Arlen's songs is certainly one of his finest. At fifty-six measures (preceded by a short verse) the chorus of "Now I Know" is a genuine Arlen tapeworm, written at a time the composer was following his expansionist instincts in several such songs with Johnny Mercer. On the broadest level, the chorus of "Now I Know" has the form A(16) A′(28) A″(8) Coda(4). But such an analysis cannot capture the way A begins each segment similarly (as in Example 3.14) but then defies our expectations to spiral off in different directions.

The first sixteen measures, which divide cleanly into 8 + 8, could be represented as AB. Yet when the first four-measure phrase of A reappears ("Now I know why I go" becomes "Now I know why it's so"), we retrospectively feel we might just have heard a single large A of sixteen measures and that we are now hearing the start of another A. But after the first four measures, this A continues in an entirely different manner; it seems to morph before our ears into a kind of massive bridge section lasting twenty-four measures

**Example 3.14** "Now I Know"

(or twenty-eight if we count the initial "Now I know" phrase). We have the first hint of a return when the head motive of A recurs with the words "Never dreamed." But the continuation is once again different, now incorporating a phrase from the bridge ("far away from the usual drone" becomes "that I'd fall so wholeheartedly"). After eight measures we rather suddenly find ourselves in a brief, four-measure coda ("Now I know love is all").

Koehler did not have much occasion to put words to Arlen tapeworms, a challenge that fell mainly to later collaborators. But in "Now I Know" he rises to the occasion. His gift, already noted, for building lyrics from short verb phrases that mirror Arlen's melodic ones is evident in the first phrase, where "Now I know" and "why I go" parallel Arlen's identical three-note figures. Koehler tries to give structure to the ever-expanding bridge-like section with a series of rhymes: "thrill/hill," "drone/own," and "feet/sweet/meet." He marks the final brief return to the head motive of A ("Never dreamed") by avoiding any rhyme scheme. Then to conclude the song he creates a double rhyme and brings back the title phrase: "that I'd *fall* quite so wholehearted*ly*" / "Now I know love is *all* that it's cracked up to *be*."

*\*\*\**

In the spring of 1934, as Arlen and Koehler were completing work on the new Cotton Club Parade, the composer was approached by Yip Harburg to write music for a revue to be produced by the Shuberts, for which Ira Gershwin would also participate as lyricist. Arlen was conflicted about taking the job, because it would mean at least temporarily abandoning his partnership with Koehler. Rather than telling Koehler in person, Arlen decided to write a letter and give it to him at a rehearsal. He was probably surprised at the reaction: Koehler read the letter on the spot and told Arlen, "You'd be a fool if you didn't do it." Koehler, we recall, was eleven years older than Arlen and already a veteran of the business. He recognized a good opportunity when he saw it. Following this exchange, still feeling bad, Arlen got quite drunk and spent the evening with a friend, extolling Koehler as a person and collaborator.[67]

After an intensely productive five years that had generated some of the most original numbers in the American Songbook, both Arlen and Koehler sensed the composer was ready for the next chapter, a different "groove" (to use his term). The new Shubert revue, *Life Begins at 8:40*, would provide just that and would mark the beginning of sustained associations with Harburg and Ira Gershwin that would prove just as critical to Arlen's career as his work with Koehler.

# 4

# Arlen and Yip Harburg

Well before the breakup scene between Arlen and Koehler related at the end of the last chapter, Arlen had found his next major collaborator. Arlen and E.Y. ("Yip") Harburg met backstage at *Earl Carroll's Vanities* of 1930, on which each had worked with other partners. Harburg immediately recognized the originality of Arlen's music. "I liked his stuff; it was rather new," he later recalled. "It was sort of a challenge to me, an enigma."[1] In the fall of 1932, while Arlen was still working with Koehler on Cotton Club songs, he and Harburg were brought together to create "Satan's Li'l Lamb" and "It's Only a Paper Moon." For the former, Johnny Mercer is credited as co-lyricist; for the latter, Billy Rose.

Despite some periods of hiatus, the association with Harburg would prove Arlen's longest-lasting and most fruitful, yielding about 150 songs (Figure 4.1). The pair worked on the scores for four Broadway shows, *Life Begins at 8:40* (1934), *Hooray for What!* (1937), *Bloomer Girl* (1944), and *Jamaica* (1957). They wrote songs for numerous films, including *The Singing Kid* and *Stage Struck* (1936), *The Wizard of Oz* and *At the Circus* (1939), *Cabin in the Sky* (1943), and the animated feature *Gay Purr-ee* (1962). Table 4.1 lists twenty-six songs that hint at the variety of styles Arlen and Harburg explored together—lyrical, folksy, child-like, satirical, and (occasionally) bluesy. Arlen's instinct to try out a different groove would pay off handsomely: his songs with Harburg display a far broader range than those written with Koehler.

## "It's Only a Paper Moon"

"It's Only a Paper Moon" is to Arlen-Harburg what "Get Happy" was to Arlen-Koehler, a first effort (although "Satan's Li'l Lamb" preceded it by a few months) that captures the special qualities of their collaboration. The lyrical, gently swinging tune created by Arlen for "Paper Moon" differs from the intense Broadway spiritual "Get Happy" and from other jazz- and blues-tinged

**Figure 4.1** Yip Harburg and Harold Arlen, ca. 1937 (Photograph by Adolph Altman, courtesy of the Yip Harburg Foundation)

Arlen-Koehler songs. Harburg's lyric for "Paper Moon" has no Black dialect, evokes no Harlem milieu; it is a poetic reflection on illusion and romantic love.

"Paper Moon" came about when Billy Rose was producing a play called *The Great Magoo* about a barker and dancehall girl who work on Coney Island. Rose wanted a song—it would be the only one in the show—that the barker would compose in recognition of how love has overcome his disillusionment with the world. Harburg's biographers attribute such themes to his life-long belief in a "cosmic romanticism," in which illusions can be redeemed by human relationships, especially love.[2] "Harold had a tune," Harburg recalled. "He had the whole tune. And I got an idea—there's a guy who sees the lights of Broadway, thinks the whole world is that."[3] In the song, whose original title in *The Great Magoo* was "If You Believe in Me," the real world seems "honky-tonk" and "phony." Yet "it wouldn't be make believe / If you believed in me." Like Koehler before him, Harburg shows a special gift for concise, memorable phrases. The governing image of the song, "paper moon," though not coined by Harburg, becomes the springboard to a series

Table 4.1  Harold Arlen and Yip Harburg: Selected Songs

| SONG TITLE | ORIGINAL FILM/SHOW | DATE |
|---|---|---|
| "It's Only a Paper Moon" | *The Great Magoo* (lyric co-credited to Billy Rose) | 1932 |
| "Fun to Be Fooled" | *Life Begins at 8:40* (lyrics co-credited to Ira Gershwin) | 1934 |
| "Let's Take a Walk Around the Block" | | |
| "You're a Builder Upper" | | |
| "Last Night When We Were Young" | n/a | 1935 |
| "I Love to Sing-a" | *The Singing Kid* | 1936 |
| "You're the Cure for What Ails Me" | | |
| "Fancy Meeting You" | *Stage Struck* | 1936 |
| "Buds Won't Bud" | *Hooray for What!* | 1937 |
| "Down with Love" | | |
| "In the Shade of the New Apple Tree" | | |
| "Over the Rainbow" | *The Wizard of Oz* | 1939 |
| "If I Only Had a Brain" | | |
| "Munchkinland" | | |
| "Lydia the Tattooed Lady" | *At the Circus* | 1939 |
| "Happiness Is a Thing Called Joe" | *Cabin in the Sky* | 1943 |
| "The Eagle and Me" | *Bloomer Girl* | 1944 |
| "Right as the Rain" | | |
| "Evelina" | | |
| "Cocoanut Sweet" | *Jamaica* | 1957 |
| "Take It Slow, Joe" | | |
| "Push de Button" | | |
| "Paris Is a Lonely Town" | *Gay Purr-ee* | 1962 |
| "Little Drops of Rain" | | |
| "I Could Go On Singing (Till the Cows Come Home)" | *I Could Go On Singing* | 1963 |
| "Looks Like the End of a Beautiful Friendship" | n/a | 1976 |

of brilliantly original metaphors: "cardboard sea," "canvas sky," "muslin tree," and the most unexpected of all, "Barnum and Bailey world." (Even though Rose gets co-credit for the lyrics, it seems more than likely, given the song's imagery, that Harburg was the main creative force behind them.)

**Example 4.1** "It's Only a Paper Moon"

In "Paper Moon" Arlen's presented Harburg a challenge he would pose again later with the tune for "Over the Rainbow": an initial octave melodic leap underpinned by a harmonic shift, in this case with a syncopated rhythm (Example 4.1). Harburg responded deftly, fitting the lower octave notes with the lead-in phrase "Say, it's" and then placing the important qualifying adverb "only" on the high note, where it also coincides with a dissonance (a diminished seventh) and calls attention to the fragility of make-believe. Listeners might not realize that Harburg places a comma after "Say." They might thus hear the opening phrase as hypothetical: "Say it's," meaning "Suppose it's only a paper moon." The comma renders the sense more ambiguous, and the tone informally conversational, possibly "Look! It's only a paper moon, not a real one." (A singer could communicate this nuance, perhaps with a short breath or pause after "Say.") That comma, which is more explicit in the second A section ("Yes, it's only a canvas sky"), and the dissonance on "only" help set up the idea that love can break through make-believe.

*The Great Magoo* closed after eleven performances, but the song, now retitled "It's Only a Paper Moon," took on a new life—and became a hit—when it was interpolated into the score of a 1933 Paramount film musical *Take a Chance* and recorded by several prominent bands and vocalists, including Paul Whiteman (with Peggy Healy; Victor 2440).

## On to Broadway: *Life Begins at 8:40*

"Paper Moon" had no immediate successor, for through early 1934 Arlen was still working closely with Koehler on Cotton Club shows. Then Arlen was approached by Harburg to collaborate on a full-scale Broadway revue produced by the Shuberts. Exhausted from work on the latest *Ziegfeld Follies*, Harburg sought assistance with the lyrics from Ira Gershwin, who had free time since his brother George was busy embarking on *Porgy and Bess*. Thus was born the trio—Arlen, Harburg, and Ira Gershwin—that created the score for *Life Begins at 8:40*, a wide-ranging extravaganza of comedy, song, and dance that parodied theater, film, literature, opera, operetta, politics, censorship, romance, travel, Freemasons, the French, and more. Two of the performers around whom the show was conceived, Bert Lahr and Ray Bolger, were vaudeville veterans who would go on to star in *The Wizard of Oz*. The show's title alludes to the best-selling self-help book *Life Begins at Forty* by Walter B. Pitkin, published in 1932. Ira Gershwin recalled that after seeing the book on a table in the apartment of the revue's director John Murray Anderson, he suggested calling the new production *Life Begins at 8:40*, a reference to the normal curtain time for Broadway shows (ten minutes after the posted 8:30 pm start).[4]

*Life Begins at 8:40* represents a genuine collaboration between two experienced lyricists who had known each other since high school.[5] Harburg and Gershwin shared the credit for all the numbers; neither would ever claim sole authorship. "Ira would come in with one idea, I'd come in with an idea, Harold would come in with a tune," was how Harburg described the process to Max Wilk.[6] Michael Feinstein, who was Ira Gershwin's assistant in the lyricist's later years, gives a more detailed assessment: "Ira and Yip were so close that they had no issues about working together or about credit. Sometimes they would work together, other times they worked separately with specific assignments, and then one might offer a suggestion or such to polish a lyric, but there was never a differentiation in credit. Often, though, there were separately written lyrics."[7]

It remains intriguing to speculate which lyrics might have been created separately. Feinstein surmises that Gershwin was responsible for "Let's Take a Walk Around the Block," whose lyrics indeed have a certain urbane (and urban) quality characteristic of Gershwin. Nick Markovich, archivist at the Yip Harburg Foundation, suggests that a similarity in the lyrics for *Life Begins at 8:40* to others written by Harburg could point to sole authorship.[8] Harburg likely provided the lyrics for "Things," a song for Lahr very much in the discursive-improvisatory style that Harburg and Arlen would write for him in "Song of the Woodman" (1936) and, most famously, "If I Were King of the Forest" from *The Wizard of Oz* (1939).[9] "Fun to Be Fooled" is almost certainly by Harburg, because it explores the beguilingly illusory or make-believe nature of romantic love in a way similar to "Paper Moon." It also shares a title with "It's Fun to Be Fooled," a song Harburg wrote with composer Dana Suesse, most likely in 1933. The image of "that Old Debbil Moon" in the bridge of "Fun to Be Fooled" is one Harburg would return to later in "Old Devil Moon," written with Burton Lane for *Finian's Rainbow*.

Ultimately, the unifying factor in all the songs written for *Life Begins at 8:40* is Arlen himself. Twenty-nine years old as he began work on the show, he was considerably junior to his two collaborators, both thirty-eight. "I'd already had my turn at the luck wheel, in the Cotton Club," Arlen told Wilk in the early 1970s. "I wanted to break out of that and try my luck on Broadway."[10] As he reported in a similar vein to John Lahr, "This show [*Life Begins at 8:40*] really meant something. I wanted to set sail on Broadway. I wanted people in the profession to know that I could write things they didn't expect of me."[11] We sense here the same ambition to "complete the circle" and find a new "groove" Arlen expressed in the comments cited in Chapter 1. Bolger later told Arlen's biographer Jablonski that *Life Begins at 8:40* "was the freshest score that had been on Broadway in a year. Harold's music was completely different from anyone else's."[12] Bolger claimed that even after thirty years he was still able to sing all the songs, even those he did not perform.

There are twenty-two different musical numbers in *Life Begins at 8:40*, including extended ensembles (notably the Act 2 finale) of the kind Harburg and Arlen would later write in the Munchkinland sequence for *The Wizard of Oz*.[13] Undoubtedly the creation of some individual numbers in *Life Begins at 8:40* followed the pattern typical of Arlen's collaborations, in which lyricists wrote to the music. But the process was more fluid and interactive than anything Arlen had experienced up to this time. Gershwin and Harburg would map out some larger scenes that included patter, quasi-recitative, and dialogue, to which Arlen would fit music. It is no wonder the composer relished—and rose impressively to—the challenge of *Life Begins at 8:40*.

The music ranges across many styles, including:

- waltzes, as in the duet "C'est la Vie" written for Bolger and Lahr, in which two men who are in love with the same girl contemplate suicide by jumping off a bridge on the River Seine
- a rhumba in "Shoein' the Mare," which refers to a popular Cuban dance
- a Kern- or operetta-like ballad in "What Can You Say in a Love Song?," which features a characteristic modulation from the tonic F up a major third to A

- an extended mock-aria, "Things"
- an 1890s parlor song, "It Was Long Ago"
- a blues song, "I Couldn't Hold My Man," in which Arlen quotes his own "Stormy Weather" and the Gershwins' "The Man I Love"

Obvious parody is not part of the songs from *Life Begins at 8:40* that became popular outside of the show, including "Fun to Be Fooled," "Let's Take a Walk Around the Block," and "You're a Builder Upper." Some of these numbers show Arlen continuing to develop further the pure line and lyrical style of "Let's Fall in Love."

We get one of the best impressions of Arlen and his music at this time from an article published in August 1934 during Boston tryouts for *Life Begins at 8:40* by Isaac Goldberg, a Harvard-educated critic who had written the first biography of George Gershwin in 1931.[14] Goldberg describes Arlen as "decidedly of a new generation" among popular song composers, not like the stereotypical "somewhat civilized thug who chisels out tunes on a piano with one finger." Arlen's songs "have a true melodic feeling for wide, yet smooth skips." And Arlen

> plays, by the way, as unostentatiously as he sings—as unselfconsciously as most people write, in privacy, a letter. His music, too, has this—shall we call it epistolary?—character. Arlen (and this is one of the reasons I am inclined to herald him as one of the new hopes for our better popular music) has a rare combination of tenderness and humor. In other words, he has both the necessary sensuousness and the wise-crackiness of the Broadway wit.[15]

Few writers have captured better than Goldberg the special qualities of Arlen's music or music-making.

"Fun to Be Fooled," which Goldberg presciently singled out as a potential hit, projects as well as any song in *Life Begins at 8:40* the special combination of tenderness and humor, sensuousness and wit that emerges in Arlen's collaborations with Harburg. The composer's strong sense of line gives the entire A section a coherent arc. The principal notes of the melody (in G major) rise gradually from B up to D, before descending to the lower octave D (Example 4.2). "Fun to Be Fooled" has a standard AABA form which Arlen tweaks with asymmetrical dimensions: A(14) A(14) B(8) A′(8). Instead of an expected 8 + 8 measures, the initial A sections divide into segments of 8 + 6, an imbalance that Harburg exploits to capture a complex emotional

**Example 4.2** "Fun to Be Fooled," melodic arc

**Example 4.3** "Fun to Be Fooled," continuation of A section

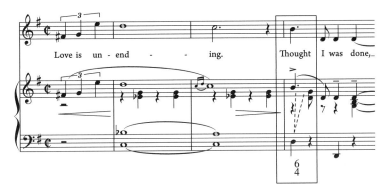

trajectory. For the first eight measures, we learn how much "fun" (repeated three times) it can be to be fooled into believing "love is unending." But then a truncated six-measure unit comes up literally short as the singer admits that even as he or she imagined being "done" with such ideas, it is "fun being fooled again."

Harmonically, the first four measures of "Fun to Be Fooled" travel a conventional path, from the tonic G to the dominant D. But the next four feature more sophisticated voice-leading and chromatic elements (Example 4.3). Arlen avoids any hint of closure by using a second-inversion rather than root-position tonic chord. The D in the bass pushes the song forward to complete of the melodic arc shown in Example 4.2. Praising the "versatility" of Arlen's music for *Life Begins at 8:40*, Jablonski suggests that there is "not a blue note in the entire score."[16] In fact, Arlen ends the first A on a blues-inflected tonic with the prominent melodic flatted seventh F♮ ("fooled again"). And earlier in A (as shown in Example 4.3, on "-end-") Arlen surprises us with a C minor chord that has a flatted third and seventh (E♭, B♭), suggesting that the "fun" has already gotten a touch bluer. These moments make for a perfect correspondence with Harburg's lyrics, which as in "Paper Moon" convey how deceptive love can be.

## "Last Night When We Were Young"

*Life Begins at 8:40* played 237 performances on Broadway, a good run for its day. The next phase of Arlen's collaboration with Harburg would take him back to Hollywood: in September 1935 the team was signed to a three-film agreement with Warner Bros. Arlen and Harburg moved in together at a house the lyricist had rented from the renowned opera baritone and now Hollywood star Lawrence Tibbett. The films they worked on at this time, all released in 1936, would include *The Singing Kid*, starring Al Jolson, and two directed by Busby Berkeley and starring Dick Powell and Jane Blondell, *Stage Struck* and *Gold Diggers of 1937*. But the greatest number of the period, "Last Night When We Were Young," would never find a home on the screen.

At the bottom of an undated one-page jot for "Last Night," sent to his friend Robert Wachsman as a gift, Arlen provided a bemused epitaph for the tune:

> Written at the Croyden in N.Y.
> Meddled with in Beverly
> and buried at 20th Century Fox—[17]

"Croyden" refers to the Croydon apartment-hotel on the Upper East Side in New York where Arlen lived in the early 1930s and created the song. Beverly is of course Beverly Hills, where Harburg added the lyrics. And 20th Century Fox is where the song was first recorded by Tibbett for his film *Metropolitan* (1935), from which it was then cut (▶ 4.1). Tibbett's operatic approach contrasts strongly with the tenderness of Judy Garland, who many years later recorded and filmed "Last Night" for a scene in *In the Good Old Summertime* (1949) made by the same studio; it too was cut (▶ 4.2). Garland told Jablonski that her version inspired Frank Sinatra, who recorded "Last Night" for the MGM film *Take Me Out to the Ball Game* (1949); that scene was also removed.[18] "Last Night" would later become one of Sinatra's signature songs when he recorded it with Nelson Riddle for the album *In the Wee Small Hours of the Morning* (1955), which we will consider in Chapter 11.

According to Harburg, Arlen had shown the music for "Last Night" to Jerome Kern, George Gershwin, and Johnny Mercer, each of whom found it too complicated and esoteric for a general audience.[19] While the film producers who cut it seemed to agree, Arlen had faith: when he was later asked, as often happened, to identify his favorite among his own songs, he usually named "Last Night When We Were Young."[20]

As we have seen, Arlen readily breaks open standard song forms if he feels the music demands it. But "Last Night" hews closely to a conventional thirty-two measure AABA' structure, perhaps to balance or offset the extraordinary harmonic and melodic ideas. The A section is characterized mainly by small conjunct and chromatic melodic gestures. The underlying harmony rarely settles into stable, consonant chords. The tonic G major appears in root position only near the end of the A section, and then obliquely as part of a progression that pushes toward the dominant seventh. The relationship between the outer voices (melody and bass) frames and guides the dissonance throughout the song. The main melodic notes often form a ninth or a tritone with the bass: A–G, F♯–E, E–D, and E♭–A (Example 4.4).

Arlen builds the bridge from two parallel four-measure phrases. Both begin with an octave leap (and the same words, "To think") that breaks free from the narrow, chromatic melodic intervals that dominated the melody of A (Example 4.5). In the first phrase, the melody starts on D, consonant with the underlying Dm7 chord. The second phrase, over the identical harmony, is set a whole step higher, on E, which forms a ninth above the bass, thus

**Example 4.4** "Last Night When We Were Young," dissonances between vocal line and bass

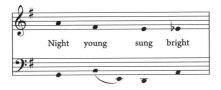

**Example 4.5** "Last Night When We Were Young," bridge

intensifying the bridge and emphasizing the dissonant intervals that dominate the sound world of "Last Night."

The final A' of "Last Night" is a brilliant synthesis of the earlier A and B sections. The first two measures ("So now let's reminisce") are similar to the first two measures of the original A, providing a clear sense of return. But in the third measure Arlen returns abruptly to the material of the bridge: the music for "and recollect the sighs and the kisses" is identical, except for the upbeat, to "To think that spring had depended." The last four measures remain in the thrall of the bridge, beginning with an octave leap on E. But now Arlen goes further, harmonizing the upper E ("clung") with the most dissonant harmony in the song, A–D–E–G–B♭ (Example 4.6). On the third beat, the B♭ and D resolve, respectively, as suspensions (2–1 and 4–3) to A and C♯, thus forming a more conventional A7. This chord in turn moves to a D7, with a lingering ninth resolving at last in an inner voice, E–E♭–D, as the tonic harmony arrives definitively for the first time in the song.

The complex yet deeply expressive music of "Last Night" inspired lyrics whose quality impressed even their author, never the most modest of artists: "When I heard that tune, the whole pathos of the human situation, of the human race, is in that musical phrase," Harburg recalled. "Old Harold gave it to me. I rode in on the coattails of his genius."[21] Harburg responded not only to the music's strong sense of loss, created by dissonance and by the absence of a stable tonic, but also to its exploration of temporality and memory in the final A'. His title phrase "Last night when we were young" compresses outer (chronological) and inner (emotional) time. The lovers were "young" only in a metaphorical sense; it was their love that was new. But their separation,

**Example 4.6** "Last Night When We Were Young," climax in A' section

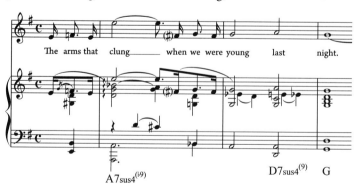

which is perhaps permanent, has suddenly made the world "old." Harburg constructs the first three stanzas (corresponding to the musical AAB) as a kind of narrative, describing what has happened from last night to today. The fourth stanza, created for A', is now hortative, as the poet tells his lover that they now must rely on memory: "So now let's reminisce / And recollect the sighs and the kisses." Recollection is precisely what Arlen has achieved by having the B or bridge music overtake A after the second measure of A'.

The last lines of the lyric are a masterstroke: Harburg rhymes "clung" with "young" and in the process reverses the elements of the title phrase to become "when we were young / last night." Harburg is responding to Arlen's melodic gesture (see Example 4.6), which now places the original motive for "when we were young" in the *first* part of the phrase and changes the direction of its resolution. Where at the opening of the song the phrase turned downward (G–F♯) into a dissonance, here the same words resolve upward, from F♯ to a G that becomes part of the tonic chord.

## Individual Hollywood Gems

Over the twenty-eight years extending from 1935 through 1962, Arlen and Harburg would write songs for ten Hollywood films and four Broadway shows, including three book musicals with integrated songs and plot. The bulk of this work was completed before 1944, making for an astonishingly productive decade.

The film *Stage Struck* (1936) furnished "Fancy Meeting You," sung by the leads Dick Powell and Jeanne Madden. The structure of the chorus is ABA'B' in a standard thirty-two measures. Arlen's music for the A section displays an imaginative economy that never falls into monotony. An arching figure that arpeggiates the tonic triad A♭ appears four times in close succession (Example 4.7a and b show the second and fourth occurrences). The first three times, the theme ends by going from E♭ up to F, the sixth degree ("be true," "[meet]-ing you," "world began"), and seems to be about to do the same a fourth time ("[pre] historic man"), when Arlen surprises us with a G♭.

At the end of A', to transition to the final B', Arlen alters that wayward G♭ to a G♮ on "Zoo," which lies within the song's key (Example 4.7c). The last four measures of B' depart from the original, to lead the song to a conclusion. The melody rises to its highest note, F♮, and then drops in one of Arlen's signature octave leaps on "Fancy" (Example 4.7d). Arlen thus encapsulates

**Example 4.7** "Fancy Meeting You," transformations of melody

in a single gesture the melodic ambitus of the song, then brings the tune to its final cadence. Underneath that leap, in the tenor range of the piano, a beautiful countermelody descends by step across a complete octave from E♭ (partially shown in Example 4.7d).

Harburg's lyrics grow out of the song's placement in *Stage Struck*. Powell and Madden, clearly falling in love, are visiting an aquarium where they observe a schoolmarmish docent explaining to a group of school students how humans evolved from fishes. She speaks in crisp rhymed couplets: "Mother Nature had a plan / To make a molecule a man. . . . We finally began to climb, / From fish to fowl to heights sublime." (Such couplets are a Harburg specialty that would reappear in the Munchkinland segment of *The Wizard of Oz*: "And she's not only merely dead, / She's really most sincerely dead.") Powell interjects his own couplets, speaking directly to Madden: "So there was you and there was me, / Fin-to-fin in the salty sea." Moving from speech into song, Powell then segues into the verse, which suggests that he and Madden have met before, "way back in history." The B section culminates in the kind of striking phrase that only Harburg could create: "We awoke! And love climbed up our family tree."

## *Hooray for What!*

In 1937 Arlen and Harburg had the chance to work on their first stage musical as a dedicated composer-lyricist team, the anti-war parody *Hooray for What!*, produced by the Shubert brothers. The basic concept was Harburg's, reflecting his concern with the rise of fascism and dictatorship in Europe. The musical, with a book by Howard Lindsay and Russel Crouse, was a vehicle for the comic actor Ed Wynn, playing a hapless American chemist who inadvertently invents a lethal gas. Military men, spies, and arms manufacturers from around the world try to steal the formula. One spy copies it while discreetly looking in a mirror. Because she gets it backward, the formula turns out to make laughing gas, and (of course) all ends happily.

*Hooray for What!*, which had a respectable run of two hundred performances, was one of the first stage productions designed and directed by Vincente Minnelli, before his move to Hollywood. Agnes de Mille, also early in her career, was signed as choreographer. Although she left during the Boston tryout, de Mille's ten-minute "Hero Ballet," with music by Arlen, remained in the show. (It anticipates her Dream Ballet for *Oklahoma!* by six years.)[22]

The score of *Hooray for What!* contains some fine Arlen and Harburg numbers in a range of styles: a waltz ("Life's a Dance"), a blues-style song ("Moanin' in the Mornin'"), a love song ("I've Gone Romantic on You"), an anti-love song ("Down with Love"), a patriotic ballad ("God's Country"), and a folksy tune ("In the Shade of the New Apple Tree"). Three songs that were dropped from *Hooray for What!* became durable hits in other contexts. The witty take on unrequited love, "Buds Won't Bud," was recorded by Judy Garland in 1940. "Napoleon's a Pastry," extensively reworked, was introduced by Lena Horne in the show *Jamaica* (1957). And perhaps most memorably, "I'm Hanging on to You," a soft-shoe number, was outfitted with new lyrics to become "If I Only Had a Brain" in *The Wizard of Oz*. Even though the types of numbers in *Hooray for What!* may be similar to those in *Life Begins at 8:40*, the 1937 score shows the team of Arlen and Harburg coming into its own, with musical and poetic languages that are still more mature. Perhaps no song displays this mastery better than "Buds Won't Bud," which has an unusually complex evolution.

"Buds Won't Bud" reflects what Harburg's biographers call a "tenacity with what he considered a good lyric."[23] In the early 1930s he wrote versions of it for two different songs, "You Didn't Do Right By Me," composed by Dana Suesse, and "'Cause You Won't Do Right By Me," with music by Lewis Gensler.[24] Two years later Harburg revised the lyrics further for "'Cause You Won't Play House," with music by Morgan Lewis. Arlen would almost certainly have been familiar with Lewis's "'Cause You Won't Play House," which was sung in a revue, *New Faces of* 1934, that ran from March to July 1934, closing a month before *Life Begins at 8:40* would begin its Broadway run. (Suesse's version was never published.)

The lyrics for the first A section of "'Cause You Won't Play House" begin almost identically to the Arlen number, then deviate after the first two lines to culminate in the title phrase (Example 4.8). Lewis's setting features prominent syncopation and a melody built from downward leaps of sevenths, supported by dissonances that delay any real articulation of the tonic F major until the bridge. This is sophisticated and engaging music. Yet when Harburg gave Arlen this lyric for *Hooray for What!*, he obviously felt that the words had achieved neither their best poetic form nor optimum musical setting.

The approach of Arlen and Harburg to "Buds Won't Bud" was likely different from when the composer would bring in a pre-existing, highly crafted

**Example 4.8** Morgan Lewis and Yip Harburg, "'Cause You Won't Play House"

tune, as in "Last Night When We Were Young." We can imagine the two partners strategizing on how to improve on the Suesse and Lewis songs. For his part, Harburg drops the articles beginning each of the first three lines, creating a punchier and more salient syntax. He also triples up on the verb phrases within the first few measures ("Buds won't bud, breeze won't breeze, and dew won't dew"), where the Lewis version had only two. In "Buds Won't Bud" Harburg sustains the song's basic idea and verbal rhythm more effectively than in "'Cause You Won't Play House," keeping the parallelism of subject and verb from the first lines. That is, as with "bud," "breeze," and "dew," Harburg treats "love" as both subject and verb: "When the love you love *won't* love you."

Arlen, a composer partial to large vocal leaps and dissonant harmonies, must have been intrigued by Lewis's setting. But, in line with Harburg's revision of the words, he took the music of "Buds Won't Bud" in a very different direction. Both composers retain a standard eight-measure A section. But where Lewis sticks to square two-measure units, Arlen articulates the form more fluidly. The A of "Buds Won't Bud" is not easy to parse, but might be represented as 3 + 2 + 2 + 1. The initial three-measure phrase mirrors Harburg's three-fold verbs, and the final one-measure unit is the piano break or interlude. It does not form part of the preceding vocal phrase, which has already cadenced firmly on the tonic ("won't love you").

Where Lewis's melody exulted in wide leaps, Arlen's tune is a model of economy. It initially moves back and forth between two notes, C and B♭, allowing our attention to be drawn to the harmonization (Example 4.9). The melodic C is the ninth of a B♭ dominant thirteenth chord that is reiterated across the opening measures. By sitting on the chord so insistently, Arlen

**Example 4.9**  Arlen-Harburg, "Buds Won't Bud"

makes it sound almost stable, while the E♭ tonic to which it resolves (on "bud") seems unstable.[25]

Even as they improved on the Lewis-Harburg version, Arlen and Harburg went through their own process of revision, involving the song's bridge. As published in the *Harold Arlen Songbook* "Buds Won't Bud" has a bridge in which Arlen and Harburg double down on the syncopations and word play of the A section ("moods won't mood," "foods won't food"). They extend the bridge beyond the conventional eight measures with four measures that extend the singer's woes ("And to make it all seem worse / My heart is beating in reverse").[26] This version of "Buds Won't Bud," which likely dates from its original incarnation in *Hooray for What!*, seems never to have been recorded. In 1940 Arlen and Harburg rewrote the bridge and some of the verse for Garland to sing in the MGM film *Andy Hardy Meets a Debutante*.[27] Garland recorded the song for the soundtrack in March 1940, but it was cut from the film; the following month she made a studio recording for Decca, which was released in June.[28] For the Garland/MGM rewrite of "Buds Won't Bud," Arlen and Harburg shortened the bridge to a more traditional eight measures and eliminated the "X won't X" tropes carried over from the A section. With this revision both composer and lyricist reined in some of their most characteristic impulses, Arlen's for extended or asymmetrical formal units and Harburg's for intricate word play.

The evolution of "Buds Won't Bud" did not end in 1940. Maintaining his "tenacity" toward this lyric, Harburg created yet another version of the chorus for Ethel Waters and Dooley Wilson to sing as a duet in the MGM film *Cairo* of 1942. Waters first sings the song solo in its 1940 revision (a great performance, with some additional scat vocals). After she and Wilson fall for each other, they sing together a chorus for which Harburg changes the "don'ts" to "dos" (▶ 4.3):

> Buds do bud
> Breeze do breeze
> And flies do flea
> Dew does dew

Harburg has managed to get still more poetic mileage from his basic conceit, and yet the device does not pale. This 1942 version makes for an effective coda to the story of one of Arlen and Harburg's finest achievements.

Two other songs from the rich score of *Hooray for What!* deserve some discussion. "Down with Love" is distinctive in the Arlen canon for its expansive energy. The verse is one of Arlen's longest and most complex, at thirty-two measures almost a song unto itself, with a structure resembling that of a typical chorus, AABC. The music of the verse ventures far from the tonic C major, as if, in Alec Wilder's words, the song seeks to "get rid of all its harmonic fervor."[29] The chorus still has plenty of fervor, though. It is dominated by a march-like repeating bass line that descends by step—something unique among Arlen's songs. Above it, the main melodic figure bursts forth and each time seems to peak at the beginning of its third bar ("shoes," "blues," "pain" "[cello-]phane"), leaving the piano to absorb the shock and complete the rest of the four-bar phrase.

The chorus of "Down with Love" has a traditional AABA′ structure, but because of the broad *alla breve* meter the A section lasts sixteen measures rather than a normal eight. As in "Fun to Be Fooled" (but without the unequal 8 + 6 articulation) Arlen halves the proportions after the first two As. Thus B ("Away, take it away") lasts only eight measures, as does the final A′ ("Down with eyes romantic"). These truncations bring "Down with Love" to a total of forty-eight measures, rather than sixty-four if all phrases were kept in proportion. The design is A(16) A(16) B(8) A′(8). From the bridge on, Arlen has in effect accelerated the phrase rhythms, intensifying the song's energy as it proceeds.

"In the Shade of the New Apple Tree" gently reimagines a hit number from 1905, "In the Shade of the Old Apple Tree" by Harry Williams and Egbert van Alstyne. The Arlen-Harburg song is perhaps best known today for its pivotal role in the history of the Hollywood musical. Late in 1937 or early in 1938, Arthur Freed, a member of the MGM music staff, was scouting for a composer-lyricist team to write the score for a film. Attending *Hooray for What!* on Broadway, he particularly admired "In the Shade of the New Apple Tree" for its lilting, folk-like tune and homespun yet elegant lyrics. Those were exactly the qualities Freed wanted for *The Wizard of Oz*; a few months later Arlen and Harburg were signed to the film.

"In the Shade of the New Apple Tree" has little of the harmonic intensity of "Buds Won't Bud" or the explosive rhythmic energy of "Down with Love." But Arlen inserts some chromatic details, including blue notes, that complicate the country-style simplicity and draw in our ears. Though completely different in mood, "In the Shade of the New Apple Tree" unfolds in the same proportions as "Down with Love": the two broad A sections last sixteen measures each, while the bridge and final A′ extend only eight measures each. Here Arlen reworks A′ so that it seems to flow seamlessly out of the bridge. The real return comes in the last four measures with an echo of the end of the original A—which Harburg appropriately underlays with the song's title.

## *The Wizard of Oz*

No songs by Arlen and Harburg occupy a larger place in the public's affection than those written for *The Wizard of Oz*. The conception, planning, and production of the film took almost eighteen months, a long time by Hollywood standards of the day. The budget eventually swelled to almost $3 million, the most MGM had ever spent on a film. The costs and delays were exacerbated by frequent changes of screenwriters, cast, and director, and by on-set accidents.[30] The presence of Arlen and Harburg and their songs—they were signed with a fourteen-week contract in May 1938—was one of the most consistent aspects of the process along the film's bumpy road to release in August 1939. Harburg was also closely involved with parts of the screenplay of *The Wizard of Oz*. He wrote the spoken lead-ins to songs and even entire segments of dialogue, including the scene in the Wizard's throne room when Dorothy and her companions receive their "diplomas."

Six songs from *The Wizard of Oz* were issued by Leo Feist, the publishing arm of MGM, most outfitted with verses written by Arlen and Harburg for this purpose: "Over the Rainbow," "If I Only Had a Brain (/Heart/Nerve)," "Ding-Dong! The Witch Is Dead," "The Merry Old Land of Oz," "We're Off to See the Wizard," and "The Jitterbug." But Arlen and Harburg's score for *The Wizard of Oz* contains more than these numbers, notably the extended Munchkinland sequence, with its blend of spoken dialogue, rhymed couplets, and songs; the choral "Optimistic Voices"; and the quasi-aria "If I Were King of the Forest," tailored for Bert Lahr as the Cowardly Lion in the vein of earlier comic numbers Arlen and Harburg had written for him.[31]

Arlen claimed *The Wizard of Oz* as his favorite among his scores "because it was written for a children's classic and we happened to capture it perfectly." He told Jablonski, "Though it is not a big score, everything it says it says well lyrically and musically."[32] In the radio interview with Dave Garroway partially cited in Chapter 1, Arlen spoke with pride about "branching out" in *The Wizard of Oz*: "And then when I got *Wizard of Oz*—how and why on earth they picked on me, being a blues writer and going from Harlem to the land of Oz, I'll never know—but fortunately there again I was lucky to prove that I could branch out and do again what I call the pure line. And that was very simple and childish."[33] "Simple and childish" is a modest understatement to describe the range of songs in *The Wizard of Oz*. Most fall into what Arlen would call the "lemon-drop" category, meaning the lighter or lighthearted numbers sung in the land of Oz.[34] Several of these are clearly based on dances, including marches ("Ding-Dong! The Witch Is Dead," "We're Off to See the Wizard"), waltzes ("Come Out, Come Out, Wherever You Are), soft shoe ("If I Only Had a Brain"), and swing ("The Jitterbug").

We have examined "Over the Rainbow" in detail in Chapter 2. Here we can note that as the only ballad in the score, it is the outlier in *The Wizard of Oz*. That bothered MGM's executives, who after one of the early previews of the film insisted that the song be cut because it slowed up the action and because they could see no reason why Dorothy would be singing such a dreamy, romantic number in a farmyard. By most accounts it was Freed, the associate producer, who rescued "Over the Rainbow," telling the studio chief Louis B. Mayer, "The song stays—or I go! It's as simple as that."[35]

Mayer and his associates were mistaken, of course, because the song fully captures Dorothy's troubled but hopeful state of mind at that point in the plot. "Over the Rainbow" is one of the earliest "I Want" songs, the kind of number that appears near the beginning of a musical film or show in which the protagonist expresses the desires or plans that will motivate his or her actions. Freed asked Arlen and Harburg for a number similar to "I'm Wishing" and "Someday My Prince Will Come" from *Snow White and the Seven Dwarfs*, the 1937 Disney animated film which MGM was seeking to surpass with its new live-action musical. Later well-known examples of "I Want" songs include "Wouldn't It Be Loverly" from *My Fair Lady* and "The Wizard and I" from *Wicked*.[36]

"The Jitterbug" was the first song Arlen and Harburg completed for *The Wizard of Oz*. It was likely intended to realize a concept from the very earliest stages in the film's development, when Dorothy is described as "an orphan in Kansas who sings jazz." Her musical style was to contrast with that of the "Princess of Oz, who sings opera."[37] The Jitterbug," based on a popular dance of the 1930s, was planned for a scene in the haunted forest when the Witch sends biting insects that make Dorothy and her companions jump and "jitter." Arlen and Harburg would surely have been familiar with Cab Calloway's song of that title that was incorporated into a 1935 musical short film *Cab Calloway's Jitterbug Party*. Arlen and Harburg's "Jitterbug" features strong melodic syncopations in the A section ("Who's that hiding?") and insistent on-the-beat dactylic rhythms (long-short-short) in the bridge ("Oh, the bats and the bees"). With its complicated choreography, the "Jitterbug" scene took five weeks to film, but was cut from *The Wizard of Oz* during the first preview, being deemed too peripheral to the plot.

In working up the six-minute Munchkinland sequence, which extends from Dorothy's arrival in Oz to her setting out on the Yellow Brick Road, Arlen and Harburg drew on their earlier experiences with extended numbers. In the finale of *Life Begins at 8:40*, "Life Begins at City Hall (Beautifying the City)," brief song reprises are interspersed with other short numbers, spoken dialogue, and rhythmically-notated patter. Near the end of the 1936 film *The Singing Kid*, a star vehicle for Al Jolson, the elaborate reprise of "I Love to Sing-a," where the action spills from a recording studio out into a busy city street, is another long sequence of about six minutes, with spoken dialogue and rhymed couplets.[38] For the Munchkinland scene, the composer and lyricist started from an outline of numbers prepared earlier by Roger Edens.[39] The final version has eleven segments:

1. "Come Out, Come Out" (Glinda)
2. "It Really Was No Miracle" (Dorothy and the Munchkins)
3. "We Thank You Very Sweetly" (Munchkins and Glinda)
4. "Ding-Dong! The Witch Is Dead" (Munchkins)
5. "As Mayor of the Munchkin City" (Munchkins)
6. "As Coroner I Must Aver" (Munchkin)
7. "Ding-Dong! The Witch Is Dead" reprise (Munchkins)
8. "The Lullaby League" (Munchkins)
9. "The Lollipop Guild" (Munchkins)
10. "We Welcome You to Munchkinland" (Munchkins)
11. "Follow the Yellow Brick Road / You're Off to See the Wizard" (Munchkins)[40]

Embedded in the scene are "Ding-Dong! The Witch Is Dead" and its reprise. "Ding-Dong! The Witch Is Dead" blends the simple and sophisticated differently from "Over the Rainbow." The form is again a standard AABA'. The high-stepping march tune remains solidly in the key of C, but, as in "Over the Rainbow," the diatonic framework is enriched by unexpected chromatic notes and harmonies. Two striking moments make use of a "blue" B♭ in the melody. It first appears at the cadence of the A section ("wicked *witch* is dead"), clashing with a B♮ in the chordal accompaniment (Example 4.10a).

**Example 4.10** "Ding-Dong! The Witch Is Dead," blue note B♭

Then in the analogous spot at the end of A′, Arlen intensifies the effect by ending the phrase on the melodic B♭ ("witch is *dead*"), harmonized with a surprising Gm7 chord (Example 4.10b).

*The Wizard of Oz* marks a unique moment in the career of Arlen and Harburg. Only on one later occasion would they seek to recapture its spirit, with the score for the 1962 animated film *Gay Purr-ee*, starring Judy Garland as the cat Mewsette (to be discussed below). Soon after completing work on *The Wizard of Oz*, Arlen and Harburg wrote four numbers for the MGM Marx Brothers film released in the same year, *At the Circus*. To paraphrase Arlen (as quoted above), that the pair could move so smoothly from the merry land of Oz to the zany world of the circus is a tribute to their versatility. The renowned "Lydia the Tattooed Lady" that they wrote for Groucho Marx remains one of popular music's great "list" songs, the kind of number which unfolds like a catalogue or litany.

## *Cabin in the Sky*

In 1943 Arlen and Harburg were brought together by Freed at MGM to contribute songs for a film version of the Black-cast musical *Cabin in the Sky*, whose stage score of 1940 had been written by Vernon Duke and John Latouche. *Cabin in the Sky* was one of eight Black-cast musicals produced in Hollywood between 1929 and 1959.[41] Although created under the aegis of studios dominated by white producers and creators, and although trading in some stereotypes of Blacks (poor and rural, hapless but contented), some of these films also made sincere attempts to depict their stories and cultures. In them, Black singers and actors also received extraordinary exposure.

The film *Cabin in the Sky* has a star-studded cast, including Ethel Waters (reprising her role from Broadway), Eddie "Rochester" Anderson, and Lena Horne. Louis Armstrong and Duke Ellington make appearances. Directed by Vincente Minnelli, *Cabin in the Sky* would be the largest-budget Hollywood musical to date with a Black cast. The plot involves Little Joe, a man with a weakness for gambling, and his patient, loving wife Petunia. On his deathbed after being shot by a creditor, Joe is given a chance to reform. The Lord's Angel and Lucifer Jr. battle over his soul, and he yields to the evil side. But this whole redemption scenario turns out to have been a feverish dream: Joe wakes up and is happily reunited with Petunia.

Duke was not available to revise or add to his score—he was serving in the U.S. Coast Guard—and in any case, according to Harburg, Freed felt Duke would not be the right composer to evoke Black vernacular musical styles. He approached Harburg, who turned to Arlen, a composer who had strong relationships with Black musicians, including Waters and Horne. The production team for *Cabin in the Sky* retained three of the Duke-Latouche songs from the stage musical, including one of Duke's biggest hits, "Taking a Chance on Love." Harburg and Arlen wrote eight additional numbers, three of which appeared in the film.[42] One that was dropped, "I Got a Song," would be put into the show *Bloomer Girl* the following year. While Arlen was well-equipped to fulfill the commission for *Cabin in the Sky*, it was more of a challenge for Harburg, who he lacked the track record of Koehler in jazz- or blues-inspired lyrics. One notable exception is "Save Me Sister," which Arlen and Harburg created for *The Singing Kid* (1936). Sung by Al Jolson, Wini Shaw (both in blackface), Cab Calloway, and a chorus, this ambitious multi-part number switches fluently between jazz and the Broadway spiritual.

"Happiness Is a Thing Called Joe," sung by Ethel Waters in *Cabin in the Sky*, was likely a "trunk" song, drafted previously by Arlen with no lyric in mind. According to Harburg, Arlen felt the song was "too ordinary" and had little interest in developing it, while the lyricist "loved that tune" and urged the composer to finish it.[43] Harburg and Arlen would often remember things differently, including the genesis of "Happiness Is a Thing Called Joe." In later years, Arlen told a friend that Harburg came to him one day with a poem that he had found in a women's magazine, which had a line about "happiness is a thing called . . ." (Arlen couldn't recall what that something was). Harburg

**Example 4.11** "Happiness Is Just a Thing Called Joe"

suggested putting in "Joe." Based on this version of the story, Jablonski suggests that "it is more likely that the melody was crafted to Harburg's final lyric."[44] My hunch, based in part on the fact that Harburg rarely failed to claim credit for something where he could, is that Arlen did indeed present him with a complete or near-complete song.

The form of the chorus of "Happiness Is a Thing Called Joe" is AA′, in which A is a standard sixteen measures, but A′ is modified and extended, first to twenty measures and then, with a coda in the second ending, to twenty-eight. As such, the song counts as a mini-tapeworm, where Arlen felt an impulse to break the form. Arlen begins the chorus by echoing the blues motive that opens an earlier Arlen song associated with Waters, "Stormy Weather" (Example 4.11) (▶ 4.4). Here the motive is contained within the upbeat ("It seems like," "A thing called"), moving up to the tonic C on the downbeat. But as in the earlier song, Arlen gives prominence to the blue note (here D♯). The motive saturates the first twelve measures of the A section, before the melody finally eases into a simpler figure that sits on the sixth degree, A, for "When they know Little Joe's passing by."

The first four measures of A′ are identical to A, but Arlen introduces new material for the next four-measure phrase ("Then he'll kiss me"), which moves to the subdominant F. The subsequent phrase ("Troubles fly away") tilts further toward the flat side, ending on a B♭6 chord. After these twelve measures of A′, despite the variations in the tune and harmony, we expect the next phrase to be the final one of a sixteen-measure A′. But this is where Arlen's tapeworm instincts kick in. Although he brings the harmony around to the tonic C, the voice pauses on the note above, D, which is approached from a blue note E♭ ("all I need to know," Example 4.12a). This gesture leaves us in the air, feeling the song cannot end here. And so Arlen fashions yet another four-measure phrase to bring the tune firmly home to C ("Jes' a thing called Joe," Example 4.12b). But the story is not yet over: that earlier melodic D was just a foretaste, or a kind of feint. In a second ending to the chorus, Arlen cadences on the melodic C, then adds an eight-measure coda that spirals up to and concludes on the high D, which earlier formed the climax

**Example 4.12** "Happiness Is Just a Thing Called Joe," comparison of melodic cadences

of the song ("Christmas ev'rywhere"). The last harmony we hear is a Cmaj6 chord with the added D ("Little Joe," Example 4.12c).

Ending on a melodic second (or ninth above the bass) would likely have been common in jazz arrangements or improvisations of the 1940s. But writing it into the score, as Arlen does, is more distinctive, providing another example of what Wilder and Bolger address in comments cited in Chapter 1: that Arlen's background in jazz arranging led him to be more "thorough" than other composers in notating these kinds of effects.

Harburg was rightly proud to point out how he structured the lyrics for "Happiness Is a Thing Called Joe" around internal rhymes and assonance, the kind of subtle techniques that, he argued, "make a song live":

> It seems like happin*ess* is *jes'* a thing called Joe
> He's got a *smile* that makes the *lilacs* wanna grow.[45]

These devices fit perfectly the contour of Arlen's melody, specifically the motivic "rhyme" created by the neighbor notes, C ("Hap-")–B ("pi-")–C ("-ness")–B ("is")–C ("Jes'"), and the many later transformations and transpositions of this figure, including in A′: E♭ ("*fly*")–C ("a-")–D ("way")–C ("an'")–E♭ ("*life*"). Harburg also accommodates Arlen's new material in A′ with the triple ending rhyme now corresponding to each of the four-measure phrases "go" / "know" / "Joe."

The balance of lyricism, sophistication, and bluesiness lifts "Happiness Is Just a Thing Called Joe" well above the more generic songs created by Duke and Latouche for the stage version of *Cabin in the Sky*, including two taken over into the film, "Taking a Chance on Love" and "Honey in the Honeycomb." Wilder, although an admirer of Duke, calls the former "a contrivance, practically a potboiler" while the latter "continues to sound like an assignment."[46] We need not share Wilder's harsh assessment to reaffirm the soundness of Freed's instinct to turn to Arlen and Harburg for the film.

## *Bloomer Girl*

*Bloomer Girl* has one of the finest scores from the "Golden Age" of book musicals that extended from the early 1940s through the 1960s. It premiered on Broadway in October 1944 and enjoyed a good run of 654 performances, the longest of any Arlen show. *Bloomer Girl* suffered by comparison with *Oklahoma!*, which preceded it by some eighteen months. Both have distinctly American locales and stories: *Bloomer Girl* is set in upstate New York just before the Civil War, *Oklahoma!* in the former Indian Territories in 1906. The producer of *Bloomer Girl*, John C. Wilson, enlisted several members of the creative team from *Oklahoma!*, including the choreographer Agnes de Mille (who had worked on *Hooray for What!*) and the orchestrator Robert Russell Bennett. For *Bloomer Girl*, de Mille created a substantial Civil War Ballet analogous to the Dream Ballet of *Oklahoma!* Celeste Holm, who originated the role of Ado Annie in *Oklahoma!*, left that show to take the lead role of Evalina in *Bloomer Girl*.

But parallels between the shows pale beside the genuine contrasts. While *Oklahoma!* deals with social-cultural conflict between farmers and cowmen, or between frontier and city ways, *Bloomer Girl* is more explicit—and for its time bolder—in treating themes of war and the rights of women and African Americans.[47] The mixed-race cast of *Bloomer Girl* (not a feature of *Oklahoma!*) was still an unusual phenomenon on Broadway in 1944.[48] Evelina, the independent-minded daughter of a prominent manufacturer of hoop skirts, is drawn to the political and social beliefs of her aunt Dolly Bloomer, based on an historical figure and activist for a number of causes, including women's rights, abolition, and a newer, more comfortable style of women's clothing, long loose trousers that came to bear her name. The musical's subplot involves an escaped slave called Pompey, sheltered by Dolly and eventually freed by his owner, a Southerner who comes to share the values of (and falls in love with) Evelina. Embedded in Act 2 of *Bloomer Girl* is a small show-within-a-show when Dolly and her followers stage a performance of *Uncle Tom's Cabin*, with several short musical numbers.

*Bloomer Girl* offered Arlen yet another opportunity to "branch out" and "complete the circle." Harburg reports that the composer was "intrigued with the period; with the skirts, with the charm of the music of the time.... So he was happy to jump ... into a new medium of old Americana."[49] The melodic and harmonic styles of this "Americana" idiom—a largely white one—furnish *Bloomer Girl* with its distinctive sound world. (The orchestrator Bennett also deserves much of the credit.) This American sound was not entirely new for Arlen, who drew in part on his film work and his previous book musical with Harburg, *Hooray for What!* Many of the songs in *Bloomer Girl* share the characteristics of "In the Shade of the New Apple Tree," a song that has been described as "amiable," "quaintly turn-of-the century," and "lightly nostalgic."[50] These include "Pretty as a Picture," "Welcome Hinges," and "Farmer's Daughter," as well as the three fine waltz numbers, "When the Boys Come Home," "The Rakish Young Man with the Whiskers," and "Sunday in Cicero Falls." Another song, "Lullaby (Satin Gown and Silver Shoe)," revisits what Arlen called the "simple" and "childish" spirit of *The Wizard of Oz*. The march song "It Was Good Enough for Grandma" shows that Arlen and Harburg had not lost the touch they had applied to "Ding-Dong! The Witch Is Dead" and "We're Off to See the Wizard."

Contrasting with the white Americana songs of *Bloomer Girl* are those sung by the Black cast members, including "The Eagle and Me," "I Got a Song" (originally written for *Cabin in the Sky*), and a stunning, brief blues-like solo "Oh, Lord" sung within the choral number "Liza Crossing the Ice." The mix of styles recalls *Show Boat*, where numbers inspired by blues ("Can't Help Lovin' Dat Man") and spirituals ("Ol' Man River") contrast with those evoking operetta ("Make Believe," "You Are Love") and the music hall ("Life Upon the Wicked Stage").

As so often with Arlen, the stylistic divide in *Bloomer Girl* is not absolute. "The Eagle and Me," a paean to freedom sung by Pompey, partakes of several idioms. A substantial verse recalls "Down with Love" in its scope and variety. While setting up the syncopated melodic-rhythmic pattern for the chorus, it follows Pompey's train of thought as he reflects on why he wants freedom. "That's it!" he exclaims midway as he realizes that the Bible "has it writ." The verse for "The Eagle and Me" is in a different key from the chorus, here in A♭, acting as a dominant to the chorus's E♭. The chorus has a standard AABA form, where the A projects the Americana idiom. Harburg draws his images of freedom from the natural world, animate ("eagle," "possum," etc.) and inanimate ("river," "ivy"). The song's bridge shifts to jazz-tinged harmonies, and Harburg's lyric changes gear accordingly, zooming out from the everyday with one of his most striking poetic images. The human spirit, he writes, has desired freedom "Ever since that day / When the world was an onion." When asked how he came up with those lines, Harburg later recalled a geology class: "I remembered the instructor saying [the earth] had layers of layers like an onion. And I never forgot that image of the world."[51]

The one true ballad in *Bloomer Girl*, "Right as the Rain," manages to be deeply expressive and still share the show's "amiable" aesthetic. It has a conventional thirty-two-measure structure that divides into two parallel segments (AA′), followed by an eight-measure coda. As usual, Arlen fills in and sometimes blurs the frame with many distinctive details. He generates the main tune from a single motive, a long note followed by a dotted rhythm (Example 4.13a). That figure, or a slight variant, occurs six times in A, supported by harmonies that are initially, for Arlen, quite simple: the first eight measures have only one non-diatonic sound, the hint-of-a-blue-note B♭ in the G harmony at "*So* real." Chromaticism increases and the melodic range begins to expand in the second eight measures of A. Rather than coming to a cadence (or even half-cadence) at the end of A, Arlen moves directly to A′ ("I only know" leads into "it's right"), which deviates from A.

The literal return of the opening phrase comes in the second eight-measure segment of A′ rather than in the first, where we might have expected it; and now Arlen places it an octave higher, creating the song's climax (Example 4.13b). The notes are identical to the original phrase, but the harmonization is completely different, consisting of chords that will lead us via a sequence of descending fifths (A–D–G–C) to the final cadence. The coda, continuing the syncopated accompaniment of the last part of A′, retraces the song's melodic trajectory from middle C to the C an octave higher. (This

**Example 4.13** "Right as the Rain," comparison of A and A′ sections

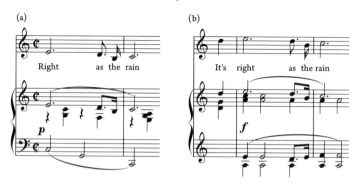

is the same strategy Arlen uses in the coda of "Over the Rainbow," starting on the lower note that began the song and rising up to the higher octave.)

The lyrics for "Right as the Rain" project homespun sincerity; Harburg avoids the world-as-onion kind of metaphor that is his specialty. Employed as far back as at least the 1890s, the colloquial expression "right as rain" has meant "quite right, safe, comfortable."[52] In drawing on it for his title phrase, to characterize the love growing between Evelina and Jeff Calhoun, Harburg also deploys the natural imagery that is part of the world of *Bloomer Girl*. That quality is also captured by Harburg's characteristic use of alliteration. He is willing to repeat "right" within the first eight measures to create a gentle pattern of alliteration ("right," "rain," "real," "right"), which then continues later on a smaller scale with "spring"/"snow," "gave"/"glow," and "falls/fill."

Arlen and Harburg made ten demo recordings for *Bloomer Girl* in the spring of 1944. (Such disks were created to attract financial backers for new musical productions.) The demo for "Right as the Rain" reveals how some details that make the song so elegant came fairly late in the creative process. Arlen prefaces the song with a spoken comment intended for John Wilson, the producer: "Jack, this is incomplete, but we thought you'd like to know where we're heading. I hope you understand."[53] Arlen first plays the song complete on the piano (without coda), then begins to sing to his own accompaniment (▶ 4.5). The lyrics for the A section are in the form we know. But A′ is still a work in progress. Arlen sings "It's right as the breeze / That dares to kiss your cheek" with an exact melodic reprise of the opening phrase, and then hums the rest of the song except for the moment when, seemingly improvising, he inserts the title phrase at the melodic return (at what is now "that falls from above").

Arlen's dummy lyrics were replaced by Harburg's much improved "It's right to believe / whatever gave your eyes this glow," lines which animate the syntactic structure by pushing the main verb phrase ("can't be wrong") to the end. In the final version of the song, Arlen underlays "whatever gave" with an arpeggio rising from C to A, which is absent in the demo and provides welcome variation to the melody. When filling out the rest of the lyrics, Harburg had the inspired but logical idea to repeat the opening line for the higher-octave reprise in the second half of A′. The demo recording of "Right as the Rain" gives us a valuable glimpse into the workshop of Arlen and Harburg, revealing the truly symbiotic nature of their creative process.

## *Jamaica*

Harburg, whose books and lyrics often veer politically far to the left, was blacklisted in 1950. Although work did not completely dry up, he spent lean years fighting accusations about his beliefs and actions, which continued to inform his creative work. In 1956 he and Arlen teamed up again for their last Broadway show, *Jamaica*, which premiered in October 1957. The book, written by Harburg and Fred Saidy, touches on themes close to Harburg's political heart. The locale is Pigeon's Island (near Jamaica), whose authentic, rural values, based in nature and community, are set against the urban mechanization and corporate capitalism of America. The two main characters are a poor fisherman, Koli, who loves his homeland, and a beautiful girl, Savannah, who dreams of living in New York with its modern conveniences and fancy life styles. Eventually she chooses to remain with Koli.

*Jamaica* was intended as a vehicle for Harry Belafonte, who was eager to be in an Arlen musical. ("I consider Harold Arlen one of the three great geniuses of American music," Belafonte told Jablonski. "The other two [are] George Gershwin and Leonard Bernstein.")[54] With his best-selling 1956 album *Calypso* (RCA Victor LPM-1248), which featured his signature number "Banana Boat (Day-O)," Belafonte became a prominent figure in the calypso craze that overtook the United States in the 1950s.[55] Though Arlen admired Belafonte, he was reluctant to take on the musical, feeling he had already explored the Caribbean sound in *House of Flowers* from 1954 (which we will examine in Chapter 8). Arlen liked "Marianne" and "Jamaica Farewell" but believed calypso songs lacked "a strong melodic nature" and would prove "theatrically uninteresting." "You couldn't build an entire show on them," he remarked.[56] In the end, though, Arlen yielded to pressure from Harburg and Saidy.

Arlen and Harburg completed most of the score for *Jamaica* in the summer of 1956. Early in 1957 Belafonte had to withdraw from the show because of vocal problems that required a throat operation. At Arlen's suggestion, the producer David Merrick turned to Lena Horne, whose professional relationship with the composer dated back decades. The book was extensively rewritten around Horne's character Savannah, who then also assumed the bulk of the musical numbers. On stage Horne apparently delivered them in a stand-and-sing style characteristic of her cabaret engagements, which sapped *Jamaica* of dramatic potential.

Shane Vogel suggests that the revisions to the book of *Jamaica* removed much of the bite of Harburg and Saidy's social-political critique, rendering the show "a typical instance of midcentury Broadway Caribbeana: a tourist production that traded on recycled notions of an undifferentiated Caribbean landscape and a tropical aesthetic of pseudo-calypso rhythms, moonlight romance, and folk simplicity."[57] This assessment, written from a vantage point sixty years after the show's premiere, seems harsh; but it is largely justified. Harburg himself claimed to be "brokenhearted" by the mangling of his work, and he skipped opening night.[58] For his part, Arlen felt the score of *Jamaica* "fell short of his mark" and lacked the "musical unity" of *Bloomer Girl*, *St. Louis Woman*, and *House of Flowers*, although he "had a fondness for individual songs."[59]

Among the songs in *Jamaica* Arlen could be proudest of was "Cocoanut Sweet," an exquisite ballad infused with elements of Caribbean music that avoid stereotype. "Cocoanut Sweet" is to *Jamaica* what "Right as the Rain" is to *Bloomer Girl*: a love ballad (without verse) whose lyrics seek to capture local color and whose music subtly reflects the timbre of the score. Arlen reimagines a standard thirty-two-measure frame as A(8) B(8) C(8) A'(8). "Cocoanut Sweet" begins conventionally, with an A section that divides that into two parallel four-measure phrases, modulating to the dominant then back to the tonic. Where we might anticipate a second A, however, Arlen begins a new melody, B (marked "grandioso"), which captures the conversational rhythms and narrow melodic ambitus of some calypso music, including the song "Jamaica Farewell," adapted by Irving Burgie (a.k.a. Lord Burgess) from West Indian folk sources (▶ 4.6; Example 4.14).

After eight measures of B, Arlen introduces another new segment (C, marked "firmly"), which nuances calypso with blue notes. At the return

**Example 4.14** Comparison of (a) Arlen-Harburg, "Cocoanut Sweet" and (b) Irving Burgie, "Jamaica Farewell"

**Example 4.15** "Cocoanut Sweet," comparison of A and A' sections

(A'), Arlen retains the original accompaniment for two measures but gives the tune a different shape; it now rises in triplets through the tonic triad (E–G–C–A) instead of moving stepwise in uneven rhythms and within a narrow range (B–C–B–A) (Example 4.15).

Harburg's lyrics for the A section of "Cocoanut Sweet" create a sensory overload of taste, smell, and color:

> Cocoanut sweet
> Honey-dew new
> Jasmine an' cherry an' juniper berry
> That's you.

The first line sits apart from the main rhyme ("new"/"you") and the internal rhymes ("dew"/"new," "cherry"/"berry"). In the second half of A, Harburg creates an elegant and unexpected internal rhyme for the third line: "Face that I *see in* the blue Carib*bean*." Harburg shifts the style and content of the lyrics for each successive section of the song. For B (partially shown in

Example 4.14), he creates internal rhymes with "smile," "I'll," and "isle." For C, the blues-colored segment, Harburg introduces more disruptive natural images—wind, hurricane, and drought—before returning to gentler ones as the music moves toward A′.

"As a song representative of Arlen's versatility," Jablonski wrote in 1961, "'Take It Slow, Joe' has yet to be discovered."[60] Indeed, this number from *Jamaica* does not loom large in the Arlen canon. Yet it shows the same imaginative recasting of a standard form as the other songs we have examined. "Take It Slow, Joe" is headed with the indication "Blue Mood," and it is certainly the bluesiest song in the score. The design is a subtly tweaked A(16) A′(22). A′ remains almost identical to A, not just through its first eight measures, but into the ninth ("If it's love"). At that point Arlen surprises us by building quickly to a climax on a high E♭ ("Let it grow") before dropping to C a tenth below (Example 4.16a). That C is harmonized by a subdominant F7 chord, which pushes us into "overtime." Six measures beyond the standard sixteen return us to the tonic and the high C through a pair of remarkable descending vocal glissandi (Example 4.16b). As in "Happiness Is Just a Thing Called Joe," these extra measures, marked "hesitatingly," then "pleadingly," manifest Arlen's tapeworm impulse at its most subtle: far

**Example 4.16** "Take It Slow, Joe," (a) climax and (b) conclusion with melodic glissandi

from supplemental, they become indispensable to the compositional arc of the song.

## End of a Beautiful Partnership

Arlen and Harburg's last large-scale project together was the score for the animated film *Gay Purr-ee,* which they completed in August 1961. It brought them together with Judy Garland almost a quarter century after *The Wizard of Oz*. In *Gay Purr-ee* (released in October 1962) Garland sang the character of Mewsette, a country cat who looks for adventure in a rough-and-tumble Paris, where she is rescued by Jaune Tom, played by Robert Goulet. "Recording 'Gay Purr-ee' is the most pleasure I've had since 'The Wizard of Oz,'" Garland wrote to Arlen. "The songs are magnificent."[61] Arlen tailors Garland's numbers to the qualities of a voice he had known so well over so many years. At one extreme is "Paris Is a Lonely Town," a sultry, blues-tinged forty-six-measure tapeworm that has some of qualities of an earlier torch song tapeworm Arlen had written for Garland, "The Man That Got Away" (to be examined in Chapter 7). "Paris Is a Lonely Town" fits no traditional form. As so often with Arlen, the song begins with a conventional eight-measure A, divided into parallel four-measure phrases. But then come twenty-four measures of new and continually evolving material ("For the loveless clown"), into which are woven hints of the opening motives. There is a literal return the first two measures of A ("The chimneys moan"), which then swerve to a different continuation and a climax ("River, river"). In the song's striking conclusion, the title phrase is broken up such that "lonely" and "town" are separated by three instrumental measures taken from the song's introduction.

At the other extreme in *Gay Purr-ee*, "Little Drops of Rain" revisits the style of "Over the Rainbow." Arlen marks the chorus "tender and childlike" (Example 4.17). The piano accompaniment, placed in a high register with pedal points and repetitive figuration in the left hand, evokes a tinkling music box; it is similar to the bridge of "Over the Rainbow," where Arlen imitates a child's piano exercise. Also like "Over the Rainbow," "Little Drops of Rain" sticks to a basic AABA, thirty-two-measure structure. The final A adjusts only the last two notes to bring a final vocal cadence on the tonic. As in the earlier song, the music remains mainly diatonic, intensifying into

**Example 4.17** "Little Drops of Rain"

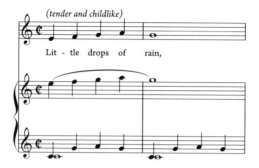

chromaticism only at the end of the bridge. Arlen called "Little Drops of Rain" "as simple a song as can be written," adding "but these are the hardest to write."[62]

*Gay Purr-ee* received neither much attention nor much acclaim, though Howard Thompson in the *New York Times* praised "Paris Is a Lonely Town" as a "knockout" and "one of Mr. Arlen's great blues numbers written for the screen."[63] After *Gay Purr-ee* Arlen and Harburg would reunite for two very different songs: their last Hollywood number, "I Could Go On Singing (Till the Cows Come Home)," written for Garland to sing in the film of that name, also her final Hollywood performance (released in March 1963); and "Silent Spring," inspired by the publication of the landmark book by Rachel Carson that drew a nation's attention to the environmental effects of pesticides.

As in *A Star Is Born*, Garland is cast in *I Could Go On Singing* as a professional vocalist, and she performs the title song diegetically to a worshipful concert audience at the climax of the film. As always, Arlen writes to the special qualities of Garland's voice: the very first phrase of the chorus rises up an octave to have her belt high, sustained notes on "cows come home."

"Silent Spring" is the relatively rare Arlen song written to a completed lyric, Harburg's eloquently poetic vision of the threat described by Carson. After imagining a desolate world in which "children hide and roses tremble," Harburg urges "silent men" to "take heart, take wing, and sing away this silent spring." Arlen's song unfolds in his later, sparser style (to be explored more fully in Chapter 10). It is in a pure C major, the tonal analogue of an unpolluted spring. "Silent Spring" is entirely diatonic except for one note coinciding with the first appearance of the word "spring." This E♭, harmonized with a diminished seventh, sounds in this context less like a Arlenesque blue note than a sudden and ominous gesture. The form of "Silent Spring" is A(16) A′(16)

B(16) A″(9). The final A″ functions both as a coda and as a foreshortened return, with which Arlen and Harburg convey a sense of urgency.

∗∗∗

The last two numbers on which Arlen and Harburg collaborated, both completed in 1976, are "Promise Me Not to Love Me" and "Looks Like the End of a Beautiful Friendship."[64] In the fall of 1981 the first of these was slotted into a revival of *Bloomer Girl* at the Goodspeed Opera House in Connecticut. It is sung in Act 2 by Dolly Bloomer when she recalls having turned down the prospect of marriage many years earlier because her suitor made it clear his career would take precedence over her professional aspirations. "Promise Me Not to Love Me" (▶ 4.7) displays some of the most characteristic traits of both Harburg and Arlen. The lyrics convey a typical Harburgian paradox: the poet asks his lover "not to love me as I love you" because "the pain of so much wanting" is unbearable. Arlen's melody has an appropriately "painful" shape, with angular, unexpected leaps. The harmony ranges chromatically, beginning well away from the tonic, which arrives in root position only at the end of the song. Yet the words do not really fit the situation Dolly is describing in *Bloomer Girl*; and the musical style, spare but complex in a way characteristic of later Arlen, does not blend well with the show's nostalgic Americana sound world. The Goodspeed production of *Bloomer Girl* took place in the absence of composer and lyricist: Harburg had died in a car accident six months earlier, and Arlen was too ill to attend.

The title of "Looks Like the End of a Beautiful Friendship" is a twist on Humphrey Bogart's renowned final line from *Casablanca*. This song was not destined for any film or show. Its words represent, Harburg noted, "the feeling that life is a series of trials and errors, and that there was still a next time."[65] The lyrics read, in part: "Here's to our beautiful illusions / May they still be there . . . / For my next affair." The "beautiful illusions" are a Harburg trope dating back to his very first collaboration with Arlen, "Paper Moon." But for the composer and lyricist there would be no next affair. The poignant lyrics and gently lilting tune acknowledge the end of a prodigious partnership extending back almost a half century.

# 5
# Arlen and Johnny Mercer

On October 5, 1932, the musical revue *Americana* introduced "Satan's Li'l Lamb," a song with music by Harold Arlen and lyrics attributed jointly to E.Y. Harburg and a twenty-two-year-old newcomer named John Mercer.[1] This represented the first collaboration between Arlen and either lyricist. As we have seen in the last chapter, Arlen soon began a productive and long-lasting partnership with Harburg. Although as a bluesy number "Satan's Li'l Lamb" is a harbinger more of Arlen-Mercer than Arlen-Harburg, it would be another nine years before Arlen would team up again with Mercer, by then an accomplished songwriter known by "Johnny" (Figure 5.1).

Figure 5.1 Harold Arlen and Johnny Mercer in the 1940s (Johnny Mercer Papers, Popular Music and Culture Collection, Special Collections and Archives, Georgia State University Library)

**Table 5.1** Harold Arlen and Johnny Mercer: Selected Songs

| SONG TITLE | ORIGINAL VENUE | DATE |
|---|---|---|
| "Satan's Li'l Lamb" | *Americana* (revue) | 1932 |
| "Blues in the Night" | *Blues in the Night* (film) | 1941 |
| "This Time the Dream's on Me" | | |
| "That Old Black Magic" | *Star Spangled Rhythm* (film) | 1942 |
| "Hit the Road to Dreamland" | | |
| "My Shining Hour" | *The Sky's the Limit* (film) | 1943 |
| "One for My Baby (And One More for the Road)" | | |
| "Ac-cent-tchu-ate the Positive" | *Here Come the Waves* (film) | 1944 |
| "Let's Take the Long Way Home" | | |
| "Out of This World" | *Out of This World* (film) | 1945 |
| "Any Place I Hang My Hat is Home" | *St. Louis Woman* (show) | 1946 |
| "Come Rain or Come Shine" | | |
| "I Had Myself a True Love" | | |
| "I Wonder What Became of Me" | | |
| "Legalize My Name" | | |
| "A Woman's Prerogative" | | |
| "Goose Never Be a Peacock" | *Saratoga* (show) | 1959 |
| "A Game of Poker" | | |
| "Love Held Lightly" | | |

Between 1941 and 1959, Arlen and Mercer would create over 160 songs for eight films, two stage musicals, and one "blues opera" (see Table 5.1).[2] In Arlen's collaborations with Mercer, the jazz- and blues-inspired dimensions of his style, honed in the late 1920s and early 1930s with Ted Koehler, reach a new level of maturity and integration. By the time he and Mercer began their partnership, Arlen no longer had to prove a point, no longer had to show how "hot" he could write. He was also no longer associated with the Cotton Club; the songs written with Mercer for Hollywood contain no local references to Harlem. Mercer was a native of Savannah, Georgia, and by his own admission his lyrics reflected that Southern background. The collaboration with Mercer inspired Arlen to work on the largest compositional scale, creating ambitious tapeworms that are some of his greatest songs. Mercer proved his ideal partner on this quest, and there is no finer example than the first product of their renewed collaboration, "Blues in the Night."

## "Blues in the Night"

Through the 1930s Mercer was active on Broadway and in Hollywood in multiple roles, as composer, lyricist, and performer. As lyricist he collaborated principally with Hoagy Carmichael ("Lazybones"), Richard Whiting ("Too Marvelous for Words"), and Harry Warren ("You Must Have Been a Beautiful Baby"). In 1941 Warner Bros., seeing the potential of a great pairing, brought Mercer together with Arlen to write songs for a film to be titled *Hot Nocturne*, about a small group of high-minded white jazz musicians who seek to avoid commercialism and practice the purest form of their art. The film was renamed *Blues in the Night* after Arlen and Mercer created the song with that title for a scene in which the band is thrown in jail after a drunken fight in a bar. There a Black inmate (acted and sung by the baritone William Gillespie) begins a song, backed only by a discreet chorus. "Boy, that's the blues," the band's leader Jigger enthuses, "the real lowdown, New Orleans blues." (▶ 5.1)

The copyist's manuscript of the "Blues in the Night" prepared for Warner Bros. (dated May 29, 1941), bears the inscription "New Orleans Blues" just to the left of the title. Indeed, "Blues in the Night" is the closest Arlen comes to writing a "real lowdown" blues. Although he was often characterized as a blues composer, he had never sought to write one with the conventional harmonic and formal structure. When the challenge came to do so, Arlen said to himself, "Any jazz musician can put his *foot* on a piano and write a blues song! I've got to write one that sounds authentic, that sounds as if it were born in New Orleans or St. Louis."[3] Arlen set about doing "a little very minor research" and came up with the idea of incorporating two different twelve-bar blues within the formal parameters of standard popular song.[4] The result, a tapeworm which extends to fifty-eight measures, merits Alec Wilder's characterization as "a landmark in the evolution of popular song."[5]

Mercer's skills as a musician, which surpassed Harburg's and Koehler's, helped him to keep complex tunes in his mind's ear while he worked out lyrics, as Arlen makes clear:

> After we got a script and the spots for the songs were blocked out, we'd get together for an hour or so every day. While Johnny made himself comfortable on the couch, I'd play the tunes for him. He has a wonderfully retentive

memory. After I would finish playing the songs, he'd just go away without a comment. I wouldn't hear from him for a couple of weeks, then he'd come around with the completed lyric.[6]

Arlen worked on the music for "Blues in the Night" for almost two days (a long stretch for him) and played it for Mercer. Mercer went away and came back with some lyrics typed on a sheet that is as illuminating as Koehler's for "Stormy Weather" (Figure 5.2). None of Mercer's ideas seemed to Arlen a good fit for the opening musical phrase, which the lyricist had drafted as "Whenever the night comes / I'm heavy in my heart / I'm heavy in my mind—Lawd!" Arlen recalled: "But then I saw those words, 'My mama done tol' me,' way down at the bottom of the pile. I said, 'Why don't we move that up to the top?' It sure worked."[7]

Mercer's lyric sheet largely confirms Arlen's memory. We can see that at the bottom right of the page, Mercer scrawled, "My mamma done said dere's blues in de night," words which do not fit any particular musical phrase and thus appear to be (at this point) a concept. Mercer may have first replaced the parenthetical "I'm heavy in my heart," in the middle of the song, with "My momma done told me," changing the monosyllabic "said" to "told me." When Arlen suggested he "move that up," Mercer wrote the fuller phrase "My momma done told me / When I was a small child" next to his typed lines at the top of the page. Mercer then revised "a small child" to "in knee pants," a far more poetic metaphor for childhood.

In crafting his lyrics, Mercer drew on the sounds of his own childhood in Georgia. "I heard a lot of that [blues] down South," Mercer recalled. "'Blues in the Night' is right out of Savannah, my background and all the things I heard when I was a boy and experienced."[8] Indeed, the lyrics for "Blues in the Night" draw on many Southern and/or blues tropes: the unfaithful woman (or man, in the version for a female singer), weather, nature, birdsong, geographical place names, and railroad whistles.[9] ("Trains are a marvelous symbol," Mercer once said. "Someone's always coming in or leaving on one, so it's either sadness or happiness.")[10] Whistling and humming, which Arlen and Mercer call for in the published sheet music, were also common among blues singers.

The singer Margaret Whiting was a teenager when she heard Arlen and Mercer introduce "Blues in the Night" before a group of Hollywood royalty at one of her mother's regular Saturday night gatherings (her father Richard

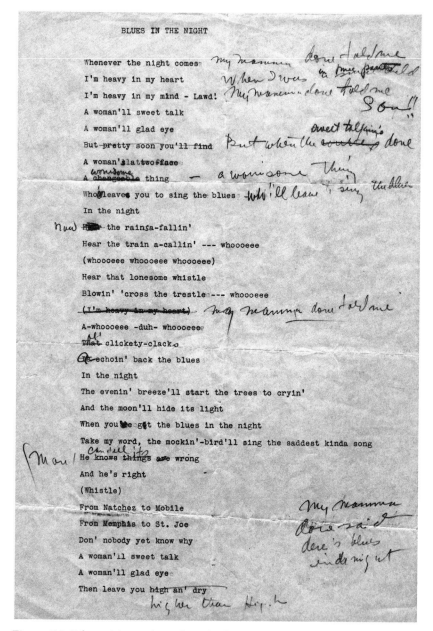

**Figure 5.2** Johnny Mercer, lyric sheet for "Blues in the Night" (Johnny Mercer Papers, Popular Music and Culture Collection, Special Collections and Archives, Georgia State University Library)

Whiting had died in 1938). Whiting's recollections make clear the impact the song had on the assembled guests:

> Harold sat down at the piano and played a few blues chords and Johnny began to imitate a train whistle. . . . He began to sing:
>
> > *My mama done tol' me*
> > *When I was in knee pants.*
> > *My mama done tol' me, Son! . . .*
>
> The room grew very still. I looked around. Mel Tormé's mouth was hanging open. Judy [Garland] had her head down and just her eyes were peering up at Arlen. Everyone in the room knew something great was happening. Just to watch Arlen and Mercer perform was a treat. . . . We had them play it nine times.
> When it was over, we couldn't get Mel Tormé up off the floor, and for the first time Martha Raye didn't have anything funny to say. Everyone wanted to sing it. Judy and I rushed to the piano to see who could learn it first.[11]

On their own, Arlen and Mercer were each recognized as great performers of their music; Whiting makes clear how special it was to hear them together. (This is definitely a moment in the history of popular song when I wish I'd been in the room.)

"Blues in the Night" is a true tapeworm, whose form can be represented as A(12) B(12) C(8) C′(10 [8 + 2]) A′(16 [12 + 4]). The A and B segments each follow the harmonic structure of a classic twelve-bar blues: I(4 measures)–IV(2)–I(2)–V(2)–I(2). Although A and B have different tunes, Arlen links them by bringing back the opening figure associated with "My mama done tol' me" as a melodic and rhythmic riff in the fourth and eighth measures of B (Example 5.1). This same vocal line ties together the last three measures of A, B, and A′ ("A worrisome thing" and "Ol' clickety clack"). These recurrences reflect Arlen's compositional impulse to lend coherence to a sprawling song.

Example 5.1 "Blues in the Night"

Because the A and B of "Blues in the Night" are both structured on the blues, they can be heard to function, at least subliminally, as AA (or AA′) within a standard song form. As such they create the expectation of a bridge section, a role assumed by the C ("The evenin' breeze'll start") and C′ ("Take my word") segments, where, as if to emphasize a formal shift, Arlen and Mercer abandon the twelve-bar blues structure and revert to the standard eight-bar unit of popular song. The two-bar extension of C′, where the vocal line is indicated to be whistled, is based on the four-bar piano introduction and thus acts as a transition to the return (Example 5.2a).[12] In the four-bar tag at the end of A′ the singer hums this same melody and then a compressed version of the three-bar phrase that had ended the A, B, and A′ segments (Example 5.2b). At such moments we can appreciate the "thoroughness" of Arlen, as reflected by Wilder's comments cited in Chapter 1; the song is a "finished product" that includes all the important compositional details.

The distinction between the "blues" and "popular song" segments of "Blues in the Night" goes well beyond the number of bars in each. In the blues-inspired portions Arlen makes use of a walking bass, a prominent blues "topic," or musical gesture associated with the genre. That bass disappears in the bridge-like C segments, which have a more standard bass-and-chord pattern.

The film *Blues in the Night* was released on November 15, 1941. By then, the title song had already been recorded no fewer than six times (not including the soundtrack performances), by Judy Garland and by bands led by Artie Shaw, Woody Herman, Charlie Barnet, and Cab Calloway. By the spring of 1942, more recordings appeared, from Tommy Dorsey, Benny Goodman, Glenn Miller, Guy Lombardo, and by vocalists including Dinah Shore, Bing Crosby, and Joe Turner. The Woody Herman recording rose to the top of the Billboard Charts by February 1942. "Blues in the Night" was nominated for

**Example 5.2** "Blues in the Night"

an Academy Award as Best Song, but was beaten out by Jerome Kern and Oscar Hammerstein's "The Last Time I Saw Paris," a sentimental wartime favorite. Both Kern and Hammerstein apparently felt that "Blues in the Night" should have won. "Tell Johnny he was robbed," Hammerstein told a friend.[13]

"Blues in the Night" would soon be picked up by Black singers in the South, worlds away from Hollywood. In July 1942, less than a year after the song was released, Muddy Waters told folklorist Alan Lomax that "Blues in the Night" was in his repertory and was one of the most popular songs among blues musicians in his region of Mississippi.[14] On this same field trip Lomax encountered a group of young girls who wanted to sing "Blues in the Night" for him in addition to the spirituals they were recording.[15] The way in which "Blues in the Night" and other songs created for Hollywood or Broadway were absorbed into Southern musical cultures shows that for much of the twentieth century the categories (and geographies) of popular music were far more permeable than is often claimed.[16]

## Two Tapeworms: "That Old Black Magic" and "One for My Baby"

In the four wartime years that followed *Blues in the Night*, from 1942 to 1945, Arlen and Mercer would collaborate on six more films, producing a wealth of songs that found their way into the American Songbook.[17] "That Old Black Magic" and "One for My Baby (and One More for the Road)," each in a different way, match the scope and ambition of "Blues in the Night."

"That Old Black Magic" is a "hypermetric" tapeworm, in which two measures are perceived as one: A(16) A′(16) B(16) A″(27, with second ending).[18] Arlen stretches the final A″ beyond its expected length, thus extending to seventy-five what would be a normal sixty-four measures in the hypermetric frame. As often happened, Mercer was presented by Arlen with a wordless song; he came up with the image of "black magic," inspired by the Cole Porter song "You Do Something to Me" (1929). The image of "voodoo" in Porter's line "Do do that voodoo that you do so well" struck Mercer as too great an idea "to be wasted on one word in a song."[19]

"That Old Black Magic" appears in *Star Spangled Rhythm* (1942) as part of a series of skits being produced for Navy soldiers on shore leave. It is sung by Johnny Johnston and danced by Vera Zorina, as choreographed by her husband George Balanchine. Scored in a lyrical style by Paramount's orchestrators (Charles Bradshaw and Leo Shuken) and conducted liltingly by Robert Emmet Dolan, "That Old Black Magic" lacks here the smoldering energy that came to be associated with it in later arrangements. In the film version we hear little trace of one of its signature features, probably the longest pedal point (a sustained bass note) in popular song: an insistent bass E♭ that lasts fifteen measures, stops for one measure, then resumes for six more. That E♭ and a repeated eighth-note rhythmic pattern underpin a syncopated melody that is equally insistent, parking itself for long stretches on the note G.[20] The pedal point also subsumes any implied harmonic shifts, including those to the dominant ("weave so well" and "the same old witchcraft"). When the E♭ pedal is interrupted at last, the effect is stunning (Example 5.3a). The bass suddenly drops a whole step to D♭, just as "that elevator starts its ride" downward. The move to D♭ is at once surprising and logical: Arlen has prepared it earlier with the melodic "blue" note D♭ in the first phrase of A′ ("that *I* feel inside"), which replaces the original low B♭ of "has *me* in its spell" in A (Example 5.3b).

In the B section Arlen's compositional instincts help him avoid too much of a good thing. He abandons the repeated notes and rhythms, the syncopations, and the long pedals; he introduces more chromaticism and speeds up the harmonic rhythm. The melody loses its narrow ambitus; it is now marked by Arlen's trademark octave leaps at "stay away," "Aflame with such."

Example 5.3 "That Old Black Magic," bass and melodic D♭

**Example 5.4** "That Old Black Magic," melodic climax and octave leap

In the modified return, A″, the once disruptive blue note D♭ reaches its compositional fulfillment when it is repeated and syncopated over four measures ("The mate that fate had me created for"). The song's climax arrives as the melodic D♭ pushes to E♭ a whole step above. Arlen's octave leap then reappears ("ev'ry time your *lips meet* mine") to point the melody down toward its original register (Example 5.4). Again, Mercer responds in kind, with "down and down I go." Arlen grounds the song by sitting on the low E♭ for the last eight bars, a gesture that seems necessary and even inevitable. With the additional eight measures in A″ the composer was apparently accommodating the lyricist, rather than the other way around. Wilder reports Arlen telling him that "because of Mercer's conviction that the lyric needed to tell a longer story in order to make its point with sufficient drama, he [Arlen] extended the melody that much more and thereby a better song was written."[21]

"One for My Baby (And One More for the Road)," premiered by Fred Astaire in another wartime film, *The Sky's the Limit* (1943), is a sixty-measure tapeworm that draws on the blues and the torch song, genres that both involve frustrated or unrequited love. Arlen originally conceived it without a specific purpose or lyric in mind, as what he called a "wandering song."[22] He told Wilk that he wrote "One for My Baby" as if "it were natural to me to write that kind of song, but then I started thinking, 'Jesus, how could a lyric-writer *dig* this, or even understand it?' Because I'd started in one key—I didn't even realize it at the time—and I wound up in another key. Unlike anything I'd ever done, or heard."[23] Ending in a key different from the initial one makes "One for My Baby" an unusual example in the popular song repertory of what has been called progressive or directional tonality.[24] The structure of "One for My Baby" is A(16) A(16) B(8) A′(20, with second ending). The first A section is in E♭ major; the second A is an exact transposition up a major third in G major. But Arlen never returns to the opening E♭ major: both the B section and the final A′ remain in G major. The main theme seems to "wander" as much as the harmony, bouncing along in dotted rhythms (Example 5.5).

**Example 5.5** "One for My Baby"

As with "Blues in the Night," but less obviously, Arlen embeds blues within the traditional broader structure. "One for My Baby" sits on the tonic harmony for the first eight bars, shifts to IV for two bars, then back to the tonic for two, then to the dominant for two, then back to the tonic. At some point we realize that we are hearing a nonstandard but still recognizable blues, with the initial tonic section twice the normal length: I(8 bars)—IV(2)—I(2)—V(2)—I(1 + modulatory transition to A′).

The wandering tapeworm "One for My Baby" appears in a legendary Hollywood song-and-dance scene from *The Sky's the Limit*. Astaire plays the triple-ace pilot Fred Atwell who has been jilted by his girlfriend and drowns the experience in drink. Mercer fashions a rambling, conversational lyric distinctive for being a meta-narrative, a narrative at one remove (▶ 5.2). As Philip Furia has observed, Mercer has the singer "drunkenly allude to a story he never tells."[25] As viewers of the film we know Atwell's backstory, but he never shares it with the bartender Joe, who learns only that the flying ace has "got a little story you oughta know" and fancies himself "a kind of poet" who's "got a lotta things to say." The filmed sequence of "One for My Baby" moves between three bars that Atwell frequents; Joe, the bartender of the lyrics, is played by three different actors. This montage (directed by Edward Griffith and choreographed by Astaire) reflects brilliantly the disjointedness of Atwell's storytelling.[26]

The renowned interlude where Astaire dances on top of the bar, breaking glasses and eventually the mirror, occurs in between the B and A′ sections of the song. After the dance, Astaire winds up his tale with Mercer's summational lyric: "Well, that's how it goes / And, Joe, I know you're getting anxious to close." A few lines later the lyric places "One for My Baby" self-consciously within the tradition of the torch song: "This torch that I've found, / Must be drowned."[27] Arlen rightly admired the achievement of his partner: "John put on that [melodic] line the best torch-song lyric of our time. The *right* lyric."[28] For his part, Astaire recalled that while *The Sky's the Limit* was being filmed, "One for My Baby" did not strike him as an "immediate hit" and yet "has become a standard classical popular song and one of the best pieces of material that was written specially for me."[29]

## Arlen-Mercer Ballads: "My Shining Hour" and "Out of This World"

Although Arlen and Mercer are usually best remembered for their jazz- and blues-inspired songs or the Broadway spiritual "Ac-cent-tchu-ate the Positive," the team also produced superb ballads. Here we will consider two outstanding examples, one very compact, the other a tapeworm.

"My Shining Hour" is introduced by the female lead Joan Leslie (dubbed by Sally Sweetland) at a soldiers' club near the beginning of *The Sky's the Limit* and then suffuses the background score. Although the song gets a short comic reprise from Astaire with altered lyrics, its prevailing tone is serious, almost devotional. "My Shining Hour" is one of the few standards whose verse vocalists tend regularly to perform, perhaps because it sets up the chorus so artfully.[30] The verse's three-note motive, gentle but insistent, always begins on the second beat, whether in the voice ("This moment, this minute") or the accompaniment (Example 5.6). The verse features asymmetrical or off-the-grid phrasing. The first large phrase, ending on "sky," is seven measures long, the second six, thus making for a broader segment of thirteen measures.

At the beginning of the chorus, the three-note motive and irregular phrasing yield to a broad melody that, uncharacteristically for Arlen, is always anchored on downbeats and divided into clear four- and eight-measure units. After the relative instability of the verse, the hymn-like chorus serves to comfort, to reassure. At a standard thirty-two measures, the chorus of

**Example 5.6** "My Shining Hour," verse

**Example 5.7** "My Shining Hour," melodic repetition in C section

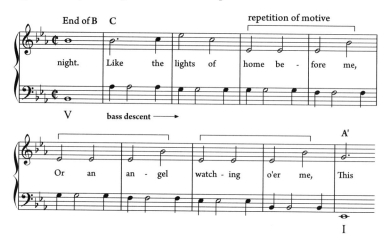

"My Shining Hour" is not a tapeworm, but like one it unfolds fluidly, without literal repetition. The form could be represented as ABCA′. The C section acts as a kind of bridge; it prolongs the dominant over a mainly stepwise descending bass that underpins Arlen's striking triple use of the melodic phrase E♭–E♭–E♭–B♭ ("home before me," / "Or an angel" / "watching o'er me") (Example 5.7). Arlen's linear bass motion (functionally unstable) and melodic repetition (stable) balance each other with an elegance that few other songwriters could achieve.

In "My Shining Hour" Mercer, who explored so many aspects of the American vernacular, tempers his muse to the hymn-like qualities of Arlen's tune. Mercer evokes images of hope from World War I–era songs like "Keep the Home Fires Burning," with its lines "There's a silver lining / Through the dark clouds shining."[31] As Furia points out, the phrase "as time goes by" in the verse makes a nod to an earlier song of that title that became a wartime favorite in the film *Casablanca*.[32] As befits the mood of "My Shining Hour," the rhyme scheme of the chorus is initially simple: the A and B segments align as *abab* ("hour" / "bright" / "flower" / "night"). But Mercer breaks this pattern in the second sixteen measures, C and A′. For C, Mercer uses a reiteration of "me," with an added elegant internal rhyme using three different versions of an "or" sound ("[be-] fore" / "Or" / "o'er"). In A′ there is no rhyme at all: Mercer brings back the opening phrase of the chorus to match the return of the analogous part of the tune and follows it with "Till I'm with you again."

The ballad "Out of This World" (1945) lies at the opposite extreme from "My Shining Hour." At seventy-five measures, it is one of Arlen's largest tapeworms. Like "That Old Black Magic," "Out of This World" is hypermetric; its segments have double the standard number of measures. Yet even within these broader dimensions, Arlen continually adjusts the number of bars: A(16) A′(20) B(18) A″(21). Section A is divided cleanly into four-bar units. In A′ the last four-bar unit is extended by the addition of a full cadence to the tonic, with the vocal phrase "than I." As sometimes happens in Arlen tapeworms, the A and A′ sections of "Out of This World" feel so complete that they might almost constitute an entire song. And yet the bridge, containing the song's climax, is still to come.

The large dimensions of "Out of This World" are enabled by a kind of tension different from "That Old Black Magic." There a long and static tonic pedal anchors the rhythmic, harmonic, and melodic activity. In "Out of This World," the tonic is not confirmed until the strong cadence at the end of A′, even though its identity is never in doubt. The harmonies are continuously inflected by altered pitches, especially the flatted third and seventh. Although these are nominally blue notes, the song has little blues-like sound. We have moved literally "out of the world" of any conventional E♭ major, into a tonal realm that seems to blend elements of Mixolydian and Dorian modes (which incorporate those blue notes) (Example 5.8). Chords do not progress as much as float, held in place by the strong bass motion from E♭ to B♭ and by the tight inner-voice half-step motion in the left hand, F–G♭–G♮–G♭.

The bridge of "Out of This World" is oriented around, but never settles into, C minor, which is articulated with closely-spaced minor sixth chords contrasting with the modal harmonies of the A section. One striking

**Example 5.8** "Out of This World"

**Example 5.9** "Out of This World," bridge

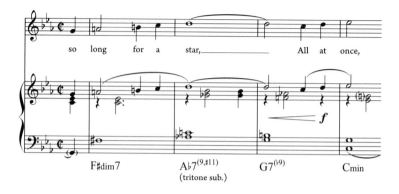

cadential progression comprises a diminished seventh chord (F♯–A–C–E♭), rare in the song up to this point, leading (at "star") to a five-note whole-tone chord (A♭–B♭–C–D♯–G♭), then a dominant ninth and a resolution to the local tonic C minor (Example 5.9). The harmony is shaped by the linear bass motion F♯-A♭-G. The whole-tone chord at "star" is known in jazz theory as a tritone substitution, which relies on the invariance in inversion of the tritone embedded in any dominant seventh chord. Here that tritone is G♭/F♯–C, which is part of both a D7 and A♭7 chord, thus allowing the latter to assume the function of the former.[33] There is no finer example than "Out of This World" of how Arlen's musical language can be at once accessible and complex.

## *St. Louis Woman*

The score that Arlen and Mercer wrote for *St. Louis Woman*, an all-Black-cast show and the first of their two Broadway musicals, is one of the finest ever created for the stage. *St. Louis Woman* ran for only 113 performances on Broadway in the spring and early summer of 1946. It fell victim to a range of problems, including conflict over its depictions of Blacks; changes of cast, director, and choreographer; and frequent rewrites of the book, which never attained a fully convincing dramatic form. Before looking in more detail at some of the show's greatest music, we should begin further back in its history, for which there is a wealth of sources that offer a window onto the complex intersections of race and the American stage (especially the musical stage) at mid-century.

Most Black-cast shows or films of the 1930s and 1940s, including *Porgy and Bess*, *Carmen Jones*, and *Cabin in the Sky*, were the products of white men. *St. Louis Woman* is distinctive for the creative involvement of Black writers. It was based on the 1931 novel *God Sends Sunday* by Arna Bontemps, a leading figure of the Harlem Renaissance. The novel traces the life of Little ("Li'l") Augie, from his childhood in Louisiana; through his successful career as a jockey in St. Louis in the 1890s, which unravels because of alcohol and violence, including murder; to his later years living in poverty in a small town in Southern California, from which he flees south to Mexico after being involved in a second murder. Despite the lurid plot elements related here, Bontemps's novel is written in an elegantly understated, poetic style, which was noted and praised by critics.[34]

Music, especially the blues, features strongly in *God Sends Sunday*, where characters hear or sing versions of W.C. Handy's "St. Louis Blues," as well as "Rocking Chair Blues" (made popular by Bessie Smith), and "Vesta and Mattie's Blues." A funeral scene includes the ballad "The Lonesome Road" (composed in 1927) and the hymns "At the River" and "We Shall Sleep, But Not Forever." The novel also includes an extended scene involving a cakewalk dance competition.

Soon after the publication of *God Sends Sunday*, Bontemps and his friend and fellow Harlem writer Countee Cullen began to collaborate on a dramatized version, which at first bore the novel's title, then was called *Leaving Time*, and eventually *St. Louis Woman*. A first draft in three acts was completed by October 1931.[35] The authors dropped the novel's framing portions in Louisiana and Los Angeles, restricting the action to St. Louis and to Augie's career as a jockey. The play depicts his relationship with Della Green, the death of Della's abusive lover Biglow Brown at the hand of his spurned girlfriend Lila, a curse placed on Augie by the dying Biglow, and Augie's sinking fortunes on the track. At the end of early drafts of the play, Della leaves Augie when his luck runs out and he begins losing races. In subsequent drafts Bontemps and Cullen added a happy ending, a scene at the racetrack in Saratoga, New York, where Augie, once again a successful jockey, reunites with Della. From the beginning the authors had the idea of including music in the play, including some of the same numbers that appear in *God Sends Sunday*.

In the first half of 1932, Will Marion Cook (who, as we saw in Chapter 3, encouraged Arlen to write "Get Happy"), took an interest in producing *St. Louis Woman* as a work of musical theater, with a score he would compose and lyrics by his son Mercer. Newspapers announced a production that would go into rehearsal in July for an August premiere.[36] But the show, billed in the press as a "folk opera," never materialized. In the fall of 1932, Cook, apparently dissatisfied with the script, asked the poet Sterling Allen Brown to rework it. The project foundered for various reasons, including Cook's ill health, although he continued to pursue it well into 1934, despite resistance from the original authors.

In the meanwhile, in November 1933, Bontemps and Cullen's play was produced by the amateur Gilpin Players of Cleveland and received a positive response from the press.[37] The authors eagerly looked forward to professional stagings, which would not, however, occur until over a dozen years later with the premiere of the Arlen-Mercer musical. In 1935, the Federal Theatre Project for New York, one of the regional programs established by the Works Progress Administration, contracted to produce the *St. Louis Woman* at Harlem's Lafayette Theater in early 1936.[38] Nothing came of this plan, nor of a desire expressed in 1938 by Orson Welles to produce the play, most likely for his Mercury Theater Company. Late in 1938, a prominent figure of the Harlem Renaissance, Langston Hughes, entered the picture. Living at that time in Los Angeles, Hughes began, with the permission of its original authors, to revise *St. Louis Woman* for a production to be directed Clarence Muse, head of the local "Negro Unit" of the Federal Theatre Project.

Hughes retained the basic structure of Bontemps and Cullen's play, but developed elements of spectacle, including music, dance, and incidental, anonymous characters ("a blind beggar," "a crawdad vendor"). In a brief note at the head of his version, Hughes describes *St. Louis Woman* as "a play of life in the Negro sporting world of St. Louis in the 1890s, the period when the Blues were born. Folk songs, Blues, and the popular songs of the day are employed in the production. Incidental background music of guitars, mandolins, and banjos."[39] Hughes adds a prologue with brief appearances of the main characters, described by him as "character flashes ending in blackouts." He removes the change of locale to Saratoga in Act 3, keeping the action in St. Louis but still reuniting Della and Augie. Handy's "St. Louis Blues" makes an appearance at the very end, and Hughes swaps in other blues and hymns for the ones in Bontemps and Cullen. Hughes also includes the character "Black Patti" (as the singer Siseretta Jones was known) performing "The Last

Rose of Summer," and a guitarist playing and singing the ballad "Frankie and Johnnie" as a kind of commentary on the murder of Biglow by Lila.

The Los Angeles staging of *St. Louis Woman* never took place, and funding for the Federal Theatre Project was soon ended by Congress. The hopes of Bontemps, Cullen, and Hughes for productions in New York and Chicago over the next few years also came to naught. But in 1943 Cullen returned to the play, reviving the idea of turning it into a musical. He began drafting lyrics, which the jazz musician Lucky Roberts would set to music. When Cullen shared the latest plan with Bontemps in June 1943, Bontemps wrote back in a letter that deserves quoting at some length:

> Thanks for going ahead with the new ST. LOUIS WOMAN campaign. A musical version would, as you know, make me supremely happy. And if Lucky Roberts has anything like "Moonlight Cocktail" in his repertoire, then praise be! I definitely would like to come in with some lyrics. What's more, I would like to help revise the play before it goes into a possible production. I went over it a couple of nights ago and felt that here and there it could stand some dusting off—especially in view of the current movement to dignify Negro roles on screen and stage. Generally speaking, I'm quite willing to stand on Little Augie's dignity as a character, but I fear we have made a few concessions to tradition (just a few), and I think they should be ironed out before the thing goes before the public.[40]

Bontemps's comment about "the current movement to dignify Negro roles" reflects his awareness that things had changed since he had published *God Sends Sunday* and begun his collaboration with Cullen on *St. Louis Woman*, well over a decade earlier. For some years, organizations like the NAACP and the Los-Angeles-based Interracial Film and Radio Guild had argued against the stereotypical roles assigned to Black actors on film and stage, which depicted Blacks as lazy, dishonest, violent, profligate, drunk, and holding jobs like maids, porters, and butlers.[41] *St. Louis Woman*, as Bontemps implies, has its share of such roles.

Although Bontemps appears never to have contributed lyrics to the 1943 version of *St. Louis Woman*, about a dozen of Cullen's survive. The words for Della's first song, "I'm a St. Louis Woman," give a good idea of his approach:

> I'm a St. Louis Woman,
> And loving is my game;

> I'm hard to get and hard to hold
> And twice as hard to tame.
> I wear diamonds to my knuckles,
> My shoes have silver buckles,
> And everywhere the men all stare
> To see me walk.[42]

These lyrics reinforce the very image of Della as a Black seductress that Bontemps, in his letter to Cullen, identified as in need of moderating. Indeed, when Mercer wrote his own lyrics for Della's introductory number two years later, "Any Place I Hang My Hat Is Home," a more nuanced impression of her emerges, as a "free and easy" spirit who has to "roam." It is Della's love for Augie that changes her mind and leads her to settle down with one man.

By September 1943 a newspaper announced that Roberts had completed his music for *St. Louis Woman*.[43] None of it appears to survive, and this musical version went no further. In June 1944 Bontemps wrote to Hughes, "I have given up on *St. Louis Woman* in its present incarnation." He reported to Hughes his disappointment with Roberts's songs: "Surely they can't be as bad as they sound to me."[44] We can imagine that Roberts's musical style, based in early ragtime, lacked the range Bontemps and Cullen anticipated for the show.

The fortunes of *St. Louis Woman* at last shifted with the intervention of the white Hollywood and Broadway establishment. A producer named Edward Gross had come across the play and felt it had promise as a stage musical. In the spring or summer of 1945 Gross took the idea to Arthur Freed, the mastermind behind *The Wizard of Oz* and other MGM film musicals. Freed envisioned that the show might star Lena Horne, then under contract to MGM, and be adapted for Hollywood. He was enthusiastic enough to form a separate production company to finance *St. Louis Woman* for Broadway, and he approached Arlen and Mercer to write the score. Horne agreed to consider the lead role of Della.

At this point, well after Arlen and Mercer had begun work and other members of the creative team were being assembled, another wind ruffled the sails of *St. Louis Woman*. In late August 1945, the Interracial Film and Radio Guild, after reviewing the script, wrote to Roy Wilkins, head of the NAACP in New York, voicing opposition to *St. Louis Woman* because it "presents the same old stereotyped tripe concerning the Negro and depicts the Negro in his worst light."[45] Walter White, the secretary of the NAACP and its main spokesperson, took up the protest. Although he had not seen the play, he wrote to Cullen and Bontemps in early September:

> [F]rom the very disturbed reports which have come to me the story deals exclusively with Negroes who are not only immoral but amoral. I understand the cast consists wholly of pimps, prostitutes and characters of that type who, in the female versions sleep only with the men who have the fattest bankrolls, and in the male version think no more of treachery and murder than they do of taking a drink of water. . . . Appearance on Broadway in the year of our Lord 1945 of a play which may conceivably be made later into a moving picture which perpetuates all these stereotypes of the Negro could be disastrous.

A live reading of the play by Cullen at White's apartment in Harlem on September 14 only confirmed White's and Wilkins's suspicions. Wilkins wrote to White on September 15: "I was glad to have the opportunity of hearing the manuscript 'St. Louis Woman' read last night by Countee Cullen, but I am still of the opinion that it would be very unfortunate if this play were produced on Broadway and still more unfortunate if it were made into a film." Wilkins acknowledges that plays and films "with these kinds of plots," like *Cabin in the Sky* and *Porgy and Bess*, tend to get backing from producers. But, he argues, "There ought to be a new deal for the Negro in the entertainment field. Surely in 1945, as we start out after the end of the war for democracy and human dignity, we ought not to be pushing the same old stereotypes of the race on the stage."

The last sentence is significant, suggesting as Bontemps did in his earlier letter to Cullen, that the stereotypical representations of Blacks were no longer acceptable. Adding to the frustration on the part of Wilkins, White, and others was that *St. Louis Woman* was the product of Black writers. Shortly after the reading of *St. Louis Woman* in September 1945, White wrote to Cullen about a new "hard-hitting" and "uncompromising" play by two white authors that avoided such caricatures: *Deep Are the Roots*, by Arnaud d'Usseau and James Gow, about a Black army lieutenant returning home to the South after the war. "What irony it is that white people should do a play of that sort," White observed, "while two colored authors should do one which portrays every cliché and every hoary myth about the Negro which our enemies have attempted to perpetuate."

The most immediate effect of the campaign against *St. Louis Woman* was the withdrawal of Lena Horne in the fall of 1945. Horne had been urged to take the part by Freed and others in the Hollywood and Broadway establishment because the show offered many roles for Blacks at a time when few were seen on stage. She had tentatively agreed to do the show because she had "fallen in love with the music" before seeing the script. But then she recoiled at the character of Della. "I was caught between two very important forces in my life," she recalled, "the opinion of the Negro community and the opinion of people who had been important in my career."[46]

Despite all the institutional and personal efforts to block the show, the development of *St. Louis Woman* proceeded. A relatively unknown singer, Ruby Hill, was chosen for the role of Della that Horne had turned down. The Nicholas brothers, Harold and Fayard, tap dancers with substantial Hollywood careers, were cast, respectively, as Augie and Barney (a fellow jockey). Pearl Bailey made her Broadway debut as Butterfly, Barney's girlfriend. Rex Ingram, a leading film and stage actor, was Biglow Brown, the abusive bar owner and jealous lover of Della. (There is some irony to Ingram's participation in *St. Louis Woman*, since he was Chairman of the National Sponsoring Committee of the Interracial Film and Radio Guild, which had expressed opposition to the script.) Augie's sister was Juanita Hall, who would later play Asian roles in *South Pacific* and *Flower Drum Song* and would appear as Madame Tango in Arlen's *House of Flowers*. June Hawkins was Lila. The production and creative team, some associated with MGM, was all white: Arlen and Mercer; the director and set designer Lemuel Ayres; and the choreographer Anthony Tudor.

But even with an accomplished cast and team in place, the path of *St. Louis Woman* to and on Broadway would not be smooth. Cullen died unexpectedly in January 1946, just two days before the start of rehearsals. Revisions to the book, deemed too sprawling in plot and imbalanced in terms of the placement of music, now fell mainly to Bontemps. After out-of-town tryouts in New Haven and Boston, the producer Gross brought in Rouben Mamoulian, who a decade earlier had directed *Porgy and Bess*, and, more recently, *Oklahoma!* and *Carousel*. Ayres's role was now reduced to set and costume design. Tudor was replaced by Charles Waters, who had choreographed MGM musical films. During rehearsals some cast members complained that gestures Mamoulian called for in certain scenes were, in the words of Pearl Bailey, "too Negroid."[47] Mamoulian reshaped the book's two acts into three, with a better distribution of musical numbers. Each act now ended with an ensemble: for Act 1 a cakewalk dance, for Act 2 a choral funeral scene reminiscent of *Porgy and Bess*, and for Act 3 an offstage horse race viewed and reacted to by the cast onstage in a manner that, judging from the script, anticipates the Ascot Gavotte scene in *My Fair Lady*.

*St. Louis Woman* opened on March 30, 1946, to mixed reviews in both the white and Black press. John Chapman of the *New York Daily News* was an outlier among New York critics in praising the show, calling it "the best Negro musical in many seasons, and the best new musical of this season up to this late date."[48] Writing for Black newspapers in Los Angeles and Norfolk, Virginia, John M. Lee condemned *St. Louis Woman* as a "thinly veiled vaudeville show" and "another one of those phony folk-lore plots with singing and dancing breaking out all over the place." As if echoing the concerns voiced months earlier by White, Wilkins, and other leaders of color, Lee cautioned producers contemplating Black productions for Broadway that "it is no longer profitable to exhibit Negro performers as versatile curiosities."[49] Indeed, *St. Louis Woman* closed less than two months later, on July 6.

In April 1946 Capitol Records, the company begun by Mercer, recorded eleven numbers for a *St. Louis Woman* cast album, which remains a vivid document of the original production. In 1998 a near-complete score was reconstructed from various sources—the original orchestrations had been lost—for a concert performance at New York's *Encores!* series and a subsequent recording.[50] We thus have a good if imperfect picture of the rich score, whose twenty-five surviving numbers include a children's song, a lullaby, an elaborate cakewalk dance, a spiritual sung at a funeral, various blues-inspired songs, shorter ballads, and extended tapeworms. Here we will look more closely at three that represent some of Arlen and Mercer's finest work.

## "Come Rain or Come Shine"

"Come Rain or Come Shine," the best known number from *St. Louis Woman* and one of the most popular standards, is sung by Della and Augie at the beginning of Act 2, when they commit to each other and move in together. The song was the result of a single evening's work in the late summer or autumn of 1945 at Arlen's New York apartment. Mercer arrived and went into the study, while Arlen stayed in the living room and, in his own words, "toyed around with an idea, then came down and played it for him [Mercer]." Arlen's melody appealed to Mercer, who immediately came up with a lyric, "I'm gonna love you, like nobody's loved you," for the opening phrase. He paused, and Arlen spontaneously interjected, "Come hell or high water." Mercer responded, "Of course, why didn't I think of that?—'Come rain or come shine.'" Before Mercer left the apartment, they had completed the song.[51]

Like "My Shining Hour," "Come Rain or Come Shine" has a conventional thirty-two-bar frame with a fluid inner structure difficult to represent with letters. Because the final eight measures are closely related to the opening eight, we might analyze the song as ABAA'. But in "Come Rain or Come Shine" repetition and contrast take place on the micro-level of *four* rather than eight bars, creating an impression of continuous variation of small units:

```
A   a    ("I'm gonna love you")
    a'   ("High as a mountain")
B   b    ("I guess")
    b'   ("But don't ever")
A   a    ("You're gonna")
    a"   ("Happy together")
A'  a'''  ("Days may be cloudy")
    c    ("I'm with you")
```

The fluid harmonic language of "Come Rain or Come Shine" complements the formal design. The song begins in F major and ends in D major; as such, it displays the progressive tonality discussed above in the context of "One for My Baby." But where the earlier song just hopped from E♭ major into G major, "Come Rain or Come Shine" is more continuous and ambiguous. After the initial *aa'* segments, there are few stable harmonies until the D-major triad at the end.

The shifting tonality of "Come Rain or Come Shine" accompanies a vocal line that is often anti-melodic, consisting of the chant-like repetition of a single note. But as the profusion of prime marks in the above formal analysis suggests, the melody is varied incrementally each time. In the very last iteration (*a'''*), Arlen subjects the repeated note D to his signature octave leap and underpins it with a distinctively voiced dominant seventh chord and a sinuous chromatic countermelody (Example 5.10). Such passages reveal how Arlen's music can be at once concise and rich.

Mercer's lyrics for "Come Rain or Come Shine" play on the opposition implied in the title. The phrase "I'm gonna love you like nobody's loved you" sets up the idea of direct opposition ("I"/"you" and "I"/"nobody") developed

**Example 5.10** "Come Rain or Come Shine," A′ section

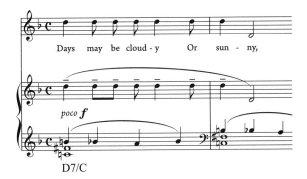

in many subsequent lines, including the recurring title phrase "come rain or come shine" and in the frequent pairs of contrasting images: "high"/"deep," "happy"/"unhappy," "cloudy"/"sunny," and "in"/"out of." At the reprise of the *a* phrase, Mercer inverts one of the original oppositions: "I'm gonna love you" becomes "You're gonna love me." The song's pile-up of antonyms is resolved only in the final, reassuring line: "I'm with you always."

## "I Wonder What Became of Me"

"I Wonder What Became of Me" was originally to be sung by Della the beginning of Act 3 of *St. Louis Woman* but was dropped from the show.[52] It represents a wistful moment for the normally confident Della, who is blamed for Augie's bad luck when he continues to lose horse races. Mercer's lyrics are among the most expressive and elegant in *St. Louis Woman*. Della sings of bright lights, of champagne, and of merrymaking in which she feels incapable of taking part because "along the way something went astray."

The form of "I Wonder What Became of Me" reflects Della's state of uncertainty, as Arlen tinkers with the lengths of the individual segments of a standard frame: A(12) A′(8) B(8) A″(16). Della's mood is also conveyed by harmonic ambiguity, few strong cadences, and another instance of progressive tonality. "I Wonder What Became of Me" begins in, or more accurately *around*, the key of E♭ major (there is no root-position E♭ chord in the song) and concludes in A♭ major. The very first harmony is an inverted B♭6 chord, which initiates a sequence of chromatically descending, gently pulsating quarter-note chords (Example 5.11a). Eleven measures into A″, instead of

**Example 5.11** "I Wonder What Became of Me," (a) opening and (b) transition to coda

cadencing on E♭ from its dominant, Arlen deflects the harmony to A♭ (at "And I can't explain"; Example 5.11b). This moment feels like the beginning of a coda, which in many songs and pieces of classical music dips toward the subdominant on the way to a final close in the tonic. Yet Arlen never returns to E♭: the harmonic trajectory of "I Wonder What Became of Me" thus conveys quite literally the sense of "becoming" implied in the song's title.

## "I Had Myself a True Love"

"I Had Myself a True Love," sung by Lila in Act 1 of *St. Louis Woman* after her rejection by Biglow, is one of Arlen's longest tapeworms, at sixty-four bars. Wilder calls it "very nearly an aria," which "would be highly acceptable as a concert song." He rightly describes the accompaniment as showing significant "compositional concern," specifically "the use of thematic material in the cadences, the shifting styles in the left hand of the piano, the dynamic markings, [and] the introduction."[53] The song's structure can be represented as A(8) B(8) A′(8) C(8) D(13) A″(8) C′(11). In actual number of bars, it divides into thirty-two-bar halves, which do not, however, align symmetrically with the formal divisions ABA′C and DA″C′, because of the thirteen-bar length of D. The first thirty-two bars could in themselves constitute a song in a standard form. They end with a strong cadence in the tonic and with a melody and lyrics that refer back to the opening: the last four bars of C, concluding with "I had a true love."

What follows, section D, initially seems analogous to the substantial interludes Arlen provided for some other songs, notably "Stormy Weather." But unlike interludes, the D section in "I Had Myself a True Love" becomes an integral part of the overall developmental plan. Arlen changes the piano accompaniment to pulsing repeated chords that descend chromatically, one of his trademark accompaniment figures that also appears in "I Wonder What Became of Me." The segment builds to a big climax at "With that gal in that damn ol' saloon," concluding with the dominant and leading to a return, A″.

The return breaks the form in a fashion rare even for Arlen. The climax of the preceding D section is Lila's despairing question and self-provided answer: "Where is he while I watch the risin' moon? / With that gal in that damn ol' saloon." As A″ begins (Example 5.12), she seems too overcome with emotion to sing the melody. Her "voice" is assumed by the right hand of the piano (or orchestra) playing the original tune in octaves. The singer enters only in the second measure with a new phrase, "No, that ain't the way it used to be," where the initial "No" is held achingly for four beats. This pattern is then repeated with the next phrase, "No, and everybody keeps telling me" (▶ 5.3).

Arlen and Mercer wind down "I Had Myself a True Love" with a return of C that has the exact same lyrics as before ("There may be a lot o' things I miss"), another unusual feature of the song. The music is identical for only the first four bars, however; at the start of the final four (plus coda), a fermata on the word "Now" makes the vocalist pause, somewhat as with the earlier "No" (Example 5.13). A fermata like this is often the signal for a cadenza, a passage improvised by the soloist. And that is essentially what Arlen and Mercer provide, as the singer seems at last to find her own voice.[54] At the low E♭ ("upon a [time]"), Arlen resumes the musical phrase from the original C section, as the piano again doubles the voice ("time I had"). But piano and voice part ways again as the voice climbs back up to

**Example 5.12** "I Had Myself a True Love," the return at A″

**Example 5.13** "I Had Myself a True Love," the final four bars of the C′ section

its concluding note on the high E♭ ("love"), which is sustained for almost four measures. Underneath, the piano fashions a coda with the pulsating chords and melody of the D section, assuming a voice that seems to comment upon the song that has just ended.

## Afterlives of *St. Louis Woman: Blues Opera*

The long saga of *St. Louis Woman*, which began with the Bontemps-Cullen play of 1931, did not end with the closing of the Arlen-Mercer musical on Broadway in July 1946. Two virtually simultaneous but separate developments in 1953–1954 brought *St. Louis Woman* back to life. In 1953, MGM, which still retained rights to the show, announced a musical film of *St. Louis Woman*, to be produced by Freed and featuring Frank Sinatra and Ava Gardner as Augie and Della, with Sammy Davis Jr. and Eartha Kitt being considered for other roles. The screenplay went through several drafts.[55] As reported in the press, Sinatra and Gardner were to "wear perfect brown makeup that has been created by ace cosmeticians of Hollywood."[56] The film of *St. Louis Woman* was never made, in part, it was reported, because of the divorce between Sinatra and Gardner, but also surely because of the controversy that would likely have arisen in the mid-1950s with the casting of two white singer-actors in blackface (or a lighter-shade brownface) for roles originated by Black performers.

In any event, MGM's plans were overtaken by the project to turn *St. Louis Woman* into a "blues opera." The catalyst was Robert Breen, director and co-producer of the Everyman Opera Company, which had been created to bring the Gershwins' *Porgy and Bess* on tour through the United States, South America, Europe, and Middle East.[57] In the latter part of 1953, Breen was scouting for companion pieces—including a possible new commission—the troupe could perform in alternation with *Porgy and Bess*. He put together a list of songs in the style he envisioned for such a work and showed it to Cab Calloway, who was playing the role of Sportin' Life. Calloway told him all the songs on the list had been written by Arlen. Breen approached Arlen and suggested expanding *St. Louis Woman* into an operatic work along the lines of *Porgy and Bess*, scored almost continuously and filled out with additional numbers and recitative.

The moment seems to have been right for Arlen, who would later write, "The idea of writing a full-length musical work in the language of the Blues—a synthesis of all the varied expressions that can be found in this style of music—had been in my mind for a long time."[58] Breen brought in the composer, conductor, and arranger Samuel Matlowsky (his name is sometimes spelled Matlovsky) to assist Arlen. Together they created the score for what was at various times called *Blues Opera* (or *Blues-Opera*, or *The Blues*) or *Free and Easy* (the opening phrase from Della's song "Any Place I Hang My Hat Is

Home"), or both, with one functioning as subtitle for the other. The surviving sources of *Blues Opera* in its first incarnation (1954–1958) are vast. They include a full piano-vocal score, copyist versions of nine additional songs by Arlen, several versions of the libretto, correspondence between Breen and the major creative figures (including Bontemps, Arlen, Mercer, and Matlowsky), demo recordings by Arlen of some of the individual numbers, and a virtually complete set of demos of the piano-vocal score.[59]

Although the high-flying world of St. Louis's Targee Street and the Rocking Horse Saloon bear little resemblance to the gritty and downtrodden Catfish Row, the characters and plot of the musical *St. Louis Woman* display clear parallels with those of *Porgy and Bess*. These similarities were enhanced when the show was refashioned as a companion opera. Augie, Della, and Biglow have their counterparts in Porgy, Bess, and Crown. Leah and Count Ragsdale occupy roles analogous to Serena and Sportin' Life, respectively. Leah is a devout woman and president of the local "betterment society"; Ragsdale is a flashy gambler who tries to lure Della away from Augie and is described in one version of the *Blues Opera* libretto as "genial, smooth, insinuating, suave."

Breen hoped to stage *Blues Opera* in Paris in December 1954, followed by a Broadway production in 1955. But the search for financial backing and the negotiations with MGM over the rights, which lasted until November 1956, delayed the production. At the request of the conductor Andre Kostelanetz, an Arlen admirer who saw the score, Matlowsky arranged a twenty-five-minute orchestral suite of music from *Blues Opera*, which Kostelanetz and the New York Philharmonic recorded in October 1957 and played at Carnegie Hall in November.[60]

In March 1959, the producer Stanley Chase, who had brought the Brecht-Weill *Threepenny Opera* to the New York stage in 1954, took over the *Blues Opera* project. Breen stayed on as director. The main title of the work was changed to *Free and Easy*, with *Blues Opera* sometimes retained as a subtitle. In April 1959, casting and rehearsals began, with an eye toward a European premiere in December. Harold Nicholas assumed the role of Augie he had played in the original *St. Louis Woman*. Sammy Davis Jr. would take over the role when it came to New York. Quincy Jones and Billy Byders rescored *Free and Easy* for an eighteen-piece jazz ensemble, which was also to play onstage as part of the action.

The company left for Europe on November 15, to begin rehearsals in Brussels in advance of an opening in Amsterdam. As rehearsals and revisions progressed, Chase and Breen frequently clashed about the opera's stage-worthiness and readiness for opening. *Free and Easy* debuted in Amsterdam on December 15, 1959. The reviews were mainly favorable, but the production was still riven by disputes between producer and director. Chase appointed as "acting director" the choreographer Donald McKayle, who in his memoirs described the opera as having "no real second act" and as "a sleeping monster that refused to move out of its state of hibernation."[61] *Free and Easy* moved on to Paris, where it opened on January 15, 1960. Again the reviews in the local press were positive, but audiences dwindled, and the early closing of the show on February 7 scuttled plans to bring *Free and Easy* to other European cities and eventually back to the United States.[62]

Although no complete score or recording emerged from the years of work on *Blues Opera/Free and Easy*, the ample sources can give us a good sense of the work.[63] The surviving libretti—the earliest detailed outline or "spine" is dated January 15, 1954—are divided into two acts and follow the basic outlines of *St. Louis Woman*, but with numerous characters added (anonymous figures like "Flower Vendor" and "Blind Man") and others removed. The Matlowsky piano-vocal score confirms the description by Arlen's biographer Jablonski of "a smoothly flowing work combining the elements of opera, ballet, and drama all fused into one."[64] Matlowsky created overtures for each act, as well as many instrumental passages to impart continuity or to accompany dance, bits of spoken dialogue, or pantomime action. About a dozen of the original songs from *St. Louis Woman* appear (including some numbers cut from the show), to which are added other Arlen songs, most written earlier with Mercer ("Blues in the Night," "That Old Black Magic," and "Accentuate the Positive" among them) or with Ted Koehler ("I Gotta Right to Sing the Blues" and "Ill Wind"). Relatively few numbers are sung complete, with the exception of "Any Place I Hang My Hat is Home," "I Had Myself a True Love" and "Come Rain or Come Shine." Most appear as fragments, sometimes only in a phrase or two.

To this imported music Arlen and Matlowsky added new passages of recitative or parlando of varying lengths, about nineteen in all. Breen and his wife Wilva would read Arlen portions of the libretto to be set in this way, and Arlen would create melodies with harmonic accompaniment. Sometimes he would notate these himself; in other cases Matlowsky took the music down from Arlen's performance. According to Jablonski, the arranger "was most impressed with Arlen's natural feeling for sung dialogue, and Arlen, in turn, appreciated Matlowsky's musicianship and understanding of what they were trying to accomplish."[65] Example 5.14 shows a characteristic passage

**Example 5.14** *Blues Opera*, recitative composed by Arlen for Della in Act 2

of recitative, sung by Della in Act 2, with an interjection by Augie. It reveals Arlen's gift for a vocal style that can be both lyrical and conversational, one that he had demonstrated time and time again in his songs, including those originally written for *St. Louis Woman*, like "I Had Myself a True Love" examined above.

After the piano-vocal score for *Blues Opera* was completed, and well into 1958, Arlen continued to write new material, including eight numbers that tend more toward song than recitative and are some of the strongest

**Example 5.15** "Flower Vendor," from *Blues Opera*

materials for the new work. At this point Mercer had pretty much ceased active involvement in the project, and some of the new lyrics are attributed in the sheet music to "W.B. Dreen," almost certainly a nom de plume for one or both of the Breens. One of the most striking new Arlen numbers is "Flower Vendor" (▶ 5.4; Example 5.15), whose languid chordal accompaniment and hauntingly simple, incantatory melody recall Gershwin's "Summertime."

As a work that occupied Arlen's energies and enthusiasm over many years, *Blues Opera* merits study and hearing.[66] Yet the piano-vocal score, as well as the surviving demos and the tapes of the Paris performance, do not necessarily show Arlen's talents in the best light. As I have been arguing in this book, Arlen is above all a master architect of the individual song. Whether thirty-two bars or an extended tapeworm, the best of Arlen's numbers take us on an emotional journey that can seem at once unexpected and inevitable. The songs that were grafted onto *Blues Opera* from other contexts lose something of that power, in part because they are truncated, in part because they are assigned to the opera's characters in ways that seem arbitrary. Little is gained dramatically by Lila singing "I Gotta Right to Sing the Blues" and Della "Blues in the Night" one after the other; or by having Augie perform "One for My Baby," or Ragsdale "Ill Wind." The songs carried over from *St. Louis Woman* for Augie, Della, and Lila retain more of their original force. But others are detached from their original characters. *Blues Opera* reassigns "A Woman's Prerogative" and "Legalize My Name," written for and sung so memorably by Pearl Bailey as Butterfly in *St. Louis Woman*. The former (ten measures only) is now performed by Ragsdale, the latter by Leah. In the opera, Butterfly has become a minor role.

Then there is the question of who is the main "composer" of *Blues Opera*. The title page of the piano-vocal score specifies "Music [by] Harold Arlen" and "Musical Adaptation [by] Samuel Matlowsky." But "adaptation" clearly encompasses a broad range of actual composition. With the exception of the Minuet that ends Act 1, a piece Arlen had written in 1939 (as "American Minuet"), Matlowsky provided the instrumental passages, including the overtures, the dances (the long cakewalk segment), and the accompaniment to the pantomimed action (such as the "Killing Sequence"). Matlowsky's work, including the *Blues Opera Suite*, is competent and often imaginative. But even with some of the fine new recitatives and songs Arlen created, the Arlen that we value most as a songwriter gets lost in the shuffle.

As we have seen, elements of the blues are common in Arlen's music, and it was perhaps logical for him to wish to develop them into a larger work. But while his blues style can make for great individual songs, or even a great show like *St. Louis Woman*, it is less effective when spread out over a three-hour work that is sung almost throughout. The same argument could be, and has been, leveled against *Porgy and Bess*, the inspiration and model for *Blues Opera*. But as an opera *Porgy and Bess* is tighter, more coherent. The Gershwins were working "from scratch" with a stronger libretto and with original music. They did not pad the score with other numbers from their catalogue.

## *Saratoga*

Arlen's last produced Broadway musical was *Saratoga*, written in 1959 with Mercer, who later called it a "B-O-M-B."[67] For Jablonski, "from its inception *Saratoga* was a mistake."[68] The show, based on Edna Ferber's *Saratoga Trunk*, was planned to give Arlen and Mercer the stage triumph that had eluded them for almost fifteen years. Adapted and directed by Morton DaCosta, who had come off a big success with *The Music Man* in 1957, *Saratoga* would be a star-studded, visually rich musical to rival Kern and Hammerstein's *Show Boat*, the 1927 show based on Ferber's earlier work. The leads were Carol Lawrence, fresh from her starring role as Maria in *West Side Story*, and Howard Keel, a distinguished baritone who had starred in the MGM films of *Show Boat* and *Seven Brides for Seven Brothers*. Cecil Beaton, who had worked on *My Fair Lady* and *Gigi*, designed sets and costumes.

Arlen and Mercer created the score for *Saratoga* during the spring and summer of 1959. From its out-of-town previews in October to its Broadway opening in December, *Saratoga* underwent many revisions, especially to its book, which was long and unwieldy, filled with too many characters and elaborate production numbers. Songs were removed; others added. Arlen, already under stress with revisions of *Blues Opera*, suffered an emotional breakdown and checked into a New York hospital; he never attended the premiere of *Saratoga*, which closed after eighty performances. Compounding its own shortcomings, *Saratoga* had the misfortune to open during a Broadway season that saw the arrival of *Gypsy* and *The Sound of Music*.

Like so many film or stage productions with Arlen's music, *Saratoga* contains some fine numbers, as was noted by critics who condemned the show but called the songs "one and all good" or "simply wonderful."[69] As always, Arlen attempted to create a special sound world. Yet perhaps because of the extensive revisions to the show and the composer's exhaustion during this period, the sonorities of *Saratoga* are less distinctive than in *Bloomer Girl* or *St. Louis Woman*.

The best-known number from *Saratoga* is the blues-inflected "Goose Never Be a Peacock," sung by the acclaimed Black contralto Carol Brice. Its initial melodic arc is pure Arlen: a bold octave descent, a rise to the flatted seventh, a descent to the flatted third, and a concluding drop to the lower fifth. Arlen and Mercer also created two fine ballads for *Saratoga*, "You for Me" and "Love Held Lightly." The former reflects an Arlen style of the 1950s, in which the piano accompaniments are sometimes sparser and less contrapuntal, featuring sustained chords and harmonic motion by whole step. In this regard "You for Me" resembles "It's a New World" from *A Star Is Born*, to be examined in Chapter 7.

One of the cleverest aspects of the score of *Saratoga* is how "A Game of Poker" and "Love Held Lightly," two songs with little apparent relationship, are first sung separately and then superimposed. Irving Berlin, the Gershwins, and Frank Loesser had all written such "double" or "counterpoint" songs.[70] The precedents most relevant for Arlen and Mercer come from *The Music Man*, the hit staged by DaCosta just two years before *Saratoga*. There the composer-lyricist Meredith Willson accomplishes the double-song feat multiple times, with "Goodnight, Ladies"/" Pick-a-Little, Talk-a-Little," "Lida Rose"/"Will I Ever Tell You," and "Seventy-Six Trombones"/"Goodnight, My Someone." It seems likely that DaCosta asked Arlen and Mercer to fashion something similar for *Saratoga*. (Arlen would write another double song, with Martin Charnin, for the unfinished show *Softly*, to be discussed in Chapter 10.)

Arlen manages the combination with characteristic subtlety (▶ 5.5). At first the two songs differ harmonically (Example 5.16). In "A Game of Poker,"

**Example 5.16** "Game of Poker" and "Love Held Lightly," aligned to show harmonic correspondences

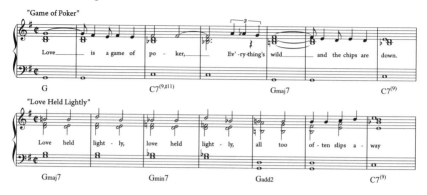

two measures of tonic alternate with two of an enhanced subdominant (C–F–B♭–D); "Love Held Lightly" sits over a tonic pedal, shifting from major to minor. The harmonies begin to align in the third and fourth measures of "Love Held Lightly" with a shift to the minor third B♭, which is also the seventh of C in "A Game of Poker." D is embedded as a pedal tone in both chords. From the fifth measure on, the two songs align still more closely. In "A Game of Poker" Arlen simply repeats the accompaniment pattern of the first four measures. In "Love Held Lightly," however, Arlen moves off the tonic (at "a-*way*") to end on the identical C9 chord as in "A Game of Poker" ("down").

Credit must be given as well to Mercer, since the linking of these two songs has musico-dramatic logic within the plot of *Saratoga*. The leads Clio (Lawrence), a grifter, and Clint (Keel), a gambler, are falling for each other, but hesitantly. The duet "A Game of Poker" acknowledges, with a metaphor they both understand, the risks and rewards of loving. "Love Held Lightly," sung by Clio's Aunt Belle, follows up on these sentiments, urging the couple to commit to each other. Both songs end with codas to which Mercer has fitted a last phrase that is identical:

> "A Game of Poker": "But it's sure / Worth a try / If it's love."
> "Love Held Lightly": "It will do all the rest / If it's love."

✽✽✽

On February 15, 1960, two days after *Saratoga* closed, Arlen wrote to Mercer, offering a consolatory perspective on the show's failure: "I'd like you to know . . . that you were as thoughtful as any human could be under fire.

Shameful it is that all of us were caught with the impossible task of bringing some life into the play." Arlen thought the blame should be shared: "I have felt all along that Fryer [Robert Fryer, the producer], DaCosta [the director] and we'uns were all guilty. We should have cracked our critical know-how all along the way."[71]

After a career of over thirty years, Arlen of course had plenty of critical know-how. But with a stage musical he was part of a larger team. In such contexts Arlen was rarely assertive, and never aggressive; he had a tendency to put his head down and focus on providing the best songs he could. As he told his biographer Jablonski in 1961, "a little of your flesh is taken away" when collaborating on a musical. He added, "You've got to compromise—you can't don a goatee and smock and start strutting around."[72] In the case of *Saratoga*, compromise could not rescue the anodyne book and characters, which did not play to Arlen and Mercer's strengths. There was no opportunity for numbers like "Blues in the Night," "Come Rain or Come Shine," or "One for My Baby," on which the reputation of one of the greatest composer-lyricist teams in American popular song deservedly rests.

# 6
# Arlen, Leo Robin, and Dorothy Fields

The songs Arlen wrote with Ted Koehler, Yip Harburg, and Johnny Mercer amply reflect the range and variety of his oeuvre. Though more limited in scope, his collaborations with other lyricists are no less important, both to him creatively and to the repertory of the American Songbook. Over subsequent chapters, we will look, in roughly chronological order, at some of the partnerships from the last two decades of Arlen's active career, beginning with Leo Robin (1947) and Dorothy Fields (1951–1952), then Ira Gershwin (1953–1954), Truman Capote (1954), and, finally, Dory Langdon (1962–1964) and Martin Charnin (1964–1967).[1]

Leo Robin and Dorothy Fields share a chapter in Philip Furia's *The Poets of Tin Pan Alley* as two prolific, versatile lyricists. Both had long and roughly similar careers which also paralleled, even if they rarely intersected with, Arlen's—beginning in New York in the 1920s, then moving to Hollywood in the early 1930s, where, in Furia's estimation, Robin and Fields "brought some of the witty urbanity of the golden age to film songs."[2] Even while continuing to work on the West Coast, both returned to the Broadway stage in the 1940s and after.

## Leo Robin and *Casbah*

In 1947, Arlen teamed up with Leo Robin to write songs for the film *Casbah*, a noir musical remake of an earlier film, *Algiers* (1938). Already an established figure on Broadway and in Hollywood, Robin had won an Oscar for "Thanks for the Memory," written with Ralph Rainger, and would go on in 1949 to provide the lyrics for Jule Styne's hit show *Gentlemen Prefer Blondes*, which included "Diamonds Are a Girl's Best Friend."

"Craftsman" is how Arlen and Robin described each other. Arlen admired Robin's ability to accommodate some of his most complex tunes: "We would always have healthy discussions about the songs. Leo starts working about midnight, and like all the true greats is a great craftsman. He would give me a completed lyric with his usual, 'Now, this is only a dummy,' but it always turned out to be the right one." For his part, Robin found it "refreshing and challenging" to work with Arlen, who was "not bound by the conventional formulas of the music business." Robin admired Arlen's belief that no number was insignificant, even if being written for a "throwaway" spot in a film: Arlen was "a very conscientious craftsman to whom everything he writes is important."[3]

Set in Algiers, *Casbah* focuses on Pépé le Moko (played by Tony Martin), a jewel thief who is sought by the French authorities but always protected by the locals within the walls of the old city, the Casbah. Le Moko falls in love with a beautiful woman visiting from France with her fiancé. She plans to stay with him in the Casbah but after a false report of his death decides to fly home. Le Moko pursues her to the airport, where he is shot to death by the police on the tarmac. *Casbah* has clear echoes of *Casablanca*—local expat falls in love with exotic foreigner engaged to another man—except that in the earlier film Rick (Humphrey Bogart) reluctantly renounces Ilsa (Ingrid Bergman) at the airport.

The four songs by Arlen and Robin that appear in *Casbah* are among Arlen's finest creations: "Hooray for Love," "For Every Man There's a Woman," "It Was Written in the Stars," and "What's Good About Goodbye?" "Hooray for Love" is something of an anomaly among Arlen songs: bouncy, optimistic, and with no trace of the blues. After a sixteen-measure verse, the main part of the chorus is a very compact A(8) A'(8), supplemented by an eight-measure interlude ("It's the wonder of the world"), after which AA' is repeated in full. Robin admitted he had "never written a lyric" that is "so repetitious." "I was shocked to notice that every line in the refrain ended with the word 'for love.' But it felt right!," he recalled. "Evidently Harold reacted to it in the same way because he made no comment about the repetition. He might not have even noticed it and this may be due to the fact that the rhymes come where the ear expects them to be."[4] Indeed, with the reiteration of "for love" Robin was responding ingeniously, if perhaps in part unconsciously, to Arlen's placement of the same short–long, quarter note–half note rhythm at the end of each two-measure unit of the chorus.

The harmonic language of both "For Every Man There's a Woman" and "It Was Written in the Stars" establishes a vaguely Middle Eastern color for *Casbah* similar to Arlen's "Americana" touches in *Bloomer Girl* or the blues sonorities in *St. Louis Woman*. Both songs are prevailingly in the minor key—unusual in Arlen's works and in the American Songbook more generally.

**Example 6.1** "For Every Man There's a Woman," extension in A section

And in both the tonic triad is enhanced by an added sixth that is probably intended to sound exotic but is also (this being Arlen) structurally significant.

The obvious gender stereotyping in the lyric of "For Every Man There's a Woman" perhaps dooms it from being recorded or widely performed today. But the song, which received an Oscar nomination, shows Arlen at the height of his powers, fashioning tapeworm-like extensions to the units of a standard structure: A(13) A(13) B(4) A'(13). In A, Arlen appends to the first eight measures a break-like, two-measure phrase "Woman was made for man." And then comes another four-measure extension: a new piano figure picked up by the voice as a kind of afterthought ("Where is she") (Example 6.1).

The uneven number of measures in A, thirteen rather than the fourteen we would expect (8 + 2 + 4), is created by the elision of the two extension phrases. The cadence to Fm6 on "man" (shown in the first measure of Example 6.1) serves both as the second measure of a two-measure phrase and as the first of a four-measure one. Arlen presumably built this asymmetry into this song before handing it to Robin. It is also striking that the vocal line for the final three measures of A ("Where is she? Where is the woman for me?") appears in smaller notes, as if capturing the more plaintive and less assertive quality of the tune. Robin accommodated this shift in tone with his questioning, afterthought-like phrase.

"It Was Written in the Stars" shares an enhanced minor tonic with "For Every Man There's a Woman," here E♭m6 (with added C♮). Arlen enriches this harmony with a swooping piano figure that lands in the second half of the measure on a chord at once dissonant and static, F–A♮–B♮–E♭ (Example 6.2). In the key of E♭ minor this chord could be reckoned as an altered V7/V, but here alternates with the tonic and is not part of any real progression.[5]

**Example 6.2** "It Was Written in the Stars," piano figuration with dissonant chord

**Example 6.3** "It Was Written in the Stars," opening of A, B, C, and D (coda) sections

"It Was Written in the Stars" is a fine example of how Arlen deploys form, harmony, and melody to fashion a powerful emotional arc within a song. It is a modest-sized tapeworm that unfolds with little repetition: A(8) B(8) C(8) A′(4) D(8 [+ 8 for coda]). In this way "It Was Written in the Stars" recalls "Cocoanut Sweet" from *Jamaica*. The first eight measures (beginning shown in Example 6.3) seem to set us up for another A, as in a standard form, but Arlen moves instead to a different melody, B ("And so, whether it bring joy"), which breaks open the limited ambitus of the A section, now rising up to D♮ ("You are the one"). Then comes yet another new segment, C ("Here, as in a daydream") that begins still higher, on E♭. The B and C sections rove harmonically; nowhere in the sixteen-measure span does Arlen touch down on the song's tonic, a strategy that makes the return of A′ satisfying ("It was written high above"). Yet the return is also brief, for after two measures Arlen is again on the move, modifying the original A phrase to climb up to a high D♭ ("Or I'll never be free"). The final part of the song, D, brings us yet another new melody that leads to the major tonic, E♭, before returning at the end to the original minor tonic. Where the opening phrase of A circles around a few pitches in a low vocal register and in eighth-note rhythms, the melody for D becomes an apotheosis, unfolding in broad quarter and half notes and climbing into a higher register for a Mixolydian-tinged final melodic cadence, D♭–E♭ ("shall be").

Robin deftly follows Arlen's compositional arc. His lyrics for the minor-mode A section project a somewhat uneasy attitude about accepting "what was written in the stars." In B, the singer's emotion begins to brighten, as he acknowledges that "you are the one." The lyrics for C capture the anticipation of having "my tomorrows in your hand," as reflected in the unsettled harmonies. The confirmation in D that this loving relationship is in fact "what the stars foretold" parallels Arlen's breakthrough into the major key, followed by a return to the darker tonic, which now sounds stable and no longer ominous.

"What's Good About Goodbye?" is one of Arlen's finest slow ballads. Arlen shapes the spacious formal units with melodic arcs built from shared thematic material: A(16) B(16) A′(18 + coda) (Example 6.4).[6] In both A and B, the first three of four phrases are initiated by the same rhythmic figure, an upbeat leading to a sustained note on the downbeat. The downbeat notes rise progressively, as shown in Example 6.4. In the A section, they ascend to the dominant C, which is sustained across the B section before settling on

Example 6.4 "What's Good About Goodbye," melodic arcs

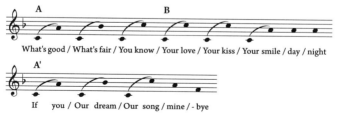

the third of the tonic, the note A. A′ begins like A but at the end descends to the tonic F. Arlen deploys his signature octave leap to great effect in "What's Good About Goodbye?," not as an isolated gesture, but fully integrated into the song's structural and expressive framework. Robin's lyric overflows with images and phrases typical of a love ballad; he presented it to Arlen "protesting that it was just a dummy."[7] But the composer rightly saw how well how in this context such clichés kept his arching melodies aloft and moving forward.

We recall how one of the distinctive features of the bridge-like segment of "My Shining Hour" (Chapter 5) was the repetition the four-note musical phrase "home before me" several times in close succession over shifting harmonies. In "What's Good About Goodbye?" Arlen does something similar, but on a larger scale. The entire sixteen-measure B section is built from slightly varied repetitions of its initial four-measure phrase "Your love could bring eternal spring" or its melodic components (Example 6.5). At the first repetition ("Your kiss could be a magic thing"), the harmonies shift but Arlen changes only one note, in the motive that ends the phrase: the minor third (E♭ in "eter-*nal* spring") becomes a major third (E♮ in "mag-*ic* thing"). Then Arlen transposes the phrase down (to yield C♯ in "Your smile could be a shin-*ing* light") and foreshortens the repetitions to involve only the closing motive, which as before shifts to a minor third (C♮ in "from day *to* day" and then "from night *to* night") (▶ 6.1). Robin follows Arlen's musical lead with ever shorter syntactical units. Meanwhile, even as the motive is repeated, the harmonies continue to float chromatically underneath. The music of "What's Good About Goodbye" unfolds with such a natural, unforced lyricism that we may not even be aware of the high level of craftsmanship—to reiterate the term Arlen and Robin employed to describe each other.

**Example 6.5** "What's Good About Goodbye," motivic transformations

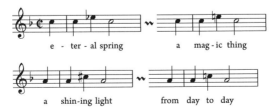

## Dorothy Fields

Dorothy Fields, a member of a distinguished theatrical family and one of the first female lyricists to rise to prominence in the early twentieth century, was Arlen's almost exact contemporary (born 1904) (Figure 6.1). Her father, Lew Fields, was half of a well-known comic vaudeville team; her brother, Herbert, contributed the books for many Rodgers and Hart musicals. Dorothy and composer Jimmy McHugh preceded Arlen and Ted Koehler as the house composers at the Cotton Club, writing shows there from 1927 through 1929, as well as songs for other revues. Fields would go on to collaborate on

**Figure 6.1** Dorothy Fields, 1951 (Photo by Walter Albertin, New York World-Telegram and the Sun Newspaper Photograph Collection, Library of Congress, Washington, D.C.)

Broadway and in Hollywood with other prominent composers, including Jerome Kern, Sigmund Romberg, Arthur Schwartz, and Cy Coleman.[8]

In the 1950s Arlen and Fields teamed up for two films, *Mr. Imperium* (MGM, 1951) and *The Farmer Takes a Wife* (20th Century Fox, 1953). Their working method differed from Arlen's with other lyricists. Fields did not, like Koehler or Harburg, recline on a sofa with eyes closed, absorbing a tune as Arlen played; nor did she, like Robin, start working at midnight. Arlen describes the somewhat business-like efficiency of their collaboration, which took place at Fields's suite in the Beverly Hills Hotel: "I'd get there about ten or eleven in the morning. Dorothy was always up early typing. We would discuss ideas—I'd play a tune and leave a lead sheet. We'd have lunch in the patio and then I'd leave. When I returned the next day, the song would be finished. It was wonderful fun."[9]

## *Mr. Imperium*

*Mr. Imperium* starred Ezio Pinza as an Italian prince (and king-in-waiting), who falls in love with an American singing actress played by Lana Turner. Fresh off his Broadway appearance in Rodgers and Hammerstein's *South Pacific*, Pinza had just embarked on what would be a very brief film career. Arlen and Fields wrote three numbers for *Mr. Imperium*: one for Pinza, one for Turner (dubbed by Trudy Irwin), and one sung as a duet.

"Let Me Look at You," the ballad for Pinza, counts as one of the greatest Arlen songs that is virtually unknown and seldom recorded. Arlen would certainly have had in his ear Rodgers and Hammerstein's "Some Enchanted Evening," Pinza's hit number from *South Pacific*, which had opened on Broadway in April 1949, barely a year before Arlen wrote his song. (The MGM copyist manuscript of "Let Me Look at You" is dated May 1950.) Although "Let Me Look at You" has an operatic sweep similarly suited to Pinza's voice, there is little question of imitation. Indeed, Arlen arguably surpasses Rodgers in originality of style and form.

As in so many Arlen numbers we have considered, tapeworm tendencies gradually take over in "Let Me Look at You," bending a standard structure to go where the music seems to lead the composer. Like the ballad "Right as the Rain" examined in Chapter 4, it builds outward and upward from an initial tune that is restricted in melodic and rhythmic range (Example 6.6). The form of "Let Me Look at You" is A(16) A′(16) B(8) A″(8), plus a long

**Example 6.6** "Let Me Look at You"

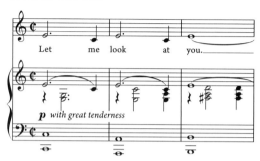

**Example 6.7** "Let Me Look at You," bridge and climax

coda for the second ending. The second half of A moves from C major to E minor ("Young and strong"), then back to the tonic. At the parallel moment in the second eight measures of A′ ("When I see such beauty and grace"), Arlen modulates to E major. But he does not cadence there, instead pushing directly into the short, chromatic B section or bridge, which provides the climax of the song (Example 6.7) (▶ 6.2). Here Arlen further explores the harmonic areas around E major before winding his way back to the C-major tonic for A″. Supporting the harmonic expansion is a metrical-rhythmic one, in which Arlen creates larger four-measure units by syncopating the melody over the bar line.

The unusually broad coda of "Let Me Look at You" stretches twenty-seven measures from the last note of the vocal part to the final double bar, dividing into two segments of sixteen and eleven measures, respectively. The piano part of the first sixteen measures replicates an introduction which Arlen wrote for the song and which appears complete in the MGM copyist scores, but was then abbreviated to an introduction of ten measures in the published sheet music. It is possible that the longer original introduction was intended as a verse to the song that was never provided with a lyric.[10] Instead, Arlen and Fields turned it into the first part of the coda, leading into a final eleven-measure reprise of the A material of the song ("Just stand alone, please do"). The piano introduction shows awkward traces of the reshuffling of material: the sixth measure moves directly and somewhat clumsily to what were the final four measures of the original introduction.

Fields's lyrics for "Let Me Look at You" recycle elements from three of her earlier "look" numbers written with Kern in the 1930s, "Just Let Me Look at You," "Lovely to Look At," and "The Way You Look Tonight." The end of the coda, "and let me look at you tonight," directly recalls all three songs. If this self-borrowing reflects some lack of inspiration, Fields makes up for it by ably navigating the increasing complexity of Arlen's musical design. For the last part of the A section, Arlen accelerates the song's rhythmic and melodic pacing, moving from broader four-measure phrases to compact two-measure ones. Fields accommodates this shift with an elegant triple rhyme and an alliteration that connects the two poetic lines ("Nonethel*ess* you *possess / p*assionate tendern*ess*"). Fields is equally skillful in handling the song's climax in the brief and intense bridge (see Example 6.7), Eight measures earlier, Fields's has already introduced the singer's more assertive, first-person "I" ("When I see such beauty and grace"). Now, she places that "I" on the downbeat and the high D♯ ("I suddenly live anew"). At moments like these we can appreciate Field's great sensitivity to the intricacies of Arlen's music.

### *The Farmer Takes a Wife*

*The Farmer Takes a Wife* was a musical remake of a 1935 film. The story takes place on the Erie Canal in upstate New York in about 1850, during a period when the railroad was beginning to replace the canal as the main mode of transporting goods. In the film, the canalmen, feeling threatened, engage in various brawls with railroad workers who come into town. At the center of the screenplay is a love triangle among Molly, a cook on a canal boat (Betty Grable); the drink- and fight-prone owner of the boat, Jotham (John Carroll); and a handsome young farmer, Dan (Dale Robertson), who gets hired to haul horses for Jotham's boat. Eventually Molly casts her lot with Dan, a practical choice (as he makes clear) since the days of canalboats are ending. Although only seven songs were used, Arlen and Fields created thirteen for *The Farmer*

**Example 6.8** "We're in Business"

*Takes a Wife*, apparently the most that Arlen composed for any single film in his career.

In *The Farmer Takes a Wife* Arlen seeks to recapture something of the feel of his 1944 score for *Bloomer Girl*, a show which was likewise situated in upstate New York in the mid-nineteenth century. (At one point during the film's number "We're in Business," in what is an affectionate nod to the earlier musical, Grable and another woman appear in bloomers and sing the line "We're Bloomer girls!" In both the show and the film, the governor of New York also appears briefly as a character.) *The Farmer Takes a Wife* falls well below *Bloomer Girl* in musical richness and variety; and Fields's folksy lyrics lack Harburg's social-political edge. Yet Arlen's fingerprints are all over the score, and there is much to admire, including in some songs that never made it into the film. Even in an ensemble-dance number like "We're in Business," which could be a formulaic effort, Arlen shows his originality. Here, when Molly and Dan celebrate their new professional partnership in renovating an old canal boat, Arlen builds a melody, challenging to sing, from a compact syncopated motive that rises and falls chromatically within a narrow range (Example 6.8).

Perhaps the song in *The Farmer Takes a Wife* that best shows Arlen's deft ability to recapture a folksy American sound is Dan's "With the Sun Warm Upon Me." Under the tune, Arlen fashions a repeating bass pattern with dotted rhythms, similar to the one he used in "One for My Baby" (as discussed in Chapter 5). But what had been a blues-inflected trope in the earlier song is now transformed by Arlen into a gently loping figure suited to the scene (Arlen marks the song "Hazily") and to Dan's farmer and horse-riding persona (Example 6.9a). There is still no hint of the blues even when Arlen does move from I to IV after four measures (Example 6.9b). The harmonic shift, typical of the blues, here sounds completely natural to Dan's down-home style.

**Example 6.9** "With the Sun Warm Upon Me"

One notable Arlen-Fields song omitted from *The Farmer Takes a Wife*, "Look Who's Been Dreaming" (which would likely have been sung by Molly or Dan), departs significantly from the score's Americana sound world. Harmonically, "Look Who's Been Dreaming" is one of Arlen's most sophisticated efforts, in some ways a harbinger of the "late" style we will explore in Chapter 10 (⏵ 6.3). The song's tonic, E♭, never appears until the final cadence. Arlen begins the first phrase on a G dominant (ostensibly V7 of C) with an altered fifth that shifts between augmented and flatted (E♭/D♭). The striking composite effect is of a five-note whole-tone cluster (G–B♮–D♭–E♭–F) (Example 6.10a). This chord resolves to another whole-tone dominant on C (C–D–E♭–A♭–B♭). With the B♭7 harmony reached on the last beat of the seventh measure (the "to-" of "today," Example 6.10b), we expect a resolution to a melodic G♮ and a tonic E♭ chord. But in one of the most astonishing moments among the songs of a composer known for his bold harmonic gestures, the melody moves (on "-day") to a G♭ underpinned by a G♭7 chord (G♭–B♭–D♭–E♮). This chord then moves up by half step to the original altered

**Example 6.10** "Look Who's Been Dreaming," (a) opening and (b) end of A section

G7 chord to begin the second A of the song ("Look who's discovered"). We can understand how with such chromatic elements "Look Who's Been Dreaming" would have sounded out of place in the score of *The Farmer Takes a Wife*. Yet it is a pity the song has not found a more regular place in the American Songbook.[11]

# 7
# Arlen, Ira Gershwin, and *A Star Is Born*

The years 1953 to 1955 comprise some of the busiest and most productive of Harold Arlen's career. With Ira Gershwin he wrote songs for the films *A Star Is Born* and *The Country Girl*; with Truman Capote, the score for the stage musical *House of Flowers*; and with Johnny Mercer, the adaptation of *St. Louis Woman* as *Blues Opera*. For the first time since the 1930s, Arlen also went into the recording studio to participate in two albums, *The Music of Harold Arlen* for Walden Records and *Harold Arlen and His Songs* for Capitol. Arlen, who would turn 50 in February 1955, kept up this level of activity even while experiencing serious illness—an ulcerated liver and esophagus (partly due to heavy drinking) that required hospitalization and surgery—and personal sorrow, with the death of his father and the emotional breakdown and institutionalization of his wife Anya. This and the next two chapters will focus on this period of intense creativity, beginning with *A Star Is Born*, Arlen's second great Hollywood hit, coming fifteen years after *The Wizard of Oz*.

In 1951, having been fired by MGM for years of unreliable behavior on and off the lot, Judy Garland sought to revive her career with a series of live one-person shows in London (the Palladium) and then New York (the Palace). When they proved enormous successes, Sidney Luft, Garland's boyfriend, promoter, and soon-to-be husband, proposed a still bigger-scale comeback: a remake of a 1937 film *A Star Is Born* into a movie musical with Garland as singer-actress in the lead role of Esther Blodgett (originally played by Janet Gaynor). Garland had already performed the role in a non-musical dramatization of *A Star Is Born* on the Lux Radio Theatre in 1942. Luft got Jack Warner of Warner Bros. to sign on, and the rest of the creative team began to come together later in 1952, including Moss Hart as screenwriter and George Cukor as director. One composer stood at the top of Garland's wish list: Harold Arlen. Although they had not worked closely together since *The Wizard of Oz*, Garland had recorded many of his songs in the interim. Ira Gershwin was a natural fit for the creative team. He and Arlen, long-time friends, had teamed up as early as 1934 for *Life Begins at 8:40* (see Figure 7.1). Gershwin had collaborated with Hart on the 1941 Kurt Weill musical *Lady in the Dark*.

*Harold Arlen and His Songs*. Walter Frisch, Oxford University Press. © Oxford University Press 2024.
DOI: 10.1093/oso/9780197503270.003.0007

**Figure 7.1** Harold Arlen and Ira Gershwin on the Gershwin tennis court, Beverly Hills, California, 1936 (Ira and Lenore Gershwin Trusts)

In *Lady in the Dark* and then later in the film *Hans Christian Andersen* (1952, with music by Frank Loesser), Hart sought to move beyond the practice, especially prevalent in Hollywood, of having songs spotted into a book or screenplay with little regard to the advancement of a plot or reflection of a character's dramatic situation. When it came to *A Star Is Born*, Hart well appreciated the challenges in adapting a backstage film into a musical whose diegetic numbers—there had to be some for a mega-star like Garland—might overwhelm narrative continuity. Hart, Arlen, and Gershwin would meet these challenges with great success.

Most Hollywood musicals have a pair of singing leads. *A Star Is Born* is an exception: aside from supporting singers and the chorus, the music was written for and is performed by Garland alone. As such, the remake reflects a major asymmetry with the original 1937 film. From the initial planning of the new *A Star Is Born*, Norman Maine, the older fading actor who is Esther's husband and foil (played by Frederic March in 1937) was to remain a speaking role. Luft and Warner sought out Laurence Olivier and Richard Burton, and then Cary Grant, who did a reading of the script for Cukor but then turned down the part. The producers eventually turned to the distinguished British actor James Mason.

Hart's early outline for *A Star Is Born* had places for seven musical numbers. Although the screenplay would evolve considerably and the film was severely cut after the premiere, the placement and the content of the musical segments remained strikingly close to Hart's original vision. I have inserted in brackets the numbers that eventually occupied the slots in his outline:

1. Benefit show—Esther and orchestra ["Gotta Have Me Go with You"]
2. "Dive" song—Esther and small group ["The Man That Got Away"]
3. Movie rehearsal song (happy type), partial; reprised complete at preview ["Born in a Trunk" sequence/medley]
4. Song on recording stage (marriage proposal with interruptions) ["Here's What I'm Here For"]
5. Honeymoon song in motel; to be reprised later ["It's a New World"]
6. Malibu beach house song (funny song; she tries to cheer Norman up) ["Someone at Last"]
7. Reprise of 5, probably sung over suicide or at end ["It's a New World"][1]

Meeting with Hart and Arlen early in 1953, Ira Gershwin hand-copied this plan almost verbatim, and the composer and lyricist set to work.[2] The development of *A Star Is Born* would last almost eighteen months and involve several creative disappointments for Arlen and Gershwin. For the no. 3 spot they drafted three different songs ("Dancing Partner," "Green Light Ahead," and "I'm Off the Downbeat"), each of which was rejected as insufficient to display Garland's talents.[3] Warner and Luft turned to Roger Edens and Leonard Gershe, who came up with the "Born in Trunk" medley, comprised of one original song and a string of previously composed numbers. Two more Arlen-Gershwin songs were cut from the film after the premiere in September 1954: "Here's What I'm Here For" (no. 4) and one that had been added between nos. 6 and 7 of Hart's outline, "Lose That Long Face."[4] Still, thanks to the continuity script and the reconstruction of most of the original film in the early 1980s, we can get a good idea of how ingeniously the songs were woven into Hart's screenplay for *A Star Is Born*.[5]

## The Songs in Context

Before looking in more detail at Arlen and Gershwin's contributions, we will explore the dramatic contexts of the songs in the film. Ronald Haver has written of *A Star Is Born* that "the song titles and lyrics were all carefully fashioned by Gershwin to work with Hart's dialogue in explaining and illuminating Esther's/Vicki's psychology.... They chart the emotional development of the character as surely as the speeches and the action advance the surface manifestation of the story."[6] Although accurate as far it goes, Haver's comment, which could apply to the music as much as the lyrics, fails to capture the subtlety of Arlen and Gershwin's achievement. Esther's "psychology" and "emotional development" are anything but straightforward in Hart's screenplay. She has both a public or stage persona (as Vicki Lester) and a private one (as Esther Blodgett). Despite her best efforts, they cannot be kept apart. Indeed, their intersection gives the film its musical-dramatic tension, which is finally resolved in the last moments of the film as Esther proudly announces a third, hybrid identity as "Mrs. Norman Maine."

The first song in *A Star Is Born*, "Gotta Have Me Go with You," already intermingles Esther's identities.[7] On the surface, it is a variety number sung by a little-known performer and two male sidekicks at a benefit concert in the Shrine Auditorium. But the dramatic context becomes more complicated when the song is moved up on the program because the star of the act scheduled before it, Norman Maine, has appeared at the theater drunk and unfit to perform. As Norman stumbles his way onto the stage, Esther rescues the situation by working him into the act: the "private" Esther has already begun to assert herself alongside the "public" one. Gershwin's lyrics capture the mutual interdependence of Esther and Norman we are witnessing onstage. He could have written a direct imperative like "You Gotta Go with Me." Instead, he comes up with the intentionally clumsier and more ambiguous "Gotta Have Me Go with You." On the one hand, with this locution Esther tells Norman that as the more established (if currently incapacitated) artist, he must take the lead in the relationship. But in an important sense these thoughts also belong to Norman, who by participating in the number is telling Esther that she has to take charge and make him "go" with her.[8]

"Gotta Have Me Go with You" begins as a diegetic number onstage and then, with the involvement of Norman, becomes a plot element, a pattern repeated several times in *A Star Is Born*. The second song, "The Man That Got Away," permeates the diegetic barrier in a different, less obvious way: Esther sings it with her band in the "dive," unaware of Norman's presence. After the episode at the Shrine Auditorium, a now-sober Norman searches for Esther and has tracked her down at a small night club on Hollywood's Sunset Strip, where she rehearses a song with a small group of musicians. Hart specified the dramatic parallels between "Gotta Have Me Go with You" and the "dive" song from his outline. In the screenplay directions for the latter he noted, "By shooting Esther from the same angle as we did when Norman approached her on the stage of the Shrine, we would, in a sense, have a reprise of that situation."[9] Like some other songs in *A Star Is Born*, "The Man That Got Away" works in ironic counterpoint to the plot. Although the romance between Esther and Norman has not yet begun, she is singing a torch song about the man that got away. Gershwin's lyrics convey sentiments Esther might feel nearer to the end of the film, when her dreams have "gone astray" and Norman's destructive behavior has put her "through the mill."

Arlen and Gershwin's number for the no. 4 slot, "Here's What I'm Here For," the scene where Norman proposes to Esther, once again fuses the diegetic and the plot-centered, and thus further blurs Esther's public-private divide. Esther first sings "Here's What I'm Here For" on the sound stage with orchestra. Then while the chorus takes up the tune, she goes to join Norman offstage for what seems to be a casual, romantic chat. We see but do not hear them conversing, as she mouths some of the lyrics. But, as planned by Norman, their private banter, which weaves together a marriage proposal and Esther's substitute lyrics ("You drink too much" instead of "I seek you out"), is being recorded. The recording is played back with Norman and an astonished Esther listening on either side of a large speaker: the private is made public. Although "Here's What I'm Here For," like all music in *A Star Is Born*, comes from Esther's mouth, its lyrics reflect the feelings of both lovers. As in "Gotta Have Me Go with You," Gershwin again displays an uncanny ear for what at first seems like awkward vernacular, now based on repetition ("here"): "Here's what I'm here for, / I'm here for you."

"Here's What I'm Here For" is the first ballad in *A Star Is Born*. The only other one, "It's a New World," occurs in Esther and Norman's honeymoon scene at the Lazy Acres Motel. "It's a New World" is solemn, almost hymn-like, indicated to be sung "with warmth and grandeur." Again, the performance of the song blends diegesis and narrative, public and private. Norman switches on the radio in the motel room and hears the disc jockey announce "Vicki Lester singing the title song from her new picture, 'It's a New World.'" Norman turns off the radio right after the beginning of the song, telling Esther "that's for ordinary folks who have to turn on the radio. . . . I've got the built-in original right in the house any time I want to hear it." Esther then sings "It's a New World" to Norman, beginning with the verse a cappella, before the studio orchestra emerges quietly in the background to accompany her in the song's chorus.

For Esther's next number, "Someone at Last," Hart creates yet another way of blending diegesis and narrative. After a long day on the movie set, she has returned to her Malibu home, where Norman has been idling, unemployed and depressed. She tells him about shooting an elaborate scene and then (according to Hart's screenplay) "launches into the production number, taking all the parts herself." As she sings, Esther leaps and dances across the living room, using furniture items as props. Her performance lifts Norman's mood. Even though their relationship is already strained by their opposite career trajectories, Gershwin's lyrics capture their genuine love for each other. As elsewhere in *A Star Is Born* he builds on verbal repetition and alliteration: "somewhere . . . someone . . . somehow."[10]

In the last original number by Arlen and Gershwin to appear in *A Star Is Born*, "Lose That Long Face" (inserted into Hart's outline between nos. 6 and 7), Esther's public and private worlds have fully collided. Humiliated at the Academy Awards by the interruption of an inebriated Norman, she is soon (perhaps the day after) back on the set to film another production number, which now becomes the most dramatically ironic song in *A Star Is Born*. Esther has to perform (in Gershwin's words) "as an irrepressibly cheerful little newsboy, unstoppably bent on making euphoric those in the scene and in the audience."[11] With "lose," "long," and "lost," Gershwin again draws upon repetition, alliteration, and seemingly clumsy syntax. (The original title of the song, maintained in the last line of the chorus, was "Get That Long Face Lost.")

For the first time in his screenplay Hart makes explicit the collapsing in on each other of Esther's diegetic and private worlds. She arrives on the set "pale" and with eyes "lack luster": "it is apparent that her heart is not in her work." As the music starts, "Esther-the-trouper comes to life, but Esther-the-woman is still not all there." The director encourages her to take a break, during which she is visited in her dressing room by Oliver Niles, her and Norman's agent, who promises to try to get Norman more acting work to build back his pride. Encouraged by this news, Esther goes back on the set and redoes "Lose That Long Face" with "a spirit born of the new hope." By splitting the takes of "Lose That Long Face" on either side of the scene in Esther's dressing room, Hart has literally juxtaposed her private and public personae.

## "Gotta Have Me Go with You" and "The Man That Got Away"

In some songs for *A Star Is Born* Arlen and Gershwin followed a typical creative pattern of music-before-lyrics. But as reported by Gershwin's secretary Lawrence Stewart, who sat in on sessions while the score was being created, "the collaboration was so close that each made suggestions about the music and words." The songs were thus "a product of reciprocal and mutual influences and responses."[12] This synergy resulted in numbers whose music as well as lyrics support the film's dramatic trajectory.

Like all lyricists who worked with Arlen, Gershwin recognized—and accommodated himself to the fact—that the composer "is no thirty-two-bar man."[13] "Gotta Have Me Go with You," the first number heard in *A Star Is Born*, is a tapeworm, distinctive not only for its forty-eight-measure chorus, but for the way the extension results directly from the insertion into the chorus of material from beginning of the verse. The structure of the chorus is: A(8) B(8) A(8) B(8) C(8) A'(8). Here the inserted verse material (a strongly syncopated melody, "Hey, you fool you") is represented as B and the bridge ("This line I'm handing you") as C. Yet this analysis obscures how A and B are linked by the continuous presence in the accompaniment of the boogie-woogie-style bass pattern. Together they thus function as a larger, sixteen-measure A, allowing a more traditional outline to emerge, with the contrasting C as a clear bridge: A(AB) A(AB) C/bridge A'.

"Gotta Have Me Go with You" directly anticipates Esther's next number, a still longer tapeworm, "The Man That Got Away," in which the second eight measures can similarly be heard as at once contrasting with and part of an expanded A. The proportions of "Gotta Have Me Go with You" resemble those of "The Man That Got Away" in that the bridge is short (eight measures) in relation to the expanded A (sixteen). In music-dramatic terms, Arlen and Gershwin's "Gotta Have Me Go with You" shows at the very beginning of *A Star Is Born* how the talented Esther can modify standard forms on the spot, so to speak, when the situation demands it; she quickly grasps the need to rescue the act. The insertion of the verse material into the chorus becomes the musical analog of Esther's working Norman's intrusion into her onstage number at the Shrine Auditorium.

"The Man That Got Away" was the biggest hit from *A Star Is Born* and one of the signature tunes of Garland's later career.[14] (Nominated for an Oscar as Best Song, it lost to Jule Styne and Sammy Cahn's "Three Coins in a Fountain.") Arlen's music—or at least its opening phrase—had its origins well over a decade earlier, when, intended for the 1941 film *Blues in the Night*, it was outfitted with a very different set of lyrics by Johnny Mercer. When Arlen first played the song's beginning to him, it struck Mercer as "a jazz tune like 'I've Got the World on a String' or something like it . . . rhythmical."[15] Mercer envisioned a song of flirtation, of visual attraction, and wrote a set of lyrics entitled "I Can't Believe My Eyes." rich in topical and geographical references. which began:

> I've seen Sequoia,
> It's really very pretty,
> The art of Goya
> And Rockefeller City.[16]

After the first two stanzas, Mercer's lyrics do not map directly onto Arlen's tune, which at that time may not have extended beyond the opening. The song languished in Arlen's trunk for years until, recognizing the music as too good to waste, he played it for Ira Gershwin in 1953 while they worked on *A Star Is Born*. Reinvented as "The Man That Got Away," with Gershwin's lyrics of intense longing and bitter loss, it became one of the great torch numbers of the American Songbook, a worthy successor to the earlier "man" song Gershwin had written with his brother, "The Man I Love."

As a tapeworm, "The Man That Got Away" fulfills the musico-dramatic promise Esther showed in "Gotta Have Me Go with You." It achieves breadth (fifty-six measures plus a five-measure coda) not by abandoning an AABA structure, but by modifying its proportions: A(16 = 8 + 8) A'(16 = 8 + 8) B(8) A"(21 = 16 + 5 as coda). The A sections are each sixteen measures, double the standard length, while the bridge B remains at eight. The vocal range remains low for most of the first eight measures as the melody moves sinuously within a narrow ambitus of a major third. It then rises quickly to its highest point, B♭, on the "-way" of "away" (Example 7.1a). The harmony here is a D7 chord with a flatted thirteenth (B♭) and a striking cross-relation: F♯ played against F♮ in the inner voices. The next phrase, "No more his eager call," beginning on C, continues the harmonic journey begun the A section (Example 7.1b). Only at "astray," thus sixteen measures into the song, do we come back to the tonic F to mark the end of A (Example 7.1c).

**Example 7.1** "The Man That Got Away," portions of A section

(a)

The man that got a - way

D7$^{(\sharp 9,\flat 13)}$

(b)

No more his ea - ger call,

Gmin7$^{(9,11)}$

(c)

Gone a - stray.

Fmaj7

Together, A and A′, each concluding on the tonic, might seem to add up to a complete thirty-two-measure song with a conventional structure. But Arlen will not let us sustain that perception for long. On the second beat of the final measure of A′ he abandons the cadential melodic F and its harmony to embark on what we now recognize as the bridge ("Good riddance! Goodbye!"). The vocal part compresses the melodic highpoints of the A sections, rising still further to E♭ and E♮ at "gone to" (Example 7.2) The ascent is accompanied by contrary motion in the piano, and "gone" is harmonized by a wrenching A♭m6 chord that subsides—"resolves" does not capture what is happening—onto a dominant seventh of F to usher in the return. The eight-measure bridge abandons the repeated syncopated rhythmic pattern of A and A″, and the melody has a more declamatory quality. It is as if the singer (the character Esther in the film) loses control as her rage boils over. When emotions run so high, she has no time for steady rhythms and a "normal" bridge of sixteen measures.

**Example 7.2** "The Man That Got Away," end of bridge

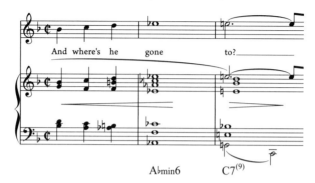

The process by which Gershwin honed the lyrics for "The Man That Got Away" is well documented in nine pages of handwritten and typed drafts.[17] Mercer had adopted an *abab* rhyme pattern for the first four lines. From the beginning, Gershwin (who likely did not know the Mercer lyrics) goes for a more direct, propulsive *aabb* rhyme scheme that arguably matches better Arlen's "insistent" music. It is hard to establish a clear order among the draft pages of Gershwin's lyrics, but the earliest ideas for the opening of the A segments include such paired couplets as:

> The tune is played out,
> The moon is in a fade-out.
> There'll be no sun-up,
> And misery is one up.

(Reprinted by permission of the Ira and Leonore Gershwin Trusts. All rights reserved.)

and

> You've lost your humor,
> You follow ev'ry rumor,
> You can't erase him,
> Yet you're too proud to chase him.

(Reprinted by permission of the Ira and Leonore Gershwin Trusts. All rights reserved.)

and, with some elements of the final version,

> The night grows dimmer,
> The stars have lost their glimmer,

> The man's a slacker,
> The blues are getting blacker.

(Reprinted by permission of the Ira and Leonore Gershwin Trusts. All rights reserved.)

Gershwin also jotted down some individual couplets like:

> You're feeling dizzy,
> The missing man where is he?

(Reprinted by permission of the Ira and Leonore Gershwin Trusts. All rights reserved.)

and

> He hypnotized you,
> You thought he idolized you.

(Reprinted by permission of the Ira and Leonore Gershwin Trusts. All rights reserved.)

and

> He may be married,
> That's why he never tarried.

(Reprinted by permission of the Ira and Leonore Gershwin Trusts. All rights reserved.)

With knowledge of the completed song, where Gershwin achieved a more consistent vocabulary of despair and hurt, we can certainly see how these couplets miss the mark.

One constant element in the drafts is the final line (or two lines, depending on Gershwin's orthography) of the first stanza, "And all because of the man that got away," which generated the song's title. It stands apart from the *aabb* couplets, which create rhyme *within* the first eight-measure unit of A. This final line reaches ahead and *outside* the unit, rhyming with the end of the second half of A ("gone astray"). In this way, Gershwin binds together the two eight-measure units into what I have argued is really a large A (rather than AB). In A' the analogous larger-scale rhyme is ("game"/"same").

## "It's a New World"

The ballad "It's a New World" lies at the expressive center—and near the temporal midpoint—of *A Star Is Born* and then returns near the end of the film during Norman's suicide scene. The song is significant in marking the emergence of a "late" style in Arlen's music, characterized by a sparseness of piano texture, less complex voice-leading, and a tendency toward root-position harmonies, which are often articulated by open fifths sustained for one or two measures and then by parallel motion. (We discuss this late style further in Chapter 10.) What gives "It's a New World" an epic quality, despite its relatively modest dimensions, is Arlen's large-scale harmonic and melodic control.

"It's a New World" extends forty measures (with an extra measure for the second ending), articulated into eight-measure segments. Though on a smaller scale than "Gotta Have Me Go with You" and "The Man That Got Away," it is no less a tapeworm in that the segments unfold without literal return or a clear formal template. The design can best be represented as A(8) B(8) C(8) D(8) A'(8). Unusually for Arlen, the A and B segments are completely diatonic, without a single accidental outside the C-major tonality, thus creating a blank canvas, as it were, which the rest of the song can fill in. And that is what Arlen does, building inexorably toward the climax at D by increasing the chromaticism and the melodic range, and by withholding the dominant harmony needed for closure.

The verse of "It's a New World," sung without accompaniment by Garland in *A Star Is Born*, elegantly anticipates the chorus's trajectory. The verse extends ten measures, divided asymmetrically as 4 + 6. The first four measures have a declamatory style ("How wonderful that I'm beholding"). Arlen creates the phrase extension to six measures by augmenting the melody to even quarter notes (at "life where all the pleasures we will prove") over a prolonged cadential progression to C. The longer note values prepare the chorus's broad melodic style of sustained half and whole notes. The verse also sets up the chorus's harmonic design. It begins diatonically, with just a hint of chromaticism in the piano's tenor line. Then, as he will do in the chorus, Arlen intensifies the harmony chromatically in the fifth and sixth measures ("polish up the stars / And mountains we move") before returning to pure C major.

As the chorus unfolds, Arlen gradually enriches C major with modal inflections and chord substitutions. The first four bars of A unfold over a static tonic-fifth pedal (Example 7.3a). The B section consists of two almost identical four-bar melodic phrases, which are, however, harmonized successively in ways that increase tension. The first phrase moves from E minor to D minor, a distinctive progression that begins to take us beyond the C-major realm of A but still lies within its diatonic-modal orbit. In the second phrase of B, Arlen adds sevenths and ninths to the same chords, thus Em7–Dm9, and before the Dm9 he inserts an F dominant ninth chord (with sharp eleventh), whose seventh, E♭, is the first chromatic note of the song (Example 7.3b).

**Example 7.3** "It's a New World"

Once introduced, chromaticism pervades the chorus. The C section begins on an Am7 and moves through harmonies that are chromatic substitutions for standard diatonic ones. The last three bars of C have a chain of descending parallel (or near-parallel chords) leading to a six-note B♭ chord on "bloom" (B♭–D–F–A♭–C–E; Example 7.3c). This chord moves back to Dm7 on the downbeat of the next measure, once again setting up the expectation of a dominant and a tonic resolution. But Arlen makes a tritone substitution (as discussed above in Chapter 5; Example 5.9): instead of a G dominant chord under the melodic G of "A [new]," we get a harmony whose root is a tritone away, on D♭. The substitution for the dominant allows Arlen to approach the tonic C via half steps in the bass, D–D♭–C, and thus continue or develop the harmonic shifts (and parallel fifths motion) characteristic of the A and B sections. Arlen's substitutions are part of his compositional strategy to withhold the real dominant until later in the song.

Although I have argued that "It's a New World" is essentially continuous, a standard frame lies behind the chorus and influences both Arlen's procedures and our perceptions of them. The third eight-bar segment, C, occupies the place of a bridge (or B) in an AABA form. Arlen exploits that position to set up a return to A in the ways we have described above. The return is only fleeting. The tonic returns in root position at "new" but is destabilized by the melodic G carried over from the preceding measure and then by the introduction of a seventh, B♭, on the second beat in the accompanying harmony.

The D section ends on a Dm7 chord ("fast") that offers Arlen the chance to move through the dominant to the tonic. Here for the first time in the song we get a dominant in root position and a full cadential progression ii7–V7–I ("fast! / You brought a new"). The tonic arrival on "new" marks the beginning of an eight-bar A′, whose first two bars are an exact return of the initial A (melody: E–F–B♮). But Arlen now collapses the original A phrase into four bars, a compression that allows him a final four-bar phrase containing the most sustained traditional progression of the song: (F)IV–(D)ii7–(G)V7–(C)I, in the second ending (Example 7.3d). The A′ section has thus restored the diatonicism of the opening.

"Don't play ballads for Ira," Arlen once remarked. "He hates having to write ballads. He'll do them very well but he doesn't like doing them."[18] ("Sing Me Not a Ballad," the Duchess commands in the 1945 Weill-Gershwin show *The Firebrand of Florence*.) In "It's a New World" Gershwin rose to the occasion with lyrics that capture both the spaciousness and intensity of Arlen's music.

He may have come to the title image by looking back to two earlier ballads of his: "Love Walked In," written with his brother George, in which the penultimate line looks toward "a world completely new," and "This Is New" written with Weill for *Lady in the Dark*, where the singer is transported "Up to another world / Where life is bliss, / And this / Is new."

To accommodate Arlen's five contrasting eight-measure units, Gershwin crafted couplets with differing rhyme schemes. The nine sheets of Gershwin's lyric drafts for "It's a New World" reveal how, as in "The Man That Got Away," he explored various possibilities for the couplets:

> I've left the shadows behind
> A new world I find
> . . .
> It's a new world I find
> With clouds silver lined
> . . .
> Now at long last I see
> A new world for me
> . . .
> I'm possessed of a key
> To a new world for me.

(Reprinted by permission of the Ira and Leonore Gershwin Trusts. All rights reserved.)

Gershwin's final version for the opening of the chorus, "It's a new world I see / A new world for me," is both simpler and subtler, with its repetition of "new world" that sets up the frequent use of the phrase or its two components in the song. The phrase appears twice in the opening A section, the section that sets out the musical and poetic material for the song. Here "new" is placed on the downbeats. The phrase "new world" is absent from the B section; at the beginning of C it is given a different metric-rhythmic configuration, with "world" on the downbeat. After these sixteen measures, which function as a kind of "development," Gershwin restores "new" to the downbeat at the beginning of the D and A′ sections in order to coincide with Arlen's root-position tonic chords.

We referred above to the hymn-like tone of "It's a New World." Some ten years after its composition, those very qualities came to the fore in a version with revised lyrics by Gershwin. Inspired by the August 1963 civil rights March on Washington, it was premiered by Lena Horne, with Arlen at the piano, at Carnegie Hall on October 5, 1963. This concert was sponsored by Harry Belafonte and the Gandhi Society for Human Rights, for the benefit of the Student Non-Violent Coordinating Committee (SNCC).[19] Horne's activities on behalf of anti-racism and human and civil rights are well known. She spoke out at time when few Blacks in Hollywood or on Broadway were in a position to do so. As we saw in Chapter 5, she turned down the lead role in Arlen and Mercer's *St. Louis Woman* because of what she felt were demeaning stereotypes. In her autobiography Horne described the 1963 Carnegie concert, in which the artists were introduced by Martin Luther King Jr., as "a real peak in my life," adding, "For once I felt the symbol had been useful."[20]

In his reworking, Gershwin keeps most of the lyrics intact but broadens the song's message of hope from the individual to the universal, from the personal to the human.[21] Thus in the verse, the "A Never-Never Land unfolding" becomes "A vision of a world unfolding." And in the chorus, "A new world, though we're in a tiny room" becomes "A new world—though it once was just a dream." (The one weak part of Gershwin's revision, for this writer, is his rhyming "just a dream" with "self-esteem," a word which does not match the poetic level of the rest of the lyric.) Horne and Arlen's performance of "It's a New World" is understated, reflecting the comfortable partnership extending back decades. Horne's approach is firm and focused, yet also conversational. Arlen fills in the broadly spaced harmonies of the piano part with melodic lines that work in elegant counterpoint to the vocal melody. Perhaps one moment stands out: the beginning of the final A, where Horne pauses determinedly on the word "Hope," more spoken than sung, before resuming musical continuity with "brings a new world to me" (▶ 7.1).

## Songs That Got Away: "Dancing Partner," "Green Light Ahead," and "I'm Off the Downbeat"

Admirers of the score of *A Star Is Born* can rejoice that the filmed sequences containing "Here's What I'm Here For" and "Lose that Long Face," though cut, survived and that the songs were published. A different fate, one that reflects the frustrations of even veteran songwriters amid the production swirl of a Hollywood film, befell the three numbers Arlen and Gershwin wrote for Hart's no. 3 slot, the "movie rehearsal" (then "movie preview"), when Esther/Vicki wows the audience in the theater and establishes her stardom.

"Dancing Partner," "Green Light Ahead," and "I'm Off the Downbeat," were never recorded or filmed for *A Star Is Born*, or published at the time. They were all rejected in favor of a fifteen-minute medley for Garland, "Born in a Trunk," that contained no Arlen-Gershwin numbers.

Looking back years later, Gershwin tells the saga in a paragraph written to introduce the lyrics of "I'm Off the Downbeat" for his 1959 book-memoir *Lyrics on Several Occasions*:

> "Downbeat" is one of three songs—all unproduced—(the other two: "Green Light Ahead" and "Dancing Partner") Arlen and I wrote for a spot in *A Star Is Born*. The situation in the film was the sneak-previewing of Vicki Lester's first movie—a showing which makes her a star overnight. All that was necessary was to put Vicki in a good number for four or five minutes, then show the audience's enthusiastic acceptance of a new star (as preview cards are signed in the lobby). Instead it was finally deemed necessary to top everything with a fifteen-minute musical (mélange) sequence using special material to introduce seven or so standards. This sequence, "Born in a Trunk," based on Miss Garland's act at the Palace Theatre, was excellent for its original purpose—vaudeville and night clubs—and, as Judy can do no wrong, received a good hand. But it added fifteen minutes to the film, held up the show, cost $300,000. Big mistake (but none of my business).[22]

We can flesh out Gershwin's account of "the big mistake." By May 1953 he and Arlen had completed most of the songs for *A Star Is Born*.[23] Still outstanding was the number for the movie preview scene, which the producers and director envisioned as a big closer for the first half of the film, preceding the intermission. Arlen and Gershwin drafted "Dancing Partner," which was rejected, as was the team's next effort, "Green Light Ahead." On September 30, 1953, Arlen, now back in New York, wrote to Gershwin of hearing all kinds of rumors about the progress of *A Star Is Born* and wanting to get the real story:

> I heard they might use an old song for the preview spot. If you have any information on that, would you be kind enough to let me know pronto as I personally would put up a mighty healthy but friendly fight. They just can't do that to us. It doesn't make sense. If they need another song in place of "Green Light" and everybody agrees, I'd be more than happy to work it out with you via phone, correspondence and recordings of a few tunes.[24]

164    HAROLD ARLEN AND HIS SONGS

Sixth months later, the movie preview music had still not been settled. In March 1954 Gershwin wrote to Jablonski that he and Arlen had by now created two songs ("Dancing Partner" and "Green Light Ahead") for that spot in the film, "both good, by anyone's standards." But both were rejected because "it seems the choreographer [Richard Barstow] couldn't get any production ideas." Gershwin continues, repeating the rumor Arlen had reported earlier: "Could be they may even interpolate an outside number which would be a shame. However, there's still a chance Arlen may be able to leave N.Y. for a week or so and we'll try to give them what they think they want."[25]

Arlen was not able to leave New York, where he was at work on *House of Flowers* and also experiencing significant health problems. But even with the composer at a distance, in early April 1954 Arlen and Gershwin gave it another shot, drafting "I'm Off the Downbeat." It is not clear whether Warner, Barstow, and their associates ever heard it. Apparently without telling Gershwin or Warner, Luft contacted Roger Edens, a composer, arranger, and a longtime Garland collaborator and mentor, about doing a big production number, still pegged at four or five minutes, for this spot in the *A Star Is Born*.[26] Edens in turn brought in a young songwriter named Leonard Gershe. Together they created "Born in a Trunk," whose lyrics ("I was born in a trunk / In the Princess Theatre in Pocatello, Idaho") have an autobiographical slant quite close to Garland's own life story, but are fundamentally different from Gershwin's other lyrics for *A Star Is Born*, which are always closely wedded to the story. "Born in a Trunk" grew into a fifteen-minute medley which certainly showcases Garland's talents but bloated *A Star Is Born* enough to necessitate the deletion of other scenes and two of Arlen and Gershwin's finest songs ("Here's What I'm Here For" and "Lose That Long Face").

How do the three songs Arlen and Gershwin wrote for the movie preview scene stack up against the film's other numbers? They are arguably, as Gershwin claimed, "good, by anyone's standards," if not at the level of "The Man That Got Away" or "It's a New World." For "Dancing Partner," several lyric drafts and one musical lead sheet in Arlen's hand survive. "Dancing Partner" has a conventional thirty-two-bar AABA' structure, as well as lyrics that explicitly address the dance theme that Barstow and the producers apparently desired.[27] The reference to a "dancing partner" who "leads me all the way" also captures, with partial irony, the complex and evolving relationship between Esther and Norman. Near the beginning of *A Star Is Born*, in the

Shrine Auditorium scene, it is Esther who rescues Norman by incorporating him into the song-and-dance sequence. And yet after this it is he who "leads" her "all the way" to bigger career opportunities, which reach a first climax in the movie preview scene.

"Green Light Ahead," Gershwin and Arlen's second attempt, is a very different kind of song. Its lyrics make no reference to dance, but optimistically urge the listener to "have your fill of fun" because "the best is yet to be." The music is in Arlen's blues style, featuring prominent flatted sevenths and thirds. As he so often does, Arlen tweaks the proportions of a standard formal design, here as A(12) A(12) B(8) A'(10). The A becomes a standard twelve-measure blues: four measures on the tonic harmony, two on the subdominant, two on the tonic, then four with a ii–V–I cadential progression. In A' Arlen retains the blues form only through the fourth measure (all tonic), then to conclude the song compresses the remainder into six measures: one measure of subdominant, one of tonic, and three of a cadential ii-V-I.

With "I'm Off the Downbeat," their final attempt, Arlen and Gershwin seem to incorporate elements of both previous songs. Its central image of the "downbeat" restores something of the dance or rhythmic element of "Dancing Partner." And lines like "Why be earthbound? / Shine and rise!" revisit the buoyantly hortatory language of "Green Light Ahead" (⏵ 7.2). The verse of "I'm Off the Downbeat" is slow and bluesy. The chorus, which picks up in tempo and mood, bears some resemblance to "Here's What I'm Here For." Both have a thirty-two-measure ABA'B' chorus dominated by a motive beginning consistently on the second beat of the measure. But where "Here's What I'm Here For" unfolds as a ballad, "I'm Off the Downbeat" is rhythmically and harmonically propulsive. Not only does Arlen begin with an empty downbeat—as Gershwin clearly noticed when crafting his lyrics and title—but he avoids any stable tonic harmony until the very end. The song (in E♭) might well have been called "I'm Off the Tonic." The chorus opens with an altered minor subdominant chord and moves in the first phrase to an altered C7, which points to an F minor that never arrives (Example 7.4).

Any of the three songs, "Dancing Partner," "Green Light Ahead" or "I'm Off the Downbeat" would have had an estimable place in the score of *A Star Is Born*, undoubtedly delivered with panache by Garland. And we might imagine the kinetic energy of the last one giving the choreographer Barstow ideas for a dance routine. But nothing Arlen and Gershwin wrote for the

**Example 7.4** "I'm Off the Downbeat"

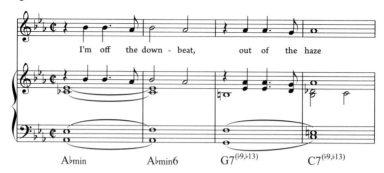

movie preview scene, with their and Hart's ever-present goal of integrating songs in the screenplay, would have passed muster as Luft and his associates developed the idea of a big production number and medley. The Edens-Gershe "Born in a Trunk" sequence sticks out in the film, even if, as Gershwin observed, Garland "can do no wrong."

# 8

# Arlen, Truman Capote, and
# *House of Flowers*

In May 1992, Peter Brook wrote to producer Roy Somlyo about the possibility of developing a "streamlined" version of *House of Flowers*, the musical Brook had directed on Broadway "in the distant past" of 1954. "It was ahead of its time," Brook noted. "[It] had one of greatest scores in musical history by Harold Arlen and weaknesses—Second Act Trouble—in the book by Truman Capote."[1] No revival resulted from this exchange, but Brook's concise assessment of *House of Flowers* still rings true: a superb music score within a flawed dramatic frame.

In these respects, *House of Flowers* resembles—and suffered a fate similar to—*St. Louis Woman* from 1946. Both are Black-cast musicals with fine scores by white composers and lyricists, and with second-act problems. The books of both shows were developed by authors from their own works, which in the transition to the musical stage lost much of the original elegance. Both shows feature stereotypes of people of color that were criticized at the time: in the earlier one, urban Blacks; in the latter, Caribbean islanders. Cast members in both shows raised concerns with the white directors, who appeared insensitive. Both *St. Louis Woman* and *House of Flowers* went through numerous cast and staff changes before, and even during, their brief runs on Broadway. Yet despite their short stage lives (113 and 165 performances, respectively), each show generated a score that would live on and attract many admirers.

## From "House of Flowers" to *House of Flowers*

In the winter of 1948 Truman Capote visited Haiti, where he spent evenings on the porches of brothels chatting with the girls.[2] From these conversations and his time on the island came the short story "House of Flowers," published in 1950.[3] In 1953, the producer Arnold Saint-Subber (he went by the shortened name Saint Subber), who had already worked with Capote on the staging of a play based on the 1951 novel *The Grass Harp*, approached him about turning "House of Flowers" into a musical. Though Capote had no experience in musical theater, he agreed, and throughout the fall of 1953 worked on the script for what he labeled "a musical play" or "a play with music," drafting lyrics for moments he felt appropriate to musicalize.[4] In November, Subber contacted Arlen about writing the songs and assisting Capote with the lyrics. Arlen at first demurred, but became intrigued as he read a draft. "I jumped at it," Arlen recalled, "because I really liked the story and, especially, because I admire Capote's work."[5]

Arlen and Capote made an unlikely pair (see Figure 8.1). At forty-eight, Arlen was a veteran of Broadway, Hollywood, and popular song; Capote, twenty-nine, was a rising author primarily of short fiction and essays. Arlen and Capote began work separately on *House of Flowers*. Arlen was in California, collaborating with Ira Gershwin on *A Star Is Born* and *The Country Girl*. Capote lived in Europe, first in Switzerland, then Rome and Paris. At this early stage *House of Flowers* evolved via transatlantic communication. Capote reports: "I would send him [Arlen] scenes and scraps of lyrics, and back came homemade phonograph records: Arlen playing melodies that the tentative lyrics had tentatively suggested, singing and talking to me."[6] Capote's lyric "scraps" and Arlen's demo disk survive for the show's biggest hit, "A Sleepin' Bee" (and will be discussed below).

When they finally met in New York in February 1954, Capote found in Arlen a generous mentor. "I had no true understanding of song writing (and Lord knows, still do not)," Capote later recalled. "But Arlen, who I suppose had never worked with an amateur before, was tolerant and infinitely encouraging and, well, just a gent about the whole thing." Capote lacked the ability of Koehler or Mercer to hear and retain music, then leave and come back later with lyrics. He would thus spend many hours—even days at a time—at Arlen's Park Avenue apartment, where, the composer remembered, the writer would "curl up on the couch: he would do his thinking and make his little notes and I would be making my large ones on a big drawing tablet."[7] (Arlen's lyricists certainly seemed to favor the couch as a venue for inspiration!) Thirty-three pages of the spiral-bound tablet are filled with drafts in the composer's hand for the lyrics of many songs in *House of Flowers*, often in partial or preliminary versions, along with a few musical "jots" made on manually drawn ledger lines. The tablet reveals the extent of Arlen's involvement in the lyrics for *House of Flowers*, for which he received co-credit.[8]

ARLEN, CAPOTE, AND *HOUSE OF FLOWERS* 169

**Figure 8.1** Harold Arlen and Truman Capote at work on *House of Flowers*, 1954; caricature by Al Hirschfeld (© The Al Hirschfeld Foundation. www.AlHirschfeldFoundation.org)

Capote came to appreciate Arlen's special qualities as a songwriter, which he describes in one of the most insightful assessments of the composer:

For him [Arlen], music is the entire story. There, in terms of sound, he is always courageous, intelligent, incapable of cliché. His songs almost invariably contain some melodic surprise, some *difficulty*—which is one of the reasons he has not had the recognition he deserves. He is too versatile and inventive to have created a large single image, an Arlen *sound*, in the sense that Porter and Gershwin have a sound. Of course, for those who really know his music, Arlen has a sound, a style, that is immediately recognizable, one more haunting and original than any of his contemporaries: a real blues in the night.

Capote's short story "House of Flowers" focuses on Ottilie, a girl from rural Haiti who works at a brothel in Port-au-Prince. At a local cockfight she meets a young country boy, Royal Bonaparte; they fall in love, and she leaves the brothel to marry and join him at his house in the mountains. Royal begins to spend more time away from Ottilie, in cafes and at cockfights. Royal's grandmother, a sorceress, casts a spell on Ottilie, who gets revenge by poisoning the grandmother's soup. Royal seeks to punish Ottilie by tying her to a tree for a day. She is visited by her companions from the brothel, who want to bring her back to the city. But Ottilie casts her lot with Royal, choosing a tumultuous and even abusive relationship over the relative security of life at the brothel.

The title of the short story refers to Royal's home, which is "like a house of flowers; wisteria sheltered the roof, a curtain of vines shaded the windows, lilies bloomed at the door."[9] Capote carries that imagery into the musical's title song, as we will see. He also makes "House of Flowers" the name of the brothel in which Ottilie and her friends work, the Maison des Fleurs. The madam of the house, who barely gets a mention in the story (where she is an anonymous "proprietress") becomes a major character, Madame Fleur. As the musical's book developed, Capote also created Madame Tango, who runs a competing brothel-cum-dance-studio across the street. In his drafts for the musical's book Capote makes the setting less specific than in the story, at first suggesting a locale "not unlike Haiti," and then a "Negro Island in the French West Indies."

For *House of Flowers*, Capote envisioned a score played by a small onstage orchestra consisting mainly of indigenous instruments and sounds: "The music accompanying this play requires an orchestra of West Indian instruments, principally drums, guitars, bells, penny-flutes and such incidental paraphernalia as conch shells and police-whistles. As the musicians occasionally function as characters, there is no pit-orchestra; they are heard either on or back-stage."[10] Although *House of Flowers* would have a pit orchestra, the score, orchestrated by Ted Royal and Peter Matz, remains essentially faithful to Capote's vision. The orchestra was enhanced by the first live appearance in the United States of a steel drum group, the Trinidad Steel Band, whose members appeared onstage as musicians and dancers.[11]

*House of Flowers* partakes of the calypso craze discussed in Chapter 4 in the context of *Jamaica*, the Arlen-Harburg show staged three years later in 1957. Shane Vogel argues that *House of Flowers* lacks the later show's social consciousness and offers only "a touristic fantasy of colonial erotics and a depoliticized calypso vision of tropical life."[12] *Mutatis mutandis*, these were the same charges leveled at the representation of Black urban life and sexual mores in *St. Louis Woman* almost a decade earlier. Such qualities certainly make these shows problematic to stage today, but it is important to stress that, like *St. Louis Woman*, *House of Flowers* helped launch or advance the careers of many young performers of color.

From the beginning, the ambitious young Subber, thirty-five years old, sought to assemble a dream team for *House of Flowers*. After securing the participation of Arlen and Capote, Subber flew with them over to Great Britain to sign up the twenty-nine-year-old director Peter Brook and the prominent artist and stage designer Oliver Messel.[13] Brook, who had directed productions with the Royal Shakespeare Company, was still little known in the United States and had not yet worked on Broadway. Pearl Bailey, who had appeared in Arlen and Mercer's *St. Louis Woman* in 1946, would assume her first Broadway lead as Madame Fleur. Juanita Hall, known for playing Bloody Mary in *South Pacific*, was Madame Tango. A nineteen-year-old Diahann Carroll made her Broadway debut as Ottilie.

George Balanchine signed on to create the dances for *House of Flowers*. Now serving as principal choreographer of the New York City Ballet, he was no longer as active on Broadway as he had been in the 1930s and 1940s. But his long-standing interest in traditions of Black dance drew him to *House of Flowers* and drew dancers to work with him.[14] Balanchine conceived no fewer than seven dance scenes for the show, an impressive number for a Broadway production.[15] *House of Flowers* marked the Broadway debuts or early appearances of a number of Black dancers, including Alvin Ailey, Geoffrey Holder, Carmen de Lavallade, Donald McKayle, Louis Johnson, Walter Nicks, and Arthur Mitchell. Some came to the show from the dance school created by Katherine Dunham, the American choreographer and dancer; others were alumni of the Martha Graham School. Some would go on to perform in the New York City Ballet, the American Ballet Theater, and the Metropolitan Opera. Ailey would form his eponymous troupe, and Arthur Mitchell would found the Dance Theater of Harlem.

The unique moment that *House of Flowers* represented for Black dancers is conveyed in an interview recorded in 2001 with Glory Van Scott, who created the role of Mamselle Cigarette (one of the women in Madame Tango's brothel):

> It was one of the most exhilarating, incredible times of my life in terms of me as this young dancer starting out. What a way to get started—at the top, not somewhere at the bottom. . . . And to recognize how wonderful an opportunity it was, and I went on from that to other companies, to . . . lots of Broadway shows, television. . . . If I could give someone a gift, certainly an artist, I would give him the gift of having that [*House of Flowers*] as a first show. . . . To experience what I experienced as an artist with [the] people that I was with."[16]

The memories of other dancers who participated in the original production of *House of Flowers* corroborate Scott's account.

One particularly notable dance sequence in *House of Flowers* was the Voudou scene in Act 2, where Ottilie visits the Houngan, or witch doctor, to learn of Royal's fate, and stumbles upon a ceremony in which the Houngan and his disciples evoke various spirits or deities. For the final segment of the Voudou scene, Holder was invited by Balanchine to recreate a dance, the Banda, associated with a demonic character in Haitian folklore, the Baron of the Cemetery, or Baron Samedi.[17]

*House of Flowers* was beset, and ultimately undermined, by disagreements among both performers and the creative and production teams. Brook offended the cast with a speech telling them he was "not prejudiced," but then made things worse by referring to "you people." Such remarks led Bailey to serve Brook with a $50,000 writ.[18] Out of town and on Broadway, Bailey would often ad lib, treating *House of Flowers* like a nightclub act. She behaved dismissively and even abusively toward some of the other cast members. Bailey appropriated numbers written for Diahann Carroll's character Ottilie, including "Don't Like Goodbyes," and insisted on additional songs, one of which was the anomalous rock-and-roll style "Indoor Girl," with lyrics by Michael Brown, inserted after the New York premiere. (Capote had been sidelined by this point.)[19]

Balanchine became fed up with the tensions and the critical remarks about his work coming from Marlene Dietrich, who was close to Arlen and would hang around the rehearsals, bringing coffee and refreshments to the cast members. Balanchine quit *House of Flowers* in Philadelphia, never again to work on Broadway. He was replaced by the twenty-six-year-old West Coast choreographer Herbert Ross, who also ended up doing most of the directing when the show got to New York, because Brook was now persona non grata among the cast. Ross appears to have retained much of Balanchine's work, but also made some dances more athletic, even perilously so: Ailey had to drop out of the show after suffering an injury during the newly added number "Slide, Boy, Slide."[20]

Reviews of *House of Flowers* in the mainstream New York press were decidedly mixed. Some critics liked the score, the sets, the dancing, and the costumes. But even the favorable ones pointed to the weakness of the book.[21] Within the Black press *House of Flowers* was both praised and condemned—praised for the lavish production values and for the opportunities it gave to performers of color, condemned for the plots and the stereotyped characters. James L. Hicks, a leading Black critic, lauded *House of Flowers* as "a fantastic fantasy of sex, song, and sin which wrings you out and leaves you limp under the impression that most of it could happen in our modern world, and is therefore good theater." He ends his review: "Go see 'House of Flowers'—you'll be happy that you did!"[22]

The opposite view emerges in an article issued in January 1955 by the Associated Negro Press News Service and picked up by a number of newspapers. "Moralists are criticizing a film and a play in which colored actors are largely used and in which they have starring roles," the article read, referring to both *House of Flowers* and *Carmen Jones*, a Black-cast film which had opened a few months before the Arlen-Capote musical. *Carmen Jones* was a Hollywood version of the stage show created in 1943, set in the American South in World War II, and for which Bizet's music was outfitted with new lyrics by Oscar Hammerstein II. The "moralists" are not named, but are said to complain that "both [productions] paint the moral life of Negroes at a pretty low level."[23] One of the moralists referred to may well have been James Baldwin, who on January 1, 1955, published in *Commentary* a damning assessment of *Carmen Jones* in these terms (he does not address *House of Flowers*).[24]

*House of Flowers* closed on May 21, 1955. An off-Broadway revival in 1968, produced by Subber with a revised book and some new songs by Arlen and Capote, failed to gain traction and ran for only a short time. In February 2003, the *Encores!* series at New York's City Center presented semi-staged performances of *House of Flowers* as part of its series of vintage musicals. Jonathan Tunick had to reconstruct the score, for which the original orchestrations were lost. The most enduring testaments to *House of*

*Flowers* remain the score and the original cast album, recorded in January 1955 (Columbia SK 86857).

## The Music of *House of Flowers*

The score for *House of Flowers* covers a wide expressive range, from slower ballads written for the romantic leads ("A Sleepin' Bee," "House of Flowers," and "Don't Like Goodbyes"), to vamp-like numbers written for Pearl Bailey as Madame Fleur ("One Man Ain't Quite Enough" and "Has I Let You Down?"), to Caribbean-style songs written for members of the ensemble ("Two Ladies in De Shade of a Banana Tree" and "Smellin' of Vanilla"). Standing somewhat apart is Ottilie's blues-inflected tapeworm "I Never Has Seen Snow," one of Arlen's greatest songs.

Although by the 1950s Arlen was renowned for songs inspired by blues and jazz, his catalogue contained only a handful of numbers evoking Caribbean music, including "'Neath the Pale Cuban Moon" (1931), based on a habanera rhythm; "Shoein' the Mare" (1934), a rumba; and "The Calypso Song" (1950). Within this Latin-tinged aesthetic of American popular song, shared by many of Arlen's contemporaries (especially Cole Porter), "Two Ladies in De Shade of a Banana Tree" from *House of Flowers* stands out for its originality. Arlen adapts a common calypso pattern, a syncopated rhythm in duple meter followed by a long note or two even notes (on "flyin' too high") (Example 8.1a), which here sounds much less formulaic than in "The Calypso Song." For the first eight measures of "Two Ladies" Arlen constrains the melody to a rapid alternation between just two notes, B and C. When the title phrase arrives, as Alec Wilder trenchantly observes, "it's like a rocket taking off after the crescendo of the preliminary sizzle. Except that the first eight measures happen to be the very best sizzle you've ever heard" (Example 8.1b).[25]

"Two Ladies" follows a standard AABA' (plus coda) form, which Arlen tweaks in his characteristic fashion. The A segments are each sixteen measures long while (as in some of the songs from *A Star Is Born*) the more lyrical bridge is only eight. In A' Arlen and Capote introduce new material, including the declamatory climax: "Look! See! Nice? Agree?" (Example 8.1c). The chorus of "Two Ladies" is sung successively by Gladiola (Ada Moore) and Tulip (Dolores Harper), and then by both in a close, fast canon, with Tulip beginning the tune two beats after Gladiola. The coda ends with eight dazzling

**Example 8.1** "Two Ladies in De Shade of a Banana Tree"

measures of rapid non-pitched, rhythmicized speech ("laze away de day while de cockatoo sings"), accompanied by clapping hands (Example 8.1d).

"Two Ladies" drew the admiration of calypso artists working in the United States. After *House of Flowers* ended its run, the song was taken up by cast member Enid Mosier (Pansy), a recognized calypso singer, and the Trinidad Steel Band. They performed together at various nightclubs in the United States and recorded an album, *Hi-Fi Calypso* (released on Columbia Records in 1956), which included their arrangement of "Two Ladies." Josephine Premice, a Haitian-American performer who was to originate the role of Tulip in *House of Flowers* but left the show in Philadelphia after being forced out by an envious Bailey, included "Two Ladies" on her 1957 Verve album *Caribe: Josephine Premice Sings Calypso*.

## "A Sleepin' Bee"

"A Sleepin' Bee," sung by Diahann Carroll as Ottilie, is the best-known song to emerge from *House of Flowers*. Richard Rodgers told Arlen's biographer Jablonski that in the years after *House of Flowers* he enjoyed hearing the song at almost every audition.[26] "A Sleepin' Bee" became a signature number for the young Barbra Streisand. The central image of "A Sleepin' Bee" comes from a passage in Capote's short story. After a conversation with her friends about how a woman knows if she is really in love, a perplexed Ottilie visits the Houngan in the hills above Port-au-Prince. He tells her that "you must catch a wild bee . . . and hold it in your closed hand . . . if the bee does not sting, then you will know you have found love."[27] In the story, Ottlile's brief encounter with the Houngan appears after six paragraphs of exposition and background. In his earliest sketches for the musical, Capote places this moment at the very opening and expands it to a full scene.

In his handwritten drafts, as well as in what appears to be the earliest typescript, Capote develops the images and phrases of what became "A Sleepin' Bee." The Houngan has been chanting and dancing around a kneeling figure in a shroud, who is then revealed to be Ottilie. When she asks him how to know if she is in love, he replies that she must catch a bee:

> A bee—what makes the honey.
> [In a casual voice, quite free of chant, and with his
> hands spread above Ottilie's head as if in benediction]
> Do a bee caught off a flower-tree
> Lie silent sleepin calm
> In the hollow of yo palm.
> Oh rest yo heart, you done found
> A love true, sweet golden as a crown![28]

The Houngan's response, although not sung, is constructed by Capote with rhymed couplets ("calm"/"palm," "found"/"crown").

The evolution of the lyrics for "A Sleepin' Bee" shows that, despite his capacity for poetic imagery, Capote indeed had "no true understanding" of how to write a popular song. He tries out several versions of a lyric. In one, he seeks to follow the standard division of popular song into verse and chorus (or "refrain," as he calls it):

> Verse
> When a lady needs to know
>     if her love is real
> But the lady don't know
>     how she should feel
> She don't figure what's in her heart
> And it seems she can't tell men apart—
> Ain't no need for such mystery

> O no, Ha! Ha! nature's got a remedy.
> 	Ask a bee! Just ask a bee!
>
> Refrain
> Is he your hero or a zero
> A gent that's all you could wish?
> The ~~mango~~ on your ~~mango tree~~
> [*changed to* The melon on your melon vine]
> Or the fishbone in your fish?
> O no longer need a lady ponder
> Is he fire or fizzle, steam or drizzle
> Ho! Ho! O no, dismiss such misery
> 	Ask a bee! Just ask a bee!
> Some women is happy to sample
> Most any example of gent
> And the pleasures he provides
> Ain't never a thorn in their sides—
> But those women can't ever be sure
> If what they're feelin is really pure
> Ho! Ho! O no, to be sure be sure to
> 	Ask a bee! Just ask a bee![29]

Capote seems to have little idea of how to distinguish a verse from a chorus and little grasp of how to make a verse that effectively sets up what follows. The draft has too much overlap or repetition between verse and refrain, including the idea that a woman cannot know what she is feeling, the exclamation "Ha! Ha!" or "Ho! Ho!," and the weak tag line "Ask a bee!" The literary gifts on display in his story and in the draft of the Houngan's speech seem to abandon Capote in the song's lyric, with its tepid rhymed oppositions like "Hero"/"zero" and "fizzle"/"drizzle," or the idea that the desired man is "the fishbone in your fish." Other drafts for the lyric show similar problems.

When Arlen received these lyrics in California, he took matters into his own experienced hands. He sent back to Capote a recording of himself playing and singing, with dummy lyrics, a tune he had written earlier and considered for use in *A Star Is Born* (▶ 8.1). Here is a full transcription of this unique source:

> In a discussion the other night, I thought that this might set quite a charming key for Miss Ottilie in the first scene with the Houngan, and I will

give you what I *think* may be workable. I'm sure the tune has enough quality and captures the mood. I hope the dummy few lines—and I call 'em that because they *are* that—mean something to you to clarify what I'm stumbling about. Now in the first scene when the Houngan and Ottilie have their dialogue before the bee caught off a flower tree, I'm going to try to read some of it. But before I do, I want you to hear one chorus of the song. Then I will do some of the dialogue, and then go into the tune as we *might* have it, and finish the scene dialogue-wise and finish the scene with the song, with a few lines of the lyric that we *can* correct later. And if this works out, as I said before . . . I'd be very pleased. [Plays chorus on piano.]

[Reads from the Capote's script:] Houngan: O many, child, many. Pluck a hair from your man's head, drop it in a glass of water. If it turns into a flower, that's one sign. Or if you find a pearl inside a coconut, that's another. But there's only one sign carries a guarantee. [Ottilie:] What do dat be, Houngan? [Houngan:] The god of hearts sets great store by *his* secrets. It'll cost you maybe a thousand francs. Ask a bee. [Ottilie:] Ask who? [Houngan:] A bee what makes the honey.

[Plays] [Speaks with the music:] "When a bee lies sleepin' / In the palm of your hand./ And true loves comes a creepin' / And your heart understands." [Ottilie:] I'm fear'd of bees. Suppose I do like you say, catch one in my hand. Suppose he sting me? [Houngan:] Then, child, you ain't in love; you just in misery. [Ottilie:] But if he don't sting me, ah, if he don't, I know I'm in love, same as all other ladies? Now, that's a fact? [Houngan:] Absolutely. [Sings:] "When a bee lies sleepin' / In the palm of your hand./ And true loves comes a creepin' / And your heart understand." [Speaks:] More lyric, we hope. [Hums melody.] [Sings:] "And true love she'll know has come for Miss Ottilie." [Speaks:] Soft curtain.[30]

Arlen intuitively grasps what Capote does not: that the original image of a bee sleeping in the palm of the hand, as found in the Houngan's poetic recitation, should be the core of the song. From this Arlen builds the first two lines (and four measures). In the next two lines, as sung on the recording, Arlen rhymes "sleepin' " with "creepin'," and then "palm o' your hand" with "heart understand." As he and Capote worked together, in person, toward the final version of the song, they retained Arlen's first two dummy lines but jettisoned the next two, replacing them with the more evocative "You're bewitch'd and deep in / Love's long look'd after land," which almost certainly come from Capote. Much more effective than "creepin,'" "deep in" creates an enjambment that leads directly to the following line. Capote's concentrated succession of "L" sounds ("love," "long," "look'd," "land") is something we might expect more from a poet than a lyricist. Although they make the lines awkward to sing, we can be grateful they remained in the song. For the rest of "A Sleepin' Bee" Arlen and Capote fashioned a superb lyric almost completely different from Capote's original draft. The final version retains one lovely image from the Houngan's speech, that of true love being "sweet golden as a crown."

In his recording for Capote, Arlen suggests with characteristic modesty that the music for "A Sleepin' Bee" "has enough quality and captures the mood" for the scene. Indeed, the song has quality to spare. Its broad melodic sweep and refined chromatic harmony make for one of the most beautifully crafted numbers in the American Songbook. The chorus has a relatively straightforward binary structure in which the last segment is extended: A(8) B(8) A′(8) B′(12). The tune of the A section unfolds in two parallel arcs (Example 8.2). The first takes flight quickly, moving up a tenth from middle C to E♭ an octave above, and then descends in gently rocking triplets to the tonic A♭. The second arc begins identically but pushes its high point a whole step higher, to F. The first two measures of "A Sleepin' Bee" are unassumingly diatonic. Arlen reserves more intense chromaticism for the climax in the second four measures. The high melodic F is so powerful because it hovers above the song's first real harmonic dissonance, a diminished seventh chord on A♭. The F, a suspension to the chord tone E♭, forms a major seventh with the piano's G♭.

**Example 8.2** "A Sleepin' Bee," melodic arcs

## "House of Flowers"

In the title song of *House of Flowers*, Capote and Arlen musicalize a passage from the short story where Royal describes his mountain home in rich detail. "House of Flowers" is one of the few numbers in the show whose lyrics do not appear in Arlen's spiral-bound tablet. They appear to predate Arlen and Capote's in-person sessions in New York in 1954, and thus in this case Arlen likely shaped his song around the work of his collaborator.[31] These may well have been the first lyrics Capote drafted for the show, working from the title and phrases in the story. Of all the lyrics in *House of Flowers* whose evolution we can trace, these remained the most consistent from inception to finished song.

Capote drafted a verse for "House of Flowers," but as with "A Sleepin' Bee" did not seem to grasp the distinction between a verse and a chorus. Once again, what he labels a "verse" overlaps directly in wording and with the subsequent "refrain":

> Verse
> My house is a house of flowers
> A breeze from the sea
> Sends poppy seed
> Scattering on my floor
> What more do I need
> when roses are, lilacs are
> a rainbow round my door?
>
> Refrain
> My house is made of flowers
> My curtains are crêpe-myrtle
> All beasts and birds
> Come live with me
> Bees and toads
> Old sea turtles
> My house a home
> For all these things
> What move and breathe and sing
> So come live with me
> I'd come live with me
> If I was you Miss Ottilie.

In the end, Arlen and Capote included no verse in "House of Flowers." But for the conclusion of the chorus they retained Royal's direct appeal to Ottilie ("Won't you come live with me," in the final version). They also created the song's bridge from four lines Capote had drafted on a separate page:

> I've never had money
> I'll never need none
> The moon is my lamp
> The clock is the sun

In "House of Flowers" Arlen characteristically reimagines a conventional AABA′ form. The song extends to forty-five measures, making it a mini-tapeworm, with a design in which the piano part becomes integral: A (10)—piano interlude (2)—A (10)—piano interlude (2)—B (12)—piano interlude (1)—A′ (8). In the piano introduction preceding the first A, Arlen introduces a distinctive idea, clearly instrumental in conception, that recurs in subsequent interludes: a rapid downward arpeggio in sixteenth notes followed by a slower chromatic rise, underpinned in the left hand by a steady pattern of a low bass note (or open fifth) alternating with a dissonant chord in a higher register (Example 8.3). With this compact musical gesture Arlen evokes, abstractly rather than pictorially, various images of motion in the lyrics—the warm winds, the spring showers, the crepe myrtle curtains, the fireflies.

In the bridge of "House of Flowers," Royal shifts from poetic description of his mountain home to a proud assertion of his values ("I've never had money and I'll never need none"); this is captured by Arlen with as strong a musical contrast as one is likely to find in any popular song. The earlier house-of-flowers piano figure gives way to a two-measure interlude with a new right-hand motive played over a stride-style bass; this is a bluesy vamp of the kind we might find in a song by W.C. Handy or Hoagy Carmichael (Example 8.4).

**Example 8.3** "House of Flowers," piano figuration

**Example 8.4** "House of Flowers," piano interlude between A and B sections

**Example 8.5** "House of Flowers," A′ section

At the end of the bridge Arlen introduces yet another piano interlude, here a tonally ambiguous riff played in octaves and halting abruptly at a fermata (Example 8.5). He then truncates A′ to accommodate the breaking of the song's poetic "frame" as Royal pleads directly to Ottilie ("Won't you come live with me"), modifying the original tune into something more like recitative, declaimed over sustained chords (▶ 8.2).

## "I Never Has Seen Snow"

"I Never Has Seen Snow," the extended ballad Ottilie sings at the end of Act 1 of *House of Flowers*, elicits one of Wilder's most fervent encomiums. He assesses "I Never Has Seen Snow" in the context of what he calls the "song-arias" from Gershwin's opera *Porgy and Bess*. For Wilder, Arlen "proves that he is capable of writing within the territory of popular music and arriving at a quality of vocal composition which is superior, I feel, to that which Gershwin achieved outside that territory."[32] We need not pit Arlen against Gershwin, or argue about what is and is not to be included in the "territory of popular music," in order to agree that "I Never Has Seen Snow" represents one of Arlen's most ambitious and powerful creations, rivaling the exquisite tapeworm "I Had Myself a True Love" from *St. Louis Woman*. In both songs, as in "House of Flowers," the piano plays an integral structural role.

Where "I Had Myself a True Love" is a song of loss and rage, "I Never Has Seen Snow" projects optimism, as Ottilie, in Capote's striking imagery, envisions her life with Royal, a lover more "beautiful" than the snow she has only imagined. The song has a substantial verse extending fifteen measures. Jablonski reports that the first line ("I done lost my ugly spell") was inspired by a comment from Arlen's doctor made when the composer was in the hospital recovering from a serious medical episode in 1954: "Harold, you poor bastard, you been took with an ugly spell."[33] In the last part of the verse, beginning with the cadence on the tonic at "the girl I was before," Arlen introduces in the piano the "slow, but steady" parallel chordal figuration that shapes the sound world of the song.

The first melodic phrase of the chorus of "I Never Has Seen Snow" ends by rising a half step from a sustained B to a short C (Example 8.6). This gesture tends to destabilize the tonic G major and push the music forward. The same two-note figure reappears in the second phrase at "love is," where Arlen explicitly connects the two notes with an upward-slanting line. On his demo and studio recordings of "I Never Has Seen Snow" (the latter to be discussed in Chapter 9), Arlen sings these B–C figures with a little upward vocal scoop or glissando. Diahann Carroll does the same on the original cast album. Their performances reflect a practice—rising in pitch at the end of a phrase—that, as discussed in Chapter 3, Arlen learned from Black singers and adopted in his earliest recordings from the 1920s. This gesture disappears from most later recordings of "I Never Has Seen Snow."[34]

**Example 8.6** "I Never Has Seen Snow," opening of A section

**Example 8.7** "I Never Has Seen Snow," bridge

The fifty-measure chorus of "I Never Has Seen Snow" has the form A(8) B(6) A′(8) B′(6) C(11) A″(11). Somewhat as in "The Man That Got Away," the B and B′ segments can be subsumed into a larger A and A″, allowing us to discern a standard frame behind the song, A(14) A′(14) B(11) A″(11), where B functions as a bridge. In the first twenty-eight measures of "I Never Has Seen Snow" Ottilie exalts her lover above any natural phenomena like snow and a twilight sky. In the bridge ("A stone rolled off my heart"), she turns to the past, explaining how and when she fell in love. Arlen begins with a correspondingly abrupt shift away from the tonic G major (Example 8.7). A melodic G♯ replaces the G♮ of the prior cadence. Harmonically, the first phrase of the bridge is built on a repeated Bm7–E7 progression that could function as ii7–V7 in the key of A. Yet it never resolves: A major and minor chords appear at several points, but always inflected or destabilized with a seventh (G♮). For the bridge Arlen also creates a more polyphonic piano texture, with distinct inner voices.

The return to A″ in "I Never Has Seen Snow" resembles that in "I Had Myself a True Love" from *St. Louis Woman* (Example 5.12). Instead of beginning with the main melody, the singer leaps up an octave from the dominant pitch D ("and though") and holds the high D for two measures while the piano plays the "lazy" piano figuration from the B section, now front-loaded to the beginning of A″ (Example 8.8) (▶ 8.3). Only in the third measure does she take up the main melody to create a real return. As in the earlier song, we sense that the singer is too overcome with emotion to begin normally. Ottilie sustains the high note on "though" much as Lila does with "No" in the phrase "No, that ain't the way it used to be."

After the title phrase "I never has seen snow" is sung on the tonic, Arlen shifts to the subdominant harmony C ("nothing' will ever be"); as in the final

**Example 8.8** "I Never Has Seen Snow," opening of A″ section

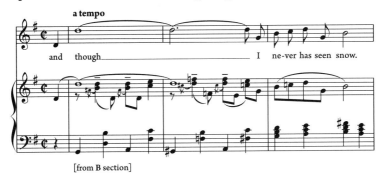

**Example 8.9** "I Never Has Seen Snow," ending

segments of many popular songs, it is part of a broad IV–V–I cadential motion that signals an ending. The last part of the progression constitutes as exquisite a moment as any in Arlen. Within a sustained subdominant chord, the right hand of the piano slides chromatically down to a blue note E♭, to which Arlen adds the blue B♭ (Example 8.9). On the downbeat he places a rest in the voice part. It is almost as if, hearing this rich chord, Ottilie is once again overcome with emotion and responds with a momentary silence before rising to the highest note of the song, G, and dropping an octave.[35]

One leaf in Arlen's tablet notebook for *House of Flowers* reveals how the composer reshaped the lyrics to accommodate the distinctive, extended musical reprise (A″) of "I Never Has Seen Snow" (Figure 8.2). Above the main text, corresponding to that of the first A, we see Arlen adding words to underlay the long high D that is a new melodic element. He first tries "+ [and] what if," which he then replaces with "and tho." As Arlen quickly realizes, the

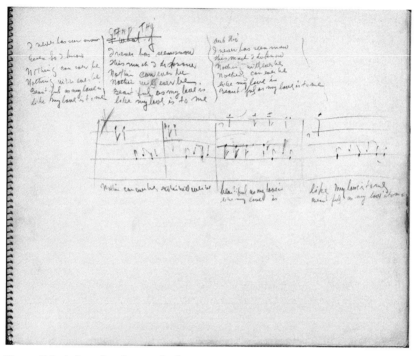

**Figure 8.2** Arlen, sketch page for "I Never Has Seen Snow," from tablet book of sketches for *House of Flowers* (Rita Arlen Collection, Music Division, Library of Congress, Washington, D.C.)

latter phrase, with one syllable and an open vowel, works much better for a sustained note. Beneath these lyrics, on hand-drawn music staves, Arlen sketches out the new portion of the tune, with lyrics, for the last four lines of the reprise.

This manuscript page reveals Arlen's craftmanship better than any other working document I have examined. Arlen may be treasured for his great tunes and sophisticated harmonies, but for him, as we saw in Chapter 1, the quality of any song depends on both words and music. When he had the chance or, in the case of his collaboration with Capote, the need to be involved with lyrics, Arlen was more than up to the task. If, as seems likely, Capote provided the striking title phrase of "I Never Has Seen Snow," it was Arlen who saw how it could be reshaped for the song's climactic reprise.

Arlen's biographer and amanuensis Jablonski is hardly an impartial critic, but even for him, as for Wilder, the composer achieves something unique in "I Never Has Seen Snow." Writing in 1961, Jablonski devotes extended commentary to the song and concludes, in an assessment that anticipates Wilder's a decade later: "'I Never Has Seen Snow' violates all the rules of popular song writing, but then it never was designed to be a 'popular song,' nor has it become one. It is, however, one of the most distinctive and distinguished songs written for the theater, concert stage, or whatever."[36]

## The 1968 Revival of *House of Flowers*

Despite the short, troubled run of *House of Flowers* in 1954–1955, Saint Subber did not give up on the show. As early as 1960 he hoped to revive it in its original form.[37] Eight years later Subber produced a scaled-down off-Broadway revival, which opened in January 1968. For this new production Capote revised the book extensively and had it issued by his own publisher Random House—a rare distinction for a musical.[38] Capote and Arlen created about eight new songs, of which five appeared in the production. United Artists released a new cast album. Despite all the effort and talent lavished on the revival of *House of Flowers*, it garnered little praise and ran for only a month and a half.

For the new production Capote took back some of the control he had lost with the original one. He resurrected scenes and lyrics from his earliest drafts, including "Jump de Broom," sung by the Houngan for Ottilie and Royal's wedding ceremony. He also introduced plot elements from the short story, most notably the character of Old Bonaparte, Royal's grandmother, who now occupies a good part of Act 2. The new production restored to Ottilie the song "Don't Like Goodbyes," which Pearl Bailey had stolen from Diahann Carroll. The only member of the original cast of *House of Flowers* to appear in the revival was Josephine Premice, who had been forced out in 1954 during out-of-town tryouts by Bailey. In the original show she played Tulip; for the revival, in a casting choice made with a touch of revenge or at least irony, she assumed Bailey's former role. But Madame Fleur now has only one solo song, a newly written "Something Cold to Drink," which replaced Bailey's "One Man Ain't Enough" in Act 1.

This new song, like most of the others Arlen and Capote wrote for the 1968 revival of *House of Flowers*, does not rise to the level of the original number. In one of the more puzzling substitutions, "Madame Tango's Particular Tango" took the place of "Madame Tango's Tango" from 1954. In the earlier number, sung by Juanita Hall and some of her girls (but not included on the original cast album), Arlen included distinctive features of a tango, including the accompanimental habanera rhythm and some parallel chromatic harmonies.

**Example 8.10** "Albertina's Beautiful Hair"

In the newer number, Arlen tilts the tango in the direction of rhythmic figures it shares with calypso. Perhaps that is what is supposed to make it "particular"; but the result lacks the sultry energy of the 1954 number.

Ottilie is given perhaps the loveliest of the additions to *House of Flowers*, a short ballad called "Albertina's Beautiful Hair," not included in the new cast album. The song appears in Act 2 when Old Bonaparte, stroking Ottilie's hair, tells her the legend of a girl from the mountains who also had lovely hair praised in song by young men. The old lady says, "Poor Albertina, she died young. But now imagine this: even when she was dead her hair kept on growin'. Sweet and heavy, longer and longer."[39] Ottilie is understandably disturbed by this story, but at Old Bonaparte's request sings the song, without accompaniment.[40] Arlen sets the words—attributed in the sheet music solely to Capote—in a hauntingly simple way that contrasts with the more stereotypical Caribbean sounds of the revised score (Example 8.10).

✻✻✻

Although *House of Flowers* had no sustained presence on stage, it yielded some of the finest songs in Arlen's catalogue. As we have seen throughout this book, Arlen always relished the challenge of working with new lyricists who he felt could push him in new directions. Arlen and Capote developed a close, almost paternal-filial bond and, in the years between the original *House of Flowers* and the revival, remained in close contact. In 1961 Arlen sent a copy of the first Jablonski biography of him, *Happy with the Blues*, to Capote, who remarked admiringly "how distinguished" it was "to have a formal biography—while <u>still</u> alive." Capote would send Arlen inscribed copies of his own latest books, as well as affectionate postcards from his travels around the world, sometimes with the greeting "Dear Dads."[41] The collaboration and friendship with Capote opened the way to Arlen's work in the 1960s with two more young lyricists, Dory Previn and Martin Charnin. These partnerships we will explore in Chapter 10.

# 9
# Arlen Sings and Plays: Recordings and Performances of the 1950s and 1960s

In Chapter 3, we examined recordings Arlen made in the 1930s of numbers written with Ted Koehler. At that stage, when Arlen often fronted for several prominent bands, he was active—and considered pursuing a career—as a vocalist. With the burgeoning success of his songwriting and his increased involvement in Hollywood and on Broadway, composition took precedence. But Arlen never stopped performing his own music, sometimes as accompanist to prominent vocalists, most often as both pianist and singer. Friends and associates often asked him to perform at private gatherings and parties, which, despite his modesty, he was willing to do. (Arlen would sometimes proactively bring along lyrics he was afraid of misremembering.)

In the 1950s, after almost two decades' absence, Arlen returned to the commercial recording studio and began more frequent, extended appearances on radio and television. (See Table 9.1 for an overview of this activity.) This was the period we explored in the previous two chapters, when he was also working on *A Star Is Born*, *House of Flowers*, and *Blues Opera*, all the while enduring several health crises.

Radio was a medium with which Arlen had long been familiar and comfortable.[1] In February 1955, he appeared for a half-hour-long segment on Dave Garroway's NBC radio show, *Fridays with Dave Garroway*. Arlen also gravitated to a recently developed broadcast medium that could show off his talents, television. Starting in 1952 he made appearances on numerous variety shows, including Steve Allen's *Tonight Show*, *The Colgate Comedy Hour*, *The Ed Sullivan Show* (and its predecessor *Talk of the Town*), the *Martha Raye Show*, and the *Perry Como Show*. Arlen also participated in television specials devoted solely to his music. In 1955 he embraced the still relatively new LP format, recording *The Music of Harold Arlen* with Walden Records and *Harold Arlen and His Songs* with Capitol. A decade later, Arlen made one more LP, with Barbra Streisand, *Harold Sings Arlen (With Friend)* on Columbia.

**Table 9.1** Arlen's Performances After 1950

| VENUE/SHOW | DATE | COMMENTS |
|---|---|---|
| Ed Sullivan's *Toast of the Town* (TV) | Sept. 28, 1952 | The Story of ASCAP (Part 1). Nine-minute segment. Arlen performs medley, with fragments of songs, ending with staged "Over the Rainbow." Viewable at Historic Films (www.historicfilms.com), HA-3. |
| The Heart Fund (Radio) | February 1953 | Sponsored by the American Heart Association. Arlen and Johnny Mercer perform in this 15-minute program. Tape held at Library of Congress, Recorded Sound Research Center, LC 1390641-3-2; source rack NCPC 02233 |
| *The Colgate Comedy Hour* (TV) | Nov. 29, 1953 | Four-minute segment hosted by Eddie Cantor. Medley of Arlen songs or portions of songs. Arlen accompanies Cantor, Connie Russell, and Frank Sinatra in other songs. |
| *Toast of the Town* | June 20, 1954 | Arlen plays medley of eleven songs, including "The Man That Got Away"; accompanies Risë Stevens in "Come Rain or Come Shine." |
| *Toast of the Town* | October 10, 1954 | Arlen plays and sings "The Man That Got Away" complete, plus a short medley of parts of other songs. |
| *The Tonight Show* with Steve Allen (TV) | Nov. 24, 1954 | Arlen, in Philadelphia for out-of-town tryouts of *House of Flowers*, plays selections from the show. |
| *The Tonight Show* | Feb. 3, 1955 | Arlen is interviewed by Steve Allen and sings medley of songs. Eydie Gormé sings "The Man That Got Away" and "A Sleepin' Bee." |
| *Friday with Garroway* (Radio) | Feb. 25, 1955 | Half-hour show. Arlen is interviewed by Dave Garroway and sings and plays "Paper Moon," "A Sleepin' Bee," and "One for My Baby." Tape held at Library of Congress, Recorded Sound Research Center, RGA 3075 A1–B2. |
| *The Music of Harold Arlen* (LP) | Released May 1955 | Two-LP set. On one Arlen performs twelve numbers. Participates in one song on the other disk. Released on CD by Harbinger Records HCD-1505 [1998] |
| *Harold Arlen and His Songs* (LP) | Released 1955 | Arlen performs twelve numbers. Released on CD by DRG Records CD-19078 (2005) |
| *The Martha Raye Show* (TV) | March 6, 1956 | A fourteen-minute segment in which Arlen performs numerous songs. |
| *Close Up!* (TV) | Feb. 28, 1957 | |
| *Perry Como Show* (TV) | Jan. 3, 1959 | |

*(continued)*

Table 9.1 Continued

| VENUE/SHOW | DATE | COMMENTS |
|---|---|---|
| *DuPont Show of the Week* "Happy with the Blues" (TV) | Sept. 24, 1961 | Hour-long show. Created in connection with publication of Jablonski's biography *Happy with the Blues.* Arlen sings "Little Drops of Rain" at the end. Available to view at Hagley Digital Archives (https://digital.hagley.org/FILM_1995300_FC362) |
| *Bell Telephone Hour:* "The Music of Harold Arlen" (TV) | Dec. 5, 1965 | A tribute for Arlen's 60th birthday, hosted by Dinah Shore, with assisting artists (including Duke Ellington). Arlen accompanies the full cast at the end for "Over the Rainbow." Available on DVD as *Harold Arlen: An All-Star Tribute*, VAI 4371 (2005) |
| *Harold Arlen Sings (With Friend)* (LP) | Released March 1966 | Arranged by Peter Matz. Arlen sings eleven numbers, is joined by "friend" Barbra Streisand for one. Columbia Records OS 2920, OL 6520 (never released on CD). |
| *The Ed Sullivan Show* (TV) | May 1, 1966 | ASCAP Salute. Arlen plays piano excerpts from "Stormy Weather" and "Over the Rainbow" |
| *The Today Show* (TV) | May 7, 1968 | |
| *Get Happy: The Music of Harold Arlen* (TV) | Feb. 25, 1973 | An hour-long special hosted by Jack Lemmon, with assisting artists. Arlen accompanies "Over the Rainbow" at the end. Tape held at Paley Center for Media, New York, B:03450 |

All these activities are as much a part of Arlen's musical identity and legacy as the songs themselves. Among other things, they are valuable for revealing how he played his own music at the piano; his chord choices and voicings, and his rhythmic and melodic figurations, often match closely the published sheet music. The musical analyst can thus confidently view the score as revealing Arlen's compositional intentions. But Arlen also frequently gives free rein to his jazz impulses, departing from the notated text and offering more evidence of how he could hear his own music—and how performers and listeners might do so as well.

Arlen's vocal style is similarly rich and revealing. By the 1950s his light tenor had darkened, but he was still able to hit high notes with precision. We recall, as discussed in Chapter 4, that in the 1930s the critic Isaac Goldberg characterized Arlen's performing style as "unostentatious" and "epistolary."[2] These qualities, as well as his focused intensity and his ability to put across the lyrics, continue into in the later years. Arlen's performances show him following the development of jazz or pop singing, at least among males, from the crooner style of the 1930s to the rhythmically and melodically freer style of the post–World War II era. Sometimes Arlen sings a tune relatively straight, as he had notated it; at other times he bends or reshapes a melody as impressively as some of the male jazz vocalists with whom he worked or who sang his music, including Johnny Mercer, Vic Damone, Frank Sinatra, Mel Tormé, and Tony Bennett.

No less a singer than Bing Crosby remarked in 1947, "I've always considered him [Arlen] one of the best stylists I've ever heard.... It's a certainty if Harold hadn't developed the remarkable facility he enjoys for writing hit tunes, he would have been an outstanding performer as a singer or as a pianist."[3] Noel Coward wrote to the composer in 1955, after receiving one of Arlen's LP albums, "I am here to tell you that I would rather hear you sing your own songs than anybody else."[4] Perhaps no one sums up better the powerful effect of an Arlen performance than Stephen Sondheim. "I heard him sing and play," Sondheim said in 1998. "And let me tell you: If you're into songwriting, they don't come any better than that. Hearing Harold Arlen play and sing makes me cry. It was a thrill—thrilling."[5]

Dave Garroway was similarly affected. After hearing Arlen perform "A Sleepin' Bee" on the February 1955 radio show, Garroway asks, with wonderment in his voice: "Where did you learn to sing? You sing like no other man in the whole world, I think." Arlen's reply modestly deflects the compliment onto his father: "Well, thank you. My dad was a cantor, and he had quite a magnificent style. He was one of the few [cantors] . . . that I think ad-libbed, as we'd call it today, a melody, like no one else. And he was a joy to listen to. And if I have anything at all, I think I got it from him."[6] In another part of the show Garroway marvels, "When you sing, you pay so much attention to the words, more than any other songwriter who composes music than I think I ever heard." Arlen responds, again with humility: "Well, I have always been a lover of lyrics. Words mean an awful lot to me. And the text should mean an awful lot to everyone, because I don't think a great song is worth a hoot unless it's a happy wedding of both [music and words]."

## Arlen's Demos

Throughout most of his career on Broadway and in Hollywood, Arlen participated frequently in "demos," or demonstration disks of his songs, many of which survive.[7] Some are private working documents, where Arlen might play through a tune in order to familiarize his lyricist with it at a point where the words were as yet unwritten or only partially complete. One especially elaborate example of this kind of demo was discussed in the last chapter: Arlen's almost-six-minute-long disk of "A Sleepin' Bee" prepared for Truman Capote, in which the composer talks through the scene from *House of Flowers*, then plays the song with provisional or "dummy" lyrics. Another similar demo is one Arlen made, probably for his lyricist Harburg, of "Cocoanut Sweet" from *Jamaica*. In it we hear Arlen playing through the song at an early stage, before lyrics were added. Here the song has an ABA' form, more conventional than the final tapeworm-like structure, and a much less inspired B melody.

Like other songwriters, Arlen recorded most of his demos to introduce songs to potential or actual producers of his films or shows. In Chapter 4 we considered one such demo, for "Right as the Rain" from *Bloomer Girl*. On it, Arlen tells the producer John Wilson that the song is "incomplete," but he wants to provide a sense of "where we're heading." He plays a complete chorus of the song, sings Harburg's lyrics-in-progress through the beginning of the second A, then da-da-dahs or hums his way through the remainder, except for where the title phrase returns.

Arlen's talents as pianist and singer made him the best salesman for his own songs; sometimes joined by his lyricists, he performs with enormous expressivity and panache. Surviving Arlen demos include those created for films over almost three decades, including *Strike Me Pink*, *The Wizard of Oz*, *A Star Is Born*, *Down Among the Sheltering Palms*, and *Gay Purr-ee*; and stage shows, including *Bloomer Girl*, *St. Louis Woman*, *House of Flowers*, *Jamaica*, *Blues Opera*, *Saratoga*, and *Softly*. These demos contain not only familiar numbers, but also songs never used, songs still in progress, or songs that were substantially reworked.

The demos for *House of Flowers* include two songs that would not appear in the show, "Can You Explain?" and "Love's No Stranger to Me," as well as "Monday to Sunday," which was revised as "Waitin'."[8] Arlen's collaborator on *House of Flowers*, Truman Capote, who had no real singing voice, joins Arlen in two delightful demos, "Has I Let You Down?" and "Can I Leave Off Wearin' My Shoes?" In the latter, Capote performs the dialogue between M. Jamison (who speaks in French) and Ottilie (▶ 9.1). The twelve surviving demos for *Softly*, the musical Arlen worked on with lyricist Martin Charnin in the mid-1960s, show Arlen still in great form as a performer, even when working with material that was doomed. These will be discussed in Chapter 10.

## Arlen's Three LP Albums

In the late 1940s Edward Jablonski and Peter Bartók (the composer's son) founded an independent company, Walden Records, to record and promote recent American music. In 1952 Walden began producing a series of disks devoted to the lesser-known songs of popular songwriters: first, songs with lyrics by Ira Gershwin (a friend of Jablonski who also helped fund the project); then, in succession, songs by Cole Porter, George Gershwin, Rodgers and Hart, and Arthur Schwartz. These albums feature many of the same musicians, including singers Louis Carlyle, Warren Galjour, and Bob Shaver, and arrangers John Morris and David Baker.[9] The caricaturist Al Hirschfeld provided portraits of the composers as cover art. During the making of these albums some of the performers kept telling Jablonski, "You know, you really have to do Harold Arlen; he's just about the greatest of all."[10] In 1954 Jablonski proposed the idea to Arlen, who agreed. That was the first contact between Arlen and the man who would become his biographer and amanuensis. As arranger they brought in Peter Matz, who was working on the dance music for *House of Flowers*.

Recognizing and wanting to celebrate Arlen's gifts as a performer, Walden produced a two-LP set, *The Music of Harold Arlen*. On one disk, twelve Arlen songs are performed by five singers, the three mentioned above, plus June Ericson and Miriam Burton, a cast member in *House of Flowers*. (Arlen joins Ericson in "Can I Leave Off Wearin' My Shoes?," speaking M. Jamison's part.) On the other disk Arlen performs a different set of numbers alone, sometimes accompanying himself on piano, sometimes backed up by Matz's quintet. Arlen sings almost all his songs in the original keys in which he wrote them or they were published—a fact which suggests that during his long compositional career he may have thought in terms of his own vocal range.

Arlen's other album of 1955, *Harold Arlen and His Songs* (Figure 9.1), was planned shortly after the Walden set was in progress. According to Jablonski, Capitol Record producer Dick Jones had been impressed by Arlen's singing on radio and television and urged the composer to prepare another disk, this time singing solo on some of his better-known songs.[11] Once again, Matz

**Figure 9.1** Album cover of *Harold Arlen and His Songs*, Capitol Records, 1955 (© Herman Leonard Photography LLC)

was the arranger. The album includes Arlen's only commercial recording of "Over the Rainbow."

Almost a decade later, in mid-1965, Arlen returned to the recording studio one last time, for a Columbia Records album produced by Thomas Z. Shepard, *Harold Arlen Sings (With Friend)*. The "friend" was Barbra Streisand, who had her breakout moment with Arlen's "A Sleepin' Bee" and whom Arlen had praised enthusiastically in his liner note for her first LP album in 1963. On this new album Arlen revisits a few numbers from his earlier LPs, but also sings some he had not recorded before, including one written with Martin Charnin, "That's A Fine Kind o' Freedom," which Streisand had premiered in April 1965 at a benefit concert for civil rights given at the Majestic

Theatre in New York, "Broadway Answers Selma." Streisand makes only two appearances on the Columbia album, joining Arlen for a duet version of "Ding-Dong! The Witch is Dead" and a solo on "House of Flowers."

Perhaps because he was not regarded primarily as a singer, Arlen's LPs seem not to have attracted much notice in the jazz and popular music press. The few comments about Arlen's singing are mixed—and sometimes patronizing. In a short review of the Capitol album in *Down Beat* in March 1956, an anonymous critic wrote, "The noted tunesmith [Arlen] plays piano and sings many of his greatest hits on this one . . . and they all possess that intangible charm so often found when a writer performs his own material. . . . It's great listening for lazy days."[12] The critic John McAndrew, writing in *Record Changer*, found the Capitol album to be "sung in fine voice, exquisite style and entrancing phrasing, [with] plenty of Arlen pianoing."[13] In the *New York Herald Tribune* in July 1955, the critic Herbert Kupferberg wrote of the Walden set that "Mr. Arlen does far better than most composers of his own works."[14] But in the *New York Times*, "J.W.," almost certainly John S. Wilson (the newspaper's longtime popular music critic), wrote of the same disks that "Arlen's singing technique is irritatingly monotonous."[15] A decade later, Wilson seems to have revised his opinion. In an expansive, sympathetic review of *Harold Arlen Sings (With Friend)* he acknowledges Arlen's place "in the top echelon" of songwriters and continues:

> Arlen also likes to sing his songs and does it unusually well. . . .[He] shows the remarkable results that can be obtained from a seemingly small and reedy voice when it is used skillfully to explore the full quality and value of every syllable in a song. Arlen builds his performances with such care and deliberation that the nuances he brings to each word become events in themselves. He gives the lyrics such a devoted sense of interpretation that one might think they were his own creation.[16]

Wilson's remarks echo those cited above from Garroway, who also admired Arlen's close attention to the lyrics.

## Arlen on Television

Impeccably dressed in a suit enhanced by either a boutonniere or a pocket handkerchief, his thick hair closely cropped, his face sometimes sporting a trim moustache and thick-framed glasses, Arlen cuts an elegant figure in his numerous television appearances in the 1950s and 60s. Often backed by an orchestra, he plays and sings some of his greatest hits, each of which is greeted by a smattering of applause from the studio audiences. In the shorter segments Arlen might perform only a few measures of each song in a medley—something to which he got accustomed but which must have been artistically frustrating. In some shows Arlen accompanies other singers in his songs, among them Frank Sinatra and Risë Stevens. In more elaborate segments, usually the concluding ones, Arlen might be joined by a group or chorus of singers and sometimes dancers (Figure 9.2).

**Figure 9.2** Harold Arlen performing "That Old Black Magic" on Ed Sullivan's *Toast of the Town*, June 1954 (Getty Images, Michaël Ochs Archives)

Several hour-long television specials were devoted solely to Arlen's music, notably *The DuPont Show of the Week* in September 1961 (narrated by Bing Crosby) and *The Bell Telephone Hour* in December 1965 (hosted by Dinah Shore). In these broadcasts, many different artists perform his songs, and Arlen himself appears at the end. In the DuPont finale, Arlen, spotlighted at the piano on a darkened stage, sings "Little Drops of Rain," a ballad recently composed for the animated film *Gay Purr-ee*. Then he accompanies the entire cast in "Hit the Road to Dreamland." In *The Bell Telephone Hour*, Arlen is at the piano accompanying the singers in "Over the Rainbow."

## Three Versions of "It's Only a Paper Moon"

One way to get a sense of Arlen's vitality as an interpreter of his own songs is through a comparison of versions of "It's Only a Paper Moon" as performed in the 1950s in three different media: on television in *The Colgate Comedy Hour* in November 1953, on radio on the Garroway show in February 1955, and on the 1955 LP *Harold Arlen and His Songs*. (Arlen sings the song in F major, a step below the published score's G major.)

In the *Colgate Comedy Hour* broadcast, Arlen sits at the piano and plays a few measures of a lively blues-style vamp. He breaks off with a series of percussive, syncopated dominant-derived chords in a high register, which are echoed a minor third higher by an offstage orchestra. Arlen then launches into one chorus of "Paper Moon" (▶ 9.2). He sings the AAB sections with only small modifications of the notated pitches but with great rhythmic energy and an instinct to stretch out certain notes ("you" in "if you believed in me"; "hang-" in "hanging"). At A′ ("It's a Barnum and Bailey world") his improvisational chops emerge more clearly.

On the Colgate segment Arlen misremembers some of the lyrics for "Paper Moon." He sings "cardboard sky" instead of "cardboard sea"; "cotton sky" instead of "canvas sky"; and "hollow world" instead of "phony world." Normally Arlen is hyper-accurate with lyrics, which he renders (as the critic Wilson noted) as if he had written them himself. But in one of his earliest television appearances, amid the glare of the lights and gaze of the cameras, even a seasoned performer like Arlen could get a bit rattled.

In the performance on Garroway's radio show, Arlen sings "Paper Moon" in a form conventional for popular song—a full chorus, followed by a repeat of the bridge and final A′. In the A′ Arlen breaks free from the notated music even more strikingly than in the Colgate show (▶ 9.3). His reworking of the bridge and the first phrase of A′ is similar, but on Garroway he continues the fluid improvisation into the final phrase ("But it wouldn't be make-believe").

On the Capitol album, Matz's imaginative arrangement of "Paper Moon," with three full choruses, allows plenty of opportunity for Arlen's jazz instincts to blossom. A bouncy figure played in unison and octaves by piano and pizzicato bass functions as an ostinato backdrop for Arlen in the A sections. On his second time through the chorus Arlen scats and hums the first two As. The bridge is then played instrumentally (as is common in jazz arrangements), and at its conclusion Arlen drops in one line from the song's verse, "The world is a temporary parking place" (▶ 9.4). The third chorus, which modulates up a whole step, is the freest and most imaginative. The bridge dissolves into a playful dialogue between singer and band, who then elide the end of the bridge and beginning of A′, moving directly from "penny arcade" to "Barnum and Bailey world" with no pause and no "It's a."

In many ways the Arlen and Matz version of "Paper Moon" is a representative pop or jazz arrangement of its time. What makes it special, and relevant to the present study, is of course the participation of the song's composer. Having written "Paper Moon" some twenty years earlier, in what is arguably a different era of popular music, Arlen now fully reinvents it with the collaboration of a sympathetic arranger who brings out the very best in him.

## Three Arlen Solos

Among Arlen's most compelling performances are those where he is alone with his piano in a recording studio. Three slower ballads on the Walden set stand out: "It's a New World," "I Never Has Seen Snow," and "Last Night When We Were Young."

### "It's a New World"

In this exquisite performance Arlen remains close to the notated melody, which he imbues with great expression, rendering the song heartfelt but never sentimental. Like Judy Garland in *A Star Is Born*, Arlen sings the verse, which is integral to the song. As we discussed in Chapter 7, the accompaniment for the chorus in this hymn-like number is sparse, featuring sustained open fifths and octaves and limited inner-voice counterpoint. In his first time through, Arlen exaggerates the bareness of the piano part, initially holding a single chord for an entire measure or more (as on the first "see"). When he gets to what I have called the D section ("A newfound promise"), Arlen animates the accompaniment with a bass-and-chord pattern that articulates each quarter note. For the final A′ Arlen returns to his notated score, with half-note motion and more inner-voice activity.

## "I Never Has Seen Snow"

As suggested in Chapter 8, this song, a tapeworm with a substantial verse and a fifty-measure chorus, is among the most carefully crafted compositions in Arlen's oeuvre. In the published score, as is common, the right hand of the piano almost always doubles the voice; but most professional accompanists, including Arlen, avoid doing so in any mechanical fashion. Arlen plays all the special piano riffs he composed into the score, including the four-measure introduction with its bold succession of widely spaced chords, the broken chromatic octave ascent in the right hand of the verse, the "lazy, but steady" G-major transition into the B section of the chorus, and the chromatic slide from G down to E♭ just before the song's final phrase. Arlen also enriches with octave doublings some of the powerful parallel chord passages that characterize "I Never Has Seen Snow." For the bridge ("A stone rolled off my heart") Arlen abandons the more intricate, chromatic voice leading in the sheet music for a rhythmic bass-and-chord pattern similar to what one hears on the original cast recording of *House of Flowers*.

In his singing of "I Never Has Seen Snow," Arlen captures many of the nuances he had written into the vocal part, including the scoop on "snow" and "love is" discussed in the last chapter, and the slowing up (*molto rall.*) and sustained note (*tenuto*) near the end of the A sections ("Cain't be so beautiful" and "Not one so beautiful"). Arlen floats in a lovely falsetto the highest note of the song, the *tenuto* G on "like" in the final phrase (▶ 9.5), revisiting the moment when he dubbed the same pitch into the *House of Flowers* cast recording of the song some months earlier to help out Diahann Carroll, who suffered from a cold.

## "Last Night When We Were Young"

This is Arlen's only commercial recording of the song he claimed to have been proudest of having composed. As with the other ballads on the Walden album, his approach blends ease and intensity. Among the three songs discussed here, Arlen strays furthest from his piano score. In place of the notated three-measure introduction of block chords in even rhythms, Arlen invents a lead-in infused with blue notes and gestures. In some ways this passage seems out of character for "Last Night When We Were Young." Perhaps Arlen improvised the introduction at the recording session, seeking to de-sentimentalize a song that might have been most familiar to listeners in Lawrence Tibbett's operatic version of 1935 (discussed in Chapter 4). He does something similar with some bluesy piano riffs in his recordings of another ballad, "Over the Rainbow."[17] In "Last Night," instead of the steady chord pattern that emphasizes the $\frac{4}{4}$ meter, Arlen opts mainly for sustained piano chords, supplemented occasionally by melodic details in a high register similar to those in the score. Arlen animates the accompaniment in the final A.

In his performance of "Last Night When We Were Young" Arlen strategically plots the climax of the voice's high E on "clung" in A'. The first time through the song, rather than make an octave leap up to that note, Arlen sings the G a minor third above the lower E. Then, after playing the bridge on the piano, Arlen returns with A' and hits the high E. But rather than increasing in volume and intensity (as most performers do), he offers the note gently, creating an anti-climax in keeping with his understated rendering of the song. He improvises an elegant little vocal flourish on the "we" of "when we were young" before moving to the final cadence (▶ 9.6).

## Some Television Highlights

Television variety hosts and producers frequently sought out Arlen in the 1950s and 60s, and it is fortunate that some of the live broadcasts survive. Watching Arlen perform his songs adds a vital dimension to our appreciation of his abilities as singer and pianist—and songwriter. His facial expressions and body language are important vehicles of communication, and we get a special bonus when the camera is positioned to capture his hands at the keyboard. As mentioned above, in many of his appearances Arlen plays and/or sings a medley consisting of short segments of his greatest hits strung together. But there are also performances of complete songs that offer him—and us—greater scope for interpretation.

## "The Man That Got Away" (1954)

Arlen performed "The Man That Got Away" twice on Ed Sullivan's *Toast of the Town* (the precursor to *The Ed Sullivan Show*) in 1954: on June 20 and October 10. In his introductory comments on the June broadcast, Sullivan describes Arlen's performance as "the first public hearing" of the song. Indeed, at that time, three months before the late September premiere of *A Star Is Born* featuring Judy Garland's iconic rendition, "The Man That Got Away" was still an unfamiliar number. Although two prominent vocalists, Frank Sinatra and Jeri Southern, released single recordings of it in June, the soundtrack album for *A Star Is Born*, as well as some singles of Garland's individual numbers, would not be issued commercially until near the time of the film's release.[18]

Sinatra and Southern both take a stylish, gently swinging approach to "The Man That Got Away"; it sounds nothing like the gut-wrenching torch number offered up by Garland, which they likely had not heard when they made their recordings. Arlen, however, would surely have known Garland's version, pre-recorded for the film in September 1953, and his performances seem an homage to hers. Indeed, as he lowers himself onto the piano seat in the October broadcast, Arlen remarks humbly and almost *sotto voce*, "Hope Judy's listening." Though he lacks Garland's unique abilities, Arlen approaches her level in conveying the emotional power and musical architecture of his song, especially in the October performance he hoped she would hear.

Arlen manages to be at once scrupulous in observing and flexible in realizing many of the most important the details of his score. In the A sections, his piano accompaniment stays close to the march-like succession of chords, played "with steady insistence." In both performances Arlen sings much of the first A segment with his eyes closed or partially closed. At certain moments, in what seems a spontaneous gesture, Arlen's hands leave the keyboard, and our eyes are drawn upward to his face as he gives special emphasis to a vocal phrase: "And never a new love will be the same" (in June) and "has seen the final inning" (in October) (▶ 9.7). Arlen begins the song's short bridge ("Good riddance! Goodbye!") with a discreet bass-and-chord pattern that corresponds in spirit if not in letter to the "easy rhythm" he specifies in the score. As we saw in Chapter 7, "The Man That Got Away" is a tapeworm that has several climactic moments, notably in the second part of the A and A′ sections and in the bridge, where the melody pushes up to E♮. Arlen plots these moments impressively, with an emphasis that never overwhelms the longer trajectory of the song.

Arlen's televised performances of "The Man That Got Away" arguably surpass the studio recording he would make the following year with Matz for the Capitol album *Harold Arlen and His Songs*. On that album, like Sinatra and many male singers, Arlen switches the gender in Ira Gershwin's lyric to "The Gal That Got Away," an alternative offered in the published sheet music. But in both 1954 television appearances Arlen stays with the original words, perhaps partly because the song was still new to the public, but also because the consonant "n" in "man" is richer and more resonant than the closed "l" of "gal." It seems like too that with the "man" version of the song Arlen can pay more direct homage to Garland's powerful version. Had she been listening, Garland would likely have recognized, in a way that she might not in the versions by Sinatra and Southern, how the composer gets at the soul of his—and now her—song.

## *The Martha Raye Show* (1956)

Perhaps Arlen's finest extended television appearance as performer and collaborator is a fourteen-minute segment from *The Martha Raye Show* broadcast on March 6, 1956. Although in her later years Raye became better known for clownish comedy, she began as a fine jazz singer.[19] She was one of numerous vocalists who had their own television variety shows in the 1950s. Raye, who had known Arlen and his music for over twenty-five years, gives him a warm and affectionate introduction, explaining that she tries to include a song of his on each show and calling him "my very favorite composer." Their medley reveals a genuine chemistry. In various combinations of solos and duets, they sing a total of fifteen numbers, most in partial versions (sometimes the final A segment, or a combination of the opening and closing sections).

First, Arlen plays and sings "Paper Moon" complete, in a version based on the Matz arrangement from the 1954 Capitol album. Then he and Raye do "Let's Fall in Love" as a duet, where she scats and then sings in harmony with the tune. Then come "That Old Black Magic," "Between the Devil and the Deep Blue Sea," "Accentuate the Positive," "Blues in the Night," "Over the Rainbow," "Come Rain or Come Shine" (again with Raye harmonizing), "The Man That Got Away," "Stormy Weather," "Happiness Is Just a Thing Called Joe," "One for My Baby (And One More for the Road)," "Hit the Road to Dreamland," and "I've Got the World on a String." The final number, sung complete as a duet, is "Get Happy." From the song's bridge on ("We're headin' cross the river"), Raye and Arlen sing in counterpoint, each with a melody that deviates from the original tune (▶ 9.8).

There are so many things to admire in watching Arlen perform with Raye—the astonishing range and variety of the songs themselves, his own abilities as vocalist and pianist, and the sheer joy of collaboration between two veteran musicians working at a high level. Nowhere is the deep continuity that runs between composer, song, and performer more palpable and more rewarding to witness.

# 10
# A Late Style? Arlen, Dory Langdon, and Martin Charnin—and Harold Arlen

Arlen's biographer Edward Jablonski entitles his chapter about the composer in the 1960s "A Man of Sorrows."[1] Arlen was indeed discouraged after the recent critical failures of what would be his last major efforts with two longtime collaborators, Johnny Mercer (*Saratoga*, *Blues Opera*) and Yip Harburg (*Gay Purr-ee*). Like many song composers of his generation, Arlen expressed skepticism about newer trends in popular music, especially rock, and he was unenthusiastic about much of what was happening musically in Hollywood, on Broadway, and on television.[2] But the composer, still only in his late fifties, was by no means a bitter old man, ready to renounce his profession. As we have seen in the last chapter, as a frequent performer of his music on radio, television, and record, he used his stature to become a prominent advocate of the American Songbook. And Arlen was still receptive to proposals for new songs or scores. As he wrote to Jablonski in 1962, "Nothing new as far as material for the theatre or movies, but ever hopeful, we go on."[3]

In the 1960s, Arlen was encouraged to "go on" by two new, younger lyricists, Dory Langdon (1925–2012) and Martin Charnin (1934–2019). Working with them successively between 1962 and 1967 on a substantial body of songs, Arlen cultivated what might be considered a "late style" of composition, still recognizably his own but distinctive in many respects. Especially in recent decades, critics have used the concept of late style to assess the works that creative artists write, paint, sculpt, or compose in their final years of productivity or life (or both). Late style has been linked to various tendencies, including experimentation, fragmentation, inwardness, subjectivity, retrospection, distillation of earlier traits into a more concentrated style, and, overall, a sense that artists well along in their careers have nothing more to prove and little need to adjust their impulses to popular taste.[4] Only recently have scholars begun to explore the concept of late style in connection with American popular song.[5] Some numbers Arlen wrote with Langdon and Charnin fit such paradigms closely; they are often

*Harold Arlen and His Songs*. Walter Frisch, Oxford University Press. © Oxford University Press 2024.
DOI: 10.1093/oso/9780197503270.003.0010

characterized by sparseness of texture, increased chromaticism, and formal experimentation. Few of them have become widely known or performed.[6]

## Dory Langdon

Dory Langdon (Figure 10.1) is perhaps best known as a singer-songwriter of the 1970s whose career unfolded in the shadow of popular figures like Joni Mitchell and Carole King.[7] She began in a different sphere, as a lyricist working in Hollywood, principally with her husband at the time, André

**Figure 10.1** Dory Previn (Langdon) and André Previn being interviewed about Harold Arlen in November 1963 for *The Twentieth Century* television show (broadcast February 1964) (Getty Images, CBS Archives)

Previn. (For much of her life, even after her divorce from Previn, Langdon was known as Dory Previn. Here I will refer to her by "Langdon," the version of her original last name "Langan" that she used professionally from the late 1950s on.) It was through Previn that Langdon and Arlen came into contact. André Previn was an enormous admirer of Arlen, with whom he was well acquainted personally. As pianist and arranger, he released two albums of Arlen songs in the early 1960s and would make one more Arlen album, with the singer Sylvia McNair, in the 1990s.[8] Interviewed together for the *Twentieth Century* episode about Arlen broadcast on television in 1964, a source already cited several times in this study, Previn and Langdon both express deep appreciation for Arlen's genius, especially his ability to shape a song as a true "composition," with little regard for formula. "Harold goes on until he feels that he has nothing more to say in the song," resulting in "kind of deliberate experimentation," Langdon observes.[9] Langdon is addressing Arlen's propensity for tapeworms, of which we find several examples among their songs.

The impetus for the collaboration appears to have come from Langdon, who was living in Los Angeles while Arlen was now settled in New York. In a letter to her, dated October 29, 1962, apparently written in response to such an invitation, Arlen notes that he has been saying "no" to producers and authors. But for Langdon: "How can I say No?" He continues, "As of today I shall dig into my file of jots and see if there is something there that meets 'our' critical taste buds—if not—I promise to hack away until I produce something—Fair Enough?"[10] "Jots," as we have seen, was Arlen's term for short musical notations of ideas, often made on fragments of music paper, that he would put down and save for possible later use.

Between 1962 and 1964 Arlen and Langdon completed six songs:

"The Morning After" (1962)
"So Long, Big Time" (1963)
"You're Impossible" (1963)
"Hurt but Happy" (1964)
"Night After Night" (1964)
"That Was the Love That Was" (1964)

None of these seems to have been destined for a specific musical show or film, and only the first three have been published.[11] For "Night After Night," Langdon added words to a tune Arlen had written back in 1935 as part of an instrumental suite, "Mood in Six Minutes."[12] "The Morning After" was written very soon after Arlen and Langdon's exchange of letters in the fall of 1962; Arlen must have found a jot to develop, or he began to "hack away" at a tune. The song received almost immediate exposure through Previn, who made two recordings, a very fine one accompanying Eileen Farrell on the album *Together with Love* (Columbia CL 1920 / CS 8720, released in December 1962) and another in his orchestral-piano arrangement on the all-Arlen album *Sittin' on a Rainbow* (Columbia CL 1933 / CS 8733, released January 1963).

In "The Morning After" the singer dreads having to face the empty day after her lover has departed. Although perhaps not as poetically melancholic, Langdon's lyrics form a counterpart to the words Yip Harburg wrote for Arlen's "Last Night When We Were Young" in 1935. The chorus of "The Morning After" has a fairly conventional ABAB form (plus coda), but it manifests one significant aspect of Arlen's late style, an intensification of chromatic jazz harmonies. The opening phrase begins well away from the tonic D major, working its way home over two measures via descending lines in the bass and inner parts (Example 10.1a). Arlen approaches D major not directly from its own dominant, which appears at the beginning of the second measure (A7), but from an enhanced A♭7 chord. This cadence undercuts the "tonic-ness" of D major, which floats rather than settles, in large part because the linear descent continues in the alto range of the piano (E–D–C♯–B) even after the D chord is reached. The vocal line of "The Morning After" concludes, after a harmonically adventurous coda, on a high E, a ninth above the tonic D and as part of a Dmaj6 chord (Example 10.1b). This effect recalls another song of Arlen's that ends similarly, "Happiness Is Just a Thing Called Joe" (discussed in Chapter 4). In this way, "The Morning After" is arguably a "late" song that harkens back to a technique or moment from an earlier work.

At ninety-five measures (including the brief piano introduction), "So Long, Big Time!" is Arlen's longest tapeworm, unique as well in that the interlude far exceeds the chorus in length—another reflection of a tendency toward experimentation among the later songs. The structure can be represented as: Piano introduction (2)—Verse (9)—[Chorus] A (10)—A′ (16 + 2 as transition)—Interlude (42)—A′ (16). In Langdon's lyric, the male protagonist, once riding high, has suffered setbacks and is leaving town, abandoning the bright lights, women, card games, and horse races. "So Long, Big Time!" might be heard to revisit another Arlen tapeworm about regretful departure, "One for My Baby." But where in the earlier number, the singer drowns his

**Example 10.1** "The Morning After," opening and conclusion

sorrows in drink, "So Long, Big Time!" is expressly defiant: "It was fun, now it's done, / But I'll never sing a loser's song."

During the interview for *The Twentieth Century*, Langdon discusses "So Long, Big Time!" in what is among the most revealing accounts of the genesis of an Arlen song. She reports that Arlen sent her the music for the chorus, which as yet had no words. It struck her as a "sad, reflective kind of song," a mood confirmed by the indication "reflectively" Arlen placed at the head of the music. Langdon says that "all I could think of for" the opening was "So long, big time," a phrase that then emboldened her to "play against" the prevailing mood Arlen had created: "Harold's songs aren't the ordinary, run-of-the-mill melodies. Why not play against it instead of writing just a very, very downbeat, reflective idea to it. . . . Why not play against it with a guy who was saying . . . "I've had it all, but it was great, and so what, and I'll never sing a loser's song? So long, big time."

Langdon sent the lyrics to Arlen, who was impressed but now came to feel the song needed expansion. He told her (she reports), "Now we've got to go back and say what happened to the fellow who sang 'So Long, Big Time.'" Langdon continues, "So then he [Arlen] sat down . . . and *really* made it a big song."[13] Arlen thus composed the forty-two-measure interlude of "So Long, Big Time!" directly in response to Langdon's lyrics for the chorus, which in turn had been written to his music. We learn from Langdon's valuable comments not only about the fluid interaction between composer and lyricist—something clearly present throughout Arlen's career but seldom documented in this way—but also about his willingness in the later years to push conventional boundaries, in this case with the longest interlude he would ever write.

With their references to "chicks," "babes," and "bookies" redolent of the Rat Pack or Mad Men era, Langdon's lyrics can seem dated today. But her short, punchy verbal phrases (as in the title) fit the strongly motivic nature of Arlen's vocal lines. As early as "Stormy Weather," with the opening three-note figure ("Don't know why") that permeates the song, Arlen shows a strong inclination for motivic economy. In "So Long, Big Time!," in a way that again can be heard as characteristic of a late style, Arlen exaggerates that tendency with an almost relentless emphasis on a two-note, short-long rhythmic figure (Example 10.2). As we have seen throughout this study, blue notes are also an indelible part of Arlen's musical language. In "So Long, Big Time!," they appear right from the first phrase (D♭, G♭) with a concentrated intensity that can be heard as another aspect of lateness.

"So Long, Big Time!" retains an edgy, syncopated style almost throughout. But Arlen and Langdon change the mood in one striking moment, at the brief transition from the end of the interlude to A'. The song's protagonist softens as he tells his interlocutor, "Buy a few beers for me / Tell 'em no tears

**Example 10.2** "So Long, Big Time," opening of chorus

**Example 10.3** "So Long, Big Time," transition from interlude

for me" (Example 10.3). Shifting the meter from a propulsive $\frac{4}{4}$ to a gentler $\frac{3}{4}$, Arlen fashions a waltz-like melodic figure repeated over chromatically descending chords. The protagonist still relies on repetition of short ideas—that is clearly his mode of expression—but the gesture is now more nostalgic than bitter.

The first recording of "So Long, Big Time!," and still the best known, was made by Tony Bennett in September 1963 and released on his album *The Many Moods of Tony* in early 1964 (Columbia CL 2141 / CS 8941). Bennett, long an admirer of the composer, had made an all-Arlen album three years earlier, *Tony Bennett Sings a String of Harold Arlen* (Columbia CL 1559 / CS 8359 [1960]). In his autobiography, Bennett recalls Arlen's direct involvement in the recording session of "So Long, Big Time!" Bennett was working through the song with the arrangers Ralph Sharon and Marty Manning "when Harold interrupted and started showing me more things I could do with the lyric, how I wasn't getting enough out of it, how I could emphasize certain words. I liked what Harold told me so much that when the album . . . came out, I gave Harold credit on 'So Long, Big Time!' for conducting his own composition."[14]

Valuable film footage of Bennett's recording session for "So Long, Big Time!," included as part of the *Twentieth Century* television broadcast, documents the interaction between composer and singer.[15] We briefly see Bennett being coached by Arlen, much as Bennett describes above, and then recording the entire song, with Arlen leading the large studio orchestra (⏵ 10.1). The players had clearly been well-rehearsed, since for much of the session Arlen seems to be mainly holding the beat. But, as in his performances as pianist and vocalist discussed in the last chapter, Arlen is totally engaged, often beaming with pleasure. The music that flowed in the process of composition is still within him, physically and emotionally.

## Martin Charnin and *Softly*

In 1964 Arlen met Martin Charnin, almost thirty years his junior. Charnin was already something of a veteran of musical theater: he had played a Jet in *West Side Story* on Broadway and had worked as lyricist on short-lived shows with Mary Rodgers and Vernon Duke. He would later go on to collaborate with Richard Rodgers on *Two by Two* and *I Remember Mama*. Charnin is best known for having written the lyrics and served as director for the hit musical *Annie*. Charnin introduced himself to Arlen by slipping into the composer's pocket a note that said "I could be good for you," a gesture that helped initiate their collaboration and also became the title for one of their early songs.[16] Together Arlen and Charnin would go on to write eleven stand-alone numbers and at least twenty for a musical, *Softly*, which was never completed or produced (Table 10.1).[17]

Arlen and Charnin created several occasion-specific songs in 1965. The composer had developed a friendship with his then-congressman, liberal Republican John Lindsay, and wrote two campaign songs with Charnin when Lindsay ran for mayor of New York City in 1965 ("John-John-John" and "Let's Give the Job to Lindsay"). Arlen and Charnin also wrote the civil-rights themed song "That's a Fine Kind o' Freedom" for Barbra Streisand to sing at a special concert, "Broadway Answers Selma!," held at the Majestic Theatre in New York on April 4, 1965, as a fundraiser for victims of the attacks on marchers in Selma, Alabama, the previous month.[18]

The stand-alone Arlen-Charnin song that best reflects aspects of the composer's late style is the dark fifty-six-measure tapeworm "Come On, Midnight." This number is essentially through-composed, that is, unfolding without clear structural repetition until the final abbreviated return: A(16) B(16) C(16) A′(8). "Come On, Midnight" may also be the most tonally adventurous of any Arlen song. The melodic line of A is comprised of chromatically descending half steps, underpinned by dissonant harmonies oriented over a C pedal point. The pedal point appears both in the bass and in an inner voice, where it is intoned throughout the song as a bell-like syncopated figure (Example 10.4a). The B section alters the melody but retains the chromaticism, dissonance, and the bell-like motive (Example 10.4b). In the C section Arlen revisits his signature octave leap (Example 10.4c). Although none of these musical features are new in Arlen, in "Come On, Midnight" they are revisited through the lens of a late style.

214　HAROLD ARLEN AND HIS SONGS

**Table 10.1** Songs by Arlen and Martin Charnin

| DATE | TITLE |
| --- | --- |
| 1964 | "I Could Be Good for You"** |
| 1965 | "That's a Fine Kind o' Freedom"*<br>"A Girl's Entitled"<br>"John-John-John"<br>"Let's Give the Job to Lindsay"<br>"Little Travelbug"<br>"Shoulda Stood in Bed"<br>"Summer in Brooklyn"<br>"This Ol' World"<br>"Come On, Midnight"**<br>"Spring Has Me Out on a Limb" |
| 1966–1967 | *Softly* (musical)<br>"Once I Wore Ribbons Here"<br>"Been a Hell of an Evening"<br>"Temples"<br>"The More You See of It"<br>"Baby-San"<br>"Pacific"<br>"Momma Knows Best'<br>Minstrel Show: "Hello," "My Lady Fair," "You're Never Fully Dressed"<br>"Yellow Rain"<br>"Happy Any Day"<br>"The Brush Off"<br>"Suddenly the Sunrise"<br>"You Are Tomorrow"<br>"Don't Say 'Love'—I've Been There and Back"<br>"I Will"<br>"We Were Always to Be Married"<br>"Why Don't You Make Me Like You"<br>"Fish Go Higher Than Tigers" |

*Published in *The Harold Arlen Songbook* (New York: MPL Communications, 1985)
**Published in *Harold Arlen Rediscovered* (New York: MPL Communication, 1996)

Like Arlen's other lyricists, Charnin found himself willing to adapt to the composer's distinctive style and tapeworm impulses. As noted in Chapter 1, he called Arlen "one of the greatest spaghetti writers of all time," whose "melodies would go places you wouldn't expect . . . You'd find yourself trying to accommodate them rather than telling him to turn it into a thirty-two-bar song."[19] As in "So Long, Big Time!" the initial melody of "Come On, Midnight" consists of two-note motives. But while in the earlier song the motives were rapid-fire and intense, here the tune is distended, spread out

**Example 10.4** "Come On, Midnight," excerpts from A, B, C sections

like putty over many measures. Charnin makes the bold move of repeating "midnight," the only word sung in the first four measures. Compact musical and syntactic units also characterize the other sections of the song ("Love was right" in B, "Move in" in C). In each case, Charnin found just the right few words to accommodate Arlen's laconic phrases.

Even as he wrote individual songs with new collaborators in the early 1960s, Arlen had no strong appetite to return to Broadway. When asked in 1964 whether he was working on anything for the musical stage, the fifty-nine-year-old composer replied, "I haven't had an assignment for two years. I talk with a lot of producers and talent and I read scripts but I'm past the age where I'll take on any script, however dubious, just to be working. I can't invest that kind of energy to close in Philadelphia."[20] But things changed by early 1965, when Arlen would tell the editor of *Cue* magazine that he and Charnin "are amassing a lively cache of music . . . and we may surprise you with a musical one of these days."[21] The musical to which Arlen refers was almost certainly *Softly*, on which he and Charnin worked for almost two years, creating at least twenty songs before the project was abandoned. Arlen's biographer Jablonski has treated some aspects of the background and music for *Softly*. But this last major creative effort of Arlen's career deserves a closer look, based on unpublished sheet music for many songs, a dozen demo recordings, and comments in a diary kept by the composer.[22]

The man who worked to bring *Softly* together was Saint Subber, whom we met earlier in this study (Chapter 8) as the producer of *House of Flowers* in 1954. In the early 1960s Subber visited Japan in search of potential properties and cast members for a musical to be set in American-occupied Japan after World War II. Eventually he settled on something created closer to home, a short story called "Softly" by the Indian-born writer Santha Rama Rau, which appeared in the *Saturday Evening Post* in December 1963.[23] Rau lived in Japan from 1947 to 1948 as the daughter of the first Indian ambassador posted there after India's independence. Though "Softly" does not appear to be autobiographical, it reflects faithfully many aspects of daily life during the Occupation and explores the complex, often fraught interactions between the Japanese and their American occupiers.[24]

The title of "Softly" comes from an expression, seemingly made up by Rau herself, for an intimate relationship between an American GI and a Japanese woman. Here is how it is explained at the beginning of the story:

> That summer, in any bar in any American billet there would be the familiar quota of men sitting alone, sipping whiskey and glumly considering how they would tell some Japanese girl that a wife (or mother, or daughter—anyway, a dependent) was arriving and that life would be different from now on. They were the men with a Personal Problem—a "pp" as it came to be called, or, as some musically minded wag had insisted, a Softly. There would be brief exchanges of this sort:
> "What's the trouble, Dick?"
> "The usual," Dick would reply. "A Softly."
> "Yeah," his friend would say sympathetically. "A Softly does it, all right."[25]

The kind of relationship characterized here as a Softly was common in occupied Japan. That a woman involved in a Softly likely knows the situation to be temporary makes it no less exploitative than the Madame Butterfly situation, in which the American marries the unwitting Japanese girl while always planning to abandon her.

The protagonist of Rau's story is Charlie Baker, an American civilian stationed in Tokyo in 1947. Charlie initially expresses little interest in pursuing a Softly, telling a colleague, "I'm writing to my wife, asking her to come to Japan with our children. I'm not in love with some Japanese girl. I just *like* the damn country."[26] But then Charlie falls for Kay, a Filipino woman who had been imprisoned during the war and then sheltered by a Japanese family. Kay takes advantage of Charlie's naivete and generosity to secretly help her Japanese fiancé, who is ill with tuberculosis. She ends up falling in love with Charlie and decides to leave her fiancé. Charlie, having committed to Kay and told his wife not to come to Japan, discovers her deception and breaks off their affair. At the ambiguous end of the story, Charlie and Kay are left with nothing, have abandoned their other partnerships as well as each other.

To adapt Rau's story into a book for a musical, Subber turned to the British playwright Hugh Wheeler, who would later go on to write the books for Sondheim's *A Little Night Music* and *Sweeney Todd*. For the music, Subber approached Arlen, perhaps imagining him as the ideal composer to infuse the score with sonorities of East Asian music, much as Arlen had done with Caribbean sounds in *House of Flowers* and *Jamaica*. Arlen brought the idea to his current collaborator Charnin, who would later recall, "We [Arlen and Charnin] were in conversation one day and he said, 'There's a project Saint Subber is going to do. He wants me to set it to music and I want to write it with you.'"[27]

By early 1966, newspapers were reporting that the show would open in the 1966–1967 season. Jason Robards was mentioned as a possible lead.[28] Subber and Wheeler went to Japan to line up cast members, and an article in *Variety* claimed that *Softly* would be "the first Broadway musical to use native Japanese actors."[29] (This claim, if largely accurate, was misleading: Miyoshi Umeki had appeared—albeit cast as a Chinese immigrant—in *Flower Drum Song* in 1958.) By April, several Japanese women were being auditioned for the show in New York. The distinguished choreographer Hanya Holm, known for *Kiss Me Kate* and *My Fair Lady*, was signed on to *Softly*. She visited Japan for twelve days to study local cultural and dance traditions. In New York in late May or early June 1966 Holm held auditions for *Softly*. In a June 5 radio interview with dance critic Walter Terry, she expressed enthusiasm for the new show.[30]

As a musical, *Softly* would have fit into an array of stage and film works from the 1950s and 60s with plots set in post-war occupied Japan. One of the most popular was the long-running Broadway play *The Teahouse of the August Moon*, adapted by John Patrick in 1953 from a novel by Vern Sneider. The play was turned into a film in 1956. In both the play and the film, Sakini, the main Japanese character, also a kind of narrator, was played in yellowface by American actors, David Wayne and Marlon Brando respectively.[31] In 1970, *Teahouse of the August Moon* was adapted into a short-lived musical, *Lovely Ladies, Kind Gentlemen*, which lasted only nineteen performances. In that show Sakini was also played in yellowface, by Kenneth Nelson. It seems clear that by visiting Japan, recruiting Japanese actors, and seeking inspiration in Japanese dance, Subber and his colleagues hoped *Softly* would attain a greater degree of authenticity and avoid the *japonisme* so blatant on stage and screen.

Despite almost two years of effort, *Softly* never came together. One problem—probably the main one—was the book. Wheeler, who at this point had little experience with musical theater, created multiple drafts that drifted ever farther from Rau's story, with characters added and dropped, and major plot points shifted. We can briefly summarize what the book drafts for *Softly* reveal.[32] In dramatizing the short story Wheeler kept the relationship between Charlie and Kay at the center, but across various drafts expanded the number of other characters and subplots. In the earliest draft, Kay is a Japanese woman passing herself off to Charlie as Filipino. In a later draft, Kay is depicted from the start as Japanese (Keiko). These changes eliminate a key aspect of the original short story—that Kay and Charlie had been on the same side in the war and are both in an important sense outsiders in Japan.

In an outline for the final scene included in the first draft and described by Wheeler as "a scene of great bitterness," Charlie breaks off with Kay and prepares to return home to the United States, an ending that is in the spirit of, but more specific than, Rau's ending. That denouement was not to endure. Appended to the outline is a further scene in which Kay and Charlie reunite—a happy ending that lasted throughout Wheeler's later drafts. Overall, the successive outlines and versions of the book for *Softly* become increasingly bloated, moving away from the central themes of Rau's story. The lack of focus and the constantly changing plot line and range of characters presented a challenge to Arlen and Charnin, who kept churning out songs. Numbers were added or dropped from the show, moved around in the book, and reassigned among characters.

From 1966 into early 1967 Arlen kept a diary whose main purpose seems to have been to document progress on *Softy*, or lack thereof. The entries fill in some details about the drawn-out and problem-ridden evolution of the show.[33] Casting the lead Charlie was one challenge. When Robards was unavailable or uninterested, Subber approached Jack Lemmon, then Lloyd Bridges (who sang an audition, without success), Frank Sinatra, and Fred Astaire.[34] None of these possibilities panned out. Finding a director also proved difficult. Gower Champion came over to Arlen's apartment in early March 1966 to hear the music, but his name reappears no further. On March 15 Arlen writes that *Softly* would be directed by Noel Willman, an Irish actor and director who had won a Tony Award for the Broadway production of *A Man for All Seasons* in 1962. His most recent effort, *The Lion in Winter*, had opened in New York in March 1966, just days before he joined the *Softly* team. "Disastrous!" was Arlen's description of a March 31 meeting with Willman, Wheeler, and Charnin; two weeks later Willman was gone from *Softly*. As late as June, Arlen was phoning Charles Walters, the Hollywood director and choreographer who two decades earlier had been brought in to help rescue the Arlen-Mercer musical *St. Louis Woman*. Nothing seems to have come of that call.

In entries from February 3 and 4 Arlen expresses concern about some of Charnin's lyrics: "I've had a few moments of frustration + anxiety about the happy wedding of lyrics + music for this show—but they didn't take hold for long enough to trouble me—but I must admit this one has me boxed in—and I don't like it." On March 15, Arlen and Charnin performed a dozen *Softly* songs for potential backers. If the demos made somewhat later are any indication, they sang and played with enormous verve. The listeners' muted reaction depressed Charnin, while Arlen typically tried to stay above it. By August 1966 Arlen notes: "More Saint [Subber], More Martin [Charnin], More [Hugh] Wheeler . . . Round + Round + I'm getting bored + annoyed." A day later, in what was a characteristic put-your-head-down-and-press-on reaction for him in such situations, Arlen writes that he is going to concentrate on the songs and "let the others have their way."

*Softly* clearly was nowhere near ready to open in fall of 1966. In December, Arlen reports in his diary what he calls "The Shocker!" Subber has told him about an entirely new story that would replace "Softly" as the source for the musical: a 1948 film *The Search* set in post-war Germany, where an American soldier (played by Montgomery Clift) helps reunite a young Czech boy and his mother who were separated in concentration camps. Charnin is apparently interested, and Arlen notes being told that eight or nine songs from

*Softly* could be imported into the new show. But he is clearly skeptical: "My reaction was zero." Arlen is willing to watch the film but remains "confused."

The plots of *Softly* and *The Search* have little in common, beside featuring a GI who becomes involved with locals in an occupied territory after World War II. There is no love story at the center of *The Search*. Among the songs created by Arlen and Charnin for *Softly*, it is hard to see how "eight or nine" could be used in the new scenario, certainly not the ones with East Asian musical elements (to be discussed below). In one of the last entries in the diary, from March 1967, Arlen reports seeing a new script completed by Wheeler. It is not clear from the context whether this is based on *The Search*. But Arlen is dumbfounded, because the show has now been turned into a "musical comedy of the 1930s."

Despite a talented creative team and a huge amount of effort that reached across the globe, *Softly* was completely dead by mid-1967. We might ask how, had it opened on Broadway, *Softly* might have fared in the company of other shows in this latter part of what has sometimes been called the Golden Age of musical theater. In general, this was not a good period for veteran composers of Arlen's generation. Irving Berlin's *Mr. President* ran only 265 performances in 1962–1963. Frank Loesser's *Pleasures and Palaces* closed out of town in 1965. Richard Rodgers's *Do I Hear a Waltz?* (1965), Burton Lane's *On a Clear Day You Can See Forever* (1965), and Jule Styne's *Hallelujah Baby!* (1967) each lasted less than three hundred performances. *Softly* might have suffered a similar fate, also the fate of most of Arlen's other shows, a short run with a score that produced a few reliable standards.

## The Songs of *Softly*

Arlen was proud of what he and Charnin achieved with the music for *Softly*. The surviving songs and the fine demo recordings confirm that, despite his dissatisfaction with some of Charnin's lyrics, the partnership energized the composer.[35] Some songs reflect the adventurous style of late Arlen, especially the highly chromatic tapeworm "Why Do You Make Me Like You?" Though there is no indication that Arlen studied Japanese music, any more than Richard Rodgers did Thai or Chinese music for *The King and I* and *Flower Drum Song*, several numbers in *Softly* incorporate East Asian musical gestures with the sophistication we might expect from the composer.

"Happy Any Day" is based on a pentatonic scale. More sophisticated in this regard is "Suddenly the Sunrise," one of the most beautiful songs in the score, sung by Charlie and Kay near the beginning of Act 2 and combining elements of late Arlen with East Asian sonorities (▶ 10.2). Charnin's wistful lyrics acknowledge the warmth and fragility of Charlie and Kay's relationship:

> Like the sunrise,
> I am like the sunrise,
> When you touched me,
> Suddenly a sunrise,
> Gone the chill of a distant day.

Arlen's piano introduction and the first eight measures of the chorus are based on parallel chords with open fourths and fifths (Example 10.5). For decades, these had constituted a standard, even stereotypical, East Asian trope in American popular music.[36] But Arlen absorbs these sonorities into his own idiom, especially the style of his later songs from the 1950s and 60s. In the introduction the parallel chords give way to the kind of sparse dissonance we find in some of Arlen's other late songs, like "Come On, Midnight," which was at some point intended for *Softly*. In the chorus of "Suddenly the Sunrise" the full right-hand open chords over a pedal fifth in the left hand reflect the style of "It's a New World," written in 1953 for *A Star Is Born*.

Formally, "Suddenly the Sunrise" shows Arlen at his most inventive. The song divides into two large segments that might be represented as A(22, plus two-measure piano extension) A′(24). The A′ section deviates from A beginning in the eighth measure, as Arlen builds to a climax at the words "If

**Example 10.5** "Suddenly the Sunrise," opening of chorus

the shadows overcome me." Here he also introduces the most chromatic vocal line and harmony of the song, representing the greatest departure from the prevailing parallel-chord style. Then, for the final eight measures, to round out the song, Arlen returns to that idiom and to the opening melodic phrase.

"Fish Go Higher Than Tigers," another number from *Softly*, incorporates Asian elements in a bolder fashion than "Suddenly the Sunrise." According to Arlen's diary, the song was composed in May 1966, well after the earliest group of songs. In this case, Charnin fashioned the lyrics first and brought them to Arlen, who was intrigued: "Doll-like lyric . . . Charming piece of material." In one of the drafts for the book of *Softly*, "Fish Go Higher Than Tigers" is to be sung in Act 1 by the Japanese orphans who are playing a game with kites. Wheeler sets the scene in some detail:

THE PLAYGROUND OF THE BOYS' CAMP

At each side of the stage is a construction of four vertical bamboo poles with a cross bar at the top. One cross bar has a paper fish flying from it, the other a paper tiger.

(NOTE: These are used in Japanese schools for a team game. The first team to have all its members reach the tops of their poles wins.)

SEVEN JAPANESE BOYS (including OMI, the youngest) in two teams, are flying kites. One team has a FISH kite, the other a TIGER kite.

THEY sing FISH GO HIGHER THAN TIGERS.[37]

Although Wheeler possibly invented the kite game, this scene represents his most thoroughgoing attempt to capture an actual Japanese practice in *Softly*.[38] The description stimulated Arlen and Charnin to create what is perhaps the most innovative song in the show. The lyrics read, in part:

>Fish go higher than tigers,
>Fish go higher than tigers ever go.
>Fish go to clouds
>That tigers never go to,
>They do.

**Example 10.6** "Fish Go Higher Than Tigers," opening of chorus

Charnin's lyrics are compact and dense, somewhat in the style of haiku, though not observing the standard three-line structure. "Fish Go Higher Than Tigers" is comprised of a chorus with ABA′ form plus an interlude. Arlen's piano introduction uses a pentatonic riff, a gesture of local color which, as in "Suddenly the Sunrise," gives way to a more jazz-oriented chordal progression. Arlen sets Charnin's words to a melody of limited ambitus, circling within and around a minor third; a static, repeating piano accompaniment; and an asymmetrical phrase structure of 2 + 3 measures, created by the addition of "ever go" (Example 10.6). All these features capture the "childlike wonder" specified in the score with a spontaneity and simplicity appropriate to playtime (▶ 10.3).

In the B section of the chorus ("Tiger can reach the sun that shines"), the sparse accompaniment consists mainly of alternating two-note clusters. Here Arlen and Charnin strikingly anticipate aspects of Stephen Sondheim's mature style, as reflected a decade later in another musical set in Japan, *Pacific Overtures*, in the similar two-note clusters (E♭–F, B♭–C) that accompany "Someone in a Tree" (Example 10.7). In many of his lyrics for *Pacific Overtures*, Sondheim likewise attempted to capture the flavor of haiku, a technique Banfield has called "lyric pointillism."[39] Although as we saw in Chapter 1, Sondheim was a great admirer and emulator of Arlen, he would likely have had no knowledge of the music for *Softly*, so there is little possibility of direct influence. For his part, Arlen was impressed with Sondheim's work, and it is revealing that, despite being disabled by Parkinson's disease, Arlen attended *Pacific Overtures* several times during its initial Broadway run in 1976.[40] Perhaps he heard in Sondheim's score a realization of something he and Charnin had attempted ten years earlier.

**Example 10.7** Comparison of "Fish Go Higher Than Tigers," B section of chorus, and Stephen Sondheim, "Someone in a Tree" (*Pacific Overtures*)

"Fish Go Higher Than Tigers," B section

ti - ger can reach the sun that shines

Sondheim, "Someone in a Tree," from *Pacific Overtures*
(steady tempo throughout)

One number in *Softly*, "You're Never Fully Dressed Without a Smile," did have something of an afterlife when Charnin recycled its title and part of the lyrics for the 1977 musical *Annie*, with music by Charles Strouse. In *Softly*, the song appears as the finale of a minstrel show put on by Japanese orphans dressed up as Uncle Sam, playing banjoes and tambourines. They were to wear white kabuki makeup instead of traditional blackface. Several of the songs featured parodic Japlish, in which "Hello" is rendered as "Herro," and so forth. Today it is uncomfortable to contemplate this part of *Softly*; even in 1966 it would surely have been offensive to many.

These problems are less obvious in "You're Never Fully Dressed Without a Smile," which Arlen and Charnin fashioned as a double or counterpoint song. As we saw in Chapter 5, such songs, in which two melodies are sung separately then superimposed, were a specialty of Irving Berlin and Meredith Willson, but rare in Arlen's work, with the exception of "Love Held Lightly"/"A Game of Poker" from *Saratoga*. In *Softly* one of the two tunes was to be sung by the Interlocutor and End Man—two roles in a traditional minstrel show—and the second by Giro, one of the Japanese orphans. Giro's song, a narrative based on the story of Adam and Eve, sets up "You're Never Fully Dressed" as a kind of verse or introduction. On the demo, we hear Charnin sing "You're Never Fully Dressed," then Arlen singing Giro's "Long, Long

Ago," before the two are combined (▶ 10.4). This demo clearly shows the enthusiasm and skill Arlen and his young collaborator brought to the ill-fated project of *Softly*.

## Harold Arlen, Lyricist

Soon after the debacle of *Softly*, Arlen became involved—again with the tireless Saint Subber—in the off-Broadway revival of *House of Flowers* discussed in Chapter 8; it would run for only a month and a half in the winter 1968. Despite these discouraging experiences, Arlen could still be energized by a new project and by a younger collaborator. In the early 1970s both came his way when Robert Breen, the initiator of *Blues Opera* (discussed in Chapter 5), introduced Arlen to an unlikely partner, Leonard Melfi (1932–2001), an avant-garde playwright associated with the LaMaMa experimental theater in Greenwich Village. Melfi and Arlen decided to collaborate on a musical for television, a medium with which Arlen was by now familiar, but for which he had not specifically composed.[41] In one of his last creative endeavors Arlen would be his own lyricist.

The musical was *Clippety Clop and Clementine*, about a young interracial couple in New York City. At the beginning both are Columbia undergraduates; they go their separate ways then reunite ten years later, when he has become a cab driver and she a purveyor of organic food. According to Jablonski, Melfi's script is an unwieldy combination of social commentary and romance. Arlen wrote eight songs for the show, for which a full draft was completed by mid-1972. But since no television producer showed interest in *Clippety Clop*, Arlen stopped work, and it became another unrealized musical in his oeuvre.

One song from *Clippety Clop* that clearly manifests Arlen's late style is the ballad "I Had a Love Once," which Jablonski suggests was written in memory of Arlen's wife Anya, who had died in 1970.[42] As with some of the other late songs we have examined, "I Had a Love Once" sounds at once retrospective and experimental. Arlen begins with two measures of syncopated C major-seventh chords in the piano, widely spaced to emphasize octaves, fourths, and fifths, and thus similar to the harmonies and voicings in "It's a New World" and "Suddenly the Sunrise." These measures may at first seem introductory, but Arlen immediately weaves them into the song when the syncopated figure alternates with the first vocal phrases, sung without accompaniment (hence the indication "Tacet") (Example 10.8).

**Example 10.8** "I Had a Love Once," opening

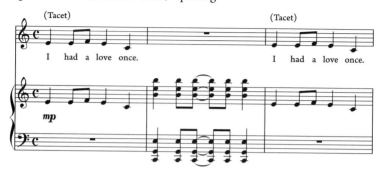

**Example 10.9** "I Had a Love Once," blue notes

Although some earlier Arlen songs (like "I Had Myself a True Love" and "I Never Has Seen Snow") integrate the piano structurally, the alternation of voice and piano in "I Had a Love Once" is unique. Arlen seems to be generating the elements of the song in real time, before our ears. Once they are in place after the initial six measures, the texture normalizes and the voice is always underpinned by the piano.

A short contrasting section ("One moment 'twas good") and the return of the opening vocal phrase yield the hint of a traditional form, A(14) B(4) A′(15), which is, however, obscured by the considerable melodic variation and reshuffling of material. In A, the phrase beginning "Roll on, you rivers" is a melodic antecedent to the consequent "Wind on, you valleys." In A′ the order is reversed when "touched by a silver stream," which reprises "Wind on, you valleys," precedes the return of "Roll on, you rivers." "I Had a Love Once" thus refracts standard form in a way typical of late style. Arlen also sprinkles blue notes throughout the song, but in a discreet way that doesn't call attention to them. The neighbor note D♯ of "*you* rivers" becomes the more distinctly "blue" E♭ in "*water*falls" and "*One moment*" (Example 10.9). These techniques reflect the meditative spirit of a late style.

After *Clippety Clop and Clementine*, as Parkinson's began to affect him from the mid-1970s, Arlen would distance himself from large projects and, with a few exceptions, from song composition more generally. His legacy would live on mainly in the many recordings of his songs by some of the greatest vocalists of the twentieth century, to be discussed in our final chapter.

# 11
## Singing the Arlen Songbook

As we saw in Chapter 9, Arlen's later performances of his own songs form a significant part of his legacy. His music also lives on prominently in the vast trove of interpretations by purveyors of the American Songbook, from Ethel Waters in the early 1930s to Audra McDonald in the present day.[1] Arlen had close personal and professional relationships with many vocalists. He wrote music for them to perform in clubs (Waters), in film (Judy Garland), on the stage (Lena Horne), or in concert (Barbra Streisand). Arlen songs were taken up by Frank Sinatra, Tony Bennett, and Ella Fitzgerald, as well as by crossover artists from the world of opera, including Eileen Farrell and Sylvia McNair. Some have made all-Arlen albums (see Table 11.1). Many have commented on how both gratifying and challenging his music is to perform.

Table 11.1 Harold Arlen Albums by Individual Vocalists (ordered by date of first release)

| ARTIST | ALBUM TITLE | COMPANY/FORMAT/ RELEASE DATE |
| --- | --- | --- |
| Lee Wiley | *Lee Wiley Sings Songs by Harold Arlen* | Schirmer 18 (4 78-rpm disks), 1943 Audiophile AP-10 (LP), 1986 Audiophile ACD-10 (CD), 1994 |
| Diahann Carroll | *Diahann Carroll Sings Harold Arlen Songs* | RCA Victor LPM-1467 (LP), 1957 RCA 0743214786925 (CD), 2003 |
| Tony Bennett | *Tony Bennett Sings a String of Harold Arlen* | Columbia CS-8359 (LP), 1960 Columbia/Sony 88883733042 [CD], 2013 |
| Ella Fitzgerald | *Ella Fitzgerald Sings the Harold Arlen Songbook* | Verve MG V-4046-2 (2 LP), 1961 Verve 314 589 108-2 (2 CD), 2001 |
| Pearl Bailey | *Pearl Bailey Sings the Songs She Loves . . . By Her Favorite Composer Harold Arlen* | Roulette SR25155 (LP), 1961 |
| Frank Sinatra | *Frank Sinatra Sings the Select Harold Arlen* | Capitol W-2123 (LP), 1964 |
| Eileen Farrell | *Eileen Farrell Sings Harold Arlen* | Reference RR-30 (LP, CD), 1989 |

*Harold Arlen and His Songs.* Walter Frisch, Oxford University Press. © Oxford University Press 2024.
DOI: 10.1093/oso/9780197503270.003.0011

**Table 11.1** Continued

| ARTIST | ALBUM TITLE | COMPANY/FORMAT/ RELEASE DATE |
|---|---|---|
| Rosemary Clooney | Rosemary Clooney Sings the Music of Harold Arlen | Concord CJ-210 (LP), 1983<br>Concord CCD-4210 (CD), 1992 |
| Richard Rodney Bennett | Harold Arlen's Songs | Audiophile AP-168 (LP), 1983<br>Audiophile ACD-168 (CD), 1993 |
| Maxine Sullivan | Great Songs from the Cotton Club by Arlen & Koehler | Stash ST-244 (LP), 1985<br>Harbinger HCD-2901 (CD), 2016 |
| Judy Kaye | Harold Arlen: "Americanegro Suite" | Premier PRCD-1004 (CD), 1990 |
| Julie Wilson | Julie Wilson Sings the Harold Arlen Songbook | DRG-5211 (CD), 1990 |
| Tom Wopat | Tom Wopat Sings Harold Arlen: Dissertation on the State of Bliss | Hyena TMF 9329 (CD), 2005 |
| Anne Burnell | Blues in the Night: Songs by Harold Arlen | Spectrum [CD], 2005 |
| Peggy Lee | Love Held Lightly: Rare Songs by Harold Arlen | Angel CDC 07777 7 54798 2 9 (CD), 1993<br>Harbinger HCD-2401 (CD), 2006 |
| KT Sullivan | Sing My Heart | DRG-91437 (CD), 1995 |
| Sylvia McNair | Come Rain or Come Shine: The Harold Arlen Songbook | Philips 446 818-2 (CD), 1996 |
| Maureen McGovern | Out of This World: McGovern Sings Arlen | Sterling S1011-2 (CD), 1996 |
| Weslia Whitfield | My Shining Hour: A Harold Arlen Songbook | HIghNote HCD-7012 (CD), 1997 |
| Del-Louise Moyer | Life's a Dance: The Songs of Harold Arlen | Alyssum, 2000 |
| Tonya Pinkins | My Shining Hour: Salute to Harold Arlen | Divinity to Infinity Unlimited, 2004 |
| Barbara Fasano | Written in the Stars | Human Child HCR-825, 2008 |
| Courtney Freed | Happy Little Bluebird: The Music of Harold Arlen | 2010 |
| Liza Pulman | Liza Pulman Sings Harold Arlen | First Night SCENECD 31 (CD), 2014 |
| Isabella Lundgren | Isabella Sings the Treasures of Harold Arlen | Spice of Life SV-0034 (CD), 2015 |
| Judy Garland | Judy Garland Sings Harold Arlen | JPS-4246 (2 CD), 2015 |
| Sylvia McNair | You Are Tomorrow: Rare Songs by Harold Arlen and Martin Charnin | Harbinger HCD-3902, 2023 |

It would be impossible in this space to explore the many singers, let alone the big bands, small ensembles, or solo pianists, who have recorded Arlen's music.[2] I will focus on a selection of distinguished tracks. Great recordings are often considered timeless, but public taste and singing styles, even those of an individual artist, change over time. Listening with a historical perspective can heighten our awareness not only of different traditions of performance, but also of the mutable nature of the songs themselves. This "replicative" dimension, as discussed in Chapter 1, provides a healthy challenge to any "realist" status of a song as a stable entity. (Complete versions of almost all the recordings discussed in this chapter are available on streaming platforms like YouTube, Spotify, Amazon Music, and Apple Music.)

## Ethel Waters: "Stormy Weather" (1933)

Ethel Waters's relationship with Arlen extended over many decades (see Figure 11.1). She recorded "Stormy Weather" for Brunswick (6564) on May 3, 1933, a month after giving the premiere at the Cotton Club. Her version contrasts strongly with the two earlier ones discussed in Chapter 3, by Frances Langford and by Arlen himself (both made in February 1933). Langford's, with Tommy Dorsey, emphasized the blues elements, even preceding the chorus with a scatted twelve-bar blues. Arlen's, with Leo Reisman, is "sweet" rather than "hot," maintaining a steady tempo and a foxtrot feel, articulating each quarter note with a bass note followed by a chord. Waters can be said to strike a middle ground between these extremes. Her "Stormy Weather" is restrained in comparison with later blues-saturated recordings of the song by Etta James, Sara Vaughan, and Ella Fitzgerald. In this respect Waters is similar to the other singer most identified with "Stormy Weather," Lena Horne.

Randall Cherry has described Waters's approach to music and lyrics as a "hybrid style," characterized by her ability to "put blues, jazz, and Tin Pan Alley sensibilities in masterful equipoise." As Cherry observes, this balance worked against her. Waters's sound "could not be categorized, to the dismay of specialty-conscious music critics and, consequently, to the detriment of Waters's own musical reputation."[3] She has been omitted from (or dismissed in) some accounts of blues and jazz vocalists.[4] But James Weldon Johnson captured her style accurately and sympathetically when he wrote in 1930:

> Miss Waters gets her audiences, and she does get them completely, through an innate poise that she possesses; through the quiet and subtlety of her

**Figure 11.1** Ethel Waters and Harold Arlen at Sardi's Restaurant, New York, 1953 (Stephen Taksler Collection, Popular Music and Culture Collection, Special Collections and Archives, Georgia State University Library)

personality. She never "works hard" on the stage. Her bodily movements, when she makes them, are almost languorous. Indeed, she is at her best when she is standing perfectly still, singing quietly. Her singing corresponds to her bodily movements; she never over-exerts her voice; she always creates a sense of reserved power that compels the listener.[5]

This description conforms with what we can imagine Waters's performance of "Stormy Weather" to have been like on the stage of the Cotton Club in 1933, and it certainly fits her recording of the song.

"Stormy Weather" was deeply meaningful for Waters—the "perfect expression" of her mood at a difficult time in her personal life. Yet she maintains an elegant decorum throughout, balancing the demands of formal structure and emotional expression, making clear the distinctions between the A sections, the bridge, and the interlude. Even though Arlen notates the song in cut time (¢), Waters gives it a distinct feel of four beats to a measure, appropriate to the "slow lament" called for by composer. Over a steady pulse from the band, she sings the first two A segments at ♩ = 80. For the bridge ("When he went away") she speeds up quite abruptly to ♩ = 104 (▶ 11.1), before slowing down with equal suddenness to something close to the original tempo at the last line ("walk in the sun once more"). With these shifts in tempo Waters seems to highlight the difference between the lament of A and the Broadway spiritual style of the bridge.

In "Stormy Weather," as in most of her recordings, Waters's enunciation is precise and controlled, with rounded "r"s in "stormy," "weather," and "bare." Waters's pitch is equally well focused, but also nuanced; she colors longer notes with a small but distinct vibrato (in the first phrase, on "wh*y*," "sk*y*," "m*y*," and "weath*er*"). Her improvisatory flourishes like "All I do is pray the Lord above will let me" in the bridge stand out all the more against the background of what Johnson called "innate poise."

Waters is the first singer—and apparently the only one before Lena Horne in 1942—to record the powerful twelve-measure interlude of "Stormy Weather" ("I walk around, heavy hearted and sad"), which does not appear in the original sheet music as published by Mills and may have been written specifically for her Cotton Club performances. Even here, in the most overtly expressive part of the song, Waters maintains her restrained approach. Only in the final phrase of the song, "keeps raining all the time," does she depart significantly from the score, with a riff starting from a tonic note at the high octave (here C), dipping below the low octave to the flatted sixth, then moving up to the flatted third above the tonic. Waters's superb sense of balance between structure and emotion has told her that this is the moment, at the very end of the song, that requires her most elaborate melodic flourish.

## Judy Garland: "Over the Rainbow" (1938, 1955) and "The Man That Got Away" (1954)

About midway through her legendary Carnegie Hall concert on April 23, 1961, after delivering a rousing version of "Come Rain or Come Shine," Judy

Garland called out, "Harold Arlen, stand up," asking the audience to recognize the composer.[6] As Arlen rose, the crowd burst into loud, extended applause, and after the noise died down, Garland commented, "We do practically all of his music all the way through the show. There is no better music."[7] Garland and Arlen had one of the most enduring associations in the history of American popular song. She was the ideal singer for much of his music, whether a ballad like "Over the Rainbow," a torch song like "The Man That Got Away"—both written expressly for her—or a rousing Broadway spiritual like "Get Happy."

"Over the Rainbow" was Garland's signature song, which she performed hundreds of times: on film, on disk, on the radio, on television, and in concert.[8] In October 1938 she recorded "Over the Rainbow" in the MGM studio for the film's soundtrack. She recorded it again for a Decca commercial release in July 1939, just before the film's release. Garland made two later studio versions, both for Capitol, in 1955 and 1960. What began in 1938 as an expression of Dorothy Gale's wistful optimism in *The Wizard of Oz* would evolve over two decades into a song of both pain and defiance, conveying the stresses of Garland's adult life, which was marked by substance abuse, depression, failed marriages, and financial difficulties.

On the soundtrack recording we hear Garland's hallmark blend of purity and richness (▶ 11.2). Although she stays close to Arlen's notated pitches, except for the short ornament on "blue" of "Skies are blue" (moving up from the main note and then back down), Garland phrases his melody with fluidity and expression. The Decca recording of "Over the Rainbow" reflects the changed context: Garland was now singing as a professional vocalist, not in the role of a Kansas farm girl. Victor Young's silky smooth orchestral backdrop differs considerably from the translucent one created by MGM's Murray Cutter for the soundtrack.

In 1955 Garland divides the opening phrase "Somewhere over the rainbow / Way up high" into three distinct units. She creates a short glottal stop or sob after "Somewhere," as if, after expressing the desire to be elsewhere, she then imagines the actual destination, over the rainbow. Garland adds another reflective pause before making her goal still more precise geographically (or meteorologically), with "way up high" (▶ 11.3). The later Garland is still clearly capable of longer phrases when she wants them. In a stunning effect, Garland in 1955 sings "There's a land that I heard of once" on a single breath, eliding the "once" that would normally be part of the next phrase. As Dorothy in the film, the singer quite naturally links the "once" to what follows, "in a lullaby," just as it appears in Harburg's lyric and in the metrical structure of Arlen's melody. She is recalling an event that is closer in time to her singing. On the 1955 recording, Garland is in a different temporal and emotional space. It is as if she knows that she heard of this land "once," at some moment in the past, but she cannot at first recall exactly where or when. Then, in that pause, she remembers: "in a lullaby."

Garland's powerful performance of "The Man That Got Away" in *A Star Is Born*, recorded on the Warner sound stage in September 1953, would become as iconic as her "Over the Rainbow." During the short instrumental introduction she sings a wordless, seemingly casual vocalise, almost as if preparing us for a mellow song. The first four measures of the A section continue this restrained idiom. Garland constantly nuances Arlen's insistent, repetitive rhythmic pattern. She adjusts the lengths of the two words "night is" by elongating the first and abbreviating the second.

As she hits the high note on the "-way" of "away," Garland begins a crescendo and opens up into more of a belter voice, which is sustained until the end of the A section. (See the more detailed analysis of "The Man That Got Away" in Chapter 7.) The same happens in A′. Garland interprets with a special intensity what is perhaps the most unusual large-scale linear feature of the song: the three highest melodic notes, rising by half step, coincide with the article "the" ("*The* writing's on the wall," "*The* dreams you dream'd") and the conjunction "for" ("*For* you've been through the mill"), and each falls on the weak fourth beat of the measure. There is thus a disjunction—intended, of course, by Arlen and Ira Gershwin—between the climactic trajectory of pitches and the metrical-syntactical design of the phrases. Rather than rushing through these quarter notes, Garland holds them out well beyond their notated value, to devastating effect.

Garland scrupulously but compellingly observes the continuity Arlen creates in the transition from the bridge back to A″. To avoid dissipating the emotional and musical intensity of the bridge, Arlen asks the singer to drop a tenth from "[gone] to," to "The," which begins A″. Garland meets the challenge vocally, taking a breath only after "rougher" (▶ 11.4).

## Lena Horne: "Cocoanut Sweet" (1957)

Lena Horne joined the chorus of the Cotton Club at age sixteen in 1933, a few months after Ethel Waters premiered "Stormy Weather" there. Eight years later, Horne would virtually take ownership of the song, recording it in 1941 for Victor and then performing it on screen in a sequence from the 1943 film musical *Stormy Weather*.[9] As we saw in Chapter 4, Horne starred in the 1957 musical *Jamaica*, whose score was essentially written around her talents by Arlen and Harburg.

The gentle ballad "Cocoanut Sweet," as recorded for the original cast album, captures many of Horne's special qualities as a singer of Arlen. The short one- and two-measure units that comprise the A section of "Cocoanut Sweet" present a challenge to any singer, as does the profusion of triplet and dotted rhythms. (See the analysis of the song in Chapter 4.) Horne achieves continuity, creating full four-measure phrases, both by scrupulously respecting the longer note values on "sweet," "new," and "you," and then by interpreting freely the triplets Arlen has notated on "Jasmine an' cherry an' juniper berry" and in analogous measures (⏵ 11.5). Horne creates contrast in the B section ("Catch me the smile") by leaning more directly into the dotted rhythms. For the C section Horne unleashes greater volume and pitch inflection to convey the bluesier feel imparted by the raised second degree ("wind," "hurricane"). She offers a splendid realization of the final A of "Cocoanut Sweet," which is less a return to than a transfiguration of the opening. She begins softly, increases in intensity at "Everything dear," pulls back briefly, vulnerably, on "nearness of you," and builds again for the climactic phrase, "How it all comes true," before gently winding down the song from "wherever we meet" to the end. (See Chapter 7 for a discussion of Horne's 1963 Carnegie Hall rehearsal with Arlen of "It's a New World.")

### Frank Sinatra: "I've Got the World on a String" (1953), "Last Night When We Were Young" (1954), and "One for My Baby (And One More for the Road)" (1958)

Frank Sinatra focused his talents on relatively few of Arlen's songs. Among Sinatra's eighty-three recording sessions of Arlen, over half involved just three numbers, "Come Rain or Come Shine" (16), "I've Got the World on a String" (14), and "One for My Baby (And One More for the Road)" (13).[10] The first two reflect Sinatra's persona as the confident swinger-lover. The third captures the more vulnerable image cultivated later in his career, as the solitary drinker, smoking a cigarette and nursing his sorrows at a bar. Friedwald has called "One for My Baby" "the perfect Sinatra saloon song."[11]

"I've Got the World on a String" was one number that helped relaunch Sinatra's career after a slump in the late 1940s and early 1950s. This topic comes up in Dave Garroway's radio interview with Arlen in February 1955, discussed earlier in this book.[12] Garroway asks Arlen which contemporary male vocalists he would pick to perform his songs. (Notably he does not ask about female vocalists, perhaps taking for granted which ones Arlen would name.) Arlen singles out Sinatra, while also nodding to Perry Como, Bing Crosby, and Tony Bennett. "Even when there were many who gave him up, I always thought he was great," Arlen remarks about Sinatra, noting that "I've Got the World on a String" "was one [song] that brought him back." "Thank goodness," remarks Garroway, before putting Sinatra's version on the air.

But it was less this particular song than Sinatra's collaboration with the arranger Nelson Riddle that helped rescue his career.[13] "I've Got the World on a String" was recorded on April 30, 1953, in Sinatra's first Capitol session with Riddle, inaugurating a series of legendary LP albums made across the decade. Here Riddle goes for a brassy big band sound, with a prominent percussion backdrop.[14] After an introductory fanfare, the band retreats as Sinatra delivers the opening phrase of the chorus in an almost conversational manner. He phrases the melodic line and shapes the dynamics to chart a descent and diminuendo to a reflective pause on "around my finger." A sudden burst from Riddle's group jolts the singer into asserting the message of the song's first A section, "What a world, what a life, I'm in love." (The chorus of "I've Got the World on a String" has a standard thirty-two measure AABA form.) Sinatra renders the second A more literally, and unlike at the opening, the band is now a constant interlocutor. After one full chorus, Sinatra repeats the bridge ("Life's a beautiful thing") and A'. This time he extends and varies the last line, now singing near the top of his range: "What world, and this is the life; hey now, I'm in love."

The following year, on March 1, 1954, Sinatra and Riddle teamed up for a session that produced "Last Night When We Were Young," which would appear in 1955 on *In the Wee Small Hours*, considered one of Sinatra's earliest "concept" albums. Sinatra appears to have recorded the song five years earlier, in 1949, for a scene cut from the film *Take Me Out to the Ball Game*.[15] Within a standard AABA' structure, Arlen unfolds a complex melodic and harmonic language that is challenging for any singer, even for one with Sinatra's technique and expressive range.

In Sinatra's rendition of "Last Night When We Were Young" the phrases flow in a broad legato, yet in a style that almost seems informal, as though he is forming thoughts as he sings. Individual words or notes (especially "ages"), are sustained for emphasis, always focused, carefully shaded, and in tune. Sinatra's diction is also impeccable: he articulates with almost no elision the cluster of consonants that link "last" to "night." Sinatra rises to the biggest climax of the song on a powerful "clung," which he holds for five full seconds. Riddle's arrangement follows Sinatra through the song's journey, providing a cushion of lush strings and solo woodwinds, but bringing in the brass for the high points, including an appropriately dissonant clash on "clung" (▶ 11.6).

On June 24, 1958, Sinatra went into Capitol's Hollywood studio with his regular pianist Bill Miller to make a test track for "One for My Baby (And One More for the Road)." A day later they were joined by Riddle and his orchestra for the recording, to be released later that year as the last number on the album *Frank Sinatra Sings for Only the Lonely*. Miller abandons Arlen's rocking bass pattern (see Example 5.5) but keeps the bluesy feel with a gentle, insistent honky-tonk accompaniment to a freely inventive right hand. Sinatra matches Miller's mood and technique with fluid but meticulous phrasing. Together they convey many different possible shades of Arlen's one-word description at the head of the song: "Lazily."

Riddle calibrates his chart to trace the song's narrative structure. He brings in the orchestra—a backdrop of strings—under the *third* phrase of the first A ("We're drinking, my friend"), then under the *second* phrase in A′ ("I'm feelin' so bad"), and finally under the *first* phrase in A″ ("Well, that's how it goes"). For that final A″, Miller is initially replaced by alto saxophonist Gus Bivona interjecting mellow thematic gestures. For the last phrase of the song ("Make it one for my baby"), Riddle's strings and Bivona's sax melt away. The singer's story, which he never really told but only said he wanted to tell, is over. We are left where we began, with Sinatra and his lone companion, the pianist Miller. Sinatra leaves Arlen and Mercer's last phrase, "the long, long road," incomplete. His mind still absorbed by the story he could not manage to tell, Sinatra intones "the long," "it's so long," "the long," "very long." His voice fades away as Miller winds down the song with a modest cadence (▶ 11.7). Friedwald has characterized this recording of "One for My Baby" as "the finest piece of acting Sinatra has ever turned in."[16] It is hard to imagine a version of "One for My Baby" that better captures the essence of Arlen and Mercer's great song.

## Ella Fitzgerald: "My Shining Hour" and "Hooray for Love" (1961)

Released in 1961, the two-LP set *Ella Fitzgerald Sings the Harold Arlen Songbook* was the sixth of the vocalist's eight composer-focused songbook albums for Verve. Arlen was pleased at the prospect of these recordings, not only because he admired Fitzgerald but also because he anticipated the involvement of Nelson Riddle, who had done elegant charts for Arlen songs (as we have seen with the Sinatra tracks) and had served as arranger for the prior Fitzgerald songbook album, devoted to Gershwin. But Verve producer Norman Granz had other ideas. Like many inside and outside the music business, he viewed Arlen primarily as a jazz and blues composer. For the Fitzgerald album Granz abandoned Riddle to bring on the big-band leader Billy May. He wrote to Jablonski in October 1959, "We intend to use Billy May because I feel these albums will probably be more in the 'blues' vein in keeping with Arlen's approach to the songs."[17] Looking back on the Fitzgerald sessions after many years, May expressed some regret about his involvement. "Working with Ella was a ball," he said. "The only problem I had was with Norman Granz. He wanted everything to be a jazz performance. We didn't see eye to eye on many things."[18] Indeed, many of the tracks on *Ella Fitzgerald Sings the Harold Arlen Songbook* are realized as full-fledged jazz numbers: the band plays a big role, and individual members take extended solos in between Fitzgerald's phrases.

Granz's enthusiasm for a jazz approach to Arlen was fully shared by Benny Green, the British music critic who in his liner notes for the original album wrote, "For an entirely satisfactory treatment of Arlen's music, you have to use jazz musicians. I am so completely convinced about this, that even if Harold Arlen himself were to scoff at the idea, I would beg his pardon and start trying to convert him."[19] Arlen in fact did scoff, expressing disappointment when he learned about May's involvement.[20] He was however quite politic in his brief comments about Fitzgerald on individual numbers cited by Jablonski in the liner notes: "She is the only vocalist who can sing the most complicated phrases in the most effortless way"; "Hooray for Ella!"; "Ella proves she can sing a song with delightful simplicity and treat the lyricists with great—and due—respect"; "Let the young ones listen, Ella is rare."[21] Reading between the lines of these remarks, we can sense that for all his praise, Arlen felt less connection to Fitzgerald's style than to that of other singers with whom he had worked closely, including Horne, Garland, and Sinatra.

Even if she does not often display the interpretive depth that many Arlen songs demand, Fitzgerald recorded some superb tracks. Every listener will have favorites among the twenty-six on the Fitzgerald-Arlen album (plus two alternative takes included on the CD reissue). Green's liner note has a lovingly detailed and insightful analysis of her "It Was Written in the Stars." He suggests—and it is hard to improve upon his commentary—that in certain "aspiring" phrases ("it shall be done," "you are the one," "I'll never be free"), Fitzgerald "takes the last note as an instrumentalist would take it, not hitting it flush in the face but approaching it with due consideration for the sentiment the lyric is trying to express as well as the actual sound of the words."

Much the same could be said of the ballad "My Shining Hour," where Fitzgerald shapes her phrases to capture both the sound and meaning of Mercer's words. May tones down his band, foregrounding the strings and giving them counterpoints that complement her legato lines. On this track, as on many on the album, Fitzgerald sings the verse, one of Arlen's and Mercer's finest, which is integral to the broader shape of song (▶ 11.8). As we saw in Chapter 5, the chorus's thirty-two measures unfold with only hints of a standard form. Fitzgerald communicates both the fluidity and the conventional aspects of the structure. In the bridge-like section ("Like the lights of home before me"), she thins her tone on "lights of home" before returning to a fuller sound for the last eight measures.

Of the up-tempo numbers on the album, "Hooray for Love" stands out, not least for Fitzgerald's liquid phrasing that imparts continuity and even logic to a lyric in which each line of the chorus ends with "for love." Fitzgerald and May also imaginatively reconfigure the eight-measure quasi-interlude ("It's the wonder of the world"). In the original song it follows the last A of AABA, then leads to a repetition of the entire chorus. Fitzgerald and May move the interlude to the front of the song, in effect creating two verses. She performs the first two phrases a cappella, each followed by an echo from May's band; they join forces for the last one ("It gets you high"). Then Fitzgerald sings the "real" verse and the full chorus. After May's band plays an almost-complete chorus, Fitzgerald sings the interlude its proper place.

## Eileen Farrell: "I Gotta Right to Sing the Blues" (1960) and "Out of This World" (1962)

Eileen Farrell was one of the first and finest of the crossover artists who moved between the worlds of opera and popular song. Her impeccable technique and full tone—she was a renowned Wagnerian soprano—enhance a genuine feeling for the lyrics of the American Songbook. Farrell's Arlen album, made later in her career (see Table 11.1), was the culmination of a long relationship with his music, dating back to the early 1940s. "I was always crazy about Harold Arlen," she wrote in her autobiography. "Harold's songs are completely singable, and always feel just right for my voice."[22]

The title of Farrell's first pop album, *I Gotta Right to Sing the Blues*, made with arranger Luther Henderson and released by Columbia Records in 1960 (CD 1465, CS 8256), derives from an Arlen song on the disk. Farrell begins it with a vocalise on a high F, swooping down two octaves in a blues-tinged arpeggio (⏵ 11.9). She sings one and a half choruses of the song, which has an AA' form. She treats the tune of the final half chorus freely and ends the track by returning the same F as the opening, now held for eleven seconds. The moment, at once surprising and persuasive, reveals Farrell's gifts in this repertory: only a trained soprano could hit and sustain that note while also transmuting it into a kind of blues wail.

Two years later Farrell collaborated with Percy Faith on a Columbia album *This Fling Called Love* (CL 1739, CS 8539; 1962). Faith is best known for plush orchestral arrangements designed for "easy listening." But the intense lyricism that Farrell brings to the Arlen-Mercer aria-like tapeworm "Out of This World" transcends any sentimentality. The song's melodic lines do indeed seem "just right" for her voice, which in the first segment of the song floats and soars above the static ostinato of fluttering string tremolos in Faith's orchestra.

### Barbra Streisand, "A Sleepin' Bee" (1961, 1962, 1963) and "House of Flowers" (1965)

By her own admission Barbra Streisand "fell in love with" Arlen's music early on. As noted in Chapter 8, she was especially fond of "A Sleepin' Bee" from *House of Flowers*, which "became my favorite song."[23] Streisand included Arlen songs on her earliest demo or audition disks in spring 1962. Of the twenty-two songs Streisand recorded live at the Bon Soir night club in New York in November 1962, five are by Arlen, the most by any composer.[24] Arlen numbers appear on each of her first four LP albums for Columbia Records.[25] Streisand joined the composer on his 1966 Columbia release *Harold Arlen Sings (With Friend)* (Figure 11.2). The admiration was mutual. The liner note of Streisand's first album, *The Barbra Streisand Album* (1963), consists solely of an encomium by Arlen, who writes in part, "Did you ever hear Helen Morgan sing? . . . Have you heard our top vocalists 'belt,' 'whisper,' or sing with that steady and urgent beat behind them? . . . I advise you to watch Barbra Streisand's career. This young lady (a mere twenty) has a stunning future. Keep listening, keep watching. And please remember, I told you so. . . ."[26]

Streisand performed "A Sleepin' Bee" for her television debut on *The Tonight Show* on April 5, 1961, a few weeks short of her nineteenth birthday. She sang it at the Bon Soir on November 6, 1962, and placed it as the final number on *The Barbra Streisand Album*, recorded in January 1963. In these versions of "A Sleepin' Bee" from her earlier years, Streisand's tone is focused, her pitch and diction precise, her phrasing direct but fluid. She traverses a wide range of expression while always remaining in control of her powerful voice. One can hear why Streisand quickly became a sensation, why she felt Arlen's music was so well-suited to her voice, and why the composer was so impressed.

Figure 11.2  Barbra Streisand and Harold Arlen in a light moment at the recording session for the Columbia album *Harold Sings Arlen (with Friend)*, 1965 (© Don Hunstein/Sony Music, Inc.; Rita Arlen Collection, Music Division, Library of Congress, Washington, D.C.)

Streisand sings "A Sleepin' Bee" in F major, a minor third below the published key of A♭. In these early recordings she performs one complete chorus and repeats the A' section ("Sleep on, bee, don't waken"), where she takes more liberties with the tune and builds to a climax. Arlen's melody begins by floating up a tenth across one and a half measures, an arc that allows Streisand to display the extraordinary colors of her voice, starting on a low A with a more covered tone near the bottom of her range, then opening up as she approaches the high C on "-in" of "sleepin." On the *Tonight Show* version she caresses the high C, sustaining it briefly beyond the written value. The second phrase begins at the same low A and now rises a step higher, to D, to which Streisand imparts a still more radiant glow (▶ 11.10). She begins the repeat of A' in a faster, jazz-inflected manner, before returning to a more lyrical style for the final phrases. Here she begins "when my one true love I has found" on a sustained D, an octave higher than notated, then arpeggiates downward on "my." For the "love" on "my own true *love*" Streisand leaps to a high F, which she hits cleanly and holds before descending for the last cadence.

Streisand's Bon Soir rendition of "A Sleepin' Bee" is more restrained and conversational than the *Tonight Show* version, as we might expect from a nightclub performance (even one being recorded for distribution, which was Columbia's original intention). Parts of the chorus are underlaid with an impressionistic, ostinato piano accompaniment by Peter Daniels. Streisand made her first studio recording of "A Sleepin' Bee" for *The Barbra Streisand Album* in January 1963. Almost all Streisand's Arlen tracks at this time were arranged by the composer's own preferred collaborator Peter Matz. Not surprisingly, many features are similar to her interpretation on *The Tonight Show* and at the Bon Soir. One important difference is Matz's imaginative arrangement, which at once cradles Streisand's voice and allows her greater freedom of phrasing.

Streisand recorded her two tracks for *Harold Arlen Sings (With Friend)* in November 1965. One was a lively duet with Arlen, "Ding-Dong! The Witch is Dead" from *The Wizard of Oz*, the other a solo performance of the ballad "House of Flowers," from the show of that name. On the liner notes for the LP, Arlen writes that "Barbra's version of 'House of Flowers' is the most moving, exciting rendition imaginable—and I'm delighted." Again, the arranger is Matz, who provides an elegant backdrop for Streisand. For the A sections of the song, Matz lays down a bed of soft strings that keep harmonic changes to a minimum, while solo woodwinds complement Streisand's flexible and at times declamatory phrases, often with variations on the distinctive accompanimental figure Arlen devised for this song (as discussed in Chapter 8). For the jazzier B section ("I never had money"), Matz brings in more brass, and Streisand increases in volume and intensity, before lowering the temperature again for the abbreviated and much altered final A.

### Sylvia McNair, "It Was Written in the Stars" (1996)

Renowned for her lucid performances of Baroque and Classical repertory in the 1980s and 90s, Sylvia McNair is also one of the premier crossover artists to work on the American Songbook. In 1994 she teamed up with pianist André Previn to make a Jerome Kern album for Philips. Then, not surprisingly, given Previn's deep admiration for Arlen, the pair turned to that composer with the fine 1996 disk *Come Rain or Come Shine: The Harold Arlen Songbook*. More recently (2022–2023) McNair recorded an album of genuine Arlen rarities written with Martin Charnin in the 1960s, some of which we examined in Chapter 10.

McNair's focused tone and precise diction, matched in this repertory perhaps only by Ella Fitzgerald, are put in the service of nuanced phrasing that can be at once, or alternately, lyrical and conversational. McNair always has in mind the larger, often complex architecture of an Arlen song. Previn, whose accompaniments and solos are as inventive as in his solo "Over the Rainbow" examined in Chapter 2, found in McNair the ideal partner for Arlen's songs. "Their harmonic and melodic complications evidently spoke to her innate musicianship," he writes in the liner notes. "No amount of unprepared key changes or harmonic twists can throw her." Previn adds, "The mostly bittersweet lyrics . . . engaged her love of text and her recognition of that peculiarly American poetic use of the vernacular."[27]

There is perhaps no more exquisite example of McNair's treatment of the "bittersweet" or her command of a song's design than in "It Was Written in the Stars." We recall from Chapter 6 how this song is a relatively compact tapeworm that builds to several successive melodic highpoints across the A, B, and C sections. McNair approaches these moments as part of a broader trajectory: "Done"–"One"–"Here." After a full-voiced phrasing of the C section's opening phrase "Here as in a daydream," perhaps the true climax of the song ("Here" is the highest melodic note), McNair pulls back slightly for "By my side you stand," as if acknowledging the fragility of the daydream. She then fashions a subsidiary climax at "Here with my tomorrows" (▶ 11.11). The D section, a kind of coda to the song, culminates in the last phrase, "What the stars foretold shall be." Rather than treat this moment as a sustained climax, like some singers (Tony Bennett, for example), McNair floats the phrase wistfully, capturing the essence of the song—that whatever happens ("joy" or "woe") is "written in the stars" and ultimately beyond our control. This sense of vulnerability, aligned with a deep musicality, makes McNair a superb interpreter of Arlen's songs.

### Audra McDonald, "I Had Myself a True Love" (2000) and "Ain' It de Truth" (2002)

In reviewing Audra McDonald's Carnegie Hall concert debut in November 2002, the *New York Times* critic Stephen Holden noted five Arlen songs on the program and wrote, "Like Lena Horne, Judy Garland and Barbra Streisand before her, Ms. McDonald has settled on Harold Arlen's songbook as the musical touchstone for her stylistic diplomacy."[28] From early in her career McDonald, a Juilliard-trained soprano, cast her lot primarily with American popular song, both classic and contemporary. We thus have less the sense of a crossover artist than with Farrell. McDonald brings her formidable technique to bear on some of Arlen's most demanding and—for a singer—rewarding numbers, especially those created for Black vocalists in *Cabin in the Sky*, *St. Louis Woman*, and *House of Flowers*. McDonald's second album, *How Glory Goes* (Nonesuch 79580; 2000), contains five Arlen numbers (not all overlapping with those sung on the 2002 concert). Her next album, *Happy Songs* (Nonesuch 79645; 2002), has four, with two of them placed strategically as the first and last tracks. In each album, the songs by Arlen outnumber those by any other composer. As Friedwald remarks, "One could easily gather the nine Arlen songs from *Glory* and *Happy* into a very delightful nine-song minialbum."[29] Such an album would indeed reveal Arlen's "touchstone" role in McDonald's repertory.

McDonald's recording of Arlen's tapeworm lament "I Had Myself a True Love" captures better than any other of which I am aware the song's narrative arc and complex form. Like any good singer approaching this song, McDonald begins "I Had Myself a True Love" plaintively and ends it in despair. But she does much more: without ever losing sight (or sound) of that larger trajectory, McDonald conveys along the way many different gradations of sadness, hope, resignation, and anger. In the A section, "The first thing in the mornin'" and "Some part of the evenin'" are parallel phrases. But McDonald holds out "some" longer than "first," as if she is momentarily more optimistic about finding "a way to be with him." Some ten measures later, in A′, she increases in volume, tempo, and frustration when singing about "those backyard whispers" of her lover's unfaithfulness. McDonald plots a similar shift in the interlude-like D section, caressing Mercer's images of tranquil domesticity (floor swept, clothes hung, pot on the stove), then excoriating her man for hanging out "with that gal in that damn ol' saloon." These rapidly changing emotions set up the climactic final A, where (as discussed in Chapter 5) the singer abandons the original tune, which is now carried by the accompaniment, and breaks into a cry of anguished denial, "No!"

McDonald's arranger Larry Hochman stays close to, but also reimagines, many of the details of Arlen's original sheet music of "I Had Myself a True Love," which already has so much richness built in. For the A sections he retains Arlen's gently rocking bass arpeggio and the elegant thematic riffs that fill out the vocal phrases. At the opening of D, Hochman transmutes the repeated, chromatically shifting left-hand chords, something of an Arlen fingerprint (and occasionally a mannerism), into soft string harmonies sustained underneath a slow octave tremolo in the right-hand of the piano. He saves the throbbing chords for the gal-in-the-saloon highpoint.

"Ain' It de Truth?" was originally written by Arlen and Harburg for Lena Horne to sing in the 1943 film *Cabin in the Sky*. The scene was cut, and they later repurposed the song for Horne in the stage musical *Jamaica*. Although few other artists have picked up "Ain' It de Truth?," McDonald makes it the first track on *Happy Songs*. McDonald, arranger Bruce Coughlin, and conductor Ted Sperling trade the sultry swing of Horne's version for an approach that is more "like a spiritual," as indicated by the songwriters, but at the same time more folksy than fervent (Example 11.1). Sperling and McDonald establish and maintain a steady beat, rarely exaggerating the syncopated rhythms, which are allowed to speak for themselves.

McDonald sings both choruses of "Ain' It de Truth?," each with its own set of lyrics. By the year 2002, when this album was released, modulation up by half step during a song might have seemed a cliché to be avoided. But McDonald and her team use it here to good effect. She sings the first chorus in the key of D♭. The second chorus begins in the same key, then at the second A shifts up to D major (▶ 11.12). The final A in this second chorus (the song has a conventional AABA form) modulates up another half step to E♭. As we

**Example 11.1** "Ain' It de Truth?"

saw in Chapter 3, in the Black church "getting happy" meant receiving the Lord's spirit. The title of McDonald's album certainly carries that connotation of "happy," as well as the more conventional one. The upward tonal shifts in "Ain' It de Truth?" make McDonald's performance a happy song in both senses: a spiritual that is cheekily irreverent.

* * *

It seems appropriate to conclude *Harold Arlen and His Songs* with McDonald's version of "Ain' It de Truth?," which raises some of the issues touched on in this book. One reason singers, Black and white, have avoided this song is surely concern over perpetuating a stereotype. "Ain't It de Truth?" falls squarely into the tradition of the Broadway spiritual as discussed in Chapter 3. Like other lyricists who worked with Arlen, Harburg evokes Black dialect in a way that might offend some listeners today. Yet McDonald and her collaborators finesse some of the potential awkwardness. She sings "the" and "that" instead of Harburg's "de" and "dat," while still managing to sound colloquial. The tempo chosen by McDonald and Sperling, a shade slower than we might expect for a spiritual, also softens any potential stereotype, as does their understated rendering of the syncopations that are a feature of the song.

McDonald's recording and her long, passionate investment with the music of Harold Arlen show us how his songs can be compelling well into the twenty-first century. That is the value of the "replicative" dimension of the American Songbook. As a music historian, I believe that no song, nor any work of music, can be fully understood outside of its original contexts. In this book I have sought to take account of some of those contexts for Arlen's songs, principally the collaborations that produced them, the shows or films in which they first appeared, and the performers (including Arlen) who sang them. Yet Arlen's music continues to find new contexts in later eras—new audiences, new performers, and, importantly, newer historical and critical approaches to appreciation. As an author writing about Arlen and his works in the third decade of the twenty-first century, I am far removed from a composer's career that began almost exactly a century ago. As such, I see myself as part of a new context for Arlen's music. I hope readers will listen to, study, and appreciate this rich repertory and thus create more contexts for perpetuating and transforming his legacy.

# Notes

## Chapter 1

1. André Previn was interviewed for the television show "The Songs of Harold Arlen," part of the CBS television series *The Twentieth Century* with Walter Cronkite, broadcast February 9, 1964 (the interview took place in 1963). This broadcast is not readily available, but the Yip Harburg Foundation has a complete transcription. I am grateful to Nick Markovich, the executive director, for sharing this with me.
2. Abel Green, "*Variety* All-Time Pop Standards," *Weekly Variety*, January 10, 1962, 185, https://varietyultimate.com/archive/issue/WV-01-10-1962-1. This list was transcribed and annotated by Charles Hamm in *Yesterdays: Popular Song in America* (New York: Norton, 1979), 489–492.
3. "New Song List Puts 'Rainbow' Way Up High," *CNN Entertainment*, March 7, 2001, http://www.cnn.com/2001/SHOWBIZ/Music/03/07/365.songs/. "AFI's 100 Years . . . 100 Songs: Greatest American Movie Music," http://www.afi.com/100Years/songs.aspx.
4. "The Songs of Harold Arlen."
5. Edward Jablonski, *Harold Arlen: Happy with the Blues* (New York: Da Capo Press, 1986 [orig. ed. 1961]), 121.
6. Jablonski, *Happy with the Blues*, 218.
7. "The Songs of Harold Arlen."
8. Alec Wilder, *American Popular Song: The Great Innovators, 1900–1950*, 3rd ed. (New York: Oxford University Press, 2022), 286.
9. Jablonski, *Happy with the Blues*, 91.
10. Sondheim is quoted in James Lapine, *Putting It Together: How Stephen Sondheim and I Created "Sunday in the Park with George"* (New York: Farrar, Straus & Giroux, 2021), 233. For more on Sondheim and Arlen see also Stephen Sondheim, *Finishing the Hat: Collected Lyrics (1954–1981) with Attendant Comments, Principles, Heresies, Grudges, Whines, and Anecdotes* (New York: Knopf, 2010), 222; Steve Swayne, *How Sondheim Found His Sound* (Ann Arbor: University of Michigan Press, 2005), 77–88; and Mark Eden Horowitz, *Sondheim on Music: Minor Details and Major Decisions*, 2nd ed. (Lanham, MD: Scarecrow, 2010), 100, 192.
11. Gene Lees, *Portrait of Johnny: The Life of John Herndon Mercer* (New York: Pantheon, 2004), 49.
12. Horowitz, *Sondheim on Music*, 168.
13. Jablonski, *Happy with the Blues*, 234–235.
14. It is striking (and perhaps reflective of what I've identified as Arlen's anonymous immortality) that in his discussion of "Unusual and Extended Standard Forms," the jazz theorist and analyst Dariusz Terefenko does not mention a single

example by Arlen. See Terefenko, *Jazz Theory: From Basic to Advanced Study*, 2nd ed. (New York: Routledge, 2018), 297–302.
15. Jablonski, *Happy with the Blues*, caption to Frontispiece.
16. Many Arlen jots are preserved in the Rita Arlen Collection at the Music Division, Library of Congress.
17. The date of the 1930s is strongly suggested by the music paper, which bears the imprint of George and Arthur Piantadosi, Inc., the publishing firm that gave Arlen his first contract in 1929. In 1930 Piantadosi merged with Remick, a Warner Bros. subsidiary.
18. "The Songs of Harold Arlen."
19. See Howard Pollack, *George Gershwin: His Life and Work* (Berkeley: University of California Press, 2007), 175–192.
20. "The Songs of Harold Arlen."
21. Quoted in Jablonski, *Happy with the Blues*, 241.
22. "The Songs of Harold Arlen."
23. "The Songs of Harold Arlen."
24. Jablonski, *Happy with the Blues*, 236.
25. The most comprehensive chronological list of Arlen's songs, which includes names of lyricists, is in Jablonski's second biography of Arlen, *Harold Arlen: Rhythm, Rainbows and Blues* (Boston: Northeastern University Press, 1996), 363–384 (Appendix A).
26. Harold Arlen, ASCAP interview with Martin Bookspan [n.d.; made in the 1960s]. Rodgers and Hammerstein Archives of Recorded Sound, New York Public Library.
27. Harold Arlen, interview on "Friday with Dave Garroway," NBC Radio, February 25, 1955. Library of Congress, Motion Picture, Broadcasting, and Recorded Sound Division.
28. Philip Furia, *The Poets of Tin Pan Alley: A History of America's Great Lyricists* (New York: Oxford University Press, 1990). A second edition of Furia's book appeared from Oxford University Press in 2022, after his death, co-edited by Laurie J. Patterson. Although much expanded, it also omits many of Furia's elegant observations. In this book I cite only from the first edition.
29. This diary is part of the Rita Arlen Collection at the Library of Congress, Washington, D.C.
30. "The Songs of Harold Arlen."
31. Ira Gershwin, *Lyrics on Several Occasions* (New York: Viking, 1975), 109.
32. Martin Charnin, personal interview, May 19, 2013.
33. Brian Kane, "Jazz, Mediation, Ontology," in *Contemporary Music Review* 37 (2018): 523.
34. Kane, "Jazz, Mediation, Ontology," 524.
35. The most thorough account of Arlen's early and formative years remains Jablonski, *Arlen: Rhythm, Rainbows, and Blues*, chapters 1 and 2.
36. William K. Zinsser, "Harold Arlen, the Secret Music Maker," *Harper's Magazine* 220 (May 1960): 44.
37. Max Wilk, *They're Playing Our Song: Conversations with America's Classic Songwriters* (New York: Da Capo, 1997 [orig. ed. 1973]), 144.

38. Gershwin and Mercer are quoted in Zinsser, "Harold Arlen: The Secret Music Maker," 42.
39. Quoted in Wilk, *They're Playing Our Song*, 144. Elsewhere Harburg describes his early impression of Arlen's songs as "a combination of Hebrew and black music" (Harold Meyerson and Ernie Harburg, *Who Put the Rainbow in the Wizard of Oz? Yip Harburg, Lyricist* [Ann Arbor: University of Michigan Press, 1993], 65).
40. Jack Gottlieb, *Funny, It Doesn't Sound Jewish: How Yiddish Songs and Synagogue Melodies Influenced Tin Pan Alley, Broadway, and Hollywood* (Albany: State University of New York, 2004), 167–168.
41. In 1925 the Blue Ribbon Syncopators recorded one of Arlen's first songs, "My Gal, My Pal" (composed 1924) (Okeh, Matrix 8989): https://adp.library.ucsb.edu/index.php/matrix/detail/2000201125/8989-My_gal_my_pal and https://www.youtube.com/watch?v=HWZeoGZD2hE). I am deeply grateful to the late Phil Schaap for drawing to my attention Arlen's association with the Blue Ribbon Syncopators.
42. Donald Bogle, *Heat Wave: The Life and Career of Ethel Waters* (New York: HarperCollins, 2011), 213.
43. Jeffrey Melnick, *A Right to Sing the Blues: African Americans, Jews, and American Popular Song* (Cambridge, MA: Harvard University Press, 1999), 59, 105.
44. John McWhorter, "Cultural Appropriation Can Be Beautiful," *New York Times*, October 8, 2021, https://www.nytimes.com/2021/10/08/opinion/cultural-appropriation-opera.html.

# Chapter 2

1. National Geographic Resource Library: https://education.nationalgeographic.org/resource/rainbow.
2. Salman Rushdie, *The Wizard of Oz*, 2nd ed. (London: Palgrave Macmillan, 2012 [orig. ed. 1992]), 25.
3. For other close analyses of "Over the Rainbow," see Allen Forte, *The American Popular Ballad of the Golden Era, 1924–1950* (Princeton, NJ: Princeton University Press, 1995), 231–236; Rob Kapilow, *Listening For America: Inside the Great American Songbook From Gershwin to Sondheim* (New York: W.W. Norton, 2019), 227–248; and Walter Frisch, *Arlen and Harburg's "Over the Rainbow"* (New York: Oxford University Press, 2017), 53–68.
4. Aljean Harmetz, *The Making of "The Wizard of Oz"* (New York: Limelight, 1984 [orig. ed. 1977]), 81. Harburg's then-girlfriend and soon-to-be-wife Edelaine recalled that it was she who suggested "Somewhere" for the opening notes of Arlen's melody. See Walter Rimler, *The Man That Got Away: The Life and Songs of Harold Arlen* (Urbana: University of Illinois Press, 2015), 74.
5. The conflicting accounts of Arlen and Harburg about the genesis of "Over the Rainbow" are summarized in Harriet Hyman Alonso, *Yip Harburg: Legendary Lyricist and Human Rights Activist* (Middletown, CT: Wesleyan University Press, 2012), 82–83.

6. For a more detailed account of the evolution of Harburg's lyrics for the bridge, see Frisch, *Arlen and Harburg's "Over the Rainbow,"* 24–26.
7. *André Previn Plays Songs by Harold Arlen* (Contemporary Records, OJCCD-1840-2; original stereo LP, S-7586). Previn plays "Over the Rainbow" in the key of D major. In Example 2.6, I have transposed the song to E♭ to facilitate comparison with Arlen's original.
8. Jazz pianist George Shearing recasts the opening progression of "Over the Rainbow" similarly to Previn, as (ii7–V7)/iii–iii. See Shearing, *Interpretations for Piano* (Van Nuys, CA: Alfred Music, 1994), 74.
9. For a discussion of interpretations of "Over the Rainbow" by several generations of jazz pianists, from Art Tatum to Keith Jarrett, see my *Arlen and Harburg's "Over the Rainbow,"* chapter 5.

# Chapter 3

1. The best general history of American popular song remains Charles Hamm, *Yesterdays: Popular Song in America* (New York: W.W. Norton, 1979).
2. https://eh.net/encyclopedia/the-history-of-the-radio-industry-in-the-united-states-to-1940/.
3. Wilk, *They're Playing Our Song*, 142.
4. The best account of Arlen's activities as a vocalist in these years is Will Friedwald, *A Biographical Guide to the Great Jazz and Pop Singers* (New York: Pantheon, 2010), 623–627.
5. Wilk, *They're Playing Our Song*, 142.
6. On the participation of Henderson and his band in *Great Day*, see Jeffrey Magee, *The Uncrowned King of Swing: Fletcher Henderson and Big Band Jazz* (New York: Oxford University Press, 2005), 121–122.
7. Arlen's versions of this story can be found in Wilk, *They're Playing Our Song*, 142–143; and in the documentary *Somewhere Over the Rainbow: Harold Arlen* (New York: Winstar, 1999). See also Jablonski, *Happy with the Blues*, 44–45.
8. Wilk, *They're Playing Our Song*, 143.
9. On Cook, see David A. Jasen and Gene Jones, *Spreadin' Rhythm Around: Black Popular Songwriters, 1880-1930* (New York: Schirmer, 1998), 79–95; and Thomas Riis, *Just Before Jazz: Black Musical Theater in New York, 1890-1915* (Washington, D.C.: Smithsonian, 1989), 91–109.
10. Jablonski, *Happy with the Blues*, 59–60.
11. It is not clear who coined the term "Broadway spiritual," which appeared in print as early as 1941. See Nathaniel Sloan, "Stormy Relations: The Cotton Club, Broadway Spirituals, and Harlem Encounters in the Music of Harold Arlen and Ted Koehler," *Musical Quarterly* 101 (2018): 120–156, https://doi.org/10.1093/musqtl/gdy017.

12. Columbia Records matrix W145363. Available on YouTube at https://youtu.be/gDLxxRMly20.
13. *God Struck Me Dead: Religious Conversion Experiences and Autobiographies of Ex-Slaves*, ed. Clifton H. Johnson (Philadelphia: Pilgrim Press, 1969), 75.
14. Both lyrics are found on the website PD Information Project, https://www.pdinfo.com/pd-music-genres/pd-spirituals.php.
15. Jablonski, *Happy with the Blues*, 43.
16. On Youmans, see Gerald Boardman, *Days to Be Happy, Days to Be Sad: The Life and Music of Vincent Youmans* (New York: Oxford University Press, 1982).
17. Jablonski, *Rhythm, Rainbows and Blues*, 28.
18. Jablonski, *Happy with the Blues*, 60.
19. Furia, *Poets of Tin Pan Alley*, 247.
20. On the *Passing Shows*, see Jonas Westover, *The Shuberts and Their Passing Shows: The Untold Tale of Ziegfeld's Rivals* (New York: Oxford University Press, 2016). On revues more generally, see Lee Davis, *Scandals and Follies: The Rise and Fall of the Great Broadway Revue* (New York: Limelight, 2000). On Earl Carroll, see Ken Murray, *The Body Merchant: The Story of Earl Carroll* (Pasadena, CA: Ward Ritchie Press, 1976).
21. The original program for the 1930 *Vanities* can be viewed online at the Playbill Vault https://www.playbill.com/production/earl-carrolls-vanities-of-1930-new-amsterdam-theatre-vault-0000008743.
22. Brunswick 4858. The Colonial Club Orchestra's recordings of "Hittin' the Bottle" and "Out of a Clear Blue Sky" can be heard on YouTube at https://youtu.be/25M9vbexAe0 and https://youtu.be/C483y60la9o, respectively.
23. See Sally Banes and John Szwed, "From 'Messin' Around' to 'Funky Western Civilization': The Rise and Fall of Dance Instruction Songs," in *Dancing Many Drums: Excavations in African American Dance*, ed. Thomas DeFrantz (Madison: University of Wisconsin Press, 2002), 169–203.
24. The tune of the earlier Arlen-Koehler song "Gladly" (1929) features a more typical metrical displacement, a broad hemiola, creating an implied measure of $\frac{3}{2}$ across two measures of cut time.
25. See Lewis Porter, *John Coltrane: His Life and Music* (Ann Arbor: University of Michigan Press, 1998), 145–151; and Dariusz Terefenko, *Jazz Theory: From Basic to Advanced Study*, 2nd ed. (New York: Routledge 2018), 140–141.
26. On McHugh, see Alyn Shipton, *I Feel a Song Coming On: The Life of Jimmy McHugh* (Urbana: University of Illinois Press, 2009); on Fields, see Charlotte Greenspan, *Pick Yourself Up: Dorothy Fields and the American Musical* (New York: Oxford University Press, 2010).
27. Donald Bogle, *Heat Wave: The Life and Career of Ethel Waters* (New York: HarperCollins, 2011), 213.
28. Cited in Jablonski, *Happy with the Blues*, 68.
29. For some of the obstacles faced by Black songwriters, see Jasen and Jones, *Spreadin' Rhythm Around*.

30. See Michael Rogin, *Blackface, White Noise: Jewish Immigrants in the Hollywood Melting Pot* (Berkeley: University of California Press, 1998); Andrea Most, *Making Americans: Jews and the Broadway Musical* (Cambridge, MA: Harvard University Press, 2004); and Melnick, *A Right to Sing the Blues*.
31. Sloan, "Stormy Relations," 146.
32. An original program of this Cotton Club show is in the Edward Jablonski Collection at the Library of Congress. The show is discussed by Jablonski, *Harold Arlen: Rhythm, Rainbows and Blues*, 50–52; and by Jim Haskins, *The Cotton Club* (New York: New American Library, 1977), 84–88.
33. A valuable introduction to "Stormy Weather" and its history in performance is Will Friedwald, *Stardust Melodies: A Biography of Twelve of America's Most Popular Songs* (New York: Pantheon, 2002), 276–307. In what follows, I bring in some sources not discussed by Friedwald to refine an account of the song's genesis.
34. "The Songs of Harold Arlen," *The Twentieth Century* with Walter Cronkite, broadcast February 9, 1964.
35. This jot is reproduced in an undated article from a Croydon Hotel in-house magazine, "How Songs Are Made," p. 16, contained in the Edward Jablonski Papers at the Library of Congress.
36. In his preface to *The Harold Arlen Songbook* (New York: Hal Leonard and MPL Communications, 1985), Jablonski claims that "Stormy Weather" is "published here for the first time in its complete form" (2).
37. The lyric sheet was featured on an episode of the television series *Antiques Roadshow* in June 2010 (https://www.pbs.org/wgbh/roadshow/season/15/san-diego-ca/appraisals/stormy-weather-lyrics-koehler-painting—201001A41/). It is reproduced here in print for the first time.
38. A contemporary photograph of female dancers at the Cotton Club in outfits similar to those depicted on the stationery, with headdress, can be found in Haskins, *Cotton Club*, 73.
39. Jablonski, *Happy with the Blues*, 61.
40. For more detail on these breaks in Arlen's recordings with the Buffalodians, see Walter Frisch, "Arlen's Tapeworms: The Tunes That Got Away," *Musical Quarterly* 98 (2015): 149, https://doi.org/10.1093/musqtl/gdv010.
41. Wilder, *American Popular Song*, 260.
42. As related to Jablonski, *Happy with the Blues*, 74.
43. "Stormy Weather" was originally published by Mills in the key of A♭. It appears in G major in *The Harold Arlen Songbook*, 48–51. The connection between the openings of "Stormy Weather" and "West End Blues" has been noted by Sloan ("Stormy Relations," 127).
44. Arlen quotes Gershwin in comments cited by Wilder in *American Popular Song*, 260.
45. Furia, *Poets of Tin Pan Alley*, 248. John McWhorter, *Talking Back, Talking Black: Truths About America's Lingua Franca* (New York: Bellevue, 2017).
46. For a concise, informative discussion of Black English, see McWhorter, *Talking Back, Talking Black*.

47. The reference to Carmichael has been observed by Friedwald, *Stardust Melodies*, 289.
48. Ethel Waters, with Charles Samuels, *His Eye Is on the Sparrow* (New York: Doubleday, 1951), 220. Further quotations are from this page.
49. Haskins (*The Cotton Club*, 87) reproduces a photo showing Waters in a simple dark dress and the dancers in elaborate silk gowns, with Ellington and his band in the background. A different photo of the same scene is included in an excellent article by Shane Vogel about how the performances "Stormy Weather" by Walters, Lena Horne, and Katherine Dunham staged a form of Black modernism that countered the prevailingly white-dominated power structure of the musical entertainment industry. See Shane Vogel, "Performing 'Stormy Weather': Ethel Waters, Lena Horne, and Katherine Dunham," *South Central Review* 25, no. 2 (2008): 93–113, https://www.jstor.org/stable/40040021.
50. For a discussion of the early recordings of "Stormy Weather" (most readily available on YouTube), see Friedwald, *Stardust Melodies*, 282–284.
51. See *Oxford Dictionary of Proverbs*, ed. Jennifer Speake (Oxford, UK: Oxford University Press, 2015), https://www.oxfordreference.com/view/10.1093/acref/9780198734901.001.0001/acref-9780198734901-e-1127.
52. Victor 24569 and 24579, respectively. These can be heard on YouTube: https://youtu.be/4LU31uWfyHs and https://youtu.be/C9gUoGz018s, Arthur Schutt (1902–1965) was a brilliantly gifted jazz pianist much admired by Arlen during these early years. This Victor disc was their only recorded collaboration; the flip side contains Arlen and Koehler's "As Long as I Live."
53. Since this segment was never printed, I cannot confirm Arlen and Koehler called it an "interlude" (and not a "patter" or some other designation), but in scope it conforms to the interludes of "Stormy Weather" and "Another Night Alone." The only modern recording of "Ill Wind" that incorporates the interlude is by Audra McDonald, on her 2002 album *Happy Songs* (Nonesuch CD 79645-2). The conductor of that album, Ted Sperling, believes that he and his arrangers transcribed it from the Arlen-Schutt recording (personal communication, February 23, 2021).
54. Jablonski, *Rhythm, Rainbows, and Blues*, 73–74.
55. "The Album of My Dreams," a song Arlen wrote in 1929 with lyrics by Lou Davis, is sung by Bobbe Arnst in a short: made in November 1929: https://youtu.be/U2nt2-mFDQM.
56. "Get Happy" appeared as the title tune for "Merrie Melodies" from 1931–1933. The very first "Merrie Melodies" cartoon, "Lady, Play your Mandolin!" is viewable at https://youtu.be/ivARNObPZsk.
57. Jablonski, *Happy with the Blues*, 86.
58. One excellently documented study that investigates the process of "cumulative creation" by which Arlen's songs were adapted for *The Wizard of Oz* in a manner resembling an "assembly line," is Laura Lynn Broadhurst, "'Arlen and Harburg and More, Oh My!': The Cumulative Creation of the *Oz* Songs," in *Adapting The Wizard of Oz: Musical Versions from Baum to MGM and Beyond*, ed. Danielle Birkett and Dominic McHugh (New York: Oxford University Press, 2019), 53–78. A similarly

detailed, archive-based approach is taken by Todd Decker, "On the Scenic Route to Irving Berlin's *Holiday Inn* (1942)," *Journal of Musicology* 28 (2011): 464–497, https://doi.org/10.1525/jm.2011.28.4.464

59. Some of these features, including the half-diminished seventh appearing in a common inversion as a minor triad with an added sixth, can be observed in one of the best-known (and often parodied) operetta numbers, Friml's "Indian Love Call," from *Rose-Marie* (1924). That harmony is often used to add an exotic or otherworldly touch to Tin Pan Alley song, as in the bridge section of Rodgers and Hart's "My Heart Stood Still" (1927).
60. A significant exception is Will Friedwald, who devotes a large entry to Arlen in his *Biographical Guide to the Great Jazz and Pop Singers*, 623–627. Friedwald includes Arlen among a trio of "Singing Songwriters"; the others are Hoagy Carmichael and Johnny Mercer.
61. The six Buffalodian recordings made in 1926 are: "Deep Henderson" and "Here Comes Emaline" (Columbia 665-D); "Baby Face" and "How Many Times?" (Banner 1776); and "Would Ja?" and "She's Still My Baby" (Columbia 723-D).
62. Friedwald, *Biographical Guide*, 624.
63. I am grateful to Peter Mintun for sharing with me information about these rare and little studied pictorials, which were produced by a number of studios.
64. Arlen uses this term in an interview on NBC radio with Dave Garroway on February 25, 1955 (Library of Congress, Motion Picture, Broadcasting, and Recorded Sound Division, Digital File 186307-3-1).
65. R.A. Wachsman, "They Kept Their Promise," Foreword to *Americanegro Suite* (New York: Chappell & Co., 1941), 11.
66. Sloan, "Stormy Relations," 139.
67. This anecdote is related in Jablonski, *Happy with the Blues*, 88.

# Chapter 4

1. Harold Meyerson and Ernie Harburg, *Who Put the Rainbow in* The Wizard of Oz? *Yip Harburg, Lyricist* (Ann Arbor: University of Michigan Press, 1993), 65.
2. Meyerson and Harburg, *Who Put the Rainbow*, 69.
3. Meyerson and Harburg, *Who Put the Rainbow*, 66.
4. Jablonski, *Happy with the Blues*, 91.
5. On the early acquaintance of Harburg and Ira Gershwin, see Meyerson and Harburg, *Who Put the Rainbow*, 15–19. Harburg and Gershwin had collaborated on lyrics, and received joint credit, for a song written with Vernon Duke for the *Garrick Gaieties* of 1930, "I Am Only Human After All."
6. Wilk, *They're Playing Our Song*, 233.
7. Personal communication by email, June 1, 2018.
8. Personal communication by email, May 22, 2018.

NOTES TO PAGES 66–78    257

9. For a detailed description of the song "Things" and Lahr's performance, see John Lahr, *Notes on a Cowardly Lion: The Biography of Bert Lahr* (New York: Knopf, 1969), 138–141.
10. Wilk, *They're Playing Our Song*, 145.
11. Lahr, *Notes on a Cowardly Lion*, 138.
12. Jablonski, *Happy with the Blues*, 91.
13. In 2010 a reconstruction, concert performance, and recording were made of *Life Begins at 8:40* at the Library of Congress, with restoration by Larry Moore and music direction by Aaron Gandy (PS Classics CD PS-1090; full album at https://www.youtube.com/playlist?list=OLAK5uy_kN3G30oUHvM87IZyKLbGjKlewQJ1A8H3A). Some numbers written for the show seem to have been left off the recording (and perhaps are lost), which has a total of eighteen tracks (an overture and seventeen numbers).
14. Isaac Goldberg, *George Gershwin: A Study in American Music* (New York: Simon & Schuster, 1931).
15. Excerpts from Goldberg's article, originally published in the *Boston Evening Transcript*, are cited in Jablonski, *Rhythm, Rainbows and Blues*, 87–88.
16. Jablonski, *Happy with the Blues*, 92.
17. Robert Wachsman Collection, Ohio State University, Box 2.
18. Jablonski, *Happy with the Blues*, 101. If Sinatra did record and film "Last Night When We Were Young" for *Take Me Out to the Ball Game*, no outtake appears to survive. Garland's outtake from *The Good Old Summertime* has survived.
19. Meyerson and Harburg, *Who Put the Rainbow*, 95.
20. Jablonski, *Rhythm, Rainbows and Blues*, 100.
21. Meyerson and Harburg, *Who Put the Rainbow*, 96.
22. The music for the "Hero Ballet" is described by Jablonski in *Rhythm, Rainbows and Blues*, 118–119.
23. Meyerson and Harburg, *Who Put the Rainbow*, 112.
24. Gensler's music for "'Cause You Didn't Do Right By Me," written for the revue *Ballyhoo of 1932*, does not appear to survive, although a sheet with the lyrics in Harburg's hand (on Gensler's stationery) are held in the Harburg Collection at Yale University. Suesse's music, with the same lyrics, survives in a handwritten lead sheet, and she performs it in an interview recorded much later. I am grateful to Nick Markovich of the Harburg Foundation for sharing the lead sheet and recording with me. Harburg's biographers, who reproduce some of the lyrics from Harburg's sheet for "'Cause You Didn't Do Right By Me," mistakenly suggest that Suesse (rather than Gensler) wrote the song for *Ballyhoo of 1932* (Meyerson and Harburg, *Who Put the Rainbow*, 112–113).
25. For a discussion of Arlen's use of 13th chords, see Steve Swayne, *How Sondheim Found His Sound* (Ann Arbor: University of Michigan Press, 2005), 80–82.
26. *Harold Arlen Songbook* (1985), 102–103.
27. The studio's vocal score for this revision, which survives in the Roger Edens Collection at the University of Southern California, appears never to have been printed. I am

grateful to Michael Feinstein for generously sharing with me this score, as well as other information about "Buds Won't Bud."
28. Both of Garland's 1940 recordings are included on the two-CD set *Judy Garland Sings Harold Arlen* (JSP 4246).
29. Wilder, *American Popular Song*, 266.
30. The story of the film's creation has been related many times. Among the most authoritative sources are Aljean Harmetz, *The Making of the Wizard of Oz* (New York: Limelight, 1984 [orig. 1977]); John Fricke, Jay Scarfone, and William Stillman, *The Wizard of Oz: The Official 50th Anniversary Pictorial History* (New York: Warner, 1989); and Hugh Fordin, *The World of Entertainment! Hollywood's Greatest Musicals* (Garden City, NY: Doubleday, 1975). There are also many features, including commentary, outtakes, and deleted scenes, on the 75th anniversary rerelease of *The Wizard of Oz* (Time Warner Video, 2014).
31. The most comprehensive account of the genesis and development of Arlen and Harburg's songs for *The Wizard of Oz* is Laura Lynn Broadhurst, "Wizards of Song: Arlen, Harburg, and the Cumulative Creation of the Songs for *The Wizard of Oz* (1939)," PhD dissertation, Rutgers University, 2020. Broadhurst summarizes her research in "'Arlen and Harburg and More, Oh My!,'" 53–78.
32. Jablonski, *Happy with the Blues*, 239.
33. Harold Arlen, interview on "Friday With Dave Garroway," NBC Radio, February 25, 1955. Library of Congress, Motion Picture, Broadcasting, and Recorded Sound Division.
34. Jablonski, *Happy with the Blues*, 120.
35. Fordin, *World of Entertainment*, 27.
36. For a discussion of the genre of "I Want" songs, see Jack Viertel, *The Secret Life of the American Musical: How Broadway Shows Are Built* (New York: Sarah Crichton Books, 2017), 52–72.
37. Memo from Arthur Freed, January 31, 1938, reproduced in Fordin, *World of Entertainment*, 14.
38. The song "I Love to Sing-a" is most familiar from its appearance in the 1936 Warner Bros. Merrie Melodies cartoon of that name. In this short, a take-off on Jolson's film *The Jazz Singer*, "Owl" Jolson sings the Arlen-Harburg number as he seeks to break free from classical music and perform "jazz."
39. Edens's outline for the Munchkinland sequence is reproduced in Fricke, Scarfone, and Stillman, *The Wizard of Oz*, 41.
40. The full Munchkinland sequence, as performed in the film, is available as a piano-vocal score: *The Wizard of Oz: 70th Anniversary Deluxe Songbook*, arranged and transcribed by Tod Edmondson and Ethan Neuuburg (Van Nuys, CA: Alfred Music, 2009).
41. On these Black-cast musical films, see Arthur Knight, *Disintegrating the Musical: Black Performance and American Musical Film* (Durham, NC: Duke University Press, 2002). On the adaptation of *Cabin in the Sky* from stage to film, see Geoffrey Block, *A Fine Romance: Adapting Broadway to Hollywood in the Studio System Era* (New York: Oxford University Press, 2023), 108–126.

42. Two additional Duke-Latouche songs were retained as instrumentals in the film, "Love Me Tomorrow" and "In My Old Virginia Home."
43. Meyerson and Harburg, *Who Put the Rainbow*, 179.
44. Jablonski, *Rhythm, Rainbows and Blues*, 178.
45. Meyerson and Harburg, *Who Put the Rainbow*, 181.
46. Wilder, *American Popular Song*, 353.
47. For accounts of the genesis and contexts of *Bloomer Girl*, see especially Jablonski, *Rhythm, Rainbows and Blues*, 180–194; Meyerson and Harburg, *Who Put the Rainbow*, 183–213; and Sarah England, "'It Was Good Enough for Grandma, But It Ain't Good Enough For Us!': Women and the Nation in Harold Arlen and E.Y. Harburg's Wartime Musical *Bloomer Girl* (1944)," MA thesis, University of Maryland, College Park, 2013.
48. Notable shows of the era with mixed-race casts included *Show Boat* (1927), *The Cradle Will Rock* (1937), *This Is the Army* (1942), and *On the Town* (1944).
49. Meyerson and Harburg, *Who Put the Rainbow*, 188.
50. "Amiable" and "quaintly turn-of-the century" in Jablonski, *Harold Arlen: Rhythm, Rainbows and Blues*, 117–118; "lightly nostalgic" in Meyerson and Harburg, *Who Put the Rainbow*, 117.
51. Alonso, *Yip Harburg*, 129. The world-as-onion image is also one of Stephen Sondheim's favorite in all of popular song: "Lyrics don't come any better than that." See Sondheim, *Finishing the Hat: Collected Lyrics (1954–1981)* (New York: Knopf, 2010), 99.
52. See *A Dictionary of Slang, Jargon, & Cant*, ed. Albert Barrère and Charles G. Leland, vol. 2 (Edinburgh: Ballantyne Press, 1890), 178.
53. I am grateful to Ken Bloom for generously providing me with copies of these and other Arlen demo recordings.
54. Jablonski, *Happy with the Blues*, 201.
55. For an account and critique of the calypso craze, see Shane Vogel, *Stolen Time: Black Fad Performance and the Calypso Craze* (Chicago: University of Chicago Press, 2018). Vogel's chapter 4 deals specifically with the musical *Jamaica*.
56. Cited in Jablonski, *Happy with the Blues*, 200.
57. Vogel, *Stolen Time*, 133.
58. E.Y. Harburg, interview (1959), Columbia University Center for Oral History.
59. Jablonski, *Happy with the Blues*, 211.
60. Jablonski, *Happy with the Blues*, 208.
61. Jablonski, *Rhythm, Rainbows and Blues*, 313.
62. Cited in Jablonski, *Rhythm, Rainbows and Blues*, 313.
63. *New York Times*, December 6, 1962, (https://timesmachine.nytimes.com/timesmachine/1962/12/06/issue.html).
64. Arlen's biographer Jablonski writes that "Looks Like the End of a Beautiful Friendship" and the one other Arlen-Harburg song from 1976, "Promise Me Not to Love Me," had been "virtually finished in the late 1940s or early 1950s" and were revised for publication at the later date (Jablonski, *Rhythm, Rainbows and Blues*, 346). As with so many

of Jablonski's claims about Arlen, we have only his word to go on. To me, the musical style of "Promise Me" sounds like later Arlen. There survives a tape recording, most likely from the 1970s, of composer and lyricist working on the song. Arlen plays the intricate melody repeatedly (sometimes with harmonization) while Harburg tries to get it in his ear and imagine a lyric. This tape suggests real composing more than polishing. I am grateful to Nick Markovich of the Harburg Foundation for sharing this audio recording (labeled "7-7-20 Arlen Work Tape").

65. Meyerson and Harburg, *Who Put the Rainbow*, 345.

# Chapter 5

1. "Satan's Li'l Lamb" was recorded by Ethel Merman a week before the opening of *Americana*, on September 29 (Victor 24146).
2. I take the number of 164 from the inventory of songs in the Johnny Mercer Song Database at Georgia State University: https://webapps.library.gsu.edu/music/mercersong/. There are 165 titles, from which I subtracted "Satan's Li'l Lamb," the song written in 1932.
3. Max Wilk, *They're Playing Our Song*, 147.
4. According to Jablonski in *Rhythm, Rainbows and Blues* (155), Arlen's source was *Blues: An Anthology*, ed. W.C. Handy (New York: Albert and Charles Boni, 1926).
5. Wilder, *American Popular Song*, 269.
6. Jablonski, *Happy with the Blues*, 136–137.
7. *The Complete Lyrics of Johnny Mercer*, ed. Robert Kimball, Barry Day, Miles Kreuger, and Eric Davis (New York: Knopf, 2009), 117.
8. Quoted in Glenn T. Eskew, *Johnny Mercer: Southern Songwriter for the World* (Athens: University of Georgia Press, 2013), 155.
9. For blues lyrics featuring these kinds images, see, for example, the many transcribed from singers in Mississippi by Alan Lomax in *The Land Where the Blues Began* (New York: Pantheon, 1993). Lomax also reports on a number of instances of whistling and humming of blues. See also *W.C. Handy's Blues, An Anthology*. The "Blue Gummed Blues" (126) begins, "Mammy told me when a child playing mumble peg."
10. *Mercer Complete Lyrics*, 117.
11. Margaret Whiting, with Will Holt, *It Might As Well Be Spring: An Autobiography* (New York: Morrow, 1987), 64–65. Whiting also told the story (with a few different details) to Max Wilk, *They're Playing Our Song*, 134. Tormé (1925–1999) would have been barely older than Whiting at this time. Garland recorded "Blues in the Night" in October 1941 (Decca DLA-2799-A). Whiting appears never to have made a studio recording of the song.
12. In the Warner Bros. piano-vocal copyist score of "Blues in the Night," the two measures leading from C' back to A (thus, just before "From Natchez to Mobile"), no vocal part is indicated, only accompaniment. The wordless vocal line with the indication for whistling and the similar moment in the coda (indicated for humming) were created for the published piano-vocal score.

13. Jablonski, *Happy with the Blues*, 143; *Mercer Complete Lyrics*, 117.
14. Alan Lomax, *The Land Where the Blues Began* (New York: Pantheon, 1993), 413–414.
15. Peter Townsend, *Pearl Harbor Jazz: Change in Popular Music in the Early 1940s* (Jackson: University Press of Mississippi, 2007), 63. Lomax's field notes, with the mention of "Blues in the Night," are preserved at the Library of Congress in the Alan Lomax Collection, Manuscripts, Mississippi, Tennessee and Arkansas, 1941–1942 (AFC 2004/004: MS 07.02.08). I am grateful to Velia Ivanova for sharing this source with me.
16. See especially Karl Hagstrom Miller, *Segregating Sound: Inventing Folk and Pop Music in the Age of Jim Crow* (Durham, NC: Duke University Press, 2010); and David Brackett, *Categorizing Sound: Genre and Twentieth-Century Popular Music* (Oakland: University of California Press, 2016). While Miller's book deals mainly with the period from the late nineteenth century through the 1920s, his approach is also clearly relevant to subsequent decades.
17. The six films after *Blues in the Night* with Arlen-Mercer songs, some written for Fred Astaire and Bing Crosby, are: *Star Spangled Rhythm* (1942), *They Got Me Covered* and *The Sky's the Limit* (1943), *Here Come the Waves* (1944), and *Out of This World* (1945).
18. The terms "hypermeter" and "hypermeasure" have been credited to the theorist Edward T. Cone (*Musical Form and Musical Performance* [New York: Norton, 1968], 40, 80). Another hypermetric tapeworm in the American Songbook is Cole Porter's "I Get a Kick Out of You," also written in cut time, where sixty-four measures are double that of the normal thirty-two. For other examples in the repertory, including Arlen's, see Walter Frisch, "Arlen's Tapeworms: The Tunes That Got Away," *Musical Quarterly* 98 (2015): 139–170.
19. Lees, *Portrait of Johnny*, 146.
20. The pedal point and repeated rhythms are much more present in one of the earliest commercial recordings of "The Old Black Magic," by Judy Garland with David Rose and his orchestra, made in July 1942. This version has special poignancy. As biographers of Mercer and Garland often point out, Mercer was deeply in love with Garland and seems to have written this song with her in mind. Rose was Garland's husband at the time and likely aware of the relationship.
21. Wilder, *American Popular Song*, 271.
22. See Jablonski, *Happy with the Blues*, 144; and Jablonski, *Rhythm, Rainbows and Blues*, 162.
23. Wilk, *They're Playing Our Song*, 150. Arlen's memory wasn't quite correct here. Another Arlen song that begins in one key and ends in another is "Two Feet in Two Four Time" (1932): A (G-major) A (A♭ major) B (E major to A♭) A′ (A♭).
24. See *The Second Practice of Nineteenth-Century Tonality*, ed. William Kinderman (Lincoln: University of Nebraska Press, 1996).
25. Furia, *Poets of Tin Pan Alley*, 273.
26. On the Astaire dance sequence for "One for My Baby," see Todd Decker, *Astaire by the Numbers: Time & the Straight White Dancer* (New York: Oxford University Press, 2022), 202–204.

27. In the film version, as sung by Astaire, these lines are replaced with the less compelling "Don't let it be said / Little Freddie can't carry his load." See *Mercer Complete Lyrics*, 138.
28. Wilk, *They're Playing Our Song*, 150.
29. Lees, *Portrait of Johnny*, 146.
30. Wilder's analysis of "My Shining Hour," a song he admires intensely, is one of his most persuasive, and I draw here upon some of his observations (Wilder, *American Popular Song*, 273–274.
31. Eskew, *Johnny Mercer*, 167.
32. Furia, *Poets of Tin Pan Alley*, 275.
33. For an explanation and examples of tritone substitutes, see Dariusz Terefenko, *Jazz Theory: From Basic to Advanced Study*, 2nd ed. (New York: Routledge, 2018), 134–136. See also Nicole Biamonte, "Augmented-Sixth Chords vs. Tritone Substitutes," *Music Theory Online* 14/2 (2008), https://mtosmt.org/issues/mto.08.14.2/mto.08.14.2.biamonte.html.
34. On Bontemps, see Kirkland T. Jones, *Renaissance Man from Louisiana: A Biography of Arna Bontemps* (New York: Greenwood Press, 1992). *God Sends Sunday* is discussed on 72–74.
35. The information about the evolution of Bontemps and Cullen's play is taken from archival sources in the Countee Cullen Papers in the Amistad Research Center, Tulane University; and the Arna Bontemps and Langston Hughes Papers at the Beinecke Library, Yale University.
36. The various newspaper reports as well as other information about Cook's project are documented in Peter Lefferts, "Chronology and Itinerary of the Career of Will Marion Cook: Materials for a Biography" (2017), *Faculty Publications: School of Music* 66, http://digitalcommons.unl.edu/musicfacpub/66.
37. William F. McDermott, "Do You Remember the Cakewalk? Gilpin Actors Revive It in Local Premiere," *Cleveland Plain Dealer*, November 24, 1933, 10.
38. On the "Negro units" of the Federal Theatre Project, see James V. Hatch, "The Great Depression and Federal Theatre," in Errol G. Hill and James V. Hatch, *A History of African American Theatre* (Cambridge, UK: Cambridge University Press, 2003), 315–334.
39. Langston Hughes Papers, Yale University, Beinecke Library, JWJ MSS 26, Box 337, Folder 5495.
40. Letter of June 13, 1943, Countee Cullen Papers, Tulane University, Box 5, Folder 10. The Roberts song to which Bontemps refers, "Moonlight Cocktail," had been composed in 1912 as a ragtime number under a different title ("Ripples of the Nile"), and was made popular in a slower version (with lyrics added) by Glenn Miller in a recording released in 1942.
41. Walter White's activities are related by him in his autobiography, *A Man Called White: The Autobiography of Walter White* (New York: Viking Press), 200–03. The files of the NAACP at the Library of Congress are filled with letters from White and others about fighting Hollywood stereotypes.
42. Cullen Papers, Box 10, Folder 5.

43. "God Send [sic] Sunday Set to Music," *The People's Voice*, September 18, 1943, 25.
44. *Arna Bontemps–Langston Hughes Letters 1925–1967*, ed. Charles H. Nichols (New York: Dodd, Mead, 1980), 166. The story of the revisions and projected stagings of *St. Louis Woman* can be traced indirectly in the published correspondence between Bontemps and Hughes. See also Arnold Rampersad, *The Life of Langston Hughes*, 2 vols. (New York: Oxford University Press, 1968–1988), 1: 366–439.
45. This and the following quotations from Walter White and Roy Wilkins come from: Library of Congress, Papers of the NAACP, Part 18. Special Subjects, 1940–1955; Series B: General Office Files: Abolition of Government Agencies-Jews; Group II, Series A, General Office File; Folder: Films—St. Louis Woman, 1945–1947. https://congressional.proquest.com/histvault?q=001457-020-0576&accountid=10226. See also White's account in White, *A Man Called White*, 338–339.
46. Lena Horne and Richard Schickel, *Lena* (Garden City, New York: Doubleday, 1965), 187–188.
47. Pearl Bailey, *The Raw Pearl* (New York: Harcourt, Brace & World, 1968), 66.
48. Cited in Jablonski, *Rhythm, Rainbows and Blues*, 203.
49. John M. Lee, *Los Angeles Sentinel*, April 11, 1946, 18; *New Journal and Guide* (Norfolk), April 13, 1946, 14.
50. The original cast album was rereleased in 1992 on CD by Angel Records (ZDM 7 64662 2). The 1998 concert revival of *St. Louis Woman* at *Encores!* in New York, with many more numbers restored to the score, led to a CD from Mercury Records (314 538 148-2)
51. Jablonski, *Happy with the Blues*, 148–149.
52. One often reads that "I Wonder What Became of Me" was dropped from *St. Louis Woman* during out-of-town tryouts, yet it appears in the list of numbers in the original Broadway Playbill (p. 21), sung by Della at the opening of Act 3 (see https://www.playbill.com/production/st-louis-woman-martin-beck-theatre-vault-0000008295#carousel-cell211227). Jablonski reports that "I Wonder What Became of Me" "was sung opening night" (*Happy with the Blues*, 150). But it seems to have been omitted thereafter and is absent from the *St. Louis Woman* libretto as reproduced in *Black Theater: A 20th Century Collection of the Work of Its Best Playwrights*, ed. Lindsay Patterson (New York: Dodd, Mead, 1971), 1–41.
53. Wilder, *American Popular Song*, 279.
54. In the piano part of the published sheet music (as in Example 5.6), Arlen doubles the vocal line with smaller notes, suggesting that at least for this measure and a half, the piano is not to play, and the singer is to have a real cadenza.
55. Fordin, *World of Entertainment*, 556.
56. "'St. Louis Woman,' Sepia on Stage Signs Ava and Sinatra for Film," *New York Age*, October 24, 1953, 6.
57. The production, which toured between 1952 and 1956, starred William Warfield and a young Leontyne Price in the title roles. On this tour, see Peggy Noonan, *The Strange Career of Porgy and Bess: Race, Culture, and America's Most Famous Opera* (Chapel Hill: University of North Carolina Press, 2012), chapter 4. The company performed in the Soviet Union in the winter of 1955–1956. On the Russian tour,

see Michael Sy Uy, "Performing Catfish Row in the Soviet Union: The Everyman Opera Company and *Porgy and Bess*, 1955–56," *Journal of the Society for American Music* 11 (2017): 470–501. Truman Capote covered the visit in a series of articles for the *New Yorker*, reprinted as Capote, *The Muses Are Heard* (New York: Random House, 1956).

58. Quoted from the original liner notes for the 1958 LP of *Blues Opera Suite* (Columbia Records CL 1099) in CD booklet for 2003 reissue by DRG Records (DRG 19044).
59. These materials are contained in a few different collections: at the Library of Congress; the Robert Breen Papers at Ohio State University (SPEC.TRI.RB); and the Robert and Wilva Breen Papers at George Mason University (C0004). Michael Gildin has done prodigious work in sorting through these sources, and he has organized the opera's demo recordings into a sequential order that follows the vocal score. The most detailed account of the genesis and development of *Blues Opera*, clearly prepared in consultation with Arlen, is Jablonski, *Happy with the Blues*, Chapter 11. Jablonski drew here on an earlier article he had written, "Blues Opera," *Hi-Fi Music at Home*, March–April 1957, 24–25, 54, 58. See also Jablonski's later discussion in Jablonski, *Rhythm, Rainbows and Blues*, 302–305. In what follows I draw on these various sources.
60. Columbia CL 1099 (1958); remastered on CD by DRG Records 19044 (2003).
61. Donald McKayle, *Transcending Boundaries: My Dancing Life* (London: Routledge, 2002), 133.
62. Sources for the 1959–1960 *Free and Easy* include production files, posters, clippings, correspondence, scripts, and audio recordings (demos and a complete performance); they are held in the Stanley Chase Papers, University of California, Los Angeles, Series 1 (Subseries 1B) and Series 4.
63. The sources for *Blues Opera* are contained principally at the Library of Congress, the Robert Breen Papers at Ohio State University, the Robert and Wilva Breen Papers at George Mason University, and the Stanley Chase Papers at the University of California, Los Angeles.
64. Jablonski, *Happy with the Blues*, 224.
65. Jablonski, *Happy with the Blues*, 222.
66. As of this writing (February 2024), Michael Gildin, John Mauceri, and Larry Blank are engaged in preparing a fully scored performing edition of *Blues Opera*.
67. Johnny Mercer, interviewed in "The Songs of Harold Arlen," *The Twentieth Century* with Walter Cronkite (February 9, 1964).
68. Jablonski, *Happy with the Blues*, 212.
69. Jablonski, *Happy with the Blues*, 217–218.
70. Irving Berlin wrote at least fourteen counterpoint songs for his shows, including "Simple Melody" from *Watch Your Step* (1912), "I Wonder Why"/"You're Just in Love" from *Call Me Madam* (1950), and "Old-Fashioned Wedding" from a revival of *Annie Get Your Gun* (1966). See Jeffrey Magee, *Irving Berlin's Musical Theater* (New York: Oxford University Press, 2012), 23. Examples by other composers include George and Ira Gershwin's "Mine" from *Let 'Em Eat Cake* (1933) and Frank Loesser's "Inchworm" from *Hans Christian Andersen* (1952).

71. Letter of February 15, 1960, Johnny Mercer Collection, Georgia State University.
72. Jablonski, *Happy with the Blues*, 236.

# Chapter 6

1. In this period Arlen also worked on two films with lyricist Ralph Blane, *My Blue Heaven* (1950) and *Down Among the Sheltering Palms* (1953).
2. Furia, *Poets of Tin Pan Alley*, 214.
3. Jablonski, *Happy with the Blues*, 164–165.
4. Jablonski, *Happy with the Blues*, 165.
5. This chord could also be understood as a French sixth, but such an interpretation would assume a resolution to E major.
6. Alec Wilder has a different and, it seems, miscounted parsing of the song: A(18) B(14) A(18). Wilder, *American Popular Song*, 280.
7. Jablonski, *Happy with the Blues*, 165.
8. The best recent account of Dorothy Fields's career is Charlotte Greenspan, *Pick Yourself Up: Dorothy Fields and the American Musical* (New York: Oxford University Press, 2010).
9. Jablonski, *Happy with the Blues*, 172.
10. I am grateful to Michael Feinstein for sharing with me the MGM copyist scores and his theory about an unlyricized verse.
11. Peggy Lee, a great singer and Arlen enthusiast, leads off her late album *Love Held Lightly: Rare Songs by Harold Arlen* (1993, Harbinger Records; released on CD as HCD-2401 [2006]) with "Look Who's Been Dreaming."

# Chapter 7

1. The outline is given in Ronald Haver, *A Star Is Born: The Making of the 1954 Movie and its 1983 Restoration* (New York: Applause, 2002 [orig. 1988]), 42. Haver's is the most comprehensive and detailed study of the film, but is marred by his failure to identify the sources of many of his quotations and stories.
2. Gershwin's version of Hart's outline, as well as lyric drafts for five songs ("Gotta Have Me Go With You" [alternate title, "You've Got to Have Me Go With You"], "Lose That Long Face" ["Get That Long Face Lost"], "It's a New World," "Here's What I'm Here For" ["What Am I Here For?"], and "The Man That Got Away"), are contained at the University of Texas, Austin, Harry Ransom Center, Jablonski-Stewart Gershwin Collection, Series II, box 6, folder 7. Other drafts and some piano-vocal scores are in the George and Ira Gershwin Collection at the Library of Congress, Boxes 35–36. Arlen's biographer Jablonski reproduces Gershwin's outline in Jablonski, *Rhythm, Rainbows and Blues*, 235.

3. Haver, *A Star Is Born*, 189. Six songs from *A Star Is Born* were published as *Selections from A Star Is Born* in 1954 (reprinted New York: MPL and Hal Leonard, 1983). "The Man That Got Away" was reprinted in *The Harold Arlen Songbook* (New York: MPL and Hal Leonard, 1985). "The Man That Got Away," "It's a New World," "Green Light Ahead," and "Someone at Last" are included in *Harold Arlen Rediscovered* (New York: MPL and Hal Leonard, 1996).
4. Arlen recalled that of the "Lose That Long Face" was the rare song from in *A Star Is Born* where the lyrics were written first, before the music See Robert Kimball and Alfred Simon, *The Gershwins* (New York: Atheneum, 1973), 243. Perhaps this reversal of the normal creative process was due to the fact that the number was added later.
5. In addition to the nine songs Arlen and Gershwin completed or drafted for *A Star Is Born*, they wrote the "Trinidad Coconut Oil Shampoo Commercial," which was recorded by Garland with piano and filmed, but never used. It appears on the CD *Judy Garland: A Star Is Born* (Sony, CK 65965).
6. Haver, *A Star Is Born*, 57.
7. The continuity script for *A Star Is Born* is available electronically through Alexander Street Press: Moss Hart, Robert Carson, and Dorothy Parker, *A Star Is Born (1954): Continuity Script* (Alexandria, VA: Alexander Street, 1954), https://search.alexanderstreet.com/view/work/bibliographic_entity%7Cbibliographic_details%7C2959061.
8. In the continuity script for *A Star Is Born*, Hart labels this number "You Better Have You for Me," which may represent an earlier version of the lyric's title. See *A Star Is Born (1954): Continuity Script*, 8. For more on this lyric, see also Philip Furia, *Ira Gershwin: The Art of the Lyricist* (New York: Oxford University Press, 1996), 215.
9. *A Star Is Born (1954): Continuity Script*, 18. "The Man That Got Away" sequence was shot and reshot multiple times over a number of months. Cukor's goal—unusual for the time and challenging to achieve—was to capture the song in one, uninterrupted take.
10. An earlier title and first line for the song, "Somewhere in the Sometime," had a still different play on "some-." See *The Complete Lyrics of Ira Gershwin*, ed. Robert Kimball (New York: Knopf, 1994), 375.
11. Ira Gershwin, *Lyrics on Several Occasions* (New York: Viking, 1959), 216.
12. Lawrence Stewart, "A Tribute: Ira Gershwin and 'The Man That Got Away,'" *Dictionary of Literary Biography Yearbook 1996*, 171.
13. Gershwin, *Lyrics on Several Occasions*, 109.
14. In 2004 the American Film Institute ranked "The Man That Got Away" as no. 11 in the "100 top movie songs of all times." Garland's performance of Arlen and Harburg's "Over the Rainbow" was no. 1. See "AFI's 100 Years . . . 100 Songs" https://www.afi.com/afis-100-years-100-songs/.
15. *Gershwin Complete Lyrics*, 150.
16. *Gershwin Complete Lyrics*, 150.
17. See above, n. 2.

18. Quoted in Kimball and Simon, *The Gershwins*, 243.
19. Basic information about the Carnegie Hall concert is contained in the program archive at Carnegie Hall: https://www.carnegiehall.org/about/history/performance-history-search?q=&dex=prod_PHS&pf=Frank%20Sinatra_.
20. Lena Horne and Richard Schickel, *Lena* (Garden City NY: Doubleday, 1965), 290.
21. The revised lyrics are printed in *Gershwin Complete Lyrics*, 374–75. Also included is the text of a telegram sent by Horne to Gershwin on September 12: "Dear Ira, I can't tell you how beautiful and how inspiring the lyrics are to me. I will be so proud to sing them."
22. *Gershwin Complete Lyrics*, 376. This paragraph and the lyrics for "I'm Off the Downbeat" were in the end not included in *Lyrics on Several Occasions*.
23. In a letter to Jablonski from May 12, 1953, Gershwin writes of "finishing the songs for Garland a couple of weeks ago," although he does not specify which songs. Edward Jablonski Papers, Library of Congress, Box 46, Folder 5.
24. Letter of September 30, 1953, quoted courtesy of Michael Feinstein.
25. Letter of March 30, 1954, in Edward Jablonski Papers, Library of Congress, Box 46, Folder 6.
26. Haver, *A Star Is Born*, 189.
27. I am grateful to the superbly gifted Eric Comstock for realizing "Dancing Partner" for me from Arlen's lead sheet.

# Chapter 8

1. Letter in Peter Brook Collection, Victoria & Albert Museum London, THM/452/4.
2. This information and other background on Capote comes from Gerald Clarke, *Capote: A Biography* (New York: Simon and Schuster, 1988), esp. chapter 31. I also draw upon Arlen biographer Edward Jablonski's accounts of *House of Flowers* in *Happy with the Blues*, Chapter 9; and *Rhythm, Rainbows and Blues*, chapter 17.
3. The story "House of Flowers" is included in *The Complete Stories of Truman Capote*, ed. Reynolds Price (New York: Random House, 2004), 197–212. Price mistakenly gives the date as 1951; the story was originally published in 1950 in the literary journal *Botteghe oscure* 6 (1950): 414–429.
4. The earliest surviving drafts for the play or libretto (undated) are Capote's handwritten sheets contained in the Truman Capote Papers, Manuscripts and Archives Division, New York Public Library, Astor, Lenox, and Tilden Foundations, Box 34, folder 8. The earliest surviving typescript draft (also undated), for which only Act I survives, is in the materials given by Steven Suskin to the Music Division of Library of Congress in 2010. It is located in the Ira and Leonore S. Gershwin Fund Collection. On the cover of this typescript is written "Property of Harold Arlen," which suggests that this is the copy that Arlen first read and that persuaded him to take on the project.
5. Jablonski, *Happy with the Blues*, 183.

6. This and the following quotations from Capote appear in William Zinsser, "Harold Arlen: the Secret Music Maker," *Harper's Magazine* 220 (May 1960): 45–46. Zinsser's extensive citations resemble almost word-for-word the thoughts Capote recorded in an undated handwritten document, "Recollections of Harold Arlen" (Truman Capote Papers, New York Public Library, Box 34). Capote must have shared this document or a transcript, or more likely the thoughts in it, directly with Zinsser.
7. Jablonski, *Happy with the Blues*, 185.
8. Arlen's tablet is in the Rita Arlen Collection, Music Division, Library of Congress, Washington, D.C.
9. *Complete Stories of Truman Capote*, 203.
10. Capote Papers, New York Public Library, Box 34, folder 8. All citations from the Capote Papers in this chapter are included by kind permission Alan Schwartz, attorney for the Capote estate.
11. See Geoffrey Holder, "Drumming on Steel Barrel-Heads," *Music Journal* 13/5 (May–June 1955): 9, 20, 24. Holder, one of the original dancers in *House of Flowers*, was responsible for bringing the Trinidad Steel Band to the United States for this production.
12. Shane Vogel, *Stolen Time: Black Fad Performance and the Calypso Craze* (Chicago: University of Chicago Press, 2018), 144.
13. While in London, Arlen and Capote performed for Brook a number of the songs they had already written; these versions are preserved on demo recordings.
14. See Sally Banes, "Balanchine and Black Dance," in Banes, *Writing Dancing in the Age of Postmodernism* (Middletown, CT: Wesleyan University Press, 2011), 53–68.
15. The seven scenes are listed in an inventory prepared by dance scholar Tommy DeFrantz after interviewing a number of dancers from the original production of *House of Flowers* for Popular Balanchine Dossiers, New York Public Library, Jerome Robbins Dance Division, Series III, Boxes 38–39.
16. Glory van Scott, audiotaped and transcribed interview, Popular Balanchine Dossiers.
17. See Celia Weiss Bambara, "Did You Say Banda? Geoffrey Holder and How Stories Circulate," *Journal of Haitian Studies* 17 (2011): 180–192. Holder went on to portray Baron Samedi in a chilling sequence in the 1973 James Bond film *Live and Let Die*. Even Shane Vogel, who is so critical of *House of Flowers*, admires the Banda episode as a partially redemptive "moment of rupture" in the show's touristic exoticism (Vogel, *Stolen Time*, 142).
18. Michael Kustow, *Peter Brook: A Biography* (New York: St. Martin's, 2005), 81.
19. Pearl Bailey offers her own take on *House of Flowers* in her autobiography *The Raw Pearl* (New York: Harcourt, Brace & World, 1968), 68–70. She claims as "untrue" the reports that "Pearl did not cooperate." Bailey paints herself not as Diahann Carroll's competitor, but as her mentor.
20. Some brief and soundless film clips of dance excerpts from the original *House of Flowers* survive. They are contained among the Ray Knight films owned by Miles Kreuger at the Institute of the American Musical in Los Angeles, and films made by Arnold Weissberger, held at the Library for the Performing Arts, New York Public

Library. Other excerpts (provenance unknown) appear in the PBS documentary *Free to Dance* (originally aired in 2001). The account of Ailey's injury—he failed to wear his knee pads when sliding across the stage—is reported by the dancer who was called in to replace him, McKayle, *Transcending Boundaries*, 71.

21. Critical reaction to *House of Flowers* from the white mainstream press is summarized and sampled in Jablonski, *Happy with the Blues*, 256–257. See also Steven Suskin, *Opening Night on Broadway: A Critical Quotebook of the Golden Era of the Musical Theatre, Oklahoma! (1943) to Fiddler on the Roof (1964)* (New York: Schirmer, 1990), 319–323.
22. James L. Hicks, "'House of Flowers' is Pert Fantasy of Sex, Song, Sin," *Baltimore Afro-American*, January 15, 1955, 7.
23. "Moralists Hit Carmen Jones, House of Flowers," *Atlanta Daily World*, January 6, 1955.
24. James Baldwin, "Life Straight in de Eye: *Carmen Jones*: Film Spectacular in Color," *Commentary* 20 (January 1, 1955): 74–77; reprinted as "*Carmen Jones*: The Dark is Light Enough," in Baldwin, *Notes of a Native Son* (Boston: Beacon Press, 1955).
25. Wilder, *American Popular Song*, 284.
26. Jablonski, *Rhythm, Rainbows and Blues*, 259.
27. *The Complete Stories of Truman Capote*, 199.
28. *House of Flowers*, typescript draft, Library of Congress. A handwritten draft of this same passage is in the Truman Capote Papers, The New York Public Library, Box 34, folder 8. This scene was cut from the original *House of Flowers*, but largely restored by Capote and Arlen for the 1968 off-Broadway revival, for which a new libretto was published: Truman Capote and Harold Arlen, *House of Flowers* (New York: Random House, 1968).
29. Capote Papers, New York Public Library, Box 34, folder 8.
30. Transcribed from the audio recording included as a bonus track on the 2003 CD release of the original cast recording *House of Flowers* (Columbia SK 86857). Arlen's comments are discussed and also partially transcribed in Jablonski, *Rhythm, Rainbows and Blues*, 246–247. Jablonski reports that the music for "A Sleepin' Bee" "dates back to before *A Star Is Born*, for which it had been only momentarily considered and discarded." (Jablonski, *Happy with the Blues*, 192). I have not been able to confirm this assertion independently, but Arlen often resurrected great "trunk" songs, as in the case of "The Man That Got Away," discussed in Chapter 7.
31. Capote seems to confirm this in reporting to Jablonski that "When Arlen came in everything had to be changed except for the actual characters and the lyrics for the title song." (Cited in Jablonski, *Happy with the Blues*, 186.)
32. Wilder, *American Popular Song*, 283.
33. Jablonski, *Happy with the Blues*, 183.
34. Audra McDonald tends to articulate distinct pitches (especially on "love is") in her interpretation of "I Never Has Seen Snow" (*How Glory Goes*, released in 2000; Nonesuch 79580-2).

270    NOTES TO PAGES 185–195

35. During the recording of the original cast album of *House of Flowers* in January 1955, Diahann Carroll, suffering from a cold, was unable to reach that high G. Arlen himself sang it for her, and his voice was dubbed into the tape for that one note in a way that is audible on the album (Jablonski, *Rhythm, Rainbows and Blues*, 258).
36. Jablonski, *Happy with the Blues*, 194.
37. Jablonski, *Rhythm, Rainbows and Blues*, 258.
38. Truman Capote and Harold Arlen, *House of Flowers* (New York: Random House, 1968).
39. Capote and Arlen, *House of Flowers*, 79.
40. Capote and Arlen, *House of Flowers*, 82.
41. Some of these materials, from Arlen's legacy, were sold at auction by Doyle on March 22, 2022. See https://doyle.com/auctions/22bp01-rare-books-autographs-maps/catalogue/, lots 96–102. The letter from Capote quoted here is lot 100.

# Chapter 9

1. Earlier radio appearances of Arlen include a December 1933 show with the Paul Whiteman Orchestra; a promotional *Wizard of Oz* broadcast of June 1939, Maxwell House Good News (available on CD from Jass Records J-CD-629 [1991]); several wartime broadcasts; and some appearances on CBS radio in the late 1940s. Some of these broadcasts have been preserved at the Library of Congress and in the collection of J. David Goldin at the University of Missouri-Kansas City, Special Collections.
2. Jablonski, *Rhythm, Rainbows and Blues*, 87.
3. Bing Crosby, letter to Robert Wachsman, December 15, 1947, Rita Arlen Collection, Music Division, Library of Congress.
4. Noel Coward, letter to Arlen, Rita Arlen Collection, Music Division, Library of Congress.
5. Quoted Swayne, *How Sondheim Found His Sound*, 84.
6. Transcribed by the author from a recording held at the Library of Congress, Recorded Sound Research Center, RGA 3075 A1–B2. Arlen also talked about the influence of his father's cantorial style in his interview with Wilk, *They're Playing Our Song*, 144.
7. There is no central repository of Arlen demos. Arlen's biographer Jablonski appears to have shared them with a number of people. I am grateful to Michael Feinstein, Ken Bloom, Bill Rudman, Michael Gildin, and Howard Green for generously providing me with digital copies of many demos.
8. Peggy Lee recorded "Can You Explain?" and "Love's No Stranger to Me" on her album *Love Held Lightly: Rare Songs by Harold Arlen* (Harbinger Records, 1993; released on CD as HCD-2401 [2006]).
9. All these albums have been remastered and released on CD by Harbinger Records.

10. Quoted in liner notes by Bill Rudman and Ken Bloom to *The Music of Harold Arlen: The 1955 Walden Sessions* (Harbinger, HCD-1505 [1998]).
11. Jablonski, *Rhythm, Rainbows and Blues*, 266.
12. "Packaged Goods," *Down Beat* 23: 5 (March 1956): 17.
13. John McAndrew, "Star Studded Shellac," *Record Changer* 14:10 (January 1957), 30.
14. Herbert Kupferberg, "Records: On Broadway and Off," *New York Herald Tribune* (July 10, 1955): E10.
15. J.W., "Jazz Debut: De Forest Offers Some Rarely Heard Tunes," *New York Times* (October 9, 1955): X20.
16. John S. Wilson, "The Songwriter as Singer," *New York Times* (May 1, 1966): 146
17. See my *Arlen and Harburg's "Over the Rainbow"* (New York: Oxford University Press, 2017), 94–96.
18. Both Southern and Sinatra made their recordings in May 1954. Southern's was released on Decca L 7701, Sinatra's on Capitol F 2864.
19. See the extended entry about Raye in Friedwald, *Biographical Guide*, 379–385.

# Chapter 10

1. Jablonski, *Rhythm, Rainbows and Blues*, 321.
2. See Arlen's comments as reported in an interview with Jack O'Brian of the *New York Journal-American* in early 1962, cited in Jablonski, *Rhythm, Rainbows and Blues*, 329–330.
3. Jablonski, *Rhythm, Rainbows and Blues*, 330.
4. The term "late style" appears to have been coined by Theodor W. Adorno for Beethoven. See Theodor W. Adorno, "Late Style in Beethoven," in Adorno, *Essays on Music*, ed. Richard Leppert (Berkeley: University of California Press, 2002), 564–567. See also an influential study that explores late style across a range of artists and media: Edward Said, *On Late Style: Music and Literature Against the Grain* (New York: Pantheon, 2006).
5. James Leve discusses aspects of a late musical style in Richard Rodgers's penultimate musical *Rex* (1976) in "Disability and Lateness in Musical Theater," paper presented at the virtual conference StageStruck!, May 12–15, 2021.
6. Several of Arlen's late songs, including "Come On, Midnight" and "I Had a Love Once," both discussed in this chapter, were recorded by Peggy Lee on her own late album *Love Held Lightly: Rare Songs by Harold Arlen* (Harbinger Records HCD 2401 [1993/2006].
7. See the obituary by Bruce Weber in the *New York Times*, February 14, 2012, https://www.nytimes.com/2012/02/15/arts/music/dory-previn-songwriter-is-dead-at-86.html. There is as yet no full-scale biography of Dory Langdon.
8. The solo piano album is *André Previn Plays Songs by Harold Arlen* (Contemporary Records M 3586 [1960]; remastered on CD as OJCCD-1840-2 [1994]). As pianist and arranger, Previn made *Sittin' on a Rainbow: The Music of Harold Arlen*

(Columbia CS 8733 [1963]; reissued by Sony on CD in 2013). The album with McNair is *Come Rain or Come Shine: The Harold Arlen Songbook* (Philips 446 818-2 [1996]).

9. Previn and Langdon (identified as Dory Previn) appear at several points in the show "The Songs of Harold Arlen," *The Twentieth Century* with Walter Cronkite, broadcast February 9, 1964. These comments occur at 45:15 and are transcribed in Jablonski, *Rhythm, Rainbows and Blues*, 325.

10. Letter from Arlen to Dory Previn, October 29, 1962, courtesy of Joby Baker and Leslie Shatz.

11. "The Morning After" and "So Long, Big Time" are in *The Harold Arlen Songbook* (New York: MPL Communications, 1985). "You're Impossible" is in the companion volume *Harold Arlen Rediscovered* (New York: Harwin Music, 1996).

12. Jablonski, *Rhythm, Rainbows and Blues*, 94–95.

13. Langdon's comments on the genesis of "So Long, Big Time!" begin at 3:59 in "The Songs of Harold Arlen."

14. Tony Bennett, with Will Friedwald, *The Good Life: The Autobiography of Tony Bennett* (New York: Pocket Books, 1998), 160.

15. The footage of the recording session for "So Long, Big Time!," which includes the entire song, begins at 5:13 in the 1964 television broadcast, "The Songs of Harold Arlen," *The Twentieth Century* with Walter Cronkite.

16. Jablonski, *Rhythm, Rainbows and Blues*, 329.

17. A collection of fifteen Arlen-Charnin numbers, including eight intended for *Softly*, has been recorded by Sylvia McNair, with the pianist Kevin Cole, on *You Are Tomorrow: Rare Songs by Harold Arlen and Martin Charnin* (Harbinger Records HCD 3902, 2023)

18. See https://www.barbra-archives.info/broadway-answers-selma-1965. Streisand recorded the song on her 1968 album *What About Today?* (Columbia CS 9816).

19. Personal interview with the author, May 19, 2013.

20. Jablonski, *Rhythm, Rainbows and Blues*, 326–327.

21. Jablonski *Rhythm, Rainbows and Blues*, 329.

22. About *Softly*, see Jablonski, *Rhythm, Rainbows and Blues*, 333–336. The Library of Congress contains some numbers for *Softly* submitted for copyright deposit. The demo recordings were kindly made available to me by Bill Rudman.

23. Santha Rama Rau, "Softly," *Saturday Evening Post* 236/43, December 7, 1963: 52–53, 56, 66, 69–72, 76, 79–84, 86–87.

24. Rau wrote an essay-memoir about her time in Japan: "Japan," in her *East of Home* (New York: Harper & Brothers, 1950), 1–70.

25. Rau, "Softly," 52.

26. Rau, "Softly," 52.

27. Martin Charnin in an interview with Bill Rudman, cited courtesy of Bill Rudman.

28. Sam Zolotow, "Robards May Star in Arlen Musical," *New York Times*, January 11, 1966, https://www.proquest.com/historical-newspapers/robards-may-star-arlen-musical/docview/117116311/se-2?accountid=10226.

29. *Variety*, February 11, 1966: 6.
30. The Hanya Holm Papers at the New York Public Library contain two pages with Holm's notes on the auditions, giving her evaluation of thirty-six dancers with "Yes" or "No." The radio interview with Walter Terry was broadcast on WNYC on June 5, 1966, as part of his series "Invitation to Dance." It is available through New York Public Library Digital Collections.
31. For a survey of some of the American films of this era set in occupied Japan, see W. Anthony Sheppard, *Extreme Exoticism: Japan in the American Musical Imagination* (New York: Oxford University Press, 2019), chapter 6, "Singing Sayonara: Musical Representations of Japan in Postwar Hollywood."
32. Wheeler's typescript drafts of *Softly* are held in the Hugh Wheeler Collection, Howard Gotlieb Archival Center, Boston University.
33. The diary, written in a National brand datebook, is held in the Rita Arlen Archives, Music Division, Library of Congress.
34. Lemmon, Bridges, and Sinatra are mentioned in Arlen's diary. The approach to Fred Astaire, as recalled by Charnin, is reported in Rimler, *The Man That Got Away*, 160.
35. Recordings of all the songs for *Softly* discussed in this section are available on the album *You Are Tomorrow* (see note 17).
36. See Sheppard, *Extreme Exoticism*, 70–73.
37. Hugh Wheeler Collection, Box 18, draft of February 12, 1967.
38. I have asked several Japanese men who grew up in the country during a somewhat later period (the 1950s and 60s) whether they recalled such team games with kites being played at school. They did not.
39. Stephen Banfield, *Sondheim's Broadway Musicals* (Ann Arbor: University of Michigan Press, 1993), 260.
40. As reported by Sondheim in Swayne, *How Sondheim Found His Sound*, 84.
41. Arlen's musical *Bloomer Girl* had been adapted for a television broadcast in 1956 as part of the Producers' Showcase series. This live telecast has been reissued on DVD (VAI 4555 [2012]).
42. Jablonski, *Rhythm, Rainbows and Blues*, 343–346.

# Chapter 11

1. Two of the most useful databases, searchable by composer or number, are SecondHandSongs (https://secondhandsongs.com/) and the Jazz Discography (https://www.lordisco.com/).
2. For a discussion of jazz pianists' interpretations of "Over the Rainbow" see Frisch, *Arlen and Harburg's "Over the Rainbow"*, chapter 5, "Ivory Rainbows."
3. Randall Cherry, "Ethel Waters: The Voice of an Era," in *Temples for Tomorrow: Looking Back at the Harlem Renaissance*, ed. Geneviève Fabre and Michael Feith, 99–124

(Bloomington: Indiana University Press, 2001). For an example of the dismissive criticism of Waters in comparison to other blues singers, see Angela Davis, *Blues Legacies and Black Feminism: Gertrude "Ma" Rainey, Bessie Smith, and Billie Holiday* (New York: Pantheon, 1998), 152–153.

4. For an example of the dismissive criticism of Waters in comparison to other blues singers, see Angela Davis, *Blues Legacies and Black Feminism: Gertrude "Ma" Rainey, Bessie Smith, and Billie Holiday* (New York: Pantheon, 1998), 152–153.
5. James Weldon Johnson, *Black Manhattan* (New York: Knopf, 1930; reprint, New York: Da Capo, 1991), 210.
6. This famous concert was captured on a two-disk LP set, *Judy at Carnegie Hall* (Capitol WBO/SWBO-1569).
7. Garland's remarks begin at 4:15 on the "Come Rain or Come Shine" track.
8. For an extended analysis of Garland's performances of "Over the Rainbow" see Frisch, *Arlen and Harburg's "Over the Rainbow"*, 75–83.
9. Horne would make a number of later recordings of "Stormy Weather." For a discussion of Horne's performances of the song, see Friedwald, *Stardust Melodies*, 294–297.
10. See the Sinatra "sessionography" prepared by Richard Cook and Steve Albin http://www.jazzdiscography.com/Artists/Sinatra/.
11. Friedwald, *Biographical Guide*, 422.
12. "Friday with Garroway," Library of Congress, Recorded Sound Research Center, RGA 3075 A1–B2.
13. See Friedwald, *Biographical Guide*, 422.
14. For details of this session, including Riddle's personnel, see Sinatra sessionograpy, https://www.jazzdiscography.com/Artists/Sinatra/capitol1.php.
15. As discussed in Chapter 4, this recording and outtake do not appear to survive; they are not listed in Sinatra's sessionographies.
16. Friedwald, *Biographical Guide*, 422.
17. Letter of October 30, 1959, from Norman Granz, Edward Jablonski Collection, Library of Congress.
18. Quoted by Douglas Ramsey in liner notes for 2001 CD reissue *Ella Fitzgerald Sings the Harold Arlen Songbook* (Verve 314 589 108-2). All references are to these notes, which have no pagination.
19. Benny Green, original liner notes from 1961, reprinted in 2001 CD reissue.
20. Jablonski, *Rhythm, Rainbows and Blues*, 311.
21. Original liner notes included in *Ella Fitzgerald Sings the Harold Arlen Songbook* (Verve 314 589 108-2).
22. Eileen Farrell and Brian Kellow, *Can't Help Singing: The Life of Eileen Farrell* (Boston: Northeastern University Press, 1999), 138.
23. Barbra Streisand, *Just for the Record* (Columbia, C4K 44111), 8. On Arlen as her "favorite composer," see also Streisand, *My Name is Barbra* (New York: Viking, 2023), 50–51, 66, 120.
24. All the Bon Soir recordings are now available on Barbra Streisand, *Live at the Bon Soir* (Sony Music Entertainment, 2023).

25. For detailed information on all of Streisand's recordings, see the excellent website curated by Matt Howe, Barbra Archives (https://www.barbra-archives.info/music).
26. *The Barbra Streisand Album* (Columbia CS 8807, CL 2007). https://www.barbra-archives.info/barbra-streisand-album-1963
27. André Previn, "A Lighthouse of Musicianship," in booklet accompanying *Come Rain or Come Shine* (Philips 446 818-2, 1996).
28. Stephen Holden, "Audra McDonald Casts Her Spell on Sadness," *New York Times*, November 5, 2002, Section E, p. 5.
29. Friedwald, *Biographical Guide*, 318.

# Selected Bibliography

Adorno, Theodor W. "Late Style in Beethoven." In Adorno, *Essays on Music*, edited by Richard Leppert, 564–68. Berkeley: University of California Press, 2002.

Alonso, Harriet Hyman. *Yip Harburg: Legendary Lyricist and Human Rights Activist*. Middletown, CT: Wesleyan University Press, 2012.

Bailey, Pearl. *The Raw Pearl*. New York: Harcourt, Brace & World, 1968.

Baldwin, James. "*Carmen Jones*: The Dark is Light Enough." In Baldwin, *Notes of a Native Son*, 47–55. Boston: Beacon Press, 1955.

Bambara, Celia Weiss. "Did You Say Banda? Geoffrey Holder and How Stories Circulate." *Journal of Haitian Studies* 17 (2011): 180–192.

Banes, Sally. "Balanchine and Black Dance." In Banes, *Writing Dancing in the Age of Postmodernism*, 53–69. Middletown, CT: Wesleyan University Press, 2011.

Banes, Sally, and John Szwed. "From 'Messin' Around' to 'Funky Western Civilization': The Rise and Fall of Dance Instruction Songs." In Thomas Defrantz, ed., *Dancing Many Drums: Excavations in African American Dance*, 169–203. Madison: University of Wisconsin Press, 2002.

Banfield, Stephen. *Sondheim's Broadway Musicals*. Ann Arbor: University of Michigan Press, 1993.

Bennett, Tony, with Will Friedwald. *The Good Life: The Autobiography of Tony Bennett*. New York: Pocket Books, 1998.

Biamonte, Nicole. "Augmented-Sixth Chords vs. Tritone Substitutes." *Music Theory Online* 14/2 (2008).

Block, Geoffrey. *A Fine Romance: Adapting Broadway to Hollywood in the Studio System Era*. New York: Oxford University Press, 2023.

Boardman, Gerald. *Days to Be Happy, Days to Be Sad: The Life and Music of Vincent Youmans*. New York: Oxford University Press, 1982.

Bogle, Donald. *Heat Wave: The Life and Career of Ethel Waters*. New York: HarperCollins, 2011.

Bontemps, Arna, and Langston Hughes. *Arna Bontemps–Langston Hughes Letters 1925–1967*. Edited by Charles H. Nichols. New York: Dodd, Mead, 1980.

Brackett, David. *Categorizing Sound: Genre and Twentieth-Century Popular Music*. Oakland: University of California Press, 2016.

Broadhurst, Laura Lynn. "'Arlen and Harburg and More, Oh My!': The Cumulative Creation of the *Oz* Songs." In Danielle Birkett and Dominic McHugh, eds., *Adapting the Wizard of Oz: Musical Versions from Baum to MGM and Beyond*, 53–78. New York: Oxford University Press, 2019.

Broadhurst, Laura Lynn. "Wizards of Song: Arlen, Harburg, and the Cumulative Creation of the Songs for *The Wizard of Oz* (1939)." PhD dissertation, Rutgers University, 2020. https://www.proquest.com/dissertations-theses/wizards-song-arlen-harburg-cumulative-creation/docview/2426499642/se-2.

Capote, Truman. *The Complete Stories of Truman Capote*. Edited by Reynolds Price. New York: Random House, 2004.

Capote, Truman. *The Muses Are Heard*. New York: Random House, 1956.
Capote, Truman, and Harold Arlen. *House of Flowers*. New York: Random House, 1968.
Cherry, Randall. "Ethel Waters: The Voice of an Era." In Geneviève Fabre and Michael Feith, eds., *Temples for Tomorrow: Looking Back at the Harlem Renaissance*, 99–100. Bloomington: Indiana University Press, 2001.
Clarke, Gerald. *Capote: A Biography*. New York: Simon and Schuster, 1988.
Davis, Lee. *Scandals and Follies: The Rise and Fall of the Great Broadway Revue*. New York: Limelight, 2000.
Decker, Todd. *Astaire by Numbers: Time & the Straight White Male Dancer*. New York: Oxford University Press, 2022.
Decker, Todd. "On the Scenic Route to Irving Berlin's *Holiday Inn* (1942)." *Journal of Musicology* 28 (2011): 464–497. https://doi.org/10.1525/jm.2011.28.4.464.
England, Sarah. "'It Was Good Enough for Grandma, But It Ain't Good Enough for Us!': Women and the Nation in Harold Arlen and E.Y. Harburg's Wartime Musical *Bloomer Girl* (1944)," M.A. thesis, University of Maryland, College Park, 2013.
Eskew, Glenn T. *Johnny Mercer: Southern Songwriter for the World*. Athens: University of Georgia Press, 2013.
Farrell, Eileen, and Brian Kellow. *Can't Help Singing: The Life of Eileen Farrell*. Boston: Northeastern University Press, 1999.
Fordin, Hugh. *The World of Entertainment! Hollywood's Greatest Musicals*. Garden City, NY: Doubleday, 1975.
Forte, Allen. *The American Popular Ballad of the Golden Era, 1924–1950*. Princeton, NJ: Princeton University Press, 1995.
Fricke, John, Jay Scarfone, and William Stillman. *The Wizard of Oz: The Official 50th Anniversary Pictorial History*. New York: Warner, 1989.
Friedwald, Will. *A Biographical Guide to the Great Jazz and Pop Singers*. New York: Pantheon, 2010.
Friedwald, Will. *Stardust Melodies: A Biography of Twelve of America's Most Popular Songs*. New York: Pantheon, 2002.
Frisch, Walter. *Arlen and Harburg's "Over the Rainbow."* New York: Oxford University Press, 2017.
Frisch, Walter. "Arlen's Tapeworms: The Tunes That Got Away." *Musical Quarterly* 98 (2015): 139–170.
Furia, Philip. *Ira Gershwin: The Art of the Lyricist*. New York: Oxford University Press, 1996.
Furia, Philip. *The Poets of Tin Pan Alley: A History of America's Great Lyricists*. New York: Oxford University Press, 1990. Second edition, with Laurie J. Patterson, 2022.
Gershwin, Ira. *The Complete Lyrics of Ira Gershwin*. Edited by Robert Kimball. New York: Knopf, 1994.
Gershwin, Ira. *Lyrics on Several Occasions*. New York: Viking, 1975.
Goldberg, Isaac. *George Gershwin: A Study in American Music*. New York: Simon & Schuster, 1931.
Gottlieb, Jack. *Funny, It Doesn't Sound Jewish: How Yiddish Songs and Synagogue Melodies Influenced Tin Pan Alley, Broadway, and Hollywood*. Albany: State University of New York, 2004.
Greenspan, Charlotte. *Pick Yourself Up: Dorothy Fields and the American Musical*. New York: Oxford University Press, 2010.
Hamm, Charles. *Yesterdays: Popular Song in America*. New York: Norton, 1979.

Handy, W.C. ed. *Blues: An Anthology*. New York: Albert and Charles Boni, 1926.

Harmetz, Aljean. *The Making of The Wizard of Oz*. New York: Limelight, 1984. Orig. ed. 1977.

Hart, Moss, Robert Carson, and Dorothy Parker. *A Star Is Born (1954): Continuity Script*. Alexandria, VA: Alexander Street, 1954. https://search.alexanderstreet.com/view/work/bibliographic_entity%7Cbibliographic_details%7C2959061.

Haskins, Jim. *The Cotton Club*. New York: New American Library, 1977.

Hatch, James V. "The Great Depression and Federal Theatre." In Errol G. Hill and James V. Hatch, eds., *A History of African American Theatre*, 315–334. Cambridge, UK: Cambridge University Press, 2003.

Haver, Ronald. *A Star Is Born: The Making of the 1954 Movie and its 1983 Restoration*. New York: Applause, 2002. Orig. ed. 1988.

Holder, Geoffrey. "Drumming on Steel Barrel-Heads." *Music Journal* 13/5 (May–June 1955): 9, 20, 24.

Horne, Lena, and Richard Schickel. *Lena*. Garden City, NY: Doubleday, 1965.

Horowitz, Mark Eden. *Sondheim on Music: Minor Details and Major Decisions*, 2nd ed. Lanham, MD: Scarecrow, 2010.

Jablonski, Edward. *Harold Arlen: Happy with the Blues*. New York: Da Capo, 1986. Orig. ed., 1961.

Jablonski, Edward. *Harold Arlen: Rhythm, Rainbows, and Blues*. Boston: Northeastern University Press, 1996.

Jasen, David A., and Gene Jones. *Spreadin' Rhythm Around: Black Popular Songwriters, 1880–1930*. New York: Schirmer, 1998.

Jones, Kirkland T. *Renaissance Man from Louisiana: A Biography of Arna Bontemps*. New York: Greenwood Press, 1992.

Kane, Brian. "Jazz, Mediation, Ontology." *Contemporary Music Review* 37 (2018): 507–528. https://doi.org/10.1080/07494467.2017.1402466.

Kapilow, Rob. *Listening for America: Inside the Great American Songbook from Gershwin to Sondheim*. New York: Norton, 2019.

Kimball, Robert, and Alfred Simon. *The Gershwins*. New York: Atheneum, 1973.

Knight, Arthur. *Disintegrating the Musical: Black Performance and American Musical Film*. Durham, NC: Duke University Press, 2002.

Kustow, Michael. *Peter Brook: A Biography*. New York: St. Martin's, 2005.

Lahr, John. *Notes on a Cowardly Lion: The Biography of Bert Lahr*. New York: Knopf, 1969.

Lapine, James. *Putting It Together: How Stephen Sondheim and I Created Sunday in the Park with George*. New York: Farrar, Straus & Giroux, 2021.

Lees, Gene. *Portrait of Johnny: The Life of John Herndon Mercer*. New York: Pantheon, 2004.

Lefferts, Peter. "Chronology and Itinerary of the Career of Will Marion Cook: Materials for a Biography." *Faculty Publications: [University of Nebraska] School of Music* 66 (2017). http://digitalcommons.unl.edu/musicfacpub/66.

Lomax, Alan. *The Land Where the Blues Began*. New York: Pantheon, 1993.

Magee, Jeffrey. *Irving Berlin's Musical Theater*. New York: Oxford University Press, 2012.

Magee, Jeffrey. *The Uncrowned King of Swing: Fletcher Henderson and Big Band Jazz*. New York: Oxford University Press, 2005.

McKayle, Donald. *Transcending Boundaries: My Dancing Life*. London: Routledge, 2002.

McWhorter, John. *Talking Back, Talking Black: Truths About America's Lingua Franca*. New York: Bellevue, 2017.

Melnick, Jeffrey. *A Right to Sing the Blues: African Americans, Jews, and American Popular Song*. Cambridge, MA: Harvard University Press, 1999.

Mercer, Johnny. *The Complete Lyrics of Johnny Mercer*. Edited by Robert Kimball, Barry Day, Miles Kreuger, and Eric Davis. New York: Knopf, 2009.

Meyerson, Harold, and Ernie Harburg. *Who Put the Rainbow in the Wizard of Oz? Yip Harburg, Lyricist*. Ann Arbor: University of Michigan Press, 1993.

Miller, Karl Hagstrom. *Segregating Sound: Inventing Folk and Pop Music in the Age of Jim Crow*. Durham, NC: Duke University Press, 2010.

Most, Andrea. *Making Americans: Jews and the Broadway Musical*. Cambridge, MA: Harvard University Press, 2004.

Murray, Ken. *The Body Merchant: The Story of Earl Carroll*. Pasadena, CA: Ward Ritchie Press, 1976.

Noonan, Peggy. *The Strange Career of Porgy and Bess: Race, Culture, and America's Most Famous Opera*. Chapel Hill: University of North Carolina Press, 2012.

Patterson, Lindsay, ed. *Black Theater: A 20th Century Collection of the Work of Its Best Playwrights*. New York: Dodd, Mead, 1971.

Pollack, Howard. *George Gershwin: His Life and Work*. Berkeley: University of California Press, 2007.

Rampersad, Arnold. *The Life of Langston Hughes*. 2 vols. New York: Oxford University Press, 1968–1988.

Rau, Santha Rama. "Softly," *Saturday Evening Post* 236/43 (December 7, 1963): 52–53, 56, 66, 69–72, 76, 79–84, 86–87.

Riis, Thomas. *Just Before Jazz: Black Musical Theater in New York, 1890–1915*. Washington, D.C.: Smithsonian, 1989.

Rimler, Walter. *The Man That Got Away: The Life and Songs of Harold Arlen*. Urbana: University of Illinois Press, 2015.

Rogin, Michael. *Blackface, White Noise: Jewish Immigrants in the Hollywood Melting Pot*. Berkeley: University of California Press, 1998.

Rushdie, Salman. *The Wizard of Oz*. 2nd ed. London: Palgrave Macmillan, 2012.

Said, Edward. *On Late Style: Music and Literature Against the Grain*. New York: Pantheon, 2006.

Sheppard, Anthony. *Extreme Exoticism: Japan in the American Musical Imagination*. New York: Oxford University Press, 2019.

Shipton, Alyn. *I Feel a Song Coming On: The Life of Jimmy McHugh*. Urbana: University of Illinois Press, 2009.

Sloan, Nathaniel. "Stormy Relations: The Cotton Club, Broadway Spirituals, and Harlem Encounters in the Music of Harold Arlen and Ted Koehler." *Musical Quarterly* 101 (2018): 120–156. https://doi.org/10.1093/musqtl/gdy017.

Sondheim, Stephen. *Finishing the Hat: Collected Lyrics (1954–1981) with Attendant Comments, Principles, Heresies, Grudges, Whines, and Anecdotes*. New York: Knopf, 2010.

Stewart, Lawrence D. "A Tribute: Ira Gershwin and 'The Man That Got Away.'" *Dictionary of Literary Biography Yearbook 1996*: 165–171.

Streisand, Barbra. *My Name Is Barbra*. New York: Viking, 2023.

Suskin, Steven. *Opening Night on Broadway: A Critical Quotebook of the Golden Era of the Musical Theatre,* Oklahoma! *(1943) to* Fiddler on the Roof *(1964)*. New York: Schirmer, 1990.

Swayne, Steve. *How Sondheim Found His Sound*. Ann Arbor: University of Michigan Press, 2005.

Terefenko, Dariusz. *Jazz Theory: From Basic to Advanced Study*, 2nd ed. New York: Routledge, 2018.

Townsend, Peter. *Pearl Harbor Jazz: Change in Popular Music in the Early 1940s*. Jackson: University Press of Mississippi, 2007.

Uy, Michael Sy. "Performing Catfish Row in the Soviet Union: The Everyman Opera Company and *Porgy and Bess*, 1955–56." *Journal of the Society for American Music* 11 (2017): 470–501.

Viertel, Jack. *The Secret Life of the American Musical: How Broadway Shows Are Built*. New York: Sarah Crichton Books, 2017.

Vogel, Shane. *Stolen Time: Black Fad Performance and the Calypso Craze*. Chicago: University of Chicago Press, 2018.

Vogel, Shane. "Performing 'Stormy Weather': Ethel Waters, Lena Horne, and Katherine Dunham." *South Central Review* 25/2 (2008): 93–113. https://www.jstor.org/stable/40040021.

Waters, Ethel, and Charles Samuels. *His Eye Is On the Sparrow*. New York: Doubleday, 1951.

Westover, Jonas. *The Shuberts and Their Passing Shows: The Untold Tale of Ziegfeld's Rivals*. New York: Oxford University Press, 2016.

White, Walter. *A Man Called White: The Autobiography of Walter White*. New York: Viking Press, 1948.

Wilder, Alec. *American Popular Song: The Great Innovators, 1900–1950*. 3rd ed. New York: Oxford University Press, 2022.

Wilk, Max. *They're Playing Our Song: Conversations with America's Classic Songwriters*. New York: Da Capo, 1997. Orig. ed., 1973.

Zinsser, William K. "Harold Arlen, the Secret Music Maker." *Harper's Magazine* 220 (May 1, 1960): 42–47.

# Credits

### Harold Arlen and Ted Koehler

"Get Happy" ©1929 (Renewed) Warner Bros. & S.A. Music.
"Ill Wind" ©1934 Mills Music, Inc. Renewed 1962 Arko Music Corp.
"Let's Fall in Love" ©1933 (Renewed) Bourne Co.
"Now I Know" ©1943 Harms, Inc.
"Out of a Clear Blue Sky" ©1930 Remick Music Corp.
"Stormy Weather" ©1933 Mills Music, Inc. Renewed 1961 Arko Music Corp.

### Harold Arlen and Yip Harburg

"Buds Won't Bud" ©1937 (Renewed 1965) Leo Feist, Inc. Rights assigned to CBS Catalogue Partnership. All rights administered and controlled by CBS Feist, Inc.
"Cocoanut Sweet" ©1957 Harold Arlen and E.Y. Harburg. Renewed 1985 Harold Arlen. All rights controlled by Harwin Music Corp. and Glocca Morra Music Corp.
"Fancy Meeting You" ©1936 (Renewed) Warner Bros., Inc.
"Fun to Be Fooled" ©1934 (Renewed) New World Music Corporation.
"Happiness Is Just a Thing Called Joe" ©1942 (Renewed 1970) Metro-Goldwyn-Mayer, Inc. All rights controlled and administered by Leo Feist, Inc. All rights of Leo Feist, Inc., assigned to CBS Catalogue Partnership and controlled and administered by CBS Feist Catalogue, Inc.
"It's Only a Paper Moon" ©1933 Harms, Inc. Copyright renewed, assigned to Chappell & Co., Inc. (Intersong Music, Publisher) and Warner Bros.
"Last Night When We Were Young" ©1937 (Renewed) Bourne Co.
"Little Drops of Rain" ©1961, 1962 Harwin Music Corp.
"Over the Rainbow" ©1938, 1939 (Renewed 1966, 1967) Metro-Goldwyn-Mayer, Inc. All rights controlled and administered by Leo Feist, Inc. Rights of Leo Feist, Inc., assigned to CBS Catalogue Partnership. All rights controlled and administered by CBS Feist Catalog, Inc.
"Right As the Rain" ©1944 (Renewed) by The Players Music Corporation. All rights assigned to Chappell & Co, Inc.
"Take It Slow, Joe" ©1957 Harold Arlen and E.Y. Harburg. All rights controlled by Harwin Music Corp.

### Harold Arlen and Johnny Mercer

All songs from *St. Louis Woman* ©1946 (Renewed) A-M Music Corp. All rights controlled by Chappell & Co., Inc.

"Blues in the Night" ©1941 (Renewed) Warner Bros., Inc.
"A Game of Poker" ©1959 by Harold Arlen and Johnny Mercer. All rights controlled by Harwin Music Corp.
"Love Held Lightly" ©1959 (Renewed) Harwin Music Corp. and WB Music Corp.
"My Shining Hour" ©1943 Harwin Music Corp. (Renewed 1971 Harwin Music Corp.)
"One for My Baby," ©1943 Harwin Music Corp. (Renewed 1971 Harwin Music Corp.)
"Out of This World" ©1945 (Renewed 1971) Edwin H. Morris & Co., a division of MPL Communications, Inc.
"That Old Black Magic" ©1942 (Renewed 1969) by Famous Music Corporation

## Harold Arlen and Leo Robin

"For Every Man There's a Woman" ©1948 (renewed 1976) Harwin Music Corp.
"It Was Written in the Stars" ©1948 (renewed 1976) Harwin Music Corp.
"What's Good About Goodbye?" ©1948 (renewed 1976) Harwin Music Corp.

## Harold Arlen and Dorothy Fields

"Let Me Look at You" ©1951 Chappell & Co., Inc.
"Look Who's Been Dreaming" ©1992 Harwin Music Corp.
"We're in Business" ©1953 Twentieth Century Music Corporation
"With the Sun Warm Upon Me" ©1953 (Renewed 1981) Twentieth Century Music Corporation. All rights controlled by Harwin Music Corp.

## Harold Arlen and Ira Gershwin

All songs from *A Star Is Born* ©1954 (Renewed 1982) Harwin Music Corp.

## Harold Arlen and Truman Capote

Songs from *House of Flowers* ©1954 (Renewed 1982) Harold Arlen and Truman Capote. All rights controlled by Harwin Music Corp.
"Albertina's Beautiful Hair" ©1968 Harold Arlen and Truman Capote. All rights controlled by Harwin Music Corp.

## Harold Arlen and Dory Langdon

"The Morning After" ©1962 Harwin Music Corp.
"So Long, Big Time" ©1963, 1964 Harwin Music Corp.

## Harold Arlen and Martin Charnin

"Come On, Midnight" ©1966 (Renewed) Harwin Music Corp.
"Suddenly the Sunrise" ©1966 Harold Arlen and Martin Charnin. All rights controlled by Harwin Music Corp.
"Fish Go Higher Than Tigers" ©1966 Harold Arlen and Martin Charnin. All rights controlled by Harwin Music Corp.

## Harold Arlen as Composer and Lyricist

"I Had a Love Once" ©1973, 1985 Harold Arlen. All rights controlled by Harwin Music Corp.

## Other Composers

Morgan Lewis, "'Cause You Won't Play House" ©1934 Harms, Inc.
Vincent Youmans, "Hallelujah!" ©1927 (Renewed) Warner Bros., Inc.
Irving Burgie, "Jamaica Farewell" ©1955, 1963 (Renewed) Caribe Music and Reservoir Media Management, Inc. All Rights for Caribe Music Administered by BMG Rights Management (US) LLC. All Rights for Reservoir Media Music Administered by Reservoir Media Management, Inc.
Stephen Sondheim, "Someone in a Tree" ©1975 Rilting Music, Inc. All Rights administered by WB Music Corp.

# Index—General

*For the benefit of digital users, indexed terms that span two pages (e.g., 52–53) may, on occasion, appear on only one of those pages.*

Tables and figures are indicated by an italic *t* and *f* following the page/paragraph number.

Academy Awards
    "Blues in the Night" (nominated), 104–5
    "For Every Man There's a Woman" (nominated), 136
    "The Man That Got Away" (nominated), 153–54
    Robin for "Thanks for the Memory," 134
Adorno, Theodor W., 271n.4
African Americans. *See* Blacks
Ailey, Alvin, 171, 172–73
Akst, Harry, 29–30
Allen, Steve, 190, 191*t*
American Ballet Theater, 171
*Americanegro Suite* (song cycle), 33*t*, 59, 228*t*
American Film Institute, 1
*American Popular Song: The Great Innovators 1920-1950* (Wilder), vii–viii
American Songbook, 7–8, 40, 61, 105, 134, 135–36, 154, 179, 206, 228, 243, 246–47
Anderson, Eddie "Rochester," 84
Anderson, John Murray, 65–66
*André Previn Plays Songs by Harold Arlen* (album), 25, 252n.7, 271–72n.8
*Andy Hardy Meets a Debutante* (film), 78
Apple Music, xiii, 230
Arabic numerals in analysis, 22
Arbuckle, Roscoe "Fatty," 15*f*
Arlen, Anya (wife), 147, 225
Arlen, Harold
    albums by individual vocalists, 228*t*
    anonymous immortality of, 1
    as an arranger, 3, 5–7
    biographies of, viii
    birth of, 13
    as a Black-adjacent composer, 13–17
    Black influences on vocal style, 56
    caricature of, 169*f*
    as a collaborator, viii, 9–12
    as a composer and craftsman, 2–5
    demos of, 193–95, 270n.7
    diary of, 11–12, 215–16, 218–20, 222, 273n.33
    discouraged by critical failures, 206
    emotional breakdown of, 130–31
    health problems of, 147, 164, 190, 223, 227
    "It's Only a Paper Moon" sung by, 199–200
    Jewish background and musical influences, 13–16
    lack of definable "style," 2
    late style of (*see* late style of Arlen)
    low name recognition of, vii–viii, 1–2
    LP albums of, 195–97
    as a lyricist, 225–27
    number of songs on "The Golden 100," 1
    original name of, 13
    Parkinson's disease of, 223, 227
    performances after 1950, 191*t*
    photos of, 14*f*, 15*f*, 32*f*, 63*f*, 98*f*, 148*f*, 198*f*, 231*f*, 241*f*
    as a pianist, 3, 24–25
    on radio, 190, 270n.1
    recordings of Arlen-Koehler songs, 56–58, 57*t*
    as a singer, 3, 29, 192–93
    solos performed by, 200–2
    song output of, 1
    start of as a songwriter, 30–31

Arlen, Harold (*cont.*)
  on television, 197–99
  television highlights, 202–5
  thoroughness of, 3, 26–27, 46–47, 86, 104
Arluck, Celia Orlin (mother), 13
Arluck, Chaim (Hyman) (Arlen's orignial name), 13
Arluck, Samuel (Shmuel) (father), 13–16, 14*f*
Armstrong, Louis, 46, 47, 47*f*, 84
Associated Negro Press News Service, 173
Astaire, Fred, 107, 108–9, 218–19, 261n.17
*At the Circus* (film), 62, 64*t*, 83
Ayres, Lemuel, 118–19

Bailey, Pearl, 17, 228*t*
  in *House of Flowers*, 171, 172, 174, 175, 187, 268n.19
  in *St. Louis Woman*, 118–19, 129
Baker, David, 195
Balanchine, George, 105–6, 171, 172–73
Baldwin, James, 173
Banfield, Stephen, 223
Barnet, Charlie, 104–5
Barstow, Richard, 164–66
Bartók, Peter, 195
Baum, L. Frank, 7–8
Beatles, 18
Beaton, Cecil, 130
Beethoven, Ludwig van, 7
Belafonte, Harry, 11–12, 91–92, 161–62
*Bell Telephone Hour, The* (TV show), 191*t*, 199
Bennett, Richard Rodney, 228*t*
Bennett, Robert Russell, 87, 88
Bennett, Tony, vii–viii, 17, 192–93, 212, 228, 228*t*, 236, 243–44
Bergman, Ingrid, 135
Berkeley, Busby, 70
Berlin, Irving, 1–2, 3, 13, 16–17, 29, 40–41, 56, 224–25
  "Alexander's Ragtime Band," 29
  "Cheek to Cheek," 5
  counterpoint songs written by, 131, 264n.70
  "Everybody Step," 37–38
  "Harlem on My Mind," 41
  "How Many Times," 29–30
  "I'd Rather Lead a Band," 37–38
  *Mr. President* songs, 220
  number of songs on "The Golden 100," 1
  "Oh! How I Hate to Get Up in the Morning," 37
Bernstein, Leonard, 91
Billboard Charts, 104–5
*Biographical Guide to the Great Jazz and Pop Singers, A* (Friedwald), 252n.4
Bivona, Gus, 237
Bizet, Georges, 173
Black English, 47–48, 58, 254n.46
Blacks
  all-Black cast films and shows (*see Cabin in the Sky; House of Flowers; Porgy and Bess; St. Louis Woman*)
  Arlen's adjacency to, 13–17
  Arlen's vocal style influenced by, 56
  in *Bloomer Girl*, 87–88
  "Blues in the Night" picked up by, 105
  civil rights movement and (*see* civil rights movement)
  in the Cotton Club, 40–41, 43–44, 59
  dance influenced by, 38
  early 20th-century music influenced by, 29
  in the Federal Theatre Project, 114
  "Get Happy" influenced by traditions of, 32–34
  *Great Day* influenced by tradtions of, 30
Blake, Eubie, 29
Blondell, Jane, 70
*Bloomer Girl* (show), viii, 11, 62, 64*t*, 84, 92, 97, 131, 135–36, 259n.47
  Arlen's demos for, 194
  *The Farmer Takes a Wife* compared with, 144
  music for, 87–91
blue notes
  "Cocoanut Sweet," 92–93
  "Ding-Dong! The Witch Is Dead," 82–83, 83*f*
  "Happiness Is Just a Thing Called Joe," 85–86
  "I Had a Love Once," 226, 226*f*
  "Ill Wind," 50–51
  "In the Shade of the New Apple Tree," 79–80

"Last Night When We Were Young," 202
"Out of This World," 111
"So Long, Big Time," 211
"Stormy Weather," 47
"That Old Black Magic," 105–6, 107
Blue Ribbon Syncopators, 16
blues, 30
    "Blues in the Night," 100, 101, 104, 108
    "Can't Help Lovin' Dat Man," 88
    *God Sends Sunday*, 113
    "Goose Never Be a Peacock," 131
    "Green Light Ahead," 165
    "Happiness Is Just a Thing Called Joe," 85
    "I Gotta Right to Sing the Blues," 240
    "Ill Wind," 50–51
    "I Never Has Seen Snow," 174
    "One for My Baby," 107, 108
    in *St. Louis Woman* songs, 114–15, 135–36
    "Stormy Weather," 47–48, 49, 57, 230
*Blues in the Night* (film), 99*t*, 104–5, 153–54
*Blues Opera* (unproduced), 125–31, 128*f*, 147, 190, 194, 206, 225
Bogart, Humphrey, 97, 135
Bogle, Donald, 40
Bolger, Ray, 3, 26–27, 65–66, 67, 86
Bon Soir (nightclub), 240–41, 242
Bontemps, Arna, 113, 114–17, 118–19, 125–26
book musicals, viii, 73, 87
Botkin, Henry, 59
Bradshaw, Charles, 105–6
Brahms, Johannes, viii–ix, 7
Brando, Marlon, 217–18
Brecht, Bertolt, 126
Breen, Robert, 125–29, 225
Breen, Wilva, 127–28
Brice, Carol, 131
Bridges, Lloyd, 218–19
Brith Sholem synagogue, 13–15, 14*f*
Broadhurst, Laura Lynn, 255–56n.58, 258n.31
"Broadway Answers Selma!" (concert), 196–97, 213
Broadway spirituals
    "Ac-cent-tchu-ate the Positive," 109

"Ain' It de Truth?" 245–46
defined, 32–33
early appearance in print, 252n.11
"Get Happy," 32–33, 232–33
"Hallelujah!," 34–35
"Save Me Sister," 84
"Stormy Weather," 48
Brook, Peter, 167, 171, 172–73
Brown, Michael, 172
Brown, Sterling Allen, 114
*Brown Sugar* (show), 33*t*, 40, 56–57
Brunswick Records, 57*t*, 230
Buffalodians, 3, 16, 29–30, 46, 56, 256n.61
Burgie, Irving (Lord Burgess), 92
Burnell, Anne, 228*t*
Burton, Miriam, 195
Burton, Richard, 148
Byders, Billy, 126

*Cabin in the Sky* (film), 62, 64*t*, 83–87, 88, 113, 117, 244, 245
Cahn, Sammy, 153–54
*Cairo* (film), 78
Calloway, Cab, 40, 42, 45, 81–82, 84, 104–5, 125
calypso music
    "Cocoanut Sweet," 92–93
    *House of Flowers* songs, 171
    *Jamaica* songs, 91–92, 171
    "Two Ladies in De Shade of a Banana Tree," 174, 175
Cantor, Eddie, 191*t*
Capitol Records, 119, 147, 190, 195–96, 197, 200, 204–5, 228*t*, 233, 236, 237
Capote, Truman, 10–11, 134, 147, 167–70, 171, 172, 173–74, 187–89, 193–94, 263–64n.57
    "Albertina's Beautiful Hair," 188
    caricature of, 169*f*
    *The Grass Harp*, 167–68
    "House of Flowers" (short story), 167–68, 170, 267n.3
    "House of Flowers" (song), 180–81
    "I Never Has Seen Snow," 183, 186
    sings with Arlen, 194–95
    "A Sleepin' Bee," 175–79
    "Two Ladies in De Shade of a Banana Tree," 174–75

Caribbean sound
   "The Calypso Song," 174
   *House of Flowers* songs, 91–92, 217
   *Jamaica* songs, 217
   "'Neath the Pale Cuban Moon," 174
   "Shoein' the Mare," 174
   "Smellin' of Vanilla," 174
   "Two Ladies in De Shade of a Banana Tree," 174
Carlyle, Louis, 195
Carmichael, Hoagy, 30, 48, 100, 181–82
Carnegie Hall, 126, 161–62, 232–33, 235, 244
Carroll, Diahann, 171, 172, 175–76, 183, 187, 201, 228*t*, 270n.35
Carroll, John, 143–44
Carson, Rachel, 96–97
*Casbah* (film), 134–39
Champion, Gower, 218–19
Chapman, John, 119
Chappell (publisher), 59
Charnin, Martin, 10–11, 131, 134, 188–89, 194–95, 206–7, 243
   *Annie* songs, 213, 224
   "Come On, Midnight," 213–15
   "Fish Go Higher Than Tigers," 222, 223
   "Happy Any Day," 221
   *I Remember Mama* songs, 213
   *Softly* songs, 213–16, 217, 218–21
   songs by Arlen and, 214*t*
   "Suddenly the Sunrise," 221, 223
   "That's a Fine Kind o' Freedom," 196–97, 213
   *Two by Two* songs, 213
   "Why Do You Make Me Like You?" 220
   "You're Never Fully Dressed Without a Smile," 224–25
Chase, Stanley, 126–27
Cherry, Randall, 230
chromaticism
   "Come On, Midnight," 213
   "I Never Has Seen Snow," 184–85
   "It's a New World," 158, 160
   "Little Drops of Rain," 95–96
   "The Morning After," 209
   "Out of a Clear Blue Sky," 39–40
   "Over the Rainbow," 21
   "Right as the Rain," 89

"Stormy Weather," 49
"That Old Black Magic," 106
civil rights movement, 161–62, 196–97, 213
Clift, Montgomery, 219–20
*Clippety Clop and Clementine* (TV musical), 225–27
Clooney, Rosemary, 228*t*
*Close Up!* (TV show), 191*t*
Cohan, George M., 29
Coleman, Cy, 140–41
*Colgate Comedy Hour, The* (TV show), 190, 191*t*, 199–200
Colonial Club Orchestra, 38
Coltrane, John, 39–40
Coltrane changes, 39–40
Columbia Pictures, 53–54
Columbia Records, 173–74, 175, 190, 196–97, 208–9, 212, 228*t*, 240–41, 242
*Commentary*, 173
Como, Perry, 236
Cone, Edward T., 261n.18
Cook, Will Marion, 13, 15*f*, 16, 30–31, 114
cosmic romanticism, 63–64
Cotton Club, 10–11, 16, 31, 33*t*, 36–37, 40–49, 54, 55, 56–57, 59, 62, 65–66, 67, 99
   Black entertainers of, 40–41, 43–44, 59
   *Cotton Club Parade* (21st Edition), 40
   *Cotton Club Parade* (22nd Edition), 33*t*, 40, 41
   *Cotton Club Parade* (24th Edition), 33*t*, 40, 50
   McHugh and Fields as songwriters for, 140–41
   opening of, 40
   "Stormy Weather" lyrics on stationery of, 43–44, 44*f*, 254n.38
   Waters's premiere of "Stormy Weather" at, 48–49
Coughlin, Bruce, 245
counterpoint (double) songs, 131, 264n.70
*Country Girl, The* (film), 147, 168
Coward, Noel, 193
Cronkite, Walter, 1–2, 8, 9, 10, 42, 43–44, 249n.1, 272n.9, 272n.15
Crosby, Bing, 104–5, 193, 199, 261n.17
Crouse, Russel, 75

*Cue* magazine, 215–16
Cukor, George, 147, 148
Cullen, Countee, 113, 114–17, 118–19, 125
Cutter, Murray, 233–34

DaCosta, Morton, 130, 131, 132–33
Damone, Vic, 192–93
dance instruction songs, 38
Dance Theater of Harlem, 171
Daniels, Peter, 242
*dauerhafte Musik,* viii–ix
Davis, Benny, 29–30
Davis, Sammy, Jr., 125, 126
Decca Records, 78, 233
*Deep Are the Roots* (d'Usseau and Gow), 117
de Lavallade, Carmen, 171
de Mille, Agnes, 75, 87
Deppe, Lois, 15*f*
diegesis
    "Here's What I'm Here For," 151
    "It's a New World," 151–52
    "Let's Fall in Love," 55–56
    "Lose That Long Face," 152
    "Someone at Last," 152
Dietrich, Marlene, 172–73
directional (progressive) tonality, 107, 120, 121
dissonances
    "'Cause You Won't Play House," 76
    "Come On, Midnight," 213
    "It's Only a Paper Moon," 65
    "It Was Written in the Stars," 137*f*
    "Last Night When We Were Young," 71*f*, 72–73
    "Let's Fall in Love," 54
    "Over the Rainbow," 22, 24
    "Stormy Weather," 49
Dolan, Robert Emmet, 105–6
Dorian mode, 111
Dorsey, Tommy, 57, 104–5, 230
double (counterpoint) songs, 131, 264n.70
"Dreen, W. B.," 128–29
Duchin, Eddy, 51–52, 57*t*
Duke, Vernon, 11, 83–84, 213
Dunham, Katherine, 171
*DuPont Show of the Week* (TV show), 191*t*, 199
d'Usseau, Arnaud, 117

Dvořák, Antonín, 31

*Earl Carroll's Vanities of 1930* (revue), 33*t*, 36–40, 62
*Earl Carroll's Vanities of 1932* (revue), 33*t*
Edens, Roger, 40–41, 46–47, 58, 82, 149, 164
*Ed Sullivan Show, The* (TV show), 190, 191*t*, 198*f*, 203
Eliscu, Edward, 34
*Ella Fitzgerald Sings the Harold Arlen Songbook* (album), 228*t*, 238
Ellington, Duke, 40–41, 42, 84, 87, 191*t*
Ericson, June, 195
Everyman Opera Company, 125

Faith, Percy, 240
fake books, 27–28
*Farmer Takes a Wife, The* (film), 141, 143–46
Farrell, Eileen, 208–9, 228, 228*t*, 239–40, 244
fascism, 75
Federal Theatre Project, 114, 115
Feinstein, Michael, 66–67
Ferber, Edna, 130
Fields, Dorothy, viii, 10–11, 40, 41, 134, 140–41, 140*f*
    *The Farmer Takes a Wife* songs, 141, 143–44
    "Just Let Me Look at You," 143
    "Let Me Look at You," 142–43
    "Look Who's Been Dreaming," 145–46
    "Lovely to Look At," 143
    *Mr. Imperium* songs, 141
    "The Way You Look Tonight," 143
Fields, Herbert, 140–41
Fields, Lew, 140–41
Fitzgerald, Ella, 17, 228, 228*t*, 230, 238–39, 243
*Free and Easy* (alternate title for *Blues Opera*), 125–26, 127
Freed, Arthur, 79, 81, 83–84, 87, 116, 118, 125
Freed, Courtney, 228*t*
*Fridays with Dave Garroway* (radio show), 190, 191*t*
Friedwald, Will, 56, 235, 237, 244, 252n.4, 254n.33

Friml, Rudolf, 55
Fryer, Robert, 132–33
Furia, Philip, 10–11, 36, 47–48, 108, 110, 250n.28

Galjour, Warren, 195
Gandhi Society for Human Rights, 161–62
Gardner, Ava, 125
Garland, Judy, vii–viii, xiii, 17, 19, 70, 75–76, 103, 203, 204, 228, 228t, 238, 244, 261n.20
   in *Andy Hardy Meets a Debutante*, 78
   Arlen's songs recorded by, 232–34
   in *Gay Purr-ee*, 83, 95
   in *I Could Go On Singing*, 96
   in *In The Good Old Summertime*, 70
   in *A Star Is Born*, 96, 147, 148, 153–54, 158, 163, 164, 165–66, 200–1, 203
   in *The Wizard of Oz*, 1, 27, 95
*Garrick Gaieties* (revue), 37
Garroway, Dave, 10, 80–81, 190, 191t, 193, 197, 199–200, 236
Gaynor, Janet, 147
*Gay Purr-ee* (film), 62, 64t, 83, 95–97, 194, 199, 206
Gensler, Lewis, 76, 257n.24
George M. Cohan Theatre, 33t
*George White's Scandals* (revue), 37
Gershe, Leonard, 149, 164, 165–66
Gershwin, George, vii–viii, 1–2, 3, 4, 7, 15, 16–17, 29, 40–41, 65–66, 68, 70, 91–92, 125, 128–29, 130, 131, 182–83, 195
   admiration for "Stormy Weather," 47
   "Clap Yo' Hands," 32–33
   "Fascinatin' Rhythm," 35–36, 37, 38
   influence on Arlen, 30
   "Love Walked In," 160–61
   "The Man I Love," 68, 154
   *Rhapsody in Blue*, 30
   "Stairway to Paradise," 37–38
   "Swanee," 30
   working method, 250n.19
Gershwin, Ira, viii, 10–11, 12, 13, 15, 29, 40–41, 60, 61, 125, 130, 131, 134, 195, 238
   "Clap Yo' Hands," 32–33
   "Dancing Partner," 149, 162–63, 164–66

"Fascinatin' Rhythm," 35–36, 37, 38
"Gotta Have Me Go with You," 150, 151, 153, 265n.2
"Green Light Ahead," 149, 162–64, 165–66
"Here's What I'm Here For," 149, 151, 162–63, 164, 265n.2
"I'm Off the Downbeat," 149, 162–63, 164, 165–66
"It's a New World," 160–62, 164–65, 265n.2
*Lady in the Dark* songs, 148, 160–61
"Let's Take a Walk Around the Block," 64t, 66–67
*Life Begins at 8:40* songs, 65–67, 147
"Lose That Long Face," 149, 152, 162–63, 164, 265n.2
"Love Walked In," 160–61
*Lyrics on Several Occasions*, 163
"The Man I Love," 68, 154
"The Man That Got Away," 150–51, 153, 154, 156–57, 161, 164–65, 204, 234, 265n.2
   photo of, 148f
"Someone at Last," 152
"Stairway to Paradise," 37–38
*A Star Is Born* songs, 147–48, 149–50, 153, 162–66, 168
"This Is New," 160–61
*Get Happy: The Music of Harold Arlen* (TV show), 191t
Gilpin Players, 114
*God Sends Sunday* (Bontemps), 113, 115
Goldberg, Isaac, 68–69, 192–93
"Golden Age" of book musicals, 87
"Golden 100, The" *(Variety)*, 1
Goodman, Benny, 104–5
Goodspeed Opera House, 97
Gormé, Eydie, 191t
Gorney, Jay, 37
Gottlieb, Jack, 15–16
Goulet, Robert, 95
Gow, James, 117
Grable, Betty, 143–44
Grant, Cary, 148
Granz, Norman, 238
*Grass Harp, The* (Capote), 167–68
*Great Day* (show), 30–31, 34

*Great Magoo, The* (play), 63–64, 64t, 65
Green, Benny, 238, 239
Grey, Clifford, 34f, 34–35
Griffith, Edward, 108
Gross, Edward, 116, 118–19

haiku, 223
Hall, Adelaide, 40
Hall, Juanita, 118, 171, 187–88
Hal Leonard (publisher), xiii
Hamm, Charles, 252n.1
Hammerstein, Oscar, II, 32–33, 37, 104–5, 130, 141, 173
Handy, W. C., 29, 113, 181–82
*Hans Christian Andersen* (film), 148
Harburg, E. Y. "Yip," viii, 1, 10–11, 15, 30, 37, 59, 60, 61, 62–67, 134, 141, 144, 193–94
   "Ain' It de Truth?" 245, 246
   *At the Circus* songs, 62, 83
   blacklisting of, 91
   *Bloomer Girl* songs, 62, 88
   "Buds Won't Bud," 75–78, 77f, 79–80
   *Cabin in the Sky* songs, 62, 83–85
   "'Cause You Won't Do Right by Me," 76
   "'Cause You Won't Play House," 76–77, 76f
   "Cocoanut Sweet," 11–12, 93–94, 93f
   death of, 97
   "Ding-Dong! The Witch Is Dead," 80, 88
   "Down with Love," 75–76, 79–80
   "The Eagle and Me," 89
   "Fancy Meeting You," 74–75
   *Finian's Rainbow* songs, 66–67
   first meeting with Arlen, 62
   "Fun to Be Fooled," 68–69
   *Gay Purr-ee* songs, 62, 83, 95, 206
   "God's Country," 75–76
   *Gold Diggers of 1937* songs, 70
   "Happiness Is Just a Thing Called Joe," 11–12, 84–85, 86–87
   *Hooray for What!* songs, 62, 75–78
   "I Could Go On Singing," 96
   "If I Only Had a Brain," 75–76, 80
   "If I Were King of the Forest," 66–67, 80
   "I'm Hanging on to You," 75–76
   "In the Shade of the New Apple Tree," 75–76, 79–80
   "It's Fun to Be Fooled," 66–67
   "It's Only a Paper Moon," 62–66, 69
   "I've Gone Romantic on You," 75–76
   *Jamaica* songs, 9–10, 62, 91–92, 171, 234–35
   "The Jitterbug," 80, 81–82
   lack of rhythm, 11–12
   last large-scale project with Arlen, 95
   "Last Night When We Were Young," 11–12, 70, 72–73, 209
   last two numbers with Arlen, 97
   *Life Begins at 8:40* songs, 62, 65–67, 70
   "Life's a Dance," 75–76
   "Looks Like the End of a Beautiful Friendship," 97
   "Lydia the Tattooed Lady," 83
   Mercer compared with, 100
   "The Merry Old Land of Oz," 80
   "Moanin' in the Mornin'," 75–76
   most productive decade of, 73
   "Napoleon's a Pastry," 75–76
   number of songs written with Arlen, 62
   "Old Devil Moon," 66–67
   "Optimistic Voices," 80
   "Over the Rainbow," 8, 9, 11–12, 18–19, 20–21, 23, 24, 65, 80, 81, 233–34
   photo of, 63f
   "Promise Me Not to Love Me," 97
   "Right as the Rain," 90–91
   "Satan's Li'l Lamb," 62–63, 98
   "Save Me Sister," 84
   selected songs written with Arlen, 64t
   "Silent Spring," 96 97
   *The Singing Kid* songs, 62, 70, 84
   "Song of the Woodman," 66–67
   *Stage Struck* songs, 62, 70
   "Things," 66–67
   "We're Off to 80, 88, See the Wizard,"
   *The Wizard of Oz* songs, 62, 66–67, 80, 82, 83
   world-as-onion image, 89, 259n.51
   "You Didn't Do Right By Me," 76
Harlem, 10, 41
Harlem Renaissance, 113, 114
*Harold Arlen and His Songs* (album), 147, 190, 191t, 195–96, 196f, 199, 200, 204
*Harold Arlen: Happy with the Blues* (Jablonski), 189, 191t

*Harold Arlen Rediscovered* (Hal Leonard and MPL Communications), xiii
*Harold Arlen: Rhythm, Rainbows and Blues* (Jablonski), 250n.25
*Harold Arlen Sings (With Friend)* (album), 190, 191*t*, 196–97, 240–41, 241*f*, 242–43
*Harold Arlen Songbook, The* (Hal Leonard and MPL Communications), xiii, 42–43, 78
Harper, Dolores, 174–75
Hart, Lorenz, 4, 29, 37–38, 39–40, 41, 140–41, 165–66, 195
Hart, Moss, 147–48, 149–51, 152, 162–63, 265n.2
Haver, Ronald, 149–50
Hawkins, June, 118
Healy, Peggy, 65
*Heart Fund, The* (radio show), 191*t*
Henderson, Fletcher, 13, 15*f*, 16, 30
Henderson, Luther, 240
"Here Comes Emaline" (Charles O'Flynn, Al Sherman, Fred Phillips), 256n.61
Herman, Woody, 104–5
"Hero Ballet" *(Bloomer Girl)*, 75
Hicks, James L., 173
Hill, Ruby, 118
Hirschfeld, Al, 195
Hochman, Larry, 245
Holden, Stephen, 244
Holder, Geoffrey, 171, 172
Holm, Celeste, 87
Holm, Hanya, 217, 273n.30
*Hooray for What!* (show), 62, 64*t*, 75–80, 87, 88
Horne, Lena, 17, 116, 162, 228, 230, 232, 238, 244
  in *Cabin in the Sky*, 84, 245
  "Cocoanut Sweet" recorded by, 234–35
  in *Jamaica*, 75–76, 92, 245
  *St. Louis Woman* role rejected by, 118, 161–62
Horowitz, Mark, 4–5
*Hot Nocturne* (film). See *Blues in the Night*
*House of Flowers* (show), viii, 10, 91–92, 118, 147, 164, 167–89, 190, 195, 201, 216, 217, 240–41, 244
  Arlen's demos for, 193–95

  dance numbers for, 171–72
  earliest surviving draft for, 267n.4
  making of, 167–74
  music of, 174–87
  number of performances, 167
  reviews of, 173
  revival of, 173–74, 187–89, 225
  second-act problems in, 167
  short story basis for, 167–68
  tensions undermining, 172–73
"House of Flowers" (short story), 167–68, 170, 267n.3
Hughes, Langston, 114–15, 116
hypermetric tapeworms, 105, 111, 261n.18

*I Could Go On Singing* (film), 64*t*, 96
Ingram, Rex, 118
interludes
  "Hooray for Love," 135
  "Ill Wind," 50, 53, 255n.53
  "The March of Time," 37–38
  "Stormy Weather," 48–49, 49*f*, 53
Interracial Film and Radio Guild, 115, 116–17, 118
Irwin, Trudy, 141
"It's Fun to Be Fooled" (Suesse, Harburg), 66–67
"I Want" songs, 81, 258n.36

Jablonski, Edward, viii, 5, 34, 36, 54, 67, 69, 80–81, 84–85, 91–92, 94–95, 127–28, 130, 133, 164, 175–76, 183, 186–87, 195–96, 206, 215–16, 225, 238
  *Harold Arlen: Happy with the Blues*, 189, 191*t*
  *Harold Arlen: Rhythm, Rainbows and Blues*, 250n.25
*Jamaica* (show), 9–10, 62, 64*t*, 75–76, 137–38, 171, 217, 234–35, 245
  Arlen's demos for, 193–94
  music for, 91–95
James, Etta, 230
jazz harmonizations, 16, 30, 56, 238
  "Fish Go Higher Than Tigers," 223
  "Happiness Is Just a Thing Called Joe," 86

"It's Only a Paper Moon," 200
"The Morning After," 209
"Over the Rainbow," 24–26, 25f
"Save Me Sister," 84
"Stormy Weather," 46
Johnson, Arnold, 3, 29–30
Johnson, James Weldon, 230–31, 232
Johnson, Louis, 171
Johnston, Johnny, 105–6
Jolson, Al, 70, 82, 84
Jones, Dick, 195–96
Jones, Quincy, 126
Jones, Siseretta, 114–15
jots, 5–8, 6f, 8f, 208
    "Get Happy," 31–32
    *House of Flowers* songs, 168
    "Stormy Weather," 42–43

Kane, Bruce, 12–13
Kaye, Danny, 59
Kaye, Judy, 228t
Keel, Howard, 130, 132
Kern, Jerome, 1, 3, 4–5, 11, 13, 16–17, 29, 70, 140–41, 243
    "Just Let Me Look at You," 143
    "The Last Time I Saw Paris," 104–5
    "Lovely to Look At," 143
    "Ol' Man River," 32–33
    *Show Boat* (show), 130
    "Smoke Gets in Your Eyes," 39–40
    "The Song Is You," 39–40
    "They Didn't Believe Me," 29
    "Till the Clouds Roll By," 39–40
    "The Way You Look Tonight," 143
    "You Are Love," 37
King, Carole, 207–8
King, Martin Luther, Jr., 161–62
Kitt, Eartha, 125
Koehler, Ted, viii, 10–11, 36–40, 99, 134, 140–41, 168, 190
    Arlen's recordings of songs created with, 56–58, 57t
    breakup with Arlen, 60–61, 62
    *Brown Sugar*, 40
    "Contagious Rhythm," 36–37
    Cotton Club shows, 40–41, 65–66
    "Get Happy," 30–33, 34–35, 36–37, 47, 54, 62–63

"Get Yourself a New Broom," 41
"Happy as the Day Is Long," 41
Harburg compared with, 62, 63–64, 84
"Hittin' the Bottle," 36–37, 38
"I Gotta Right to Sing the Blues," 5–7, 127
"Ill Wind," 50, 51, 53, 127
"I Love a Parade," 54
last songs with Arlen, 59–61
"Let's Fall in Love," 55–56
*Let's Fall in Love* songs, 53–54
"Love Is Love Anywhere," 54
"The March of Time," 37–38
Mercer compared with, 100
number of songs written with Arlen, 31
"One Love," 36–37
"Out of a Clear Blue Sky," 36–37, 38–40
photo of, 32f
"Raisin' the Rent," 36–37
*Rhythmania*, 40
selected songs written with Arlen, 33t
"Stormy Weather," 36–38, 41, 42–46, 47–49, 50, 101
"This Is Only the Beginning," 54
Kostelanetz, Andre, 126
Kraft Music Hall, 55–56
Kupferberg, Herbert, 197

Lafayette Theater, 114
Lahr, Bert, 65–67, 80
Lahr, John, 67
LaMaMa experimental theater, 225
Lane, Burton, 66–67, 220
Langdon, Dory, 1, 10–11, 134, 188–89, 206–12, 272n.9
    "Hurt but Happy," 208
    "The Morning After," 208, 209
    "Night After Night," 208–9
    photo of, 207f
    "So Long, Big Time," 208, 209–12
    "That Was the Love That Was," 208
    "You're Impossible," 208
Langford, Frances, 57, 230
Lapine, James, 4
late style of Arlen, 145–46, 157–58, 206–27, 271n.4, *See also* Charnin, Martin; Langdon, Dory
Latouche, John, 83–84, 87

Lawrence, Carol, 130, 132
Lee, John M., 119
Lee, Peggy, 17, 228*t*, 270n.8, 271n.6
Lees, Gene, 4
Lemmon, Jack, 191*t*, 218–19
lemon-drop songs, 80–81
Leo Feist (publisher), 80
Leslie, Joan, 109
*Let's Fall in Love* (film), 33*t*, 53–56, 58
Lewis, Morgan, 76–77, 76*f*, 78
*Lew Leslie's Blackbirds* (revue), 37
*Life Begins at 8:40* (show), 10, 61, 62, 64*t*, 70, 75–76, 82, 147
   music for, 65–69
   origin of title, 65–66
*Life Begins at Forty* (Pitkin), 65–66
Lindsay, Howard, 75
Lindsay, John, 213
list songs, 2, 83
Loesser, Frank, 131, 148, 220
Lomax, Alan, 105
Lombardo, Guy, 104–5
"Lonesome Road, The," 113
Lord Burgess (Irving Burgie), 92
*Love Affair* (film), 33*t*
Luft, Sidney, 147, 148, 149, 164, 165–66
Lundgren, Isabella, 228*t*
Lux Radio Theatre, 147
*Lyrics on Several Occasions* (Ira Gershwin), 163

Ma, Yo-Yo, 18–19
Madden, Jeanne, 73, 74–75
Majestic Theatre, 196–97, 213
Mamoulian, Rouben, 118–19
Manning, Marty, 212
March, Frederic, 148
March on Washington, 161–62
march songs
   "Ding-Dong! The Witch Is Dead," 80–81
   "It Was Good Enough for Grandma," 88
   "The March of Time," 37
Markovich, Nick, 66–67
Martha Graham Dance School, 171
*Martha Raye Show, The* (TV show), 190, 191*t*, 204–5
Martin, Tony, 135
Marx, Groucho, 83

Marx Brothers, 83
Mason, James, 148
Matlowsky, Samuel, 125–26, 127–28, 130
Matz, Peter, 170, 191*t*, 195–96, 200, 204–5, 242–43
May, Billy, 238, 239
Mayer, Louis B., 81
McAndrew, John, 197
McDonald, Audra, vii–viii, 228, 244–47, 269n.34
McGovern, Maureen, 228*t*
McHugh, Jimmy, 40, 41, 140–41
McKayle, Donald, 126–27, 171
McNair, Sylvia, 208, 228, 228*t*, 243–44
McWhorter, John, 16–17
Melfi, Leonard, 225
Melnick, Jeffrey, 16–17
melodic arcs
   "Fun to Be Fooled," 68–69, 69*f*
   "Let's Fall in Love," 54, 55*f*
   "Over the Rainbow," 20*f*
   "A Sleepin' Bee," 179, 179*f*
   "What's Good About Goodbye?" 138*f*
melodic climaxes
   "Get Happy," 35, 35*f*
   "Last Night When We Were Young," 72*f*
   "Let Me Look at You," 141–42, 142*f*
   "That Old Black Magic," 107*f*, 107
Mercer, Johnny, viii, 10–11, 15, 59, 62, 70, 98–104, 134, 147, 156, 168, 191*t*, 192–93
   "Ac-cent-tchu-ate the Positive," 109, 127
   "Any Place I Hang My Hat Is Home," 116, 127
   "Blues in the Night," 11–12, 99, 100–4, 102*f*, 105, 127, 133
   *Blues Opera* songs, 125–26, 128–29, 206
   "Come Rain or Come Shine," 11–12, 119–21, 127, 133
   "A Game of Poker," 131, 132
   "Goose Never Be a Peacock," 131
   "I Can't Believe My Eyes," 153–54
   "I Had Myself a True Love," 123–24, 127, 244–45
   "I Wonder What Became of Me," 121
   "Lazybones," 100
   "Love Held Lightly," 131, 132
   "My Shining Hour," 110, 120, 239

number of songs written with Arlen, 99
"One for My Baby," 11–12, 105, 108–9, 120, 133, 237
"Out of this World," 240
photo of, 98f
*Saratoga* songs, 130–31, 132–33, 206
"Satan's Li'l Lamb," 98
selected songs written with Arlen, 99t
skills as a musician, 100–1
Southern background of, 99
*St. Louis Woman* songs, 112–13, 114, 116–17, 118, 119, 125, 161–62, 171, 218–19
"That Old Black Magic," 105, 107, 127, 261n.20
"Too Marvelous for Words," 100
"You for Me," 131
"You Must Have Been a Beautiful Baby," 100
Mercury Theater Company, 114
Merrick, David, 92
Messel, Oliver, 171
*Metropolitan* (film), 70
Metropolitan Opera, 171
MGM, 2, 70, 130, 147, 233
   *At the Circus*, 83
   *Blues Opera*, 126
   *Cabin in the Sky*, 83–84
   *Mr. Imperium*, 141, 142–43
   *St. Louis Woman*, 78, 79, 118, 125
   *The Wizard of Oz*, 80, 81, 116
Miller, Bill, 237
Miller, Glenn, 104 5
Mills, Jack, 40–41, 51–52, 232
Minnelli, Vincente, 75, 84
Mitchell, Arthur, 171
Mitchell, Joni, 207
Mixolydian mode, 111, 138
Monet, Claude, 18
Moore, Ada, 174–75
Morgan, Helen, 240–41
Morris, John, 195
Morton, Jelly Roll, 46
Mosier, Enid, 175
Moyer, Del-Louise, 228t
Mozart, Wolfgang Amadeus, 4–5, 27
MPL Communications, xiii
*Mr. Imperium* (film), 141–43

Muse, Clarence, 114
*Music Man, The* (show), 130, 131
*Music of Harold Arlen, The* (album), 147, 190, 191t, 195
*My Fair Lady* (show), 2, 81, 118–19, 130, 217–18

NAACP, 115, 116–17
National Broadcasting Company. *See* NBC
National Endowment for the Arts, 1
*National Geographic*, 18
NBC, 29, 190
Nelson, Kenneth, 217–18
New Amsterdam Theatre, 37
New York City Ballet, 171
New York City Center, 173–74
*New York Daily News*, 119
*New York Herald Tribune*, 197
New York Philharmonic, 126
*New York Times*, 96, 197, 244
Nicholas, Fayard, 118
Nicholas, Harold, 118, 126
Nichols, Loring "Red," 56–57, 57t
Nicks, Walter, 171
*Nine-Fifteen Revue*, 33t
*No, No, Nanette* (show), 34

octave leaps, 7
   "Come On, Midnight," 213
   "Come Rain or Come Shine," 120
   "Fancy Meeting You," 73
   "I Never Has Seen Snow," 184
   "It's Only a Paper Moon," 65
   "Last Night When We Were Young," 71, 72
   "One Love," 37
   "Over the Rainbow," 20–21
   "That Old Black Magic," 106, 107f, 107
   "What's Good About Goodbye?" 138–39
*Oklahoma!* (show), 1, 2, 75, 87–88, 118–19
"Old Devil Moon" (Lane, Harburg), 66–67
Oliver, King, 47f, 47, 56
Olivier, Laurence, 148
*On a Clear Day You Can See Forever* (show), 220
"On Any Street in Harlem," 41
"On Lenox Avenue," 41

*Out of This World* (film), 99*t*, 261n.17

*Pacific Overtures* (show), vii, 223
Palace Theatre, 147
Palladium, 147
Paramount, 56, 57*t*, 65, 105–6
*Passing Shows* (revue), 37
Patrick, John, 217–18
patter segments, 37–38
pedal point
　"Come On, Midnight," 213
　"Over the Rainbow," 23
　"That Old Black Magic," 105–6, 261n.20
*Perry Como Show* (TV show), 190, 191*t*
Piantadosi, George and Arthur (music publisher), 31
pictorials, 56
Pine Street Shul. *See* Brith Sholem synagogue
Pinkins, Tonya, 228*t*
Pinza, Ezio, 141
Pitkin, Walter B., 65–66
plagal cadences, 26
*Pleasures and Palaces* (show), 220
*Poets of Tin Pan Alley, The: A History of America's Great Lyricists* (Furia), 250n.28
*Porgy and Bess* (opera), 65–66, 113, 117, 118–19, 125, 126, 130, 182–83, 263–64n.57
Porter, Cole, 5, 17, 105, 174, 195
Powell, Dick, 70, 73, 74–75
Premice, Josephine, 175, 187
Previn, André, vii–viii, 1, 2–3, 4, 19, 25, 25*f*, 207–9, 207*f*, 243, 249n.1, 271–72nn.8–9
Previn, Dory. *See* Langdon, Dory
progressive (directional) tonality, 107, 120, 121
Pulman, Liza, 228*t*
pure line, 80–81
　"Let's Fall in Love," 54, 58, 68
　"Over the Rainbow," 10, 20–21, 27

radio, 29, 190, 270n.1
Radio Corporation of America. *See* RCA
ragtime, 16
Rainger, Ralph, 134
Rau, Santha Rama, 216–17, 218

Raye, Martha, 103, 204–5. *See also Martha Raye Show, The*
RCA, 29, 228*t*
RCA Victor, 91–92, 228*t*
Real Book, 27–28
realist approach to popular song, 12–13
*Record Changer* (periodical), 197
Recording Industry Association of America, 1
Reisman, Leo, 48–49, 57–58, 57*t*, 230
Remick, Jerome, 30–31
Remick Music, 31, 54
replicative approach to popular song, 12–13, 24–25, 230, 246–47
*Rhapsody in Blue*, 1–2, 30
*Rhythmania* (show), 33*t*, 40
Riddle, Nelson, 70, 236–37, 238
Rimler, Walter, viii
Robards, Jason, 217, 218–19
Roberts, Lucky, 115, 116
Robertson, Dale, 143–44
Robin, Leo, 10–11, 34–35, 34*f*, 134, 141
　*Casbah* songs, 134–35
　"For Every Man There's a Woman," 135, 136
　"Hooray for Love," 135
　"It Was Written in the Stars," 135, 138
　"Thanks for the Memory," 134
　"What's Good About Goodbye?" 135, 138–39
"Rockin' Chair," 48
"Rocking Chair Blues," 113
Rodgers, Mary, 213
Rodgers, Richard, 1, 4, 17, 29, 140–41, 175–76, 195, 213, 220, 271n.5
　"Harlemania," 41
　"Have You Met Miss Jones?" 39–40
　"Little Girl Blue," 37–38
　"Lover," 39–40
　"Mountain Greenery," 37–38
　number of songs on "The Golden 100," 1
Roman numerals in analysis, 21–22, 26
Romberg, Sigmund, 55, 140–41
Rose, Billy, 34, 62, 63–64, 64*t*
Rose, David, 261n.20
Ross, Alex, viii–ix
Ross, Herbert, 172–73

Royal, Ted, 170
Royal Shakespeare Company, 171
Rushdie, Salman, 18–19
Russell, Connie, 191*t*
Rust College Quartet, 32–33

Saidy, Fred, 91–92
Saint-Subber, Arnold. *See* Subber, Saint
Sandy Hook Elementary School
    shootings, 18–19
*Saratoga* (show), 2, 99*t*, 206
    Arlen's demos for, 194
    music for, 130–33
*Saratoga Trunk* (Ferber), 130
*Saturday Evening Post*, 216
Schutt, Arthur, 51–52, 53, 57*t*, 255n.52
Schwartz, Arthur, 140–41, 195
"Scotch snap" rhythm, 47
*Search, The* (film), 219–20
sequential modulation by thirds, 39–40
*Seven Brides for Seven Brothers* (film), 130
Shakespeare, William, 18, 51
Sharon, Ralph, 212
Shaver, Bob, 195
Shaw, Artie, 104–5
Shaw, Wini, 84
sheet music publishers, 29
Shepard, Thomas Z., 196–97
"She's Still My Baby," 256n.61
Shore, Dinah, 59, 104–5, 191*t*, 199
*Show Boat* (film), 130
*Show Boat* (show), 30, 37, 88, 130
Shubert brothers, 37, 60, 61, 65–66, 75
Shubert Theatre, 33*t*
Shuken, Leo, 105–6
Sinatra, Frank, vii–viii, 17, 19, 70, 125,
    191*t*, 192–93, 197–98, 203–4, 218–19,
    228, 228*t*, 235–37, 238
Sinatra, Ray, 55–56, 57*t*, 58
*Singing Kid, The* (film), 62, 64*t*,
    70, 82, 84
Sissle, Noble, 29
*Sky's the Limit, The* (film), 99*t*, 107, 108–9,
    261n.17
Sloan, Nathaniel, 41, 59
Smith, Bessie, 113
Snappy Trio, 16
Sneider, Vern, 217–18

*Softly* (unfinished show), viii, 131, 213,
    214*t*, 216–25
    Arlen's demos for, 194–95
    attempts to develop, 217–20
    short story basis for, 216–17
    songs of, 220–25
"Softly" (Rau), 216–17
Somlyo, Roy, 167
Sondheim, Stephen, vii, viii, ix, 4–5, 19, 27,
    193, 217, 223, 249n.10
*Song Makers of the Nation* (Paramount
    series), 56
song pluggers, 3, 29
*Songs of Comfort and Hope* (album), 18–19
"Songs of Harold Arlen, The" (TV show).
    *See* Twentieth Century
Sony Classical, 18–19
Sousa, John Philip, 29
Southern, Ann, 55–56
Southern, Jeri, 203–4
*South Pacific* (show), 118, 141, 171
Sperling, Ted, 245, 246
spirituals. *See* Broadway spirituals
Spotify, xiii, 230
*St. Louis Woman* (cast album), 119
*St. Louis Woman* (show), viii, 10, 16–17,
    92, 99*t*, 112–24, 130, 131, 135–36,
    147, 161–62, 171, 182–83, 184, 218–
    19, 244
    Arlen's demos for, 194
    *Blues Opera* based on, 126, 127–28, 129
    history of, 112–19
    *House of Flowers* compared with,
        167, 171
    novel as basis of, 113
    number of performances, 167
    original title of, 113
    plans for film version, 125
    reviews of, 119
*Stage Struck* (film), 62, 64*t*, 70, 73–75
*Stardust Melodies: A Biography of
    America's Most Popular Songs*
    (Friedwald), 254n.33
*Star Is Born, A* (film), viii, 96, 131, 147–66,
    168, 174–75, 177, 190, 200–1, 203,
    221, 234
    Arlen's demos for, 194
    continuity script for, 266n.7

*Star Is Born*, A (film) (*cont.*)
  non-musical dramatization, 147
  original 1937 version, 147, 148
  the songs in context, 149–52
Stark, Bobby, 15*f*
*Star Spangled Rhythm* (film), 99*t*, 105–6, 261n.17
Stevens, Risë, 191*t*, 197–98
Stewart, Lawrence, 153
Stewart, Rex, 15*f*
*Stormy Weather* (film), 234–35
Stott, Kathryn, 18–19
Streisand, Barbra, vii–viii, 175–76, 190, 191*t*, 196–97, 213, 228, 240–43, 241*f*, 244, 275n.25
*Strike Me Pink* (film), 194
Strouse, Charles, 224
Student Non-Violent Coordinating Committee (SNCC), 161–62
Styne, Jule, 11, 134, 153–54, 220
Subber, Saint (Arnold Saint-Subber), 167–68, 171, 173–74, 187, 216, 217–20, 225
Suesse, Dana, 66–67, 76–77, 257n.24
Sullivan, Ed, 191*t*, 203, See also Ed Sullivan Show, The; Toast of the Town
Sullivan, KT, 228*t*
Sullivan, Maxine, 228*t*
Sweetland, Sally, 109

*Take a Chance* (film), 65
Talbert Choir, 48
tapeworm songs, viii, 3, 12, 99, 109–10
  "Blues in the Night," 5, 100, 103
  "Come On, Midnight," 213
  "For Every Man There's a Woman," 136
  "Gotta Have Me Go with You," 153, 158
  "Happiness Is Just a Thing Called Joe," 85–86
  "House of Flowers," 181
  hypermetric, 105, 111, 261n.18
  "I Had Myself a True Love," 122–23, 244–45
  "I Never Has Seen Snow," 174, 201
  "It's a New World," 158
  "It Was Written in the Stars," 137–38, 243–44
  "Let Me Look at You," 141–42
  "The Man That Got Away," 5, 153, 154, 158, 203–4
  "Now I Know," 59, 60
  "One for My Baby," 5, 107, 108, 209–10
  "Out of This World," 111, 240
  "Paris Is a Lonely Town," 95
  "So Long, Big Time," 209–10
  "Take It Slow, Joe," 94–95
  "That Old Black Magic," 5, 105
  "Why Do You Make Me Like You?" 220
"Tea for Two" (Youmans, Caesar), 34
television, 190, 197–99, 202–5
Terry, Walter, 217, 273n.30
"Thanks for the Memory" (Rainger, Robin), 134
*They Got Me Covered* (film), 261n.17
thirteenth chords, 77–78, 257n.25
"This Is New" (Weill, Ira Gershwin), 160–61
Thompson, Howard, 96
Tibbett, Lawrence, 70, 202
Tin Pan Alley, 3, 10–11, 29, 34, 37, 39, 40–41
*Toast of the Town* (TV show), 190, 191*t*, 203
*Today Show, The* (TV show), 191*t*
*Tonight Show, The* (TV show), 190, 191*t*, 241, 242
Tony Awards, 218–19
"Too Marvelous for Words" (Whiting, Mercer), 100
torch songs
  "The Man That Got Away," 154, 232–33
  "One for My Baby," 107, 108–9
Tormé, Mel, 103, 192–93
Trinidad Steel Band, 170, 175
tritone substitution, 262n.33
  "It's a New World," 160
  "Out of This World," 111–12
"trunk" songs, 9–10, 84–85, 269n.30
Tudor, Anthony, 118–19
Tunick, Jonathan, 173–74
Turner, Joe, 104–5
Turner, Lana, 141
*Twentieth Century, The* (TV show), 208, 210, 212, 249n.1, 272n.9, 272n.15
20th Century Fox, 11, 70, 141

Umeki, Miyoshi, 217

United Artists, 187
*Up in Arms* (film), 33*t*, 59

van Alstyne, Egbert, 79
*Variety*, 1
vaudeville, 29, 37
Vaughan, Sara, 230
Verve Records, 228*t*, 238
"Vesta and Mattie's Blues," 113
Victor Records, 57*t*, 65
*Vitaphone Varieties* (shorts), 54
Vogel, Shane, 92, 171, 255n.49
voice-leading, 26–27, 69, 158

Wachsman, Robert, 59, 70
Walden Records, 147, 190, 195–96, 200
Walters, Charles, 218–19
"wandering songs," 107
Warner, Jack, 147, 148, 149, 164
Warner Bros., 31, 54, 70, 100, 147, 234
Warren, Harry, 11, 30–31, 100
Washington, George Dewey, 48
Washington, Ned, 41
Waters, Charles, 118–19
Waters, Ethel, vii–viii, 16, 17, 40, 42, 57, 78, 228, 234–35, 255n.49, 273–74n.3
  in *Cabin in the Sky*, 84–85
  at Cotton Club, 48–49
  photo of, 231*f*
  "Stormy Weather" recorded by, 230–32
Waters, Muddy, 105
Wayne, David, 217–18
Weill, Kurt, 126, 147, 160–61
Welles, Orson, 114
"We Shall Sleep, But Not Forever," 113
Wheeler, Hugh, 217, 218, 219, 220, 222
White, Walter, 116–17, 119
Whiteman, Paul, 55–56, 57*t*, 65
Whitfield, Weslia, 228*t*
Whiting, Margaret, 101–3, 260n.11
Whiting, Richard, 100, 101–3

Wilder, Alec, vii–, 3, 4, 26–27, 46–47, 78–79, 86, 87, 100, 122–23, 174, 182–83, 186–87
Wiley, Lee, 228*t*
Wilk, Max, 13–15, 29, 31, 66, 67, 107
Wilkins, Roy, 116–17, 119
William Morris Agency, 53–54
Williams, Harry, 79
Willman, Noel, 218–19
Willson, Meredith, 131, 224–25
Wilson, Dooley, 11, 78
Wilson, John C., 87, 90, 194
Wilson, John S., 197, 199
Wilson, Julie, 228*t*
*Wizard of Oz, The* (film), viii, 1, 2, 3, 7–8, 10, 18–19, 27, 59, 62, 64*t*, 65–67, 75–76, 79, 88, 95, 116, 147, 233, 242–43
  Arlen's demos for, 194
  budget, 80
  creation stories, 258n.30
  cumulative creation in song adaptations, 255–56n.58
  Munchkinland sequence, 67, 74–75, 80, 82–83, 258n.39, 258n.40
  music for, 80–83
Wopat, Tom, 228*t*
Works Progress Administration, 114
"Would Ja?" 256n.61
Wynn, Ed, 75

Yankee Six, 16
*Yesterdays: Popular Song in America* (Hamm), 252n.1
Yip Harburg Foundation, 66 67
"You Do Something to Me" (Porter), 105
Youmans, Vincent, 11, 17, 29, 30, 34–35, 34*f*, 35*f*
Young, Victor, 41, 233
YouTube, xiii, 230
"You've Seen Harlem at Its Best" (McHugh, Fields), 41

Ziegfeld Follies (revue), 37, 65–66
Zinsser, William, 13–15
Zorina, Vera, 105–6

# Index of Arlen Songs

*For the benefit of digital users, indexed terms that span two pages (e.g., 52–53) may, on occasion, appear on only one of those pages.*

Tables and figures are indicated by an italic *t* and *f* following the page/paragraph number.

"Ac-cent-tchu-ate the Positive," 99*t*, 109, 127, 204–5
"Ain' It de Truth?" 245–47, 246*f*
"Albertina's Beautiful Hair," 188*f*, 188
"American Minuet," 130
"Another Night Alone," 57*t*
"Any Place I Hang My Hat Is Home," 99*t*, 116, 125–26, 127
"As Coroner I Must Aver," 82
"As Long As I Live," 33*t*, 57*t*
"As Mayor of the Munchkin City," 82

"Baby-San," 214*t*
"Been a Hell of an Evening," 214*t*
"Between the Devil and the Deep Blue Sea," 33*t*, 57*t*, 204–5
"Blues in the Night," 11–12, 99*t*, 100–5, 103*f*, 104*f*, 133
   facsimile of lyric sheet, 102*f*
   first performance of, 101–3
   interpolation into *Blues Opera*, 127, 129
   as tapeworm, 5
   twelve-bar blues and, 2, 103–4
"Breakfast Ball," 41, 45
"Brush Off, The," 214*t*
"Buds Won't Bud," 64*t*, 75–78, 77*f*, 79–80

"Can I Leave Off Wearin' My Shoes?" 194
"Can You Explain?" 194
"C'est la Vie," 67
"Cocoanut Sweet," 11–12, 64*t*, 93*f*, 137–38
   analysis of, 92–94
   Arlen's demo of, 193–94
   Horne's performance of, 234–35

"Come On, Midnight," 213–15, 214*t*, 215*f*, 221
"Come Out, Come Out, Wherever You Are," 80–81, 82
"Come Rain or Come Shine," 11–12, 15–16, 99*t*, 121*f*, 133
   analysis of, 120–21
   Arlen's performance with Martha Raye, 204–5
   in *Blues Opera*, 127
   sung by Frank Sinatra, 235
   sung by Judy Garland, 232–33
"Contagious Rhythm," 33*t*, 36–37

"Dancing Partner," 149, 162–63, 164–66
"Ding-Dong! The Witch Is Dead," 80–81, 82–83, 83*f*, 88, 196–97, 242–43
"Don't Like Goodbyes," 172, 174, 187
"Don't Say 'Love'—I've Been There and Back," 214*t*
"Down with Love," 64*t*, 75–76, 78–80, 89

"Eagle and Me, The," 64*t*, 88, 89
"Evelina," 64*t*

"Fancy Meeting You," 64*t*, 73–75, 74*f*
"Farmer's Daughter," 88
"Fish Go Higher Than Tigers," 214*t*, 222–23, 223*f*, 224*f*
"Flower Vendor," 128–29, 129*f*
"Follow the Yellow Brick Road / You're Off to, See the Wizard," 82
"For Every Man There's a Woman," 135–36, 136*f*

"Fun to Be Fooled," 10, 64*t*, 66–67, 68–69, 69*f*, 79

"Game of Poker, A," 99*t*, 131–32, 132*f*, 224–25
"Get Happy," 31*f*, 33*t*, 35*f*, 36–37, 255n.56
   analysis of, 30–36
   Arlen's performance of, 204–5
   "It's Only a Paper Moon" compared with, 62–63
   "Stormy Weather" compared with, 47
"Get That Long Face Lost" (original title of "Lose That Long Face"), 152
"Get Yourself a New Broom," 41
"Girl's Entitled, A," 214*t*
"God's Country," 75–76
"Goose Never Be a Peacock," 99*t*, 131
"Gotta Have Me Go with You," 149, 150–51, 153, 154, 158, 265n.2
"Green Light Ahead," 149, 162–64, 165–66, 266n.3

"Happiness Is Just a Thing Called Joe," 11–12, 64*t*, 85*f*, 86*f*, 94–95, 209
   analysis of, 84–87
   Arlen's performance with Martha Raye, 204–5
"Happy Any Day," 214*t*, 221
"Happy As the Day Is Long," 33*t*, 41, 57*t*, 58
"Harlem Holiday," 41
"Has I Let You Down?" 174, 194–95
"Hello," 214*t*
"Here's What I'm Here For," 149, 151–52, 162–63, 164, 165, 265n.2
"Hit the Road to Dreamland," 99*t*, 199, 204–5
"Hittin' the Bottle," 36–37, 38
"Hooray for Love," 135, 239
"House of Flowers," 174, 181*f*, 182*f*, 242–43
   analysis of, 180–82
   Arlen's recording of, 196–97
"Hurt but Happy," 208

"I Can't Believe My Eyes," 153–54
"I Could Be Good For You," 214*t*
"I Could Go On Singing (Till the Cows Come Home)," 64*t*, 96

"I Couldn't Hold My Man," 68
"If I Only Had a Brain (/Heart/Nerve)," 64*t*, 75–76, 80–81
"If I Were King of the Forest," 66–67, 80
"If You Believe in Me" (original title of "Paper Moon"), 63–64
"I Got a Song," 84, 88
"I Gotta Right to Sing the Blues," 7, 33*t*, 57*t*, 127, 129, 240
"I Had a Love Once," 225–26, 226*f*
"I Had Myself a True Love," 99*t*, 124*f*, 127–28, 182–83, 184, 226
   analysis of, 122–24
   McDonald's performance of, 244–45
"Ill Wind," 33*t*, 50–53, 51*f*, 52*f*, 56, 57*t*, 127, 129, 255n.53
"I Love a Parade," 33*t*, 37, 54, 57*t*
"I Love to Sing-a," 64*t*, 82, 258n.38
"I'm Hanging on to You," 75–76
"I'm Off the Downbeat," 149, 162–63, 164, 165–66, 166*f*
"Indoor Girl," 172
"I Never Has Seen Snow," ix, 174, 183*f*, 184*f*, 185*f*, 186*f*, 226
   analysis of, 182–87
   Arlen's performance of, 200, 201
"In the Shade of the New Apple Tree," 64*t*, 75–76, 79–80, 88
"It Really Was No Miracle," 82
"It's a New World," 131, 149, 151–52, 159*f*, 164–65, 221, 235, 265–66nn.2–3
   analysis of, 157–62
   Arlen's performance of, 200–1
   "I Had a Love Once" compared with, 225
"It's Only a Paper Moon," 7, 62, 64*t*, 65–66, 69, 97
   analysis of, 62–65
   Arlen's performances of, 199–200, 204–5
   original title of, 63–64
"It Was Good Enough for Grandma," 88
"It Was Long Ago," 68
"It Was Written in the Stars," 135–38, 137*f*, 239, 243–44
"I've Gone Romantic on You," 75–76
"I've Got the World on a String," 2, 33*t*, 204–5, 235–36

## INDEX OF ARLEN SONGS

"I Will," 214*t*
"I Wonder What Became of Me," 16–17, 99*t*, 121–22, 122*f*, 123, 263n.52

"Jitterbug, The," 80–82
"John-John-John," 213, 214*t*
"Jump de Broom," 187

"Last Night When We Were Young," ix, 9–10, 11–12, 64*t*, 71*f*, 72*f*, 209
    analysis of, 70–73
    Arlen's performance of, 200, 202
    "Buds Won't Bud" compared with, 76–77
    Sinatra's performance of, 236–37
"Legalize My Name," 99*t*, 129
"Let Me Look at You," 141–43, 142*f*
"Let's Fall in Love," 10, 33*t*, 54*f*, 54–56, 55*f*, 57*t*, 58, 68, 204–5
"Let's Give the Job to Lindsay," 213, 214*t*
"Let's Take a Walk Around the Block," 64*t*, 66–67, 68
"Let's Take the Long Way Home," 99*t*
"Life Begins at City Hall (Beautifying the City)," 82
"Life's a Dance," 75–76
"Linda," 33*t*, 56–57, 57*t*
"Little Drops of Rain," 64*t*, 95–96, 96*f*, 199
"Little Travelbug," 214*t*
"Liza Crossing the Ice," 88
"Lollipop Guild, The," 82
"Long, Long Ago," 224–25
"Looks Like the End of a Beautiful Friendship," 64*t*, 97, 259–60n.64
"Look Who's Been Dreaming," 145–46, 146*f*
"Lose That Long Face," 149, 152, 162–63, 164, 265–66nn.2–4
"Love Held Lightly," 99*t*, 131–32, 132*f*, 224–25
"Love Is Love Anywhere," 54
"Love's No Stranger to Me," 194–95
"Lullaby (Satin Gown and Silver Shoe)," 88
"Lullaby League, The," 82
"Lydia the Tattooed Lady," 2, 64*t*, 83

"Madame Tango's Particular Tango," 187–88
"Madame Tango's Tango," 187–88
"Man That Got Away, The," ix, 5, 95, 149, 150–51, 155*f*, 156*f*, 158, 161, 164–65, 184, 265–66nn.2–3
    analysis of, 153–57
    Arlen's performances of, 203–5
    Garland's performance of, 232–33, 234
    ranking in top movie songs, 266n.14
"March of Time, The," 36–38
"Merry Old Land of Oz, The," 80
"Minnie the Moocher's Wedding Day," 33*t*
"Moanin' in the Mornin'," 75–76
"Momma Knows Best," 214*t*
"Monday to Sunday," 194–95
"Mood in Six Minutes," 208–9
"More You See of It, The," 247*t*
"Morning After, The," 208, 210*f*, 272n.11
"Munchkinland," 64*t*
"My Lady Fair," 214*t*
"My Shining Hour," ix, 99*t*, 109–10, 109*f*, 110*f*, 111, 120, 139, 239

"Napoleon's a Pastry," 75–76
"'Neath the Pale Cuban Moon," 174
"Night After Night," 208–9
"Now I Know," 33*t*, 59–60, 60*f*

"Oh, Lord," 88
"Once I Wore Ribbons Here," 214*t*
"One for My Baby (And One More for the Road)," 5, 11–12, 99*t*, 105, 108*f*, 120, 129, 133, 144, 209–10
    analysis of, 107–9
    Arlen's performance of, 204–5
    Astaire's performance of (in *The Sky's the Limit*), 108–9
    Sinatra's performance of, 235, 237
"One Love," 36–37, 37*f*
"One Man Ain't Quite Enough," 174, 187
"Optimistic Voices," 80
"Out of a Clear Blue Sky," 33*t*, 36–37, 38–40, 39*f*
"Out of This World," 99*t*, 111–12, 111*f*, 112*f*, 240
"Over the Rainbow," vii, 1, 2, 7, 9, 11–12, 18–28, 20*f*, 21*f*, 23*f*, 24*f*, 25*f*, 27*f*, 64*t*, 65, 80, 81, 82–83, 89–90, 243
    Arlen's performances of, 199, 204–5

"Over the Rainbow," (cont.)
  Arlen's recording of, 195–96
  formal structure of, 19–20
  Garland's performance of, 232–34
  harmony of, 21–24
  jazz harmonizations of, 24–26, 25f
  jot for, 8
  "Last Night When We Were Young" compared with, 202
  "Little Drops of Rain" compared with, 95–96
  as a palimpsest, 18–19
  proposed cutting of, 2, 81
  pure line of, 10, 20–21, 27
  ranking in top movie songs, 266n.14
  replication of, 13, 24–25
  texture of, 26
  voice-leading in, 26–27
  voted greatest song of 20th century, 1
  widespread appeal of, 18–19

"Pacific," 214t
"Paris Is a Lonely Town," 64t, 95, 96
"Pretty as a Picture," 88
"Primitive Prima Donna," 41
"Promise Me Not to Love Me," 97, 259–60n.64
"Push de Button," 64t

"Raisin' the Rent," 41
"Rakish Young Man with the Whiskers, The," 88
"Right as the Rain," 64t, 89–91, 90f, 92, 141–42, 194

"Satan's Li'l Lamb," 33t, 62–63, 98, 99t
"Save Me Sister," 84
"Shoein' the Mare," 67, 174
"Shoulda Stood in Bed," 214t
"Silent Spring," 96–97
"Sing My Heart," 33t
"Sleepin' Bee, A," 9–10, 168, 174, 179f, 180, 196–97, 269n.30
  analysis of, 175–79
  Arlen's demos of, 177–78, 193–94
  Arlen's performance of, 193
  Streisand's performance of, 240–42
"Slide, Boy, Slide," 173

"Smellin' of Vanilla," 174
"So Long, Big Time!," 208, 209–12, 211f, 212f, 214–15, 272n.11, 272n.13, 272n.15
"Someone at Last," 149, 152, 266n.3
"Something Cold to Drink," 187
"Song of the Gigolo," 33t
"Song of the Woodman," 66–67
"Spring Has Me Out on a Limb," 214t
"Stepping Into Love," 57t
"Stormy Weather," vii–viii, 10, 33t, 36–38, 41, 43f, 44f, 47f, 49f, 53–54, 57t, 58, 68, 85, 101, 211, 234–35, 254n.33, 254n.36, 255n.49
  analysis of, 42–49
  Arlen's recording of, 57–58
  Arlen's sketch page for, 42–43, 43f
  "I Had Myself a True Love" compared with, 123
  "Ill Wind" compared with, 50–51, 53
  interlude, 48–49
  Koehler's lyric sheet for, 43–46
  relationship to "West End Blues," 47, 47f
  Waters's premiere of, 48
  Waters's recording of, 230–32
"Suddenly the Sunrise," 221f, 221–22, 223, 225
"Summer in Brooklyn," 214t
"Sunday in Cicero Falls," 88

"Take It Slow, Joe," 64t, 94f, 94–95
"Tell Me with a Love Song," 33t
"Temples," 214t
"That Old Black Magic," 5, 105–7, 106f, 107f, 111, 127, 198f, 204–5, 261n.20
"That's a Fine Kind o' Freedom," 196–97, 213, 214t
"That Was the Love That Was," 208
"Things," 66–67, 68
"This Is Only the Beginning," 54, 55, 57t, 58
"This Ol' World," 214t
"This Time the Dream's on Me," 99t
"Trinidad Coconut Oil Shampoo Commercial," 266n.5
"Two Feet in Two Four Time," 261n.23
"Two Ladies in De Shade of a Banana Tree," 174–75, 175f

"Waitin,'" 194–95
"Welcome Hinges," 88
"We're in Business," 144f, 144
"We're Off to See the Wizard," 80, 81, 88
"We Thank You Very Sweetly," 82
"We Welcome You to Munchkinland," 82
"We Were Always to Be Married," 214t
"What Can You Say in a Love Song?" 67
"What's Good About Goodbye?" 135, 138f, 138–39, 139f
"When the Boys Come Home," 88
"Why Do You Make Me Like You?" 214t, 220

"With the Sun Warm Upon Me," 144, 145f
"Woman's Prerogative, A," 99t, 129

"Yellow Rain," 214t
"Yesterday," 18
"You Are Tomorrow," 214t
"You for Me," 131
"You're a Builder Upper," 64t, 68
"You're Impossible," 208, 272n.11
"You're Never Fully Dressed Without a Smile," 214t, 224–25
"You're the Cure for What Ails Me," 64t